Saving POUGHKEEPSIE

Debra Anastasia

OMNIFIC PUBLISHING
LOS ANGELES

Omnific Publishing
1901 Avenue of the Stars, 2nd floor
Los Angeles, CA 90067
www.omnificpublishing.com

First Omnific eBook edition, November 2014
First Omnific trade paperback edition, November 2014

The characters and events in this book are fictitious.
Any similarity to real persons, living or dead,
is coincidental and not intended by the author.

Library of Congress Cataloguing-in-Publication Data

Anastasia, Debra.
  Saving Poughkeepsie / Debra Anastasia – 1st ed.
  ISBN: 978-1-623421-70-0
  1. Poughkeepsie — Fiction. 2. Contemporary Romance — Fiction.
  3. Foster Children — Fiction. 4. Family — Fiction. I. Title

10 9 8 7 6 5 4 3 2 1

Cover Design by Micha Stone and Amy Brokaw
Interior Book Design by Coreen Montagna

Printed in the United States of America

T, J and D, it's always for you.

1

BECKY

On an unseasonably warm November evening, the three brothers sat outside Blake's house in chairs around his fire pit — something they'd taken to doing as often as possible in the last several months. The women had gone inside about an hour earlier, and Beckett guessed from the recent dousing of lights in the kids' rooms upstairs, that his niece and nephew were now tucked in their beds. Sure enough, he watched the ladies carry wineglasses and a bottle of wine past the sliding door and into the dining room.

Cole was telling a story of the olden days, so Beckett tuned back in. Of the three brothers, the religious one held his liquor the worst.

"I forgot how it started — this was before Eve and Livia and Kyle, mind you. I forget which of your guys it was, Beck. Anyway, he'd covered all his fingers with raw dough — like Pillsbury dough right from the can — do you remember?"

Beckett knew that was his cue. "Brother, that's going way back. Shit, I don't think Blake even had hair on his titties yet."

Blake rolled his eyes before grabbing his pec and puckering up a kiss in Beckett's direction.

"Okay, I remember." Beckett smiled. "Damn. That fuck up was Dildo. I have no idea what he was on, but that was a crazy night. But he had, like, a sack full of expired Pillsbury dough biscuits. And he was tripping and started cracking them open. Half of us had guns pointed at his head because he'd scared the fuck out of us, 'cause you know they pop loud as anything when you open them. He didn't care, just started stretching out the dough and wrapping it all around his body. Naked as fuck, except for his tighty whities? Right?"

Cole laughed so hard he appeared to be having trouble breathing. "And then you got pissed off..."

The laugh circled the fire. Blake smiled wide, trying two and three times to take a sip of his beer and having to stop to laugh more.

"It was the stupid song he kept singing," Beckett said, shaking his head. "I don't even know. I snapped. Dragged his dumb ass outside, and there were, like, three dogs out there that Dentist had. Remember? I dropped the doughboy out there, and next thing I know the dogs are eating the dough off of him. I'm telling you, he was tripping balls so hard, he probably thought it was all in his head."

"And they weren't hurting him, just eating the dough and licking it off of him," Cole added, slapping his thigh.

"And then Dildo started praying to the Pillsbury Dough Boy? And thanking him because he didn't wrap his dick in it?" Beckett let the image come to his head, smiling. "I'll tell you what, I'm pretty sure he's been clean ever since. Worked like a charm. I was a fucking animal back then, though. He's lucky that's all I felt like doing that night."

Blake shook his head. "Dildo still work for you?"

Beckett nodded. "Yeah, since I've been back I've been establishing the old veins, getting this beast of a town pumping again. But keeping stuff as clean as I can."

Cole and Blake nodded approvingly. "I think you may be the most merciless nickname giver ever," Cole said. "Dildo is a tall, bald guy, right? Rough. I'm surprised you didn't give us nicknames." Cole set his bottle in the cup holder on his chair.

Beckett pressed his lips together.

Blake shook his head. "Oh, he has names for us. Tell him."

Cole poked the fire with a long stick. "How'd you find out?"

"Mouse told me." Blake shrugged.

The men toasted with their bottles, as they did whenever Mouse was mentioned: the part of their tattoo who no longer existed. After years as Beckett's most essential bodyguard, financial planner, and information-stashing genius, the man had died on the job, protecting Blake because he was loyal to his boss, who he considered a brother.

"And…" Cole shot Beckett a look.

"You're unofficially known as Sparkles and Jesus." Beckett squinted as Cole pretended to be offended.

"I think it's only fair if we give you a nickname. Blake?" Cole asked.

Blake stood and added a log to the fire. It'd been burning steady since right after dinner. Being with his brothers like this was Beckett's favorite. In his wildest dreams he never pictured getting to sit with them, out in the open in Blake's backyard—as in grass behind the home where he lived.

Blake had had such trouble adjusting to having a roof over his head when they were teens, and he'd spent years homeless before he met Livia. But he wasn't the only one whose life had changed dramatically. Cole, who Beckett had pictured getting prostate checks from a cardboard cutout of the Pope in a church's basement for the rest of his life, was now happily married to a girl with the filthiest mouth he'd ever encountered.

While his brothers tossed horrible and wonderfully insulting nicknames back and forth, Beckett let his gaze find the top of Eve's ponytail bobbing in the dining room window.

They'd been together for four months now, since their run-in with Vitullo had forced them home. The two of them were occupying the same space and finding a new normal—a normal that looked like nice young neighbors on the outside but involved a lot of time reestablishing their local contacts and going over the information Mouse had accumulated for them while he was alive behind closed doors—with a side of waiting and watching for a Vitullo move.

Beckett had traded his soul to Rodolfo Vitullo for Eve's life, and though they'd eventually worked a truce that released Beckett from his service (one branded scar later), their relationship was tenuous at best. Vitullo was not someone to be trusted and forgotten, especially since he still had to be angry over the loss of his daughter, Mary Ellen, and the loss of a good chunk of his money to Sevan Harmon.

"We're going with Fluffy Beast for now, but reserve the right to change it at any time," Blake announced as he tossed a cold beer to each man before taking one of his own from the cooler next to his chair.

"Fluffy Beast, Sparkles, and Jesus." Beckett nodded. "Though the best nicknames only have one word, I'll forgive you because it's your first go-around."

Beckett popped the lid off his beverage with the side of his chair.

"Dogs have to shit," Kyle called as she let Gandhi and the Hartt family dog, Marx, out.

"Hey, babe?" Cole called.

Kyle stepped out onto the porch.

"Give me a good nickname for Beckett."

"Now you dragged out the big guns." Beckett smiled.

"I'll be right back," Kyle said.

The men stayed silent as they watched the girls inside huddle up.

Soon Kyle was back. "Okay. It's Becky."

Beckett laughed out loud and held up his beer, toasting. Kyle stepped outside with her wine glass and bare feet. Eve and Livia followed, leaving the door open so they could hear the kids. The women joined the toast to his new nickname. Beckett looked from one face to another and then glanced up at the kids' bedrooms. Everything he needed was right here. Right now. He had to make this work.

Livia filled up the dog's water while Blake dropped the beer bottles in the recycling. She laughed when he came up behind her and nuzzled her neck. "Is this a three-beer pass you're making or a four-beer?"

He laughed against her skin. "Hey, Mrs. Judgypants, how many glasses of wine did you have?"

"Once it's opened it's useless. We had to drink it." She turned in his arms. He was glowing. Being with his brothers did that to him. It might have been how unsafe they'd felt growing up, but when they were able to relax together now it was a victory, just their laughter, their easiness. "You smell like the fire."

He kissed her then, deep and demanding, and she agreed to his physical invitation. He took her hand and led her out into the backyard. She shivered a bit. The fire was almost embers, just enough to see his face while her eyes adjusted to the dark.

"Outside again?" She teased him.

"You know I love it best when you're wearing nothing but the stars."

She sighed. He still knew what to say.

Blake led her to their hammock.

"And the hammock?" She was grateful she'd chosen a long dress for the dinner party.

"You can wear the hell out of that too." Blake lifted her in his arms, and as he slid her down to her feet, he used the tips of his fingers to trail her legs, catching the hem of the dress pulling it above her waist before setting her down.

After he had her situated, he made no move to take off his own clothes, instead kneeling in front of her like he was about to pray. Within the time it took her to gasp, Blake was tasting her and using the mesh of the hammock to his advantage, slipping his fingers inside of her, slowly first then at a strong pace.

She had to beg to get him to stop after she came, tilting backward in the hammock and motioning for him on the other side. Even upside down she knew how to find him, her unconventional position allowing her to take him deeper than usual. Finally he was the one to pull away. Making his way to the other side of the hammock, he adjusted himself to enter her and used the swinging to increase their friction and speed.

Neither had noticed the endless, ominous squeaking from the hooks buried in the trees, lost in their own pleasure, but when Blake sat down next to her in the hammock, both screws pulled out from their anchors simultaneously. They hit the ground butt first with a hard thud.

First, Livia moaned with the immediate ache she felt in her tailbone. "Ow," Blake muttered, moaning right along with her. Then they laughed so hard together that they had trouble catching their breath. Blake wrapped her in his arms and reclined on the grass. She patted his chest gently, loving the tap back from his heart and his white smile. He looked amazing cloaked in stars, too.

Cole saluted Beckett's retreating car as Kyle unlocked the door to their house. He went to the alarm panel and disarmed and rearmed the system. When he'd finished she twirled on him and backed him against the wall.

"Hey, sexy" was all she needed to say to get him started.

Hands in her red hair, he kissed her lips with a slow, precious tenacity. She moaned and her hands began seeking. Sex with Kyle meant even more than it had back in the day. After trying so hard to get pregnant for so many years, to have her remember that this connection was more than just a means to an end—an elusive end—was tender and exciting.

The fact that they were adopting a baby just mere weeks from now—and still not telling anyone about it—had filled them both with the need to be close. They were excited, nervous, and hopeful. And they did those feelings best together.

Taking off each other's clothes was as easy as taking off their own after all their time together, and soon they were naked in their living room. She went to the floor, hands and knees, spinning to offer herself to him.

He felt the manly growl in his brain. She didn't want foreplay. When she was like this, she wanted him hard. He slipped behind her and felt for the spot he needed. Kyle whispered his name softly, like he was her air. He placed two kisses on the dimples at the base of her spine and let her ache for a second as he trailed his fingers from her shoulders to her thighs. Silk. She was silk. Cole eased inside her. No matter how many times he'd had her, those first seconds would click his soul into place, as if it had been loose and she was the only one who knew how to align it.

And then there was only feeling. He had to remind himself to reach around her to find where she kept her orgasms hidden, teasing one from her with his fingers. After she shuddered and lost her whisper to a shout, he let the tide wash over him as well, wrapping his arms around her hips and pulling her into his lap.

She turned and looked at him, her profile so lovely, beautiful lips still gasping for air. "I love you."

"I love you, too."

Beckett drove, so he'd been careful to have only the two beers. He was playing it safe now, trying to appease Capt. John McHugh by following all the rules he could. Of course there were a few he could never obey. With Rodolfo Vitullo still lurking in the shadows, he had to keep a few of his options open.

"I paid the bill for Mouse's storage unit yesterday," Eve informed him from the passenger seat.

His deadly love was practical as well. She scanned the road, watching like she always was.

"You know, I was thinking of heading over there tomorrow. I want to make sure we've been back through everything, know all the information we have available. You know. How we do." He put the cruise control on for the portion of Route 9 that was flat and straight.

"You mean as you're working to be Poughkeepsie PD's new best friend?" She gave him a teasing look.

"You know my brothers love it here. And fuck me, I love having them here. Nights like tonight? Shit, I would have killed anyone to have what we just did back in the day. You, my brothers? Only thing missing is Mouse."

Gandhi snored from the backseat, and Beckett smiled at Eve. He'd known enough upheaval in his life to cherish the quieter moments.

"So no breaking rules?"

He checked the side of the road for the reflective eyes of the deer that liked to come out at night.

"Nope. Becky here is a fucking Boy Scout. I pledge allegiance, pay my taxes, go to church. Tons of bullshit."

He looked back at Eve and she'd unbuttoned her shirt and pushed the cups of her lace bra under her breasts. She fondled her nipples while he watched.

"Tits!" He licked his lips.

She shook her head and bit her lip, trying to hide her smile. "Don't forget to drive."

He was halfway into the other lane and yanked the car back onto his side. She was busy sliding her jeans off her hips.

"You're not wearing your seatbelt," he added, almost frantically checking both her progress and the car's position on the road.

"That's true. I also kill people, so keep it in perspective, Becky." She began to touch herself and his balls were ready to ignite.

"My dick is about to teach you never to call me Becky again."

She laughed and took her fingers from inside herself and forced them into his mouth. "My pussy rules the world."

He licked her fingers and groaned.

Eve started in on his jeans and finding him commando as usual, she grasped his penis and pulled it free without hesitation. She went down on him hard, and Beckett wondered if she was punishing her mouth for wanting him as much as she did. Driving the car while Eve expertly handled his stick made him feel so powerful. He wanted to head butt the windshield. (He didn't.)

He almost missed their street and made wide, sloppy turns until they were parked in his driveway. Eve pulled away from his cock as soon as the wheels stopped and strolled across their front lawn buck-ass naked.

She waited for him like she was wearing clothes, relaxed.

Beckett opened his car door and let G scamper out. The dog continued on through the door Beckett opened and up the stairs, presumably to his beloved dog bed.

Eve began pressing the alarm code's buttons as he came up behind her, slipping one arm around her waist and the other around her neck.

"How you want me, baby?"

She answered by biting his forearm as they walked inside.

He spun her in his arms. When he went in for a kiss, she slapped his face.

"So that's how?" He put her hard against the wall, holding her by her throat as he slammed the front door. "You have to fight me? 'Cause I'm the toughest fucker you've ever met. Say it."

He released his grip. She tilted her head back, closing her eyes. "You're the toughest."

She never did what he told her to. "How much did you drink?" he asked.

"Enough—" she looked at him, her eyes glass "—to know you still haven't fucked me yet, Becky."

He switched his grip, using her breasts to keep her against the wall, and alternated pinching her nipples with a full-on grope. Instead of fighting him, she moaned with pleasure, hips gyrating.

"Oh, now you're a slut? How much wine to get you like this?"

She slapped him in the face again. He shook his head against the sting of it.

"Still not fucking me," she pointed out. "I'm going die of old age here." She wrinkled her nose in his direction.

"Fine." He let her go to push his pants all the way off. She tried to slip away from the wall.

"No. Here." He grabbed her by the waist and pushed her up higher, sliding her over his dick like a sword and a sheath.

He kept her aloft by her neck and kissed her lips as they turned blue. He slammed into her over and over. But he didn't like the leverage, so he took her to the stairs instead, climbing her while he climbed them. He had her pinned while he pounded into her. She made him try harder when she met him thrust for thrust, biting and clawing him, surely drawing blood.

When she was this wild, he was a monster for her. He bruised her, took her blows, and fought to give her the pleasure she made him earn.

As she came, he pulled out and used his fingers on her mercilessly, making sure her clit never ceased feeling his pressure, his demands while his fingers worked miracles inside her, anywhere he could bring her sensation. She had reached the top of her climax when he put his mouth on her, feeling and tasting her as she pulsed.

Eve was useless when he was done, having to beg him to stop. But he wasn't done; he'd never be done with her. He flipped her and took her from behind. She held on to a stair and the railing as he positioned her legs to his liking. The build was insane. The sight of her, flushed and swollen from his hands, made his cock proud.

She pulled away when he was so very close, and he tried grasping her by the shoulders, but she easily broke his hold, pushing him onto the stairs in her place.

He was just on the edge, ready, when her beautiful, sinning mouth took him and brought him beyond. His guttural screams as she finished him off could scare people, and upstairs, G began to bark.

He could do nothing more than laugh as he watched her stand and wipe her mouth, smiling at him as if he were prey.

This woman constantly surprised him. Hell, his life constantly surprised him.

Although Rodolfo Vitullo's luxuries were opulent and copious, at his age his body was failing, and worse than that, his legacy was in the hands of a man busy whining that his newest Lamborghini was too fast.

His son, Primo, had neither his father's looks nor his balls. His sister, Mary Ellen—now tragically deceased at the hands of that deadly, manipulative sex goddess of a woman—had been the ballsy one. He couldn't stop picturing the blonde, January, and how well she'd held up under torture, the swift way she'd dispatched his men in the security clips he'd taken to watching in his spare time. And honestly, his emerging plan to have her bear his son's child was probably a mistake. She was way too much woman for him.

But spare time was a funny turn of phrase, because although Rodolfo sat in one place—most frequently his study at his New Jersey estate—he was almost always ruminating around in his past. He was best at biding his time, letting weeks and months pass, then getting the ultimate revenge when his enemies let their guard down. He pondered Beckett Taylor and that mesmerizing woman's belief that they had bested him, as well as weapons dealer and international playboy Sevan Harmon's cruel betrayal of his daughter, Mary Ellen—all for naught, so it seemed, as he'd heard reports that Sevan's investments had gone belly up, and the man was basically a pauper now. Such a waste, and knowing how far Sevan had fallen did nothing to soothe his anger. Mary Ellen was still dead.

His weapons manufacturing business had investors, an array of legitimate contracts and clients, and a board of directors that would see to it that the legal part of the Vitullo legacy would carry on. But the off the books, most profitable part of his empire—the shady, murky part—needed careful management that his son was far too stupid to handle. If only he could have designed his offspring…

Perhaps the woman could carry Rodolfo's direct descendant instead. No need to sully anything with Primo. Yes, he actually liked that idea very much. If only it wouldn't have to be so clinical—yet another way his body was failing him. But nothing to be done about that. He had to think about the future. He had a few dedicated, nursemaid-style girlfriends—one in particular, Jennifer, who would cut out her own tongue if it made him happy—who he could trust to raise the child to his exacting standards. Nurse Jennifer would live in the lap of luxury while the child grew up with a full staff to attend to any needs.

In an attempt to rekindle their relationship, as well as feel out the possibilities of this January situation, he'd reached out to Beckett several times over the past few months, but his calls had been rebuffed. The young man loved that deadly woman, Rodolfo knew that much. And he also didn't have enough sense to show respect. He'd never seen such an arrogant bastard in all his years. No good sense of self-preservation.

When Nicholas knocked on the door to Rodolfo's study in the New Jersey compound, interrupting Primo's long-winded (and entirely ignored) tirade, he waved his son away. "Go buy a minivan. I can no longer tolerate the sound of your pathetic voice."

Nicholas closed the door behind Primo, likely clipping the edge of his heels in the process, based on the way he jumped just before the slam. Nicholas turned toward Rodolfo. "Sir, I've found out what I can about the girl."

Rodolfo nodded. "Let me know."

Nicholas pulled a computer out of the bag he carried and set it on the marble table. "Watch this."

Nicholas offered commentary while the computer showed a slideshow of January's life. It began with her father and mother. The mother was gorgeous and, according to the newspaper clipping, had been divorcing the father when she gave birth to an Eve Lily Hartt. No real surprise January had been using an alias along with the fake hair color. A picture from a local parade was the next item of note, and a tall dark boy who was not Beckett stood with his arm around the young Eve. David and Eve had been dating for a time when they were in a car accident that killed the man and, according to the next article, their unborn baby.

"Was she injured?" Rodolfo leaned forward.

Nicholas nodded. "Quite a bit, it seems. Those details are hard to acquire because the new HIPAA rules take a little more effort to compromise. But know I'm working on it. And we both know she's in supreme physical condition." He paused meaningfully for a moment.

Things got more interesting as Nicholas's sources became shadier and the documentation more illegal. Stolen police files elaborated on the accident: the car that hit Eve and David's had been driven by a dead man—a bullet to the head had made him a shitty driver. There was speculation, but no proof, that the drive-by that killed him was ordered by a local crime organization run by none other than Beckett Taylor.

"Son of a bitch. The boy might be better than I thought if he can make her suck his dick after that." Rodolfo sat back and crossed his good leg over his poor one. "I wonder if she knows."

Nicholas nodded. "Not to give her too much credit, but I found that information pretty easily. We have to assume she's aware of Taylor's involvement after all this time."

Details of how Eve's alliance had formed with Beckett were sketchy. She'd lived a double life after disappearing for an extended time. She'd led her father to believe she was undecided in her profession when in actuality she quickly became one of Beckett's most trusted enforcers.

Though Eve's allegiance to him made no sense, Rodolfo didn't blame Beckett for falling for her. Judging from the videos Rodolfo had hoarded, seeing her work in person would be a huge turn-on. The ensuing years were fairly flat. Taylor had left town, and the girl also disappeared for a while, then resurfaced and began working in the city. They'd reunited under unclear circumstances and all hell had broken loose, leaving Mary Ellen dead in the wake.

Though Rodolfo still seethed with hate at the thought of what Eve Hartt had cost him, he also felt a glimmer of hope. After watching her murders once again, it was even more apparent that he needed this girl. She was now the key to his future—Vitullo Weapons' future. He could almost kick himself because he'd had her in his possession once, and all he'd wanted to do was torture her. Mary Ellen had unwillingly delivered him the best hope he could ever have for a child who'd actually be able to wield the power Rodolfo would bestow.

Nicholas seemed every bit the professional businessman as he made his presentation, but Rodolfo knew that just under his calm façade, the man was deeply disturbed. Nothing made Nicholas happier than watching blood flow. He was wildly devoted to Rodolfo, because the work he was assigned not only granted him access to his deepest fantasies, but was considered a job, so he got paid. And there were some things Nicholas had to do, whether he wanted to or not, because his boss said so.

Rodolfo loved finding these little outcasts and creating what felt like a deep, symbiotic relationship with them. He'd lost count now of just how many had served him over the years. Because of their proclivities they were usually not long for this world.

He dismissed Nicholas so he could think, letting the slideshow replay in a loop. He hit the remote so her security camera footage moved in tandem on the larger screen.

It was time to take action. First he needed to store his semen, and that was enough of a task. He wanted her impregnated with his seed no matter what—even if he was dead. And maybe this would be his final act, because at this point waking up every morning was a genuine surprise. So much so that he made a phone call. He'd offer his generations their salvation today.

A doctor was soon on his way to what had to be the most unusual house call he'd made in a while.

2

JOHN BLAKE BRIDGE

Looking back, they would remember that Kyle had awakened just a few seconds before the phone call in the middle of the night. But for now, they had hastily dressed and thrown two bags in the car: one with their clothes and the other with baby needs—little diapers, bottles, onesies, and jumpers zipped up tight. The car seat was as in there as good as Cole could get it.

Kyle had a couple million concerns, and she was pretty sure she was burping up her lunch from three weeks ago. The stress was getting to her. She hadn't told her sister or father about this adoption that Beckett, of all people, had arranged. Sitting in the passenger seat now for the five-hour drive to Maryland, she was stuck right between hope and prayer. She still waited for the floor to drop out from under her—which basically seemed healthy, given the circumstances. Her previous miscarriage was the only tale to tell in her short history as a mother, despite years of trying. But now, because of Beckett and his big heart, a baby might come home in her backseat.

As Cole drove, she mentally reviewed all that had come before. Her two meetings with Chery had gone well, though at first, Kyle had been afraid the woman would change her mind. Chery was a friend and previous employee of Beckett's from his time in Maryland. He'd stepped in when he discovered she was being abused by her boyfriend, and now the boyfriend was out of the picture—permanently, Beckett had made pretty clear. And no one seemed to want to discuss it beyond that.

At their first meeting together, at a Maryland seafood restaurant this past summer, Cole and Chaos — one of Beckett's trusted men who'd taken a liking to Chery — had shaken hands. Chery had asked smart questions and did, in fact, seem clean, as Beckett had said she was, but it had taken more than an hour before they got around to talking about the baby's father, Jared. Chery had seemed embarrassed, but determined to make sure they had all the information. And she was resolute in her decision not to raise the baby.

"He and I, we were in a situation," she'd begun to explain. "I couldn't stop coming back to him. That's something you should know. And it wasn't stubbornness, more that doing things differently seemed too drastic. I'd like this baby to know when to quit something." She'd shrugged.

Kyle had smiled and looked around at all the people present before returning her focus to Chery. "I've done some things differently than I should have — for attention or whatever. I just needed to be in the center of someone's affection. And until my sister and Cole set me straight, I didn't realize how much power I had, how strong I could be. And that I had to be worth my own attention."

Cole had taken her hand at that point. "Chery, I doubt a person can live on this planet without regret," he'd told her. "It's part of the experience we're meant to have. This baby? He will be everything to us. I'll use any skill I have to help him become a man. And Kyle —"

"I'll make sure he stands up and knows what he's worth," she'd interrupted. "There won't be a day he's not loved. I'll say it with my hands — making a home for him. I'll say it with my arms — hugging him so he knows his mother is present every day. His heart will never be alone. And I'll say it out loud every day. Because it matters."

Chery had nodded and looked into the distance. She seemed as committed to the idea of adoption as anyone in her position could, so Kyle did her best to take her at her word. "Thanks for that," she'd eventually said. "Do you have a name?"

Cole had smiled and squeezed Kyle's hand. "John Blake Bridge."

"That's a strong name," Chaos had said. "Blake's after a good man," he'd told Chery as he rubbed her shoulder.

Shrugging, Cole answered, "Yeah, we had a few other front runners, but we're both happy with this."

After their meal, Chery had stood, and the rest of the group followed. She'd laid her hand over her belly, patting gently. "Well, John Blake is tiring me out."

Kyle looked down at her phone in her lap as the car sped down the highway. The number for the lawyer Beckett had connected them with was on speed dial. After some Internet searching, she'd found that the man was on the up and up—or at least his public persona as a lawyer was. Beckett had sworn he kept everything legit. Cole reached over and squeezed Kyle's hand as he drove, clearly nervous as well.

The second meeting with Chery had been the one that inspired Kyle to buy the things for the baby that were behind her in the back-seat now.

It had been Chery's sister Vere's birthday party, just a few weeks ago in October. The theme was dogs, and Chery had gone all out, decorating a local park with dog balloons, plates, and napkins, and strategically placed stuffed dogs.

Cole and Kyle knew Vere had autism, but Kyle wasn't sure what that looked like. It turned out, Vere was Vere. Some of her friends were there, and they were having a blast dancing and singing to the radio. A fruit bowl shaped like a cake was the centerpiece.

Kyle had pitched in, insisting on carrying things so Chery wouldn't have to. And she'd watched as Cole did what he did best: put people at ease. Soon enough, Vere was introducing him to her friends and her new dog, Rufus.

When finally Chery sat, Kyle sat next to her. "You did a great job. She looks so happy." Kyle didn't add that the party was just like what a good mother would do. The thought choked her, though.

Chery rubbed her stomach. "Thank you. It was a lot. There's more than getting the right things for her here. For weeks we had to go through the schedule—some things strictly required, others last-minute adds. I just wanted this day to be good for her. But asking for a whole day? Probably too ambitious. So far we're according to plan." She stretched her arms above her head. "And then afterward, we'll have to work to come down from it all, readjust to our regular day. But she does look happy."

Kyle could feel herself holding her breath as Chaos began play-ing fetch with Rufus.

"You're concerned." Chery met her gaze.

"It's just…" Kyle had bit her lips together, afraid to voice what she worried might be true.

"I'm sure," Chery said firmly. "For this decision, I'm sure. I'm not changing my mind." She'd taken Kyle's hand and placed it on her stomach. "And it's not because I don't think the baby — John — will be amazing, because he will. I just need..." the woman searched for the words "...space from Jared. And this baby, I don't want to put what I'm feeling on him. He deserves a clean slate. He deserves to be the center of someone's universe. Your universe. You won't be looking for someone else in what he does, the choices he makes. You will only see John. That's what I believe is best for him."

The baby had moved just then, kicking at Kyle's hand. "Oh my! He's so strong."

Chery leaned down as much as she could, "Say hi to Mommy, John. She loves you so much." She nodded. "That's you. Step up to the mic."

Kyle leaned down and whispered, "You're the best boy in the whole world. I love you."

Still the baby kicked at her.

"Look at that, he can't wait either. You guys are perfect for each other." Chery had patted Kyle's hand on her stomach. "This is right."

And now, barely a month later it was the middle of the night, and Cole was so focused on driving they could hardly have conversation.

She checked their list on her phone, mentally repacking the bags. "Did you remember the good camera?"

"Yes. It's in our bag." The GPS rattled off how many miles it was until the next turn.

Kyle's phone began ringing in her hands. "It's Chaos. Oh my God! It's Chaos."

"Answer it!" Cole kept his eyes on the road.

"Hello?"

Her brain flashed with every possible horrible thing that could happen.

"Hello, Mommy! Your baby boy was born exactly ten minutes ago." Chaos sounded like he was smiling.

"Everyone okay?" Kyle was actually impressed she could make words because she was sure she was hyperventilating.

"Chery and John are doing great. Can you hear him?"

Kyle hit speaker, and John's robust cries filled the car. Cole met her eyes and instantly both of them were crying with their son.

"How far away are you guys?"

Cole answered, thankfully. "Fifteen minutes."

Chaos filled Cole in on some parking procedures, but Kyle listened to the music behind him. That baby's cries were the sound of her dreams coming true.

Chaos offered a picture and sent it to Kyle's phone, but she refused to look. She needed to see him in person first. She closed her eyes and the next thirteen minutes took her back through their years of trying for a baby…red, the worst color of all…how many times she and Cole had held each other as disappointment slammed into them.

When they arrived, Cole surprised her by pulling into a doctor's reserved spot — not his usual style. The tires had barely stopped when Kyle was out of the car. Inside, the staff was ready, asking for identification, then leading them both to their first glimpse of John.

In the room sat a very tired-looking Chery. Chaos had his arms folded, watching over the bassinet.

A few steps into the room and Kyle could see the baby. Her baby. He was swaddled with a red blanket, embroidered with the name *John Blake*. Somewhere in her head, she realized this was a gift from Chery and Chaos. But instead of responding, she looked at the newborn's face.

Kyle had felt this feeling once before, when she'd first laid eyes on Cole. It was the almost audible snap of her life clicking into place. There was life before John and, thank God, from this second on, there would be an after *with* him.

She reached to pick him up before hesitating, looking to Chery. Her eyes were teary, but her voice was strong. "Go on, now. Your baby's been waiting a long time to meet you."

Kyle slipped her hand under his head and picked up her son while Cole took a picture with his phone because they'd forgotten the camera in the car. Chaos offered her his chair and moved next to Chery.

Kyle sat, holding on to John with gentle sureness. "Happy Birthday, son. I love you so much." Cole knelt next to her, putting his big hand atop hers on the red blanket. In that moment, Kyle knew she would never hate the color red again. Because of him. His eyes were brown and looked at her seriously. His lips were a beautiful color of red as well.

"Look at those cheeks!" Cole uncovered John's hand from the swaddling. They looked in shock at his tiny little hand.

"I forgot how small the new ones are." Kyle leaned over and kissed John's forehead, sniffing him.

Cole did the same before offering his lips to Kyle. Then he turned back to the boy. "Hey, son. I have so many plans for you! I've already got you a baseball glove. We're going to play catch and maybe fish."

Kyle and Cole fussed over John, sighing when he fell asleep. Chaos gave Cole a packet of information the nurse had passed to him, then shortly the nurses arrived, fitting the whole family with hospital bracelets.

"We have a room set aside for you guys," one of them explained. "Would you like to go there and let Chery get some sleep?"

Again Kyle looked, but Chery waved her on.

The nurse took John from Kyle's arms and placed him in the bassinet. "He gets to travel in style."

Kyle and Cole hugged Chaos and Chery before following the nurse out of the room. One last glance over her shoulder left Kyle shuddering. Chery had crumpled into Chaos, obviously dissolving into tears.

Cole followed Kyle's line of sight before hugging her and hurrying her on. "Look at him, he's such a miracle. I'm sure this is tough on her."

Kyle nodded and followed the nurse into their own hospital room. "I'll be back in just a few minutes to go over a few basics with you," the woman said. "And it will be time for John's bottle."

They stood at the edge of the bassinet, peering into their future. Cole leaned down and picked up the baby carefully. "I'm so in love."

Kyle grabbed his phone to take more pictures. It rang as soon as she snapped the first shot. Beckett was calling.

She answered, "Thank you. I can't even…he is so beautiful."

"Everybody's good? Awesome. Text me a picture immediately. Did you name him Beckett Taylor Bridge? Don't let me down, Fairy Princess."

She could hear him smiling. Their conversations were often laced with insults, but today this man was the reason she was a mom.

"You know, if you weren't in Cole's life, this beautiful baby wouldn't be in front of us. You're a motherfucking angel." She wiped away her copious tears, loving the sight of Cole holding his son.

"You better clean up that filthy mouth, Mommy. And I never looked at it that way before. Very nice." Kyle heard Beckett filling someone in on the birth of the child.

"Who's that?"

"Eve. She says congrats."

"Wow. Very nice indeed. Tell her thank you. I know you want to talk to your brother, so let me get my son out of his arms." Kyle accepted John's feather weight gratefully after she set the phone down on a chair.

She could only hear Cole's side, but she could easily imagine Beckett, the deadly teddy bear, reacting to the news.

"Yeah. He's great," Cole said. "Chery seems to be doing well…I think it was tough. Definitely…Chaos is a stand-up guy. No, not this one, brother. John Blake Bridge is the one we decided to go with… Eight pounds, nine ounces and twenty-one inches long. He's eating like a champ so far according to his chart…Will do. And Beck? I love you."

Kyle's eyes filled again. Those brothers didn't say it out loud much.

As Cole hung up, the nurse returned with an armful of supplies, and Kyle felt her eyes go wide. They were about to learn a few things about their newborn son.

Blake sipped his cold coffee as Livia sat in front of Kellan's high chair. Emme was busy in the next room dressing Marx, the dog Beckett had insisted they adopt from the shelter, as a frog princess. It was a simple morning—the kind of simple morning Blake could hardly have dreamed of years before, when he spent his days at the train station and his nights in handmade shelters in the woods, avoiding the sun at all costs. How far he'd come. How far they'd come together.

Marx tore into the room, stopping to roll in a desperate attempt to get the frog costume off and forcing Blake out of his memories. He shook his head and laughed as Emme came racing after him, certain if he just gave the costume a chance he'd love it.

It was also a day of big plans. Livia's list lay on the counter with almost all the items checked off. Planning for a trip to Disney World seemed like a sport to his wife. According to Cole, the love of the place ran in the family, as Kyle had been marathon packing for them as well.

Emme gave Princess Frog Dog the update after Marx collapsed in a heap on the kitchen floor with a defeated sigh: "You're going to a kennel. Daddy says it's like a dog hotel. So no biting. And no stomping your feet, because the dogs below you are trying to sleep." She pointed at the dog who gamely licked her finger. "You are so silly. And I'll pack your favorite toy and draw you a picture of us for your hotel room. Mommy, does Marx need change for the vending machine?"

Livia smiled. "No, sweetheart. The dogs get their food delivered. That reminds me…" She turned toward him. "Did you make copies of his shot record? He got the kennel cough one last visit."

Blake watched as she made sure the last bits of Kellan's food were bite size. She pointed to her spot in front of their son's high chair as her phone rang.

"My sister," she explained. "'Sup, Kyle! Are you ready to spank Mickey with me?" Livia walked out of the room.

Emme stood next to Blake, shaking her head. "What's up, big head?" he asked her. His daughter rolled her eyes before climbing into his lap. "You're not supposed to be able to make that face until you're a teenager."

Kellan tried out one of his new words, "Meme! Meme!"

Emme reached out and held his hand while putting her other hand on Blake's face, rubbing his stubble. "Mommy better be careful with all that spanking talk. Mickey will put her in Disney jail."

Blake pretended to bite her hand while she giggled. "Disney jail?" he asked.

Emme turned so she could look at him seriously. "Goofy runs it. And he's a nightmare."

Blake busted out laughing. He only stopped when he saw Livia, wearing a very shocked face, return from the other room.

"What's up?" Blake put his daughter on her feet before freeing Kellan from the high chair.

"We just became an aunt and uncle?" Her phone made the sound for a text message delivered.

"Kyle's pregnant? That's great!" Blake watched as Kellan wobbled over to his favorite toy: beads on a track. Emme went back to the dog, still talking about Disney jail.

"No, we have a nephew—as of last night. They adopted a baby in Maryland." She looked at her phone, tears in her eyes instantly. Blake drew close and put his arm around her.

The baby looked like all newborns. He read the message out loud: "Your nephew, John Blake Bridge. He's healthy and beautiful."

"Aww." Livia pulled him into a hug. "Your brother loves you so much. My dad? My dad is going to freak out! Apparently Kyle called him just before me."

"They're in Maryland? Can we swing by on the way to Florida? I'm guessing they're not coming with us now." Blake looked at the next picture, in which Cole pretended to do the brothers' handshake, wrapping forearms to connect their matching tattoos, with his son's tiny—and thankfully untattooed—arm.

"I'm so happy for them. Did you know about this?" Livia gave him a stern look.

"No, not at all. Let me call Beckett and see if he knew."

Blake went out on the porch and slid the door closed. His brother picked up on the first ring.

"Hello, you handsome motherfucker."

"And back at you, Uncle Beckett." Blake grinned.

"Right? You guys are providing the earth with a lot of gorgeous kids. Today is a beautiful day for sure."

Blake smiled wider, hearing the joy in his voice.

"How's everybody in that house? Whitebread packing her ass off?"

"She loves to pack, that's for sure. We're great," Blake said. "Did you know about this going down?" He leaned over and began to weed the flowerbeds out of habit.

"It's on the up and up, if that's what you're asking. You know Cole wouldn't have it any other way. I just helped them make the connection. You remember Chery from Maryland? Well, she was in a way and needed help, and Cole and Kyle have had…issues."

Blake stood and tossed the weeds into the woods. "I know, but it seems sudden, right?"

"We've known for a while, but they wanted to keep it quiet until it was a done deal." Beckett sounded like he was walking upstairs. "I'm headed down there in a few hours to get a peek at the little guy. And maybe change their minds about that lame-ass middle name…"

Blake shook his head. "Seriously? Blake is a very manly name. I mean Beckett, that could be a golden retriever's name. Isn't it a brand of tennis racket?"

"Son, you named *your* boy after me." Beckett seemed a little giddy.

"Oh yeah, I guess it is pretty kick ass. We're leaving for Florida in a bit, but we were thinking of swinging by and saying congrats. Livia's going to want to sniff the head and all."

"Dude."

"The baby's head, you dirty-minded bastard. It's a thing with women." Blake looked through the window to see Livia washing the breakfast dishes. She put bubbles on her hand and blew them like a kiss. The soap splattered on the window.

Beckett talked to someone in the background for a few seconds, making the case to come with him see the baby.

Blake recognized the responding female voice as his cousin's. "Whoa, you have Eve with you?"

"Yes. Yes, I do, actually. She says she can't come to Maryland, which is pissing me off. I'll text you when I change her mind and get on the road. Later, brother."

Beckett was gone before Blake had a chance to say anything further, so he went back in to Livia. "Well, it's going to be a whole reunion! You think your father can deal with Beckett? 'Cause he and Eve might be coming too."

"He'll deal. Eve, you say? Really?"

Blake counted Livia's delighted smile.

A little later that morning, Eve parked her motorcycle outside Starbucks in the crisp November air and used her credit card to pay for street parking. Beckett had given her hell for not going with him to Maryland. But although she was thrilled that Cole and Kyle were finally getting their child, the sight of a baby still killed something in her. And she could find no way to tell him that. So he was pissed, and had left strict instructions for her to take douchebags with her everywhere she went until he got back. He wanted nothing left to chance while he was out of town.

However, at the moment, instead of accompanying assholes, she had her piece on her and a knife tucked inside her jacket. It had been months since their showdown with Rodolfo Vitullo, and neither he or anyone else from Vitullo Weapons had bothered them. Well, the old man had been leaving messages on Beckett's phone, but with the intel she'd liberated from Sevan Harmon about Vitullo's not-so-savory dealings in their back pocket, they felt fairly protected. Besides, she just needed a quick cocoa.

She got in line and ordered her usual. But when she went to pay, Police Officer Ryan Morales's voice was in her ear. "Let me."

Eve nodded, keeping her eyes on the counter. She knew having to face Ryan was coming eventually, now that she lived in Poughkeepsie again. It was a miracle it had been this long, but she just wished she'd seen him coming. As they waited for their drinks, she looked him up and down — handsome, but more rugged than last time. And he still had love for her in his eyes, which made her look away.

"Ride here on the back of someone's bike?" he asked, gesturing to her helmet.

She responded with her best not-fucking-likely glare.

"You have your own?" He grabbed her drink before the barista could call Eve's name, then took the next order right out of the lady's hand.

"I do." She tapped her foot and looked at her beverage.

"Come with me to a table, and I'll let you have it." He gave her a smile.

He was trying. She hated how deeply she'd hurt him. Their undercover work together in Mary Ellen Vitullo's organization had blossomed into a complicated friendship, and for Ryan, something more.

"Fine." She followed him to a corner spot and sat, resting her helmet on the extra chair.

"This is where it all started." He slid her cup across to her waiting hand.

She said nothing, but took a sip of the piping hot chocolate.

"Fancy meeting you here." He tried again. "I was just thinking about you."

She could see women in the shop looking at him. He made a nice package in his crisp slacks and button-down shirt. She sighed.

"Listen, I'm not trying to make this awkward for you. I just wanted you to know I looked into my uncles' records, like you suggested. I unearthed some buried juvie reports." He twirled his coffee in his hands. "There was some information there I wanted to address with you. You were—"

"You didn't have to do that," she interrupted. "Why change your memories of them? You should have ignored me and left well enough alone."

His jaw tensed. "Because as much as I said I didn't believe you, I didn't think you'd..." he looked around before lowering his voice "...kill people without a reason. Now Taylor, yes. I still think he's a barnacle on a dragon's testicle."

Eve suppressed a laugh.

"Okay, whatever. I'm nervous."

She smiled at him and sighed. "You know you taught me to laugh. I didn't do it enough before you."

He stopped talking and took a sip of his coffee. They sat together, the distance between them so much greater than the table.

"You with him now?" Ryan stared out the window.

"Yeah." She crossed her legs and accidentally brushed against his under the table. "Sorry."

"For kicking me or for throwing your life away?" He leveled his brown eyes on her.

"If you thought that was a kick, we have an issue." She tried to make light of his question, but things were getting awkward. She got to the point. "You need to move past me now."

He shook his head and frowned. "I disagree. I'm not one for giving up."

"Let's review: You're a cop. I'm the exact opposite of that." Eve touched his hand. "And besides, he's where I'll always be, even if it's just in my head. You deserve better." She stood and grabbed her helmet. "That sounds fake, but I want the best for you. I really do." She shrugged, knowing he'd never understand how much she wished they could be friends. She'd miss him.

He nodded instead of answering, and Eve tossed her cup out on the way to her bike, a thousand emotions swirling through her. By the time she looked up, it was already too late.

Ryan watched her leave, silently hating how goddamn beautiful she was. It would be a hell of a lot easier to sit rejected if he didn't have a giant hard-on. And she wasn't driving a motorcycle.

Fuck me sideways. He hung his head. Damned if he hadn't lost her forever. And it sucked. *Son of a bitch.* He looked down at the table, running his hands through his hair until the red and blue lights reflecting off the walls of the coffee shop caught his attention.

He stood and turned, looking for the source, and he saw Eve kneeling on the sidewalk with her hands in the air.

Ryan walked briskly outside, where two policemen had their guns drawn and pointed at her.

"Keep your hands nice and high where we can see them," one of them admonished.

Ryan couldn't stop himself. "Hey, what's going on?"

"Step aside, sir."

"This is police business."

"Really? Then you won't have any trouble sharing." He pulled his badge out of his jacket and showed it to the men.

A look of panic flashed between them. Although they were in uniform, they had what appeared to be an unmarked car.

"What's your station house? Because I know this isn't a local situation." Ryan stepped closer to the armed men and looked at Eve. She was staying put, hands in the air.

"Sir, we're in process here. If you'll excuse us…" The first holstered his weapon and approached her carefully.

He pulled her hands behind her and grabbed his handcuffs. Ryan grabbed his cell phone from his pocket and dialed Kathy, the receptionist at the station. Eve's weapons were removed.

"Hey, cutie," she answered. "I'm headed out the door. What's up?"

"What's your badge number, partner?" Ryan wasn't above getting physical, but after staring for a moment, the man rattled off a number. Ryan repeated it to Kathy and asked her to run it. It was wrong, the way these guys were going about things. "What're the charges?" he asked them as he waited.

"This is our case, and now is not the time." The second man pulled Eve to her feet.

Ryan stared into her eyes as Kathy told him what he already knew: "There's no record of that number. You need some backup, baby?"

"Okay, sorry. I know you were leaving. Thanks for your help on that." Ryan hung up on her and turned to the men.

"I apologize — just jittery lately. You guys need any help bringing her in?"

"No, we're good. Thanks, though."

Ryan had no choice but to watch as they pulled Eve along and tossed her in the back of the car in a way very unlike what any real cop would do. He hated his powerlessness, but it didn't seem safe to escalate the situation here — too much potential collateral damage in the coffee shop behind him.

One fake cop jumped into the driver's seat, and the second slipped in next to Eve in the backseat as she righted herself. She slumped again, as if she'd been hit or shot, as the car pulled away, lights and sirens blazing, and Ryan was already running toward his truck.

3

CATCH

Eve fought through the chemically induced fog. After the first two gunshots she was able to get her eyes to stay open. Her handcuffs were too tight and her wrists were on fire. The wounds from the last time she was bound that way — courtesy of Rodolfo Vitullo — made the burning a hundred times worse.

Her feet were still free, but her mind was blurry. She was in a cop car.

No, wait. It wasn't a police vehicle. It was missing all the telltale signs of belonging to the government. The man nearest her shouted directions to the driver. She focused on that.

"Get in the tunnel! Fuck, he's coming on the opposite side. He's trying to get even with us on the left."

"Shit. He nicked that car — nope still coming. Jesus."

"Shoot out his fucking tires!"

"I'm trying. He's swerving. This asshole is good. Tapped another car. Jesus, he just jumped the median!"

"I saw him. I saw him."

The man next to her dropped his gun and leveled another at whoever was chasing them. And then her foggy brain knew who it was: Ryan. Ryan knew these men weren't cops.

"Okay, keep it steady, I gotta aim. I'mma blow his head off."

Eve tried to time her kick, but her coordination was sloppy. She managed to swing her body around and brace against the car door. She kicked him in the ribs twice before getting a solid shot at his jaw.

The man's shots went wild, and she worked her legs like pistons, hitting him in every soft spot he had. The driver made eye contact with her in the rearview mirror and said nothing, swerving to get her off balance.

Something rammed their car from the rear, metal grinding on metal until the driver slammed on the brakes. Eve tumbled to the floor, smooshed and off balance.

She took a breath and settled herself. From her awkward place on the floor, she worked on her arms. The yoga she favored helped her slide her hands from behind her back under her feet like a jump rope. As she crawled back to the seat, she had her bound hands in front of her. The man in the rear seat with her was coming around as the driver swerved from one lane to another, sending crap flying all over the car. A screwdriver rolled past her foot, and in an instant she had it.

The driver aimed his gun wildly over his head, barely missing her face as the back window of the car shattered, sprinkling crumbled glass everywhere. She kept track of both guns while bitch-slapping the closer gunman with her screwdriver-studded fist. Finally, when he'd dropped his gun a fraction, she inserted the shaft of her weapon into his temple. He fell, boneless and dead to the floor.

The car was slammed from the back again, and screeches and sparks flew everywhere as the bumpers entangled and locked together. One glance out the window told Eve they were doing at least ninety miles an hour. Cars were pulling to the side of the road and spinning out of control.

And then she locked her gaze on Ryan's. It was his truck directly behind them. His front windshield was shattered, so she couldn't miss his determined face.

Her screwdriver was so deep in the dead man there was no retrieving it now. The driver aimed his gun over his head again, trying for her. Eve used her handcuffs to pin his hand to the headrest, applying as much force as she could.

She wanted him to let go of his gun, but a wave of blurriness washed over her. The fucking drug they'd injected into her was rearing its head. The pain of the gunshot was ice combined with lightning. She screamed.

"Take that, bitch!"

The blurriness got worse, and time seemed to be getting slower as she peered over the seat. The driver was headed right for one of the scariest turns in Poughkeepsie. The flimsy guardrail would be barely a hindrance for a car traveling this fast. The view was stunning as the Hudson River rippled hundreds of feet below the edge of the road.

Move. In that moment, her mind told her she had one chance. Judging from the searing center of her pain, she'd been hit in the abdomen. That was bad news anyway, but damned if she was going to let her almost-dead body tempt Ryan into following this car off the cliff.

She crawled over the backseat, out the broken back window, and onto the trunk. It was stupid. Her blood poured out of her, making the smooth metal ridiculously slippery and hard to stay on.

The driving asshole began swerving again, trying to escape from Ryan. She used her bound hands as her anchor, pulling herself to the tippy edge. A quick jerk to the right had the car almost on two wheels. The fucker was headed for the cliff.

Seconds. That's all she had left, but the reckless maneuver had unhooked the cars, and Ryan now fell behind.

At least I can jump and he'll stop his truck. It occurred to her that Ryan would then run over her, and he would hate that. But she felt another bullet fly close to her head. *Come on. Come on.* Ryan could drive the shit out of a vehicle. The high-speed techniques cops mastered made him the far better driver. Her eyesight was going gray at the edges. *Just have to hang on until he gets a little closer.*

Ryan saw what she had in mind, and he shook his head the whole time while he peeled the rest of his windshield out of the way. It was now or never.

With a silent prayer for help from Mouse, Eve threw herself toward Ryan's truck.

She couldn't leap far enough. The gap between cars and the asphalt below was about to be her grave when Ryan literally caught her with his hood. She rolled onto the vehicle and felt his strong arm grab hers.

He pulled her into the cab while executing a hairpin turn, then let go of her once she was inside to work the shift pedal and the gearshift.

They came to a blistering stop.

"Shit!" Ryan yelled. As he pulled her into the passenger seat from the floor of the truck, he gaped at her bloody stomach. Behind him an explosion lit the truck's interior orange, and he covered her with his body.

She used the last of her strength to hug him now that he was against her. She tried to talk, but her voice wouldn't work. She ignored the searing pain to smile at him, but after that there was only black.

Beckett pulled into the Maryland hospital's parking lot five hours after he'd left Poughkeepsie and feeling off. Something wasn't right, but damned if he could figure it out. He called Eve and it went straight to voice mail.

Though she hadn't said it, he knew she'd shied away from seeing baby John because her own scars still hadn't healed, would never actually heal. Regret swelled up as Beckett's brain reminded him again that her life was painful because of him. With Herculean effort, he shook it off and refused to be anything but joyful on his brother's big day.

He met Chaos in the lobby, and the man walked him through the visiting process so he could see Chery before the baby-meeting event. When he entered her room, she was dressed and seemed poised to leave.

"Hey, pretty. How you holding up?" Beckett embraced her gently.

"I'm all right. Tough stuff, though — this thing." She didn't seem to know where to put her hands.

"You still sure this is what you want?" Beckett sat on the empty hospital bed.

She nodded. "But I feel like I'm torn up on the inside. It hurts so much." Her eyes filled, and Chaos beat Beckett to her side, rubbing her back. "But it's the right thing. He can have a clean slate. He deserves it." She shrugged as Chaos handed her a tissue.

"I can't imagine. All I know is you're fucking brave as fuck," Beckett said.

Chery laughed a little. "You're a goddamn poet."

"Where's Vere?"

Chaos answered. "She's at the day facility. We're getting her as soon as Chery's got her walking papers."

"That's cool. How's the dog working out?"

Beckett got the full story of Vere's birthday party and how much she'd loved the gift he'd sent. The dog, rescued from death row and now named Rufus, had arrived by limo, complete with tons of food and more toys than he'd ever need.

Soon enough the nurse came in with a clipboard, so Beckett gave Chery a hug and shook Chaos's hand. After asking a few questions, he was directed to a room clear on the other side of the maternity ward.

Inside, Fairy Princess was feeding baby John and beaming.

"Now that's a fucking sight. How beautiful you are." Beckett leaned against the doorframe.

"You hitting on my wife?" Cole pounded Beckett on the shoulder.

"Every chance I get. She's a sweet piece of woman." He grabbed his brother up in a hard hug. "Congratulations, Daddy. You guys getting to know each other?"

Cole held up his arm for the shake. "It's amazing. He's just…an answer to prayers. Less than twenty-four hours in, and my whole world has changed."

The handshake got a third arm as Blake entered and joined in. This was magic for Beckett, pure and simple. The world slowed down, and his cares melted away as he looked from face to face. He loved these men so fiercely, it'd probably scare them if they knew how much.

Livia came in behind Blake and busted through the boys, passing Kellan to Beckett and Emme's hand to Cole.

"Rude." Beckett teased her.

She shot him a look as she knelt in front of her new nephew in her sister's arms. "Oh, Kyle…" was as far as she got before both women were crying.

Beckett knew he wasn't the only man now looking around the room, trying to avoid tearing up himself.

Emme pulled on Cole's hand. "Why are they crying?"

Her uncle bent down. "Well, sometimes when all your dreams come true? The best you can do is cry. It's happy, not sad."

Beckett laughed as Kellan put his little hand in his mouth.

Blake patted his shoulder. "Careful, he loves to feed people."

He was about to reply that Kellan took after Uncle Cole when the boy stuffed a wet cracker in his mouth.

As he gagged it down, Beckett tried not to hurt the kid's feelings. "Yummy."

Kyle passed John to Livia and snickered. "Looks like you loved it, hot shot."

"Pipe down, sweet ass—" he noted the children and quickly covered "—ociated banker?"

Kyle hugged her niece, stole her nephew from Beckett's arms, and pointed at her son. "Look at that, big guy. You have some company."

Everyone started talking at once, and the kids got down to playing with the toys Blake pulled out of their bag. Pictures were taken in every possible combination.

Cole sheepishly asked Blake if he would come double-check the car seat just to be sure it was in right, and Beckett followed, leaving the women and children in the hospital room.

"Thanks so much for coming to see us. Means the world." Cole was every inch the proud papa. "I feel so alive when we all get to be in the same place."

"Couldn't be anywhere else, brother." Beckett slapped Cole's back as they stepped off the elevator and headed out to find the car.

"I had it parked in a reserved spot and totally forgot about it," Cole explained with a laugh. "This morning I got out here just as the doctor was waiting to pull in. He was pissed until I explained I was out of my mind." He opened the back door of his old-man car, and Blake checked the seat, showing him how the belt fastened and where it should sit on the baby's chest.

"I'll text you a picture of my handiwork before we leave," Cole promised. He and Blake slipped into daddy talk as Beckett checked his phone. Three text messages rolled in as soon as he opened it.

They were from a douchebag with bad fucking news. Word had it that Eve had been arrested. Beckett looked up, and as if the messages brought the man forth, John McHugh and Kathy approached them from across the parking lot.

After hearty congratulations, Beckett asked John for a moment. To his credit, the man squelched a look of distain and stepped aside with him.

"I just got intel saying Eve has been arrested. You know what for?" Beckett's mind was going a million miles an hour. There'd been no movement, no threats for months. Why now? Though, of all things, getting picked up by the cops was one of the safer options for Eve.

Confusion crossed McHugh's face. "Really? I think your intel is shit. Let me find out." He stepped aside and pulled out his cell phone.

Beckett noticed Kathy waiting, within earshot. "You know anything? Everyone knows the receptionists are really the brains of the place." He moved closer to her as McHugh shot him a dirty look.

"No...Eve's father is a friend of mine, so I think that would perk up my ears. But..." She bit her lip.

He urged her to continue.

"Just before we left—weirdest thing—I think one of our officers was investigating a possible impersonation of a police officer. I'm sure it's just a coincidence."

McHugh rejoined the conversation with a stern face. "Ms. Eve Hartt is not being detained, nor is there any indication she has had contact with our force. I guess your shit intel was just shit. But if you hear anything further, let me know. Now, if you'll excuse me, I have a grandson to meet." He held out his hand to Kathy, who gave Beckett a shrug.

Beckett hated the scenario that had just played out in his head. Grabbing up Eve was damn hard. She'd be looking every which way for someone out of the ordinary, like usual. But if they had badges, she might be forced to go with them. This could've been the most perfectly executed kidnapping ever.

Fuck.

Though he'd driven five hours and spent a mere forty-five minutes with his new nephew, after Beckett talked with McHugh, he left one hospital and wound up going straight to another. It had been a hurried good-bye with his brothers, but Beckett had a bad feeling. And sure enough, Morales had texted with the news that Eve had lost something like half her blood volume halfway through his five-hour trip back to New York—which made him shrink it to more like a three-hour-and-forty-five-minute trip. Poughkeepsie General had surely hoped he'd never return, but here he was: sitting in the waiting room holding his head.

Ryan launched colorful curses at him every few minutes.

"Dingleberried cocksucker...Twat waffle...Anus junkie...Clit fungus...Rectum warhorse."

The hours passed slowly. Eve was on the operating table, and the only thing keeping him from losing his mind was the fact that her own father, the best surgeon around, was piecing her abdomen back together.

At some point, he didn't even know how long ago now, the nurse had come out to tell them the drug in her system was complicating the surgery and preventing her blood from clotting. He was lucky he knew anything at all. Ryan had unwillingly filled him in with more details about her injuries about an hour after he arrived so he'd stop bothering the nurses. Beckett had then told the fancy dog spa where G was currently vacationing that he would be there at least another day.

Beckett began rocking in the plastic chair. If he lost her now, he'd not be able to live. He would drive off a cliff—maybe the same one the fucker who shot her did. And then he'd be able to spend his time in hell beating the fuck out of the man who'd hurt Eve. It had to be Rodolfo. Though why he would try to pick her up now was a mystery—one Beckett intended to solve. The man was such a calculating bastard. Or Sevan, if he had a wild thought, might have made a play for Eve as well. It could be time to get that fucker under his direct gaze to make sure he wasn't coming up with any actionable ideas. He might prove useful whether Eve lived or not. *God, let her live.*

"Sperm biter...Jizz fondler...Mucus Dumpster."

"How bad was it?" Beckett finally just had to make conversation with the ass gobbler, Ryan, or kill him. And he was the only one that really knew what the hell had happened.

Ryan sat across from him in the beige waiting room. "For shit. The worst. In the gut and then the sheer amount of blood...I've never seen so much blood. And I've been to murder scenes."

"She's tough, though." Beckett folded his hands together.

"That's for fucking sure. She took a guy out then wrestled with the driver. Plus she was toasted on whatever they gave her and had a

GSW to the torso. Then she *jumped* from their trunk to my hood at, like, ninety miles an hour. I shit my pants a little, I'm not ashamed to say." Ryan stood and began to pace.

"I want to shit in your pants too after hearing that fucking story." Beckett held his head as nausea rolled through him.

"When are they going to get done, for fuck's sake?" Ryan kicked a chair.

"It's a big job. Lots of little veins, important things. You can't miss one, you know?" Beckett rolled his head on his neck, trying to get rid of the knots of stress.

Ryan defaulted back to cursing at him while Beckett's brain ran through the scenario that had just been put there.

Eve was batshit crazy and brave like a tiger. He vowed then, in this darkest moment in time, to get to the bottom of this, to get Rodolfo or whoever it was, and make him pay.

"Tit shitter…Monkey taint…Testicle junkie."

Dr. Ted Hartt had done this surgery a million times in his nightmares. It was always Eve, and it was always life threatening.

But here, fully awake, with classical music playing in the background of his operating room, he made sure every move was professional. He didn't look at her face, didn't tear up. It was against every rule there was to operate on your own child, but he was on duty and, damn it, he was the best and everyone knew it.

Another surgeon had been called in off the golf course, but Ted had recognized the man and shook his head when he arrived. This delicate operation would be lost in his hands. Ted was simply better, and his team acknowledged that by staying by his side.

In his head he referred to her as *the patient*. He focused on the wound. He continued picking parts of her spleen out of the inside of her abdomen. He reconstructed the veins as best he could, but the lack of clotting made it difficult.

Twice they'd lost her rhythm. Twice they'd been able to shock the patient back. He wouldn't let it break him. Instead he'd nodded at the return of her heartbeat and proceeded, repairing the damage over and over. It was as if they were trying to bail out a boat that was destined to sink. The blood they gave her barely kept up with what was coming out.

It had been hours. And Ted had every intention of working for hours upon hours more. This patient would live if he had to buy her soul back from the devil himself.

4

Amen

Sometime after midnight, Blake took the call from Beckett on the balcony of their hotel room in Lusby, Maryland. As he listened, he knocked softly on the door of his brother's room, and Cole emerged looking tired and concerned.

After Kyle, Cole, and baby John—they were calling him JB now—had checked out of the hospital, they'd received a text from Beckett requesting that everyone stay out of Poughkeepsie a few extra days. Wanting to be together, Blake had cancelled the beach visit they'd planned before Disney to stay in Maryland. He'd also rescheduled his meeting with producers of the television show he was composing for, which he'd been so proud of himself for coordinating with the family visit to Florida.

Grandpa John had been on the phone for most of the day. He seemed to want to go home to handle something, but he refused to say what. Blake had overheard Kathy talking him down.

"Sweetheart, you deserve to spend time with your family," she'd said. "There'll always be something going wrong at work. You're a *policeman*."

And so John had stayed, and Blake now listened as Beckett's voice explained that the reason he'd run home so quickly was likely connected to John's situation.

After Blake assured his brother he would stay put and stay alert, he disconnected and filled in Cole. "He sounds horrible. She must be really bad off. He wants us to stay here, but he asked that you pray for her." Blake shook his head. Eve was complicated, but he'd never have been able to stand in the sun so soon if it hadn't been for her.

Cole nodded. "Can you join me?"

"Of course," Blake said.

"Dear Lord, Please protect and guide Eve at her time of recovery. Life has given her a lot of emotional wounds, and now her physical body is mirroring this pain. Please take her hand and keep her safe. Let her live to lead a life that shows her the power of your love."

Together they added, "Amen."

Blake hated that it was all they could do right now.

Eve was pretty sure she had a cotton ball for a brain. Everything was fuzzy. She opened one eye and then the other. The lights felt like they were made of her raw nerves, and she was so thirsty.

As she let her eyes adjust, she noted she was in a hospital room, and Ryan was passed out in a chair near her bed. He was way too huge to be comfortable in that position. He was carrying his hand-gun as well.

She cleared her throat, hating herself a bit when she saw how startled he was by the noise.

"Jesus! Fucking shitter." He straightened himself and was on his feet. "Sorry, fell asleep. How you doing?"

"Thirsty." Eve could barely get the word out.

He found her a cup and filled it from a pitcher close by. He added a straw and held it to her lips.

"Drink slowly. They'll probably cut my nuts off for doing this without asking anyone." Ryan apologized for the tepid water. "It's been here awhile."

She forced herself to take small sips, and her throat thanked her the whole time. She didn't stop until she got to the slurpy end of the cup.

"How long have I been here? You okay?" Eve was able to say more now that her thirst was quenched.

"It's Saturday afternoon now, so you've been here a little over a day, and I'm fine." Ryan held up his hands. "Just don't move. There are rules about all this stuff. And you have all kinds of drainage shit. Don't move. Or fart. Or laugh."

Eve tried to smile at him, but failed. "Feels like I ate a cannon ball."

"That's pretty much what you did there, Rocky." Ryan dialed his phone. "Yes, sir, she just opened her eyes. Looking good." He turned his attention back to Eve. "Your dad will be here in a minute."

"He's going to be pissed." Eve looked at her torso. The huge wound packing made her look pregnant.

"Listen, you're going to be okay. That's all that matters."

Her father pushed through the door and saw her sitting up. "Thank the Father Almighty." He exhaled audibly. "Okay, Ryan, out you go."

Ryan shrugged his apology and left the room. Her father went about the business of giving her a checkup. He did the nurse's job as well as his own, taking her temperature, checking her bandages, and listening to her heart.

"Okay, this is a button that's hooked up to your pain medicine. You press it when something hurts." He stood and smoothed back her hair.

Eve hit the button twice. "So?"

"So?" Her dad looked at her complexion and tested the elasticity of her skin to see if she was dehydrated. He was being her doctor.

The medicine flowed into her system, and she began to have nice long lapses of semi-consciousness. "Aren't you going to yell at me?" Her words began to slur.

"No, just heal. That's your job. And mine is to see to it that you do well while you take care of that. I'll be your father later." He gave her a gentle kiss on the forehead.

She was drifting off, but she could still hear him.

"I love you so much, baby girl. Never leave this earth again."

"Sir, I've finally been able to access Eve's medical records, and though I'm sorry we were not successful in acquiring her, I've discovered some disheartening things about the woman in question," Nicholas reported, looking at the floor.

Rodolfo tried not to let his anger get the best of him. Since the stroke, any time he did, he began to slur his words. But Nicholas was not saying things that filled him with joy.

"I prefer being happy." Rodolfo found his hand tingling, going a bit numb. He focused his attention on the sensation of opening and closing his left fist. "What can you do about that?"

The messenger looked nervous, but continued. "In the car accident, when she was hospitalized as a teen, Ms. Hartt's fetus was injured to the point that it needed to be removed."

"And?" Rodolfo clenched both fists now.

"Well, after the procedure her uterus hemorrhaged. They had to perform a hysterectomy." Nicholas shifted his weight from one foot to another.

Nicholas wasn't shaking yet, so Rodolfo held out hope the information wasn't as completely dire as it sounded. "She'd be unable to have my child then? Is this what you're telling me?"

"Well, yes. After extensive searching, I was able to determine that Ms. Hartt no longer has any reproductive organs, save one remaining ovary that regulates her hormones." Nicholas quickly went into this briefcase and pulled out his iPad. "But…"

"Your timing is for shit, my friend. You realize with this information we could have avoided that whole fiasco yesterday? This better be an amazing but." Rodolfo felt weary. This last thread to a viable offspring was his breath and soul.

"One of the nurses I met with seemed to have a bit more information than she was letting on. So I increased the irritants to see what would emerge." Nicholas turned the device around and a very exhausted-looking woman appeared on the screen. She was tied to a chair.

"*So now, what was that you were saying? I need it on video.*" Nicholas' voice was louder than hers in the recording.

Pain had obviously taken her far past the need for patient confidentiality. "*Her father used the time she was under to do a procedure I disagreed with.*"

"*And that was?*"

The nurse looked at the camera. "*This will end my career.*"

"*Do you need more motivation?*"

The woman's eyes darted to the lower left, where surely something Nicholas had used to harm her was waiting, and she shook her head.

"*I was just starting out. I came into the room, and the patient was unconscious. Her father was there—he works at the hospital—and there was a fertility woman extracting her ovary. I was dismissed from the room. Later, when they were gone, I checked on the patient, and she was still under. I never knew for sure, but I was pretty certain her father had taken the ovary without her knowledge. He was half out of his mind with concern. Now, years later, I realize I should have told my supervisors.*"

Nicholas turned off the video before facing Rodolfo. "Suffice it to say the nurse did not know the name of the woman in the room."

"Ask her again, then. Bring her here." Rodolfo pointed to the spot in front of him.

"That's not possible, sir. But I'm confident I found out everything she knew." Nicholas looked worried again.

She was dead, Rodolfo surmised. "So, tell me about these ovaries and what you think that means."

"Well, I'm thinking the father knew that a nineteen-year-old girl might want to procreate again someday. Ms. Hartt was barely conscious for the first week in the hospital. I think her father had her ovary frozen. I've done some research, and it seems they've made some progress with this science in Europe. There's one doctor in particular...I have his name somewhere..."

"I don't give a crap about his name," Rodolfo blustered as Nicholas shuffled papers. "Just tell me what he can do!"

"Well, at least theoretically, if the ovary truly exists, we could have it reactivated to produce mature eggs again," Nicholas explained. "Then we could fertilize them and a surrogate could bring the child into the world. Your child. With Eve Hartt. And no messy entanglements with the actual, fairly deadly woman need to happen." Nicholas smirked.

"So they take my sperm and shake it up with her unfrozen woman stuff, and we can control the pregnancy? That actually—" Rodolfo smirked as well "—has potential. If—and this is a very big if—the nurse was correct and that European doctor knows his stuff. How do we find out where this frozen ovary is? Surely her father has it well protected. And let's make that foreign doctor an offer to continue his research in a more easily accessible location." He put his hands together, letting his shaky fingertips touch.

"I could start canvasing fertility clinics, run a few Google searches to see which specialist might have been be involved? Who was friends with Dr. Hartt?" Nicholas repacked his briefcase. "And I can also reach out to the doctor. I'm sure a generous research stipend would do the trick."

"That's a place to start, but it also sounds like it'll take a while. I'll give you a month to get all the pieces in place." He waved Nicholas toward the door. "Time is of the essence, and we don't want to tip our hand, so perhaps work on the research doctor first, as we can't perform the trick without the magician, now can we? Then I'd suggest you talk to Dr. Hartt in a very inspiring setting. No?" Rodolfo smiled again, hating the slight droop he could feel on the left side of his mouth.

Beckett hovered in the hospital waiting room, his anxiety level sending him through the roof, when asshole Morales finally returned, by way of the cafeteria. Asshole.

An email had just buzzed through on Beckett's phone from one of his guys inside the police department, and now he had some intel that changed the game. The dental records of one of the dead bodies from the accident were fairly unique: every other tooth was solid gold. Because of this, the asshole had been known as Checkers, and he'd worked for Rodolfo's business in various capacities since his pubes had come in. He'd also spent quite a bit of time in the system, which is how Beckett's man recognized him. Checkers always smiled funny in his mug shots so the gold would catch the light. And Vitullo's high-priced attorney had always bailed him out. Checkers had likely been selected to impersonate an officer because he knew how it was done so well.

Giving him the middle finger with both hands, Morales announced, "Hey, crap bag. She's awake."

"Oh, thank fucks out loud." Beckett sat hard in a plastic seat.

"She was lucid and talking, you hairy prick gurgler." Morales smiled. "And she didn't ask about you once. How you like that, tampon muncher?" Morales turned back toward Eve's room and continued to give Beckett the finger behind his back.

Beckett shook his head. He hated that guy. He'd made sure to point out that Beckett wasn't related to Eve so he couldn't go into the recovery room. Morales had insisted he was on police business and needed to speak to her as soon as she was conscious. Apparently he also had an in with Ted. Of course the cop who saved your daughter from the clutches of the evil villain would be your fucking favorite. He texted the news to Blake and Cole and received jubilant replies. Morales was a fucker with a filthy mouth, but at least he'd had the decency to keep Beckett informed.

Beckett closed his eyes for a few moments, and suddenly it was hours later. He knew he should get after solving this problem, or at the very least pick up poor G, but he didn't want to leave without seeing Eve.

Twenty minutes later Morales came out, looking as haggard as Beckett felt. "She's awake, dildo biscuit. And she wants to talk to you." He used both his middle fingers to point Beckett back down the hallway.

Beckett ignored the insults and powered down the corridor. He opened her door, and there she was. He stopped for a second and let his knees get back under him. Seeing her beautiful goddamn eyes was all he needed. "Hey, killer. Looking like you're in pain." Beckett came in and kissed her on her mouth. She pinched her lips shut.

When he sat down, puzzled, she explained, "No toothbrushes yet."

"Like I care about that. Kiss me for real." He leaned in for another light kiss, and this time she kissed him back.

"Thank you so much for being alive. I was killing myself every five minutes out there." Beckett picked up her hand.

"Remember, Romeo was an asshole. Don't pull that shit." She squeezed his hand.

"How bad was it?" Beckett hated to hear, but he had to know.

She shook her head. "Without Ryan I was a goner. He caught me with his truck when I jumped."

"You're so badass. Seriously. Never do that shit again." Beckett kissed her hand and her wrist.

"Don't ask that of me. You know how this works." She hit a little button next to her.

"Did they say anything?"

"No. Hit me with a tranquilizer before I could get anything out of them. They looked convincing as cops, though. Convincing enough, anyway. And I couldn't fight back on the street, you know? It was broad daylight. Great set up. Fuckers." She was getting agitated.

"Settle down. Just take a few deep breaths." He rubbed her gently on the leg. Her stomach was bloated and bandaged. They'd gotten her good. A gunshot there should have put her six feet under.

"You can't retaliate." She looked concerned. "You don't even know who it was. And besides, I told you Mike Simmer was a stupid idea, and it blew up in both of our faces. So maybe listen this time?"

"And slicing Mary Ellen's throat was Mensa material?" He touched her cheek.

"Let's try not to respond to this like brainless assholes. Wait until we can figure it out together." Her gaze grew cloudy.

Surely she was ready to rest again. No need to put any of this on her now, Beckett decided.

"All right. I'll get proof and ammunition," he promised. "But that's only because I love you. I'm already working on it." He leaned down and gave her another quick kiss.

"Speaking of murder, my dad will kill you if he sees you in here. You better go. But thanks for staying."

Beckett nodded. She was right, and he didn't want to make the situation tense for her.

"I got it, baby. No worries." He stood and leaned over her. "I fucking love the hell out of you."

She smirked, eyes getting droopy, "I love you back."

And with that, he left her, though it felt like he'd pulled his heart right out of his chest and left it lying next to her in the bed.

Morales was waiting on the other side of the door. "Queef sucker."

"Listen, according to her I owe you one." Beckett leveled his stare at the man.

"Suck my nut juice. The only thing you owe me is walking out that damn door and not coming back." He pointed to the exit with his middle finger.

"She loves me, so you know." Beckett headed for the door.

"Anus jockey." Morales shook his head with disgust.

"Thanks, officer. You staying here until she's out?" Beckett continued ignoring the insults for now.

"Yeah, elephant dick pincher. I'm not leaving her unguarded for a fucking second. Unlike you." Morales opened Eve's door and let it swing shut behind him.

Beckett nodded at the closed door before turning to leave. That last comment stung a bit.

Perhaps because of it, and against his better judgment, Beckett spent the night in the waiting room—just to make sure. Though for his trouble he was treated to the sight of Ted Hartt coming down the corridor just as his eyes opened in the morning. He dove for the vending machines, and then took the hint that it was finally time to go.

His phone buzzed as he traveled toward the exit, and Beckett bit his tongue before he answered it. "Yes, Rodolfo?"

"Taylor. Finally you take my calls. All I had to do was play with Eve a little bit to get your attention." The old man coughed on the other end.

"You do know that by hurting her, you've made an enemy of me." Beckett could feel hate crowding words into his mouth. He'd known Rodolfo was involved, but to hear the old fuck admit it, without a care in the world...

"Actually, I was never able to meet with her, and I lost several of my people in the process, so I think it's safe to say I came out on the losing end." Rodolfo sighed. "If only I'd been able to speak to you sooner. I've been calling for months. But never mind that now. I want to clear your head, clear the air. I won't be after her again."

"I believe you not fucking *at all*." Beckett had to will himself to not crush the phone in his hand. "What the hell did you want, anyway? What was so important that suddenly doesn't matter?"

"I understand why it might be hard for you to trust me. I will tell you this, that woman killed my Mary Ellen, but she has worth. I see that now. I also know that taking her won't make a good partner out of you, and I'm still convinced we could work together quite successfully. I've been hearing my old friend Sevan Harmon is a bit down on his luck, so perhaps now would be a good time to cut him out of the trafficking through Poughkeepsie, hmmm?"

"Not interested," Beckett said. "You almost fucking killed her."

"Tone, young man. Tone. Well, that's too bad. I'll give you some time to think on it. But anyway, I'm getting older now. I need my legacy to continue. We don't need bad blood between us. She's yours. You can have her. Hell, out of the two of us—you need her more. She's loyal to you. A good quality in a hit woman." The sound of Rodolfo smacking his lips traveled the connection.

"I'm not reassured. And I'm still angry." Beckett curled his hand into a fist.

"You have my word as a businessman. Why don't you come by and we can discuss it in person. Sometime next week, maybe? I don't want to disturb your plans for the Thanksgiving holiday. She'd just kill everyone here anyway. Yours is the only leash she will accept, and I don't need to lose any more of my good men. For her to be useful, she can't be in a cage, and that's where I'd have to keep her. She's a weapon for you."

Beckett shook his head and rolled his eyes. "I'm a man of my word. Let's see how you do." He disconnected the call and slid into the driver's seat of the Challenger.

Rodolfo had spoken some sense. Eve was not someone who could be forced into anything. She was too fucking clever and driven and single minded. But something still nagged at him. What had made *now* seem like the time to steal her? Was it simply that Beckett had gone out of town? Was there some message he was missing? As much as he hated the thought, perhaps an in-person meeting with the old coot would be useful. He just needed a little time to think it through. He sent a message to Rodolfo's people that they should expect him on December third.

Whatever Rodolfo's plan was—or had been—Beckett hoped that maybe, just maybe, the old man had realized he needed to back off.

He slammed the car into gear and drove to the scene of Eve's accident, now two days past. When he surveyed the scene, sheer rage overwhelmed him. He opened the door to the Challenger and left it ajar while the car alerted him of this repeatedly. He actually stopped in his tracks and closed his eyes. He inhaled and exhaled, trying to control himself some fucking way. The bendy yoga people seemed to get off on this breathing shit, so in and out he went. He opened his eyes and looked at the jagged guardrail. The fuckers that took her had plunged to their deaths through that little slice of protection.

He blamed himself for it all. He wasn't here, wasn't protecting her. He was absent when she needed him. And most of all, his reputation hadn't been enough to scare the assailants away. Doing good seemed barely worth it if he couldn't keep his own family safe. Maybe he'd gone soft after all. In his head, the only answer was murder and plenty of it. The old way. The way he knew. If he stacked enough dead bodies on top of one another, no one would see past them to find the ones he loved. He wanted to go to Rodolfo's compound and blow men away until he was out of ammo.

He wasn't sure how long he stood looking off the road—enough time that cars began to honk, drivers cursed at him, and eventually, he grew chilly. He got back into his car. But he sat there and shot the middle finger at motorists protesting the inconvenience of his parking style, which had funneled the road down to one lane and forced drivers to time their passing of his car with the absence of oncoming traffic. Eve had asked him to wait. It was a promise that would be hard to keep. But damned if he wouldn't try.

Beckett began a huge mass text to all his known douchebags. He needed a nice quorum of loyal guys to make a more informed decision. The absence of Mouse pounded his conscience once again. The big guy would certainly have made today easier to handle.

After driving to the meeting place—an old, crapped out restaurant Beckett had thought of renovating—he found himself among the last to arrive. He entered the room and waited as the guys quieted down.

"We're being attacked," he said simply. "And it's an unprovoked attack. As most of you know, Eve was abducted a few days ago. They didn't get far with her, of fucking course. She's alive. But obviously we're going to have to retaliate against someone who would put one of my people in the back of a fake cop car and try to get out of town. They were purposeful and clever. And that'll have to be the last time we're bested."

He looked from face to face in the crowd. After more than six years out of sight, and just seven fairly inactive months back, he needed them to understand how he planned to do business. Shark stood in the back cracking his knuckles. He was a wild card. Yes, he'd helped Eve when she was working for Mary Ellen, but only when it suited him, and he sometimes had to be blackmailed to help at all.

"As I've told most of you before, working for me shouldn't be a death sentence. I'm doing shit a new way. I've learned. Surprisingly, I've aged. Situations have forced me back. Your loyalty has brought you here. I'm going to say this one more time: Being in my employ will always include a way out. I will never hunt you down and kill you after I give you the okay to leave. As of right now, there is no blood out of Beckett Taylor's organization. Despite the attack on Eve, and despite my personal feelings about the fucker who did it, my desired approach to getting shit done hasn't changed. I need you to understand that."

The men looked suspicious. As they should be. Maybe they thought he was cracked out on drugs, or drunk off his ass because of Eve's injuries. The rotten restaurant setting surely made him look more insane than he was. It was like the old days at his crappy strip mall.

"I have some intel, but now is not the time to act. Right now I need to get this town safer, which I know sounds like I'm speaking in tongues right fucking now, but hang tight. I'm interested in things being better for everyone, not just myself. Your job is to stay alert and listen. Can you all handle that?"

When they heard he had a plan, they seemed a little less tense. They nodded or grunted their understanding.

"Okay, get outta here, except for Shark, Dildo, and Treats." Beckett pointed toward the door with his pinkie. He waited as the room cleared.

The men he'd held back moved closer to the bar where Beckett had taken his stand. "Okay. I want you bitches to nose around. You find people that are just out of prison, families on hard times, old hookers, druggies that are straight. I want a file as thick as my dick of people to choose from."

Dildo, a tall, skinny guy with pale hair dared to speak first. "I'm not down for hurting kids. Or old people, hookers or not."

Beckett shook his head. "Do you not know me for shit? Jesus. That's not who I am — especially not now. Don't misunderstand. I've been looking into some abandoned properties. I want to divide you guys up and have you work with people. I want to build Poughkeepsie up while taking Rodolfo Vitullo down. He's made it clear he can't leave me, or at least people I care about, alone. And for now that's confidential, you got it?"

Shark raised an eyebrow. "You looking to kamikaze yourself? I'm not buying into that."

"No, numb nuts. I've just learned some shit these last few years while I was away. You give people a little respect, and they rise up to meet you. Not always, but sometimes. Don't mistake it for me going soft. I'll just as soon pound someone's asshole into their brain if they fucking deserve it. Do you all understand?"

The small crowd nodded. Beckett dismissed them all with a wave, but grabbed Shark's arm and held until they were alone.

"You gonna propose, big boy?" Shark gave Beckett's commanding hand a side eye. "In that case, call me Dax."

"You'd never be that lucky, asshole. I've to get a few things straight with you before we move forward." Beckett let go and crossed his arms.

"I'm all ears. And penis, so the ladies say." Shark's eyes flashed.

It was a risk, trusting this slippery sucker. But he'd been able to work with Eve when it counted, so that had to mean something. Plus, she'd shared some Mouse-gathered blackmail information that could be used to strong-arm Shark into doing what was needed. Though Beckett would rather have loyalty from this guy who excelled in getting into everyone's back pocket, his brain was filled to the brim with shit that could help in a pinch.

"Like I said, I'm changing shit," Beckett told him. "I have to make this place as safe as possible for the people in my life. I'm fair, but I'll need a commitment from you. And not wishy-washy shit like you pledge to all the other players in this godforsaken game. You have a family too." Beckett waited as the information settled. Shark's quick inhale and the tightening of his hand into a fist told Beckett all he needed to know. The nerve was hit. "No," he continued. "You took that wrong. I'm not threatening your girl and Micki. I'm saying I know you're juggling fire to provide. I get that. I submit that if we do this smart, keep the lines of communication wide open, we can get out. We can let this town be a haven for our people. I want to compile a bunch of likeminded individuals who can go to war if needed, but would rather not. Not peacekeeping shit, but not senseless, power-hungry bullshit either."

Shark was on edge, judging from his shallow breathing. "I'm listening."

Beckett nodded. "You need to leave, you go. But if you want a place to park your damn people and know you're not fucking alone in protecting them, come with me."

"I've heard a lot a shit about you, and nobody's my damn boss." Shark stepped backward, away from the conversation.

"And it's all true. Probably multiply it times a hundred. I'm nobody's fucking saint, and I don't pretend to be. But I'm shit at running away. I'm tired of the way things were—the way they are. I've got too many people who deserve to sleep at night, not be punished because they know me."

"You've got a balance here that's impossible to maintain long term," Shark countered. His wheels were clearly turning, most likely picturing a life of easy chairs and school plays.

"Impossible is just the shit nobody's tried yet," Beckett shot back. "My balls are way too big not to hope for the best. And I'm stubborn and vigilant and single-minded. I'm going to make this city a fortress." He shrugged. He wanted Shark on his side, but not enough to lube up his own asshole and grab his ankles for it.

"You need this decision now?" Shark looked at his watch.

"Yup."

"And if I say no?" His hand went to his piece.

"You leave. You never darken my door again, and I make no promises that I won't shoot you dead if we come head to head in the future, but your family is safe from me. That's my word." Beckett ran a hand through his hair, already starting to re-block his plan in his head.

"The blonde? She's worse than you. She's crazy."

"I wouldn't say that to her face if you like your dick on your body. She's in." He hoped. He was letting her heal before roping her into his newest situation.

"All right, you crazy motherfucker. I'll work with you, but only if my family is as high up on your priority list as your own."

"I can't put them that high. But the next step down, that I can cop to." Beckett held out his fist.

Shark looked at the gesture for a few beats. Finally, he nodded, tapped Beckett's fist, and used it to add some choreography to the handshake, solidifying the union in a manly way. "What do you need first?"

"I need you to find Sevan Harmon. Spend Thanksgiving with Micki and your daughter, then get on the road and find him. I'm not one-hundred-percent sure Harmon is useful, but I want every tool at my disposal when I lay this out. Rodolfo's got weak spots, and he might just be one of them."

Shark nodded, and Beckett smiled, his dimples highlighting his pleasure. *Fuck impossible.*

At the end of their second day in the Maryland hotel, Blake and his family concluded a day of outlet shopping with a dip in the hotel pool, and then met Cole and family with John and Kathy at the Chinese restaurant close by. Calamity ensued in the most endearing way—at least Blake hoped the other guests found it endearing. They set up a highchair for Kellan and a bucket seat holder for JB, blocking a bit of the walkway around the table in the process. Grandpa John looked so happy, it was damn hard to recognize him. Emme gave him her rundown on the menu, explaining the things she would be willing to eat and the reasons some of the offerings were subpar, in her opinion.

"Grandpa, this says poo-poo platter. I really don't think we should eat here." Emme set her mouth to the side and gave the adults a hard look.

Livia fastened a bib around Kellan's neck while she laughed. "Try to read the rest, pretty girl. You'll find out the ingredients."

Blake felt his phone vibrate with a text. Beckett had messaged that they could all go about their business and return at will. He felt he had things adequately under control. Blake acknowledged his brother quickly.

Halfway through dinner, both Kellan and JB were fussing, so Blake and Cole each took an armful of child and went to the parking lot for some time-honored pacing. After both the boys had settled, Cole, still bouncing, asked, "That was him on the phone?"

"Yeah. Beck says we're clear for takeoff. Eve's awake and starting to heal. He told me his people are on high alert, and the police are also ready to amp up their patrols." Kellan snuggled deeper into Blake's chest as he started to hum.

"Does it make me a jerk if I can't help but wonder if running to hotels to hide is going to come up again in our future?" Cole looked at his son.

"Well, if it does I think it makes us both jerks. So far, it's been mostly okay. Things seem under control or whatnot as far as Beckett and Eve are concerned. At least since Livia was taken, things seem calm.

I don't ask questions, though." Blake pulled Kellan's travel blanket from his shoulder and wrapped the child in it. "This nap is poorly timed."

"I'm so scared to wake him when he's asleep," Cole said, looking down at his son. "But then I'm checking a million times in a row to make sure his little chest is going up and down."

"That's normal. Sorry. You never stop agonizing over whether or not the kid's okay, or if the woman is happy. Endless cycle. Welcome, brother."

They chuckled and Blake added, "It's a crappy club of no sleep, less money, and concerns that turn into heartburn in your chest at two a.m." Kellan's breath was warm against his neck. "Worth every second, though."

"That's what I'm finding out." Cole kissed his son's forehead before continuing their previous conversation. "Should we be asking questions? I feel like I want to know what we're signed up for."

Blake looked into the distance. Back in the day he would never have questioned Beckett—it felt like a breach of the man code or whatever. But since Livia had been taken, all bets were off. Now Eve was in the hospital, and maybe they needed to know if Poughkeepsie was the best place for a safe future.

"I think we have to." Blake met his brother's eyes. There was a ton more left unsaid as the restaurant door opened, and the family came out in a whirl of laughter and questions.

After tucking the kids into car seats, the caravan prepared to move. Cole and Kyle would return to Poughkeepsie and settle home with JB. John and Kathy would follow Livia, Blake, and the kids down to Florida and proceed with the vacation as planned. The girls hugged each other hard before getting into their vehicles. Blake and Cole nodded at each other.

"I'll call you about what we were just discussing later," Blake told him.

After twenty minutes of constant talking, Blake watched as the kids let the car motion rock them to sleep. Livia noticed as well and settled with a sigh.

"Finally. Though we'll pay for *our* lack of sleep later." She rubbed the back of Blake's neck.

"Of course we will." A light mist started, and he hit the wiper blades. "I'm excited for Disney."

"Me too. Emme's going to flip over the characters. I wonder how Kellan will do?" She rustled through her bag and applied some strawberry ChapStick.

"So Cole and I were talking—" he glanced at her "—about Pough-keepsie and safety and stuff. How are you feeling about it?"

She closed one eye and exhaled. "I don't know. That's a tough one. I guess I'm shaken. I fought for a lot in Poughkeepsie. I grew up there. Married you."

She made eye contact and smiled. He counted.

"But by the same token, there's enough to worry about every day without wondering if someone after Beckett and Eve will drag our kids into the crossfire—even though I know he's trying to be a different person now. I think we could stay if it was just us, but I can't look at their faces and not want to protect them." She shrugged.

"So, do you think we should move?" Blake would do anything for her.

"I wish there was a way we could stay. And that Beckett could stay too." She looked out the window and traced a raindrop's descent on the window with her finger. "But the kids come first. I think we have to talk to Beckett."

Blake nodded in agreement even though she wasn't looking at him. She'd summed it up perfectly.

5

SEVAN

Sevan Harmon needed two things: More money, of course. Always more money. And more respect. His life was forever a chess game played on a roulette wheel. He'd had to take precise, informed, ball-dropping gambles to get where he'd been.

As he smiled at yet another topless model, toasting her with his martini, he plotted. She knelt. He was willing to bet she had no clue he was on four hit lists and at least six hundred dollars overdrawn in his bank account. Based on the impeccable tailoring of his white linen pants and the gleam of his expensive watch, he suspected she thought she was about to deliver a semi-public blow job that might result in actual cash coming from the tip of his penis. Happy December from the heart of paradise, currently found in Mexico. Screw snow, ice, and tiny, cold dicks.

As she leaned forward and tested her gag reflex to its limit, Sevan ordered himself to put his concerns out of his mind. Living for the moment, or even the second, was how he'd always made ends meet, but his balls tensed and his erection loosened as he pictured his latest venture going belly up. His resort plans in Dubai were dead in the water. He tried to focus on the woman between his legs. Her name was eluding him.

Katrina?

Lucia?

He had been so positive things would work out. He'd used the investment capital he'd "borrowed" from Mary Ellen Vitullo to get investors excited about his luxe blueprint: villas filled with the most expensive touches. And Sevan knew expensive. But after taunting Mary Ellen, Sevan had fully intended on returning her money. Maybe even getting her to marry him. He'd done some damage, but there'd never been a heart he couldn't unbreak. He'd been sure he could just wink and say, "C'mon, Mary Ellen, you know you love me." And she would've wet her panties for him. Of course, now she was dead.

Katie?

Annabelle?

He was fully flaccid now, but she was working hard, adding moans as his dick slipped around in her hands like the corpse of a slug. He took another swig of his drink and stared hard at her ass, slapping it to add some motion to the flesh her thong revealed. In the harsh sunlight, the ridge of her buttock implants showed. Swallowing, he took his hand from her ass to her breast. When she didn't notice he was touching her nipple, he knew it was numb, cut off from the rest of her body. It was acting a part as much as she was. He sighed. Damned if she wasn't like an animated mannequin. He poured the dregs of his martini over her head. She tossed her hair and pretended to like it, licking her lips until he pulled himself out of her hands and repositioned his pants.

He watched her grow furious.

"What? You no like what I do?"

He slid his sunglasses in place. English was not her first language, nor was it her last. She'd been able to interpret six different conversations using eight different languages for him during his last meeting. She was fluent in many different curses and told them all to him, professionally, as his investors backed out. They wanted their money back.

"No. You're fat. You're fake. You're not pretty. I can't even make it stand up for you." She was gorgeous. He just picked the words he knew would hurt her the most. A woman who took such care with her appearance would take these insults personally, no matter how many languages she knew. She kicked sand at him and swore him up and down before stomping off.

It was a dick move, even for him, and he knew it. Depression was starting to set in. He'd had such a high when his pockets were full of other people's money. He'd been so high that when Beckett Taylor's hot piece of ass had suggested he return Mary Ellen's money, he'd been able to agree. Or at least that's how he preferred to remember the exchange. His bank account had been bloated with investors' money. He could afford to please her, shock her even, by returning the money to Rodolfo Vitullo.

It was during that phase that Sevan had convinced himself he'd get out of the drugs and weapons business. It was interesting, when he was "rich," how he could laugh off the threats of the shady people he'd been trafficking illicit items to. But now he sank down low in his beach chair. They were all he had left.

And while he was busy pretending to be someone he no longer was, his organization was unattended, falling apart. Getting involved with these types of people was like petting a tiger. It had seemed manageable, but now he wasn't sure he could escape. He should have kept Mary Ellen's damn money.

"Blaming her 'cause you can't get it up? I feel like I'm in a bad Viagra commercial." A man sat next to him in the empty beach chair.

Sevan composed himself. "Maybe I don't play for her team? And you can kindly go fuck yourself." He knew better than to turn and look the man in his face. He tried to place the voice. He failed.

"I don't need to fuck myself. My equipment is titanium any time a woman needs it." The man tossed an envelope in his lap.

Sevan flinched despite himself.

"I'm doing a job for someone. They're looking for you. Call that number. Soon." The man stood.

Now Sevan looked him up and down. Handsome fucker. Scruffy beard, light-colored eyes that were crinkled up, trying to defeat the bright sun. Hard chest, American-style bathing trunks.

"And your boss is…?" He didn't touch the envelope.

"I don't have a boss. But I'm going to find that topless chick and satisfy the living hell out of her, Sevan."

He held up his middle finger as the man left. Exasperated, he opened the envelope. In it was an American phone number. He dialed his cell phone, which was on the verge of being shut off due to non-payment.

"This phone was ringing like a goddamn coward. This must be fucking Sevan."

This voice he did recognize. They'd done business in the past. No one would forget this asshole. "Taylor. I'm in the middle of an amazing vacation. You better tell me something worth my while. I'm on my way to shop for yachts."

"Really? They sell yachts in hell or are you really buying yourself a new fucking douche canoe?" Taylor shouted orders in the distance.

Sevan said nothing.

"Listen, get your broke ass to Poughkeepsie. You're pissing off the Dubai movers and shakers, and yes, I have friends everywhere. If you make it here alive, I might have a use for you." Taylor started what sounded like a large vehicle.

"No way. I'm staying far away from Vitullo until he's as dead as Mary Ellen." Sevan couldn't think of a more dangerous place to go.

"Shark found you, fuck monkey. He's bringing you back to town — either to me or to Rodolfo as a goddamn Christmas present. Your choice."

Taylor disconnected the call.

Sevan wanted to punch something, but the only solid thing close enough was his own goddamn face. He had to sit and wait as Shark winked at him and proceeded to perform what had to be spectacular cunnilingus on Fake Butt not even a rock toss away. He waited while she returned the favor to Shark.

Instead of being the mac daddy getting his on a semi-public beach, Sevan was busy watching and waiting, ironically, with a dick that was finally hard.

Cole was exhausted. How one little human could stay awake so long was a mystery. He felt like a zombie, and Kyle looked like one. But one glance at JB made all the surreal, am-I-awake-or-dead feelings evaporate. He was so small and so present and such a light bundle that he made Cole's heart feel so full. Kyle and he were tremendously thankful for the time they'd spent with their niece and nephew throughout the years. The diapers and feedings seemed mostly like common sense.

Still, Kyle was calmer than he was, easy with her new title. A mother in the waiting room at the pediatrician had even thought JB had to be her second or third child because she was so relaxed.

Cole had been rocking his son in the chair in the nursery, and it was time to finally put him down, but he couldn't quite get there. His protective instinct was so strong. He gazed at JB and wondered at the miracle of his thin eyelids, at the violence that had brought such a perfect example of God's love into the word. He was so staggeringly grateful for his brother. This love he had for his son was a quiet thunder in his soul.

He prayed over him all the time. Maybe it was the exhaustion taking a toll, but he felt such an understanding of the world from his place in the rocking chair. And then, out of nowhere, there was the searing hate. He almost wanted to put JB down so the emotions coursing through his veins wouldn't be wrapped around his son.

There should be forgiveness, but Cole hadn't evolved that much. He hated his mother. To think that she'd held him as a babe, the same size as JB even, and instead of love, she'd seen a means to an end. All this time he'd been blaming himself on some level, thinking that as a child he must have failed. He'd failed to make his mother fall in love with him. The cracks inside him he'd blamed on himself.

And now, holding his own child, he knew for certain it was never his fault. It was hers. She was able to hold her baby and not understand the miracle in her arms. God gave her a gift, a version of His only son, and she'd found only the evil inside herself to hurt him. She'd found the way to be an observer to his pain over and over.

Kyle padded quietly in, smiling first at JB and then putting her gaze on his. He was so very good at locking people out, but not her. He knew she saw the pain retreating into him. She gently lifted JB and kissed him on the forehead, light as a wish, before putting their son in his crib.

She pulled Cole out of his chair and led him back to their bedroom. By the time he stood by their bed, his shell was in place, all his pain and anger locked inside.

"No. I saw that. I saw you. Talk. Tell me." She pulled him onto the bed and curled up in his arms. "This is a no-silent-treatment zone."

"We should sleep. Sleep when the baby sleeps."

"No, you say what you're dealing with. And even if I can't fix it, you won't be alone with it." She kissed his lips and looked at him with sure, unfailing trust.

This woman was his strength.

He sighed. It took a while to unwind the tight grip he had on this thing. She smoothed his hair and traced his lips while she waited.

"It's just, you know, holding him is so amazing it hurts. I feel like I'm getting to look God in the face. I've never been so affected. Between JB and you, I feel like my heart is splayed open. It scares me, but even more than that…it makes me so angry at her."

Kyle nodded. He could tell she knew who *her* was.

"All this time, I figured I was lacking something she needed. But now, I know I had it, she just never cared. I was a whole person. I deserved space in her world."

He stopped. The tears were climbing his throat. His defense was always to stop — stop talking, stop feeling.

They were quiet for a while.

He tried to make her feel better. "Listen, it's not fair for me to —"

She covered his mouth, and honored his beliefs by starting to pray.

"Dear God, this man before you is a husband and father. Grant him the strength to process his newfound knowledge. Forgiveness for his mother is a task that neither he nor I may be able to grant in our lifetimes. But I thank her for bringing me this man, and through him my beautiful son. In front of you, I want to make a promise to Cole."

She put her hands on his face, framing it for a moment. She touched his forehead, his lips, and finally returned her hands to his cheeks.

"I promise you, Cole Bridge, that in honor of the little child you once were, I will never forget that JB is a gift from God. I will honor his unique, gorgeous person with enough love for both him and the memory of a little boy who deserved so much more than he got, for as long as I live and beyond."

She kissed his lips.

"Amen."

He held her close and kissed her hard, her tears salty on both of their lips. "You are so much. I have no words."

"I know," she said. "I feel that way about you too."

The love they made was tender, a promise to a brand-new family that it was, first and foremost, bound by love.

It was a lovely Wednesday morning in early December, and Beckett strolled toward his front door feeling good. He'd just handled a drug dealer stationed near a school, thanks to a tip-off from his repurposed douches, and he felt quite accomplished. Until he arrived at the front door and found it unlocked. Instantly, he was pissed.

When he entered, Eve stood in the kitchen, making a salad.

"Do we not keep you fucking safe anymore?" he demanded.

Without looking, she launched the knife she was using to chop the salad at him, barely missing his head. The blade sank into the plaster of the wall.

"I knew it was you." She smirked. He could only see her blond hair.

He cursed her in his head, because she was still healing. He wanted to put her on the counter and screw her so hard. Instead he gently slipped his hands around her waist. "How you doing?"

"Stir crazy. But you knew that." She turned and hugged him before kissing him.

Her smile was lighter fluid to his testosterone. He was full caveman for a few heartbeats. "I do know that. I remember how you took care of me when I was stir crazy." Years ago when he'd been running from the law, she'd kept him hidden, and only their rough sex kept his brain from leaking out his ears. "Which is, painfully, not an option right now." Beckett sighed. "We could go upstairs and have some nice, easy Good Housekeeping sex? Make gentle love and all that shit?" He grazed her neck with his teeth.

"That sounds awesome. Then can we decoupage? Please? Let's make cat sculptures, and they can be headstones on the graves of our dead sexuality." She laughed as he made a face at her.

"You funny today?" He gave his best smolder.

"Today, I am." She bit her lip and wrinkled her nose. The doorbell rang, and she looked slightly worried. "Speaking of funny..." She held his arms when he went to go to the door. "I made a plan with a friend for today because I know you have that meeting."

"Why are you nervous about that?" He switched the grip so he was holding her arms instead. The bell rang again. Gandhi woke himself up from his drooling nap with a bark.

"I just never got a chance to tell you that I need to start taking walks. Dad was pretty specific about my recovery."

Beckett gave her a hard stare. He knew now who was on the other side of the door. "Really? No one else could go with you?"

"He's a friend. I get to have friends." She sighed.

"How 'bout picking friends who aren't in love with you?" He let go of Eve and jumped over G on his way to the door. He swung it open to see the very predicable Ryan Morales on the other side, holding two water bottles in his gloved hands. "Rip his nut sack off, G." Beckett pointed at the man's crotch.

"Your dog can't handle that big a meal, pus chunk." Morales looked past him to Eve. "You ready?"

Beckett stepped in front of her, blocking the cop's line of view. "She was just sitting down to a salad. So, no."

It was a tension-filled moment. Beckett was not done talking to Eve at all.

She put her hand on his shoulder. "I was making the salad for later. It's done, and I'm ready to go."

Beckett gritted his teeth. Eve put her hands on his cheeks.

"Settle down." She gave him a fairly generous kiss, which made him happy.

She tugged on her jacket and gloves. Beckett added his scarf around her neck. "It's cold."

"This is what dad said I had to do. Expand the lungs and all that." She turned and walked out of his door.

He tried one more time, calling after her, "We can get a treadmill!"

Morales turned with a smirk. "Doc says fresh air's the best for her lungs." Then he mouthed "sucker" just for Beckett.

He mouthed back, "You packin'?"

Morales moved his jacket to show his police issue. Beckett knew Eve would be armed. She always was. He slammed the door behind them and cursed his way up the stairs. Damned if he was going to be a jealous pussy. Still, it burned in his chest. But it was time to suit up and get out to Rodolfo's. He was thankful Eve hadn't asked any further questions about the meeting, as it was the last place she needed to be.

As he changed, he steeled himself, thinking again of the conversation he'd had with Cole and Blake last night. It had added some direction to the wheels he already had in motion. He'd popped in to visit JB and found Blake there as well, just back from his Disney adventures. Cole was on his last day of paternity leave from the school, and Blake was showing off an iPad full of pictures. Cole had lamented, "I wish this town was more like it was when we were in foster care. I feel like it was less dangerous, or I was just ignorant?"

Beckett hadn't responded right away, just looked down at JB's sweet face in his slumber. Three kids, so fucking little, who were now pawns in a game he didn't even really want to play anymore. "I think it was a little of both, bro. A little of both."

Cole had an almost a pained look on his face when he spoke again. "Should we really even be here anymore?"

Beckett had nodded, though he wasn't sure. He loved having his brothers close, but he'd toyed with the idea of setting up a little commune in a small town in the middle of nowhere to hide from his past.

"Kyle'd really like to stay, but you know how she is about the baby," Cole continued. "She's scared." He shrugged. "And I might be too. I feel like I'm looking over my shoulder all the time."

"We don't blame you, but with who we all are…" Blake trailed off.

Message received. His brothers and their wives were concerned for their families. His plan was more of a reality now. Sevan was on his way to Poughkeepsie, and Beckett knew his instinct had been right. When he was finished, Poughkeepsie would be a castle with a moat around it if it had to be.

When he was a just a young, deadly pup he'd brought the town to its knees by being the scariest motherfucker he could be. But age had given him insight now, and his chunk of time in Maryland had taught him a few goddamn things about patience. As much as he wanted to ignore it and nuke the fucker, the half-dead Rodolfo would not respond well to brutal violence. And dead he wouldn't say anything. Beckett had to go in humble, go in respectful if he wanted answers and a way to get to the bottom of whatever this was with Eve.

He took a glance out the window and saw no trace of Eve and Morales. It was no good attacking the geezer from the exterior. That risked an all-out war with countless collateral damage. No, if he wanted to end this, he needed Rodolfo's illegal empire to implode.

Ryan grabbed her hand and held her back. "Don't go too fast right out of the gate." He let go before she could protest.

"Ugh. I hate being coddled." She did slow her steps, though—from turtle speed to snail.

"I think everyone in the entire world could figure that out." Ryan smiled at her.

"I know, I'm a whiner." She took a sip of the cold water and smiled.

"So your boyfriend didn't know I was coming?" She knew he was forcing himself to walk slowly—barely walking at all, actually. She hated this.

"It wasn't like I was hiding it. He just has a big meeting today. He was kind of mysterious about it, actually, and I didn't want to twist him up. He understands that you and I are friends." She took a deep breath, and the air was so crisp it almost hurt.

Recovery was going to take forever. Apparently the doctors and her father weren't wrong when they said she would be diminished for a few months. She'd tried to ignore their suggestions twice, and the pain had caused her to stop moving and almost stop breathing. She had a new respect for Blake and his recovery from his chest wound years ago.

She decided to change the subject. "So, you dating anyone?"

Ryan began to whistle.

"Not answering?"

He took a swig of water before tossing up a hand. "You don't want to hear what I have to say about this. And frankly, I don't want to tell you."

She gave him a look that she hoped conveyed how much she couldn't ignore the obvious obstacle to them being friends.

"I know you're with him. I get it," he said. "I'm not wearing a hair shirt or pining for you. It's just…" He shook his head. "No one knows everything about me like you do. So when we get time together? I don't have to watch what's coming out of my mouth. It's relaxing. Does that make sense?"

It did. Eve had had too many names and lives not to see the beauty of being your actual, true self. She nodded.

"And nothing I tell you will shock you — none of my stories from work. God, if I tell you I had to arrest a twelve-year-old kid yesterday, you'll get it. You'll know I hated it. And when I say something in that kid's eyes scared me, you won't think I'm a monster for predicting his life of crime and calling him a waste of time." He kicked a wayward rock out of the way. "I say that to another chick? She'll worry I'm not father material."

Eve nodded again. "Okay, I won't haunt you about dating for a little while."

"Thank you. I just need time, I think. You set that bar pretty high. I think I need some age on me to either lower that bar or get me ready to meet someone who can make me forget about you."

She took another deep breath and yelped a bit.

"You all right?" He put his hand on her back and scanned the area to make sure her noise hadn't been inspired by their surroundings.

"Just too deep. I'm good." She took more-shallow inhales while Ryan watched, looking concerned. She rolled her eyes. "I hate this shit. I feel powerless like this."

He nodded. "You want to go to the shooting range tomorrow? Let off some steam?"

"Yes, please! That would be great."

Ryan kept his hand on her back until she was breathing regularly again, then he dropped it back to his side.

Her back registered the lack of his warmth. She liked this human being so much. She really hoped their friendship could make it. There had to be another girl for him.

Beckett hated this house. Fucking New Jersey. It was as if the deaths that had built Rodolfo's empire clung to the interior. He was, however, a little flattered by how many soldiers had shown up to keep an eye on him. He kept flinching and making quick movements to freak them out. Finally he was waved forward. One of Rodolfo's top people escorted him—Nicholas, if he remembered correctly. The old fart didn't even give his guys proper nicknames.

He entered a sitting room, where the diminished man seemed to be taking an unplanned nap. Beckett clapped his hands, and he didn't respond. "I can't be lucky enough that you're actually a dead motherfucker right now."

Rodolfo opened his eyes. The shrewdness in his gaze was instant.

Beckett sighed. Nothing as easy as this moldy foreskin expiring from natural causes was happening today.

"That'll be all, Nicholas," Rodolfo said.

Beckett sighed and went forward without an invitation, sitting in the chair opposite the old man. "Give me one good fucking reason not to snap your neck right now." He leaned forward, sizing up the old fart for a kill. He could taste Eve's pain on the tip of his tongue. All he wanted was to hear the man scream.

"You'll never make it out alive? You do like breathing. How's Eve? Healing, I bet." The right side of Rodolfo's mouth lifted.

"You waited until I was out of town. Then you sent asshole Checkers to grab her. Not kill her—grab her, because you drugged her instead of blowing her brains out." Beckett let the words come out smooth like he was a hard motherfucker, though really he was picturing the worst-case scenario in his head, and it made his heart curl up. "Anyway, last I knew her name was January to you. You need to explain why you know anything about my girl. I thought we'd agreed our status was I leave you alone, you leave me alone."

"She's intriguing," Rodolfo said, as if he had not a care in the world. "I see talent in her. The videos of her coming to kill my Mary Ellen are riveting. Almost a virtuoso. So young for that talent, and she was on such a different path too—until you ruined it all for her. No children? That's a bitch. Because her offspring would be a valuable asset to anyone's business."

Beckett stood. "We're done here. This is why you wanted to see me? Do you not have anything actually useful to say? Business-wise? You do remember business, don't you? Or do you just daydream about younger ladies you'll never have now? The truce is over. Suck my dick, Vitullo." He kicked over the chair he'd been sitting in.

Nicholas slammed into the room at the sound of the noise.

Rodolfo stood slowly. "Get out, Nicholas."

"But, sir?"

The old man pointed with his shaking index finger. "Out."

Nicholas closed the door behind him reluctantly.

"*You* do not decide a truce is over. We went into this together, and we'll leave it that same way. Need I remind you that you have much to lose?" Rodolfo wiped at his mouth. "Never love more than you hate, Taylor. It makes you weak."

This old buzzard was the best of the best at being the worst. Beckett hardened himself internally. "And never assume you know every trick up my sleeve, Vitullo. I'm a crazy asshole. I don't even know what I'm doing next, so you sure as hell don't."

"Speaking of hate…as much as *January*—" Rodolfo accentuated her fake name "—physically killed my daughter, Mary Ellen wouldn't have been in such a bad situation if Sevan Harmon hadn't gotten his hooks in her. Ultimately he's to blame, as far as I'm concerned. So that should put your mind at ease," he added with a bit of a cackle, "and perhaps give us an opportunity to work together. I don't know where Sevan's keeping himself these days, but it seems no one's minding the shop in your neck of the woods. He used to have some quite profitable trade routes through there. They could use some tidying up."

Beckett narrowed his eyes. "Good to know. Just understand that nothing goes on in Poughkeepsie that I don't oversee."

"I'm not sure that's entirely true. Now that Harmon's MIA, I'm going to take a good, hard look at how to maximize what he left behind. Never stop sucking a teat that's giving milk, I always say." Rodolfo raised his eyebrows as if this were a profound statement.

Beckett closed his eyes for a moment. There were things he was good at. Claiming a town happened to be one of them. "I can't recommend that," he said. "Not in Poughkeepsie. This is your chance to avoid a war, so stay out of my way." Beckett was already out the door in his head. He wanted to take this guy down from every angle. He would mentally drain him, financially ruin him, and kill anyone who got in his way.

"Listen, you're right to be angry. I tried to take her, and I shouldn't have. I crossed the line. Like I said the other day, I won't try again. That's my word. I still see value in our truce." Rodolfo held out his hand. "It's still in place?"

It wasn't the words but the intonation that let Beckett know it was a threat and a play. He shook his head. "Don't ask me to shake the hand of the man who tried to kill my girl. I don't trust myself stepping that close to you."

Rodolfo smirked a bit. "I lost two men, remember? They were good ones too. I think we can call it even."

"She's worth twenty of your men. Maybe more, and you know it. Never touch her again."

Rodolfo's gaze followed Beckett as he backed toward the door. "Those sounded like orders instead of requests."

"Did they? Actually, orders coming from me usually have *motherfucker* attached to them. I just treated you like a tender great aunt. I'm not afraid of you, but I have respect, like I would for a twenty-three-foot alligator residing in the goddamn sewer. Nothing's killed you yet, and you've lived through a lot of shit. You want to be in my life? Then you'll have to contend with how big my balls are." Beckett sighed. Years ago he'd have left a pile of old bones on the floor like he was exiting a chicken wing joint. And damn if that wasn't still the most appealing option. But now, he had to be better at the game than anyone had ever been.

He nodded once at Rodolfo, letting the man know the truce, such as it was, remained intact, and he closed the door firmly behind him, using everything he had to keep his hands to himself like a five-year-old. In the hallway he passed Nicholas, heading toward Rodolfo's study with a glass of water and a tray of pills. The guy was the worst and just the vibe coming off of him was all wrong.

"I know you hear everything, you pansy little fucker," Beckett announced as he passed. "I don't trust you. Just so you know." He stepped up to him, and though Nicholas was a bit taller, fear crowded into his eyes. "Pussy."

On his way out of the building, Beckett gave the gathered soldiers a winning smile, clapping a few on the back to boot. By the time he got to his car, only two guys still trailed behind. He rolled his eyes before he turned to face them, and they raised their guns.

"Listen, you ladies think you have a sweet deal here with the crypt-keeper? He's an insane fucker. I'm looking for a few men, and none of his mind game bullshit. Families are safe with me, and you don't have to bleed out on a sidewalk to leave my employ. I pay better than this stingy shit as well." He saw the interest flare behind their eyes. "You've heard of me, I can tell. So find me if you're interested." With that, he hopped into his Challenger and cranked OnCue up loud.

Nicholas shook his head the whole way into Rodolfo's sitting room and placed a pill and some water on the desk. Rodolfo harrumphed about having to take the pill and maneuvered his lips into a certain configuration to keep a water-tight seal.

Nicholas waited until he was sure the task was complete before speaking. "He's a punk. Say the word, sir. I'll start the plans tonight."

Rodolfo clicked on his TV, and the credits for *The Price is Right* rolled. "We're playing the long game, Nicholas. The generational game. Find out how to create my future children. We know now that Sevan is nothing, so that's the only job you have."

Nicholas sighed as he turned, but he dared not say anything aloud. Instead he just wished silently for some kind of a release coming soon. He was getting antsy. He'd managed to make contact with the doctor in Europe, but had yet to offer him a change of venue for his research. And anyway, that man offered no option for the bloody release he craved. His services would be required for the long haul.

Before he got to the door, Rodolfo's voice stopped him.

"And never underestimate Taylor. He's driven by loyalty—a kind that makes him even scarier than you, my friend."

6

ASS

Blake folded up the Disney bags in the Thursday morning sunlight of his kitchen. Coming back from vacation had been ridiculously hard. He'd had a blast with his family, and as much as Beckett and Cole would make fun of him, he couldn't wait to go back to the land of the mouse.

"You need those to go in the recycling?" He turned at the sound of her voice. "I'm going to the garage to see if my cell phone is out there." Livia in jeans and a T-shirt still made his heart race.

"Hello, beautiful." He grabbed her and pulled her in for a kiss.

"Really? I haven't even brushed my hair today. It's me or Emme who gets ready in time for school in the morning. No time for both." She hugged him back, cuddling against his chest.

"Easier to grab from behind then." He growled in her ear and spanked her butt.

"Ow. Watch it, piano hands." She spanked him in retaliation.

"Go easy with the money maker."

"Last time I checked, I just have to keep those evil hands safe so you can continue to compose music." She spanked him again. "You can't insure everything."

"Careful." He nibbled on her ear.

"Promises, promises, Mr. Hartt." Livia smiled up at his face.

He counted, moving his lips silently.

"That's a large tally you have there, sir." Her hands found the way to his back pockets.

"Is that what we're calling it nowadays? A tally? Whatever turns you on, penguin pajamas." He pulled her into a quick dip and nuzzled her neck.

"Mommy, Daddy is being Pepe Le Pew," came a small voice from behind them. "Now you have to hit him."

Blake and Livia shook their heads and laughed.

"Your daughter."

"No, your daughter."

"I'm everyone's daughter, and Kellan just tipped over a giant box of cereal in the pantry." Emme joined her parents' hug, effectively ending their embrace.

"Did you want those bags in recycling?" Livia repeated while conceding her place in Blake's arms to Emme.

"No, thank you." He smiled at his little girl.

"So…we're keeping the bags?" Livia gestured to the neat pile on the counter.

"Yes." He tipped Emme upside down. "So I need to go to the pantry?"

Emme laughed and watched as her hair brushed the floor. "No, you don't. Kellan and Marx are eating the cereal together. It's precious."

Livia took off in the direction of the pantry.

"Precious? Really? When did you learn that one?" Blake pulled her up and set her on her feet.

"Mommy says it to the neighbor about that new dog that barks all the time. But yesterday when she was done, she said, 'Precious, my ass,' in her quiet voice. And I think *ass* is a bad word." Emme began to feel the scruff on his jaw—her favorite pastime when she had her father's attention.

He bit his lips together so he wouldn't crack up. After nodding he added, "True, that is an adult word. I bet Mommy didn't know you heard it."

Livia walked into the room with Kellan propped on her hip. He ate cereal from a small Tupperware.

"He was hungry?" Blake nodded at his son.

Livia rolled her eyes. "As usual. I'm letting the cordless vac take care of the mess." She meant the dog. "What didn't Emme hear?"

"Tell her, baby girl." Blake put his hand on Emme's head and turned it toward her mother.

"I'm not a baby." She turned to Livia. "You said a bad word. I'm not supposed to say them." Emme began dancing her feet around, spinning under his hand. Finally she stopped twirling, and he steadied her with his hand. "I heard you say, 'Precious, my ass' about Mrs. Show's new dog."

Livia nodded and gave Blake a hard look as Kellan began chanting, "Aaaa. Aaaa. Aaaaass."

"Well, now even the baby's cursing." Emme held her hands up as she shrugged.

Livia and Blake laughed so hard that he hung onto the counter, and she squatted down to steady herself.

The kids laughed a bit, not quite sure what was so hilarious, and then wandered to the living room.

"Emme, we have to leave for kindergarten in just a couple minutes," Livia called as she made her way to him. They both lay on the linoleum. "Are we insane or was that the funniest thing in the world?" she asked, catching her breath.

"We're insane." Blake held her hand as they looked at the ceiling. "And that was really funny."

"Are we saving the bags because you're sentimental?" She peeked at him, and he could feel her attention.

"I thought it would be a sweet way to pack her lunch for school, wiseass. My kindergarten game is strong."

She looked at him, gray eyes sparkling. "Oh, sure, now you curse."

"I'm not fucking animal, Livia. I'd never make the baby curse." He did his best to look disapproving. She jumped on him and began tickling.

He grabbed her hands and bit his lip before adding, "You're in a dangerous position, Mrs. Hartt."

"You liked Disney that much, huh?" She squeezed him with her legs.

He pulled her hands to his lips, kissing them both before responding, "I cannot wait to go back. I fucking loved it. Though it is amazing to be home. I love this house. I can picture you falling in love with me here—making the truckload of breakfast sandwiches for the whole platform, all that."

She smacked his arm lightly. "Now you're just showing off."

He sat up and kissed her lips until she moaned.

She murmured against his lips, "I love it, too. I hope we never have to leave."

By the day after his meeting with Rodolfo, Beckett was looking at a map on his wall where he'd outlined Poughkeepsie in black. He was going all tactical army shit this time. He'd pulled up listings of all the properties for sale in town on his computer, and the iPad had a list of all the abandoned crap in disrepair. Once Sevan's sorry ass got to town, he could point out any additional locations he'd been using to traffic his merchandise. He had two already manned by douchebags. In the meantime, Beckett had put a pin on each of his brothers' houses so he could cross-reference the vacant and dilapidated properties with their locations.

Eve was so quiet he didn't know she was in the room until she spoke. "You've been busy."

He stopped what he was doing and looked her up and down. "You look good. How'd the nap go?"

"Ugh. Demeaning. I'm sick of this. But the nap felt good." She sat on the couch next to G. He snorted himself awake before rolling onto his back for some belly rubs.

"Oh sure, all he has to do to get you to touch him is roll on his back." Beckett put down the paper he was holding and came to sit next to her.

"He's so damn cute, he doesn't even have to ask." She smiled at the drooling fur ball.

"I know." Beckett put his arm around her shoulders, reaching down and squeezing her breast.

She gave him a look. "Seriously? That's, like, such a teenage maneuver."

"I'm not afraid to go basic to get results." He kissed her lips. She bit his.

She pointed at the wall after pulling away. "What, are you on the zoning committee or something?"

"That's my master fucking plan." He looked at it and started thinking again.

"Um, care to tune a chick in?" She grabbed a handful of him to get his attention.

It worked.

"I want you feeling better before I get you involved." He gently touched her stomach, laying his hand on the scars he knew were there.

"That's not getting you laid any time soon." He could tell in an instant she was pissed.

He sighed. "Are you going to bust my balls until you're in on this?" He gestured to the wall.

"Affirmative."

He watched as her eyes darted from the iPad to the wall and back again.

"You're surrounding your family, which would make sense if you were preparing for war," she said. "Is that what's going on?"

"They took you. They would've fucking killed you if you weren't such a goddamn terminator." He grabbed her hair hard with one hand and touched her neck with the other.

"You see? That's what's wrong. Why didn't they kill me? They sedated me. That's tickling on the edge of my brain. I've been parading out there every day on those walks with Morales. And they're not fast walks, you know? A shooter should have picked me off by now." She put her hands on his chest and tapped out a restless rhythm.

"You trying to die out there, killer?" He looked down his nose at her. Fear crowded into his lungs with the air he inhaled.

"Was Rodolfo trying to make a move? 'Cause walking away doesn't seem his style. I've been looking into him — Mouse's files and all. No one got away. Snitches died in prison quick. Like real quick. On the way to lock-up quick — not *in* lock-up. So my question is, why did he want me — unless he just got bored with our truce. And why did he want me alive?" Her gaze slid back to the wall.

"My meeting was with him yesterday." He waited for her outburst. She was quiet for so long it unnerved him. "Say something."

"You went alone. Without me." Eve looked away, toward the window.

"You're who he wanted. I wasn't bringing him a special delivery of his dearest wish."

"Did you go alone? Tell me you at least brought a few douchebags."

Beckett shook his head. "No."

"Why not?" She pushed away from him, stood, and made her way to an armchair. She lowered herself into it slowly.

"I'm trying to do things differently, remember? Even now. Even after something as ridiculous as trying to snatch you up. I needed to get a look into the snake nest. I wanted to see what the fuck is up before I set my balls on fire and bust in there. That's what you and I talked about, right?" He rested his head in his hands.

"Snakes live in holes." She lifted her eyebrow.

"Fuck you. Maybe their holes lead to a nest. No one knows." He smiled at her.

"Scientists know." She returned his smile.

"You want to be a scientist and follow my snake?"

"How'd I know that was coming?"

"My snake would love to come."

"Tell me your damn plan. I'm actually quite impressed you didn't light Rodolfo's world up. But I'm pissed you went alone. Don't pull that shit again. You tell me what you're doing, and I'll tell you what I'm doing." She rested her hands on her knees.

In the past she would have crossed her legs and inhabited the hell out of that chair with her sexiness. Today she was a wounded tigress. Beckett's rage caught his tongue for a second. He forced it down.

"That's fair." He looked at his feet for a moment. It was a commitment between them, and he liked it. "I wanted to blow him to hell. I was halfway there, baby. But then I stopped. They haven't tried to kill you, like you said. Which tells me someone, somewhere is thinking. And I want to know what they're thinking about before I turn New Jersey into Chernobyl. Maybe there's another way to make this problem disappear."

He waved at the map. "This thing is about my brothers. They might want to stay in Poughkeepsie. I've bought five houses in Hawaii just in case they want to go, but if they want to stay, I need to make that possible. I got them involved in this shitty life I picked out for myself. And because they love my crazy ass, they've had choices made for them and their freaking families."

He pushed off the couch and crossed the room to sit on the arm of Eve's chair. "So I'm surrounding them," he explained. "Buying up shit and dropping douchebags in those places to keep things safe. I'm also trying to pluck assholes from Rodolfo and turn them — Trojan horse bullshit. He was too easy during our meeting. Almost apologized." He raised his eyebrows when her face registered surprise. "Right? It doesn't match up. I want him out of our lives. And hopefully, along the way I'll be able to offer some choices to a few people who have been getting it up the ass — bound to loan sharks, just outta prison, that kind of thing. So that's my plan." He met her skeptical gaze. "And you think it's stupid."

"I didn't say that, snake nest." She winked at him, and he felt hugely relieved that she was no longer angry about his lone-wolf routine. "Just let me sit here and marinate in this for a bit."

She tucked one foot under her and settled in, looking at his map.

He nodded and began again, trying to work the numbers and match the possibilities. If he used his little store in Maryland as a test case and converted that approach to the big time here in Poughkeepsie, maybe it could work. Maybe.

7

KILLER MODE

Eve lazed in the living room, hardly aware of what day it was. It was the weekend now, but what did that matter if she couldn't do much of anything during the week? She knew her recovery would be a slow process—she understood that mentally anyway. But her body felt numb half the time, and the pain meds made her groggy. She hated the whole lot of it, but she was glad to be alive and sitting on this damn couch. Beckett trotted down the stairs and smiled at her. Gandhi lolled his head the side and smiled back. Eve rubbed his belly some more.

"You're a fucking flirt, buddy. Can't blame ya, though. How you doing, killer?"

Feet in socks, jeans hanging low, Beckett pulled a T-shirt over his head in an easy way that he probably had no idea highlighted his sheer strength. But it did. The way he flashed his dimples at her when his head popped through the hole made her wonder if he actually did know.

"I'll lay on my back for you. *Allllll* day." He slid over to her on his socks and held out his hand. As he pulled her to standing, he petted his dog. Then he wrapped one arm around her waist and tenderly touched her stomach, concern in his eyes.

Turning her head, she tried to block out the memory that filled her mind. David had held her the same damn way when she'd been pregnant with Anna.

"What?"

Exhaling, she tried to let the scene escape. It didn't. "Just, some-times, I wish I could have a kid. Instead it's like where I'm supposed to create a baby? It's a demolition site. First the pieces of the wreck-age, then the hysterectomy, and now a goddamn bullet. It's like only weapons can be there."

Beckett didn't apologize or try to sympathize. He just held her.

She covered his hand with hers. "Your brothers having kids left and right has me sentimental."

He kissed her lips before raising an eyebrow.

She shook her head. She knew he would get her anything, in-cluding a baby. "You play the cards you're dealt. This is my hand."

A knock on the door sent G into a tizzy.

She turned toward it, not expecting anyone. Ryan had already dropped by for their walk. Still Beckett didn't let go of her. She motioned to the door.

He shook his head in wordless conversation. He wasn't alarmed, but wanted her to go upstairs. She nodded. He kissed her again, and she grabbed at him through his jeans. G barked more as someone rapped on the door again.

Finally she eased from his grasp, ascended the stairs, and pulled a gun from the hall closet. She sat on the top step, the skin of her stomach straining as she took her low seat.

She heard Shark's voice and slipped immediately out of her fe-male regret and into work mode. Killer mode. Beckett's plan was in motion, and it was time to face some of her past.

Beckett opened the door and didn't tell G to pipe down when he saw the fear in Sevan's eyes. "Come in, fucknuggets. Where you been?"

They inched past the dog into the living room. Eventually G turned and ran up the stairs, probably to tell Eve about the visitors.

Shark made sure Beckett knew what a huge pain in the ass Sevan was with his usual exasperated, exaggerated facial expressions. "And the worst part was we had to *drive* back because dickweed raises too many flags for air travel."

Beckett winked at him. "Thank you for your work. Why don't you go upstairs and have Eve show you around?" He nodded in the direction of the stairs, and Shark scuttled off.

Now standing alone, Sevan looked like a caged rat. Still a handsome one, but his obvious fear washed away the swagger necessary for him to be a stunner. "Well, here I am. Now what? Got a roasting spit out back for me?"

Beckett sat in an armchair and kicked his socked feet up on the ottoman. "Ironically, I have the woman who killed Mary Ellen upstairs. But Rodolfo? He blames his daughter's death on you."

Sevan sat on the couch and tried to smooth his wrinkled linen pants, which he'd paired with a loud, flower-print shirt. He'd been posing as a tourist.

"And I've contacted the developers in Dubai too," Beckett continued. "They hate you something fierce. Heard they were looking for talent to take you out."

Sevan held his head.

"As of right now, you're under my protection." Beckett unwrapped a lollipop from the decorative bowl next to his chair and popped it into his mouth. "This is delicious. Damn, I haven't had one of these in years. You like candy, Sevan?"

The man ran his hands through his hair over and over. "What? No."

"You're wrong," Beckett countered.

Sevan looked even more puzzled.

"Your answer is, '*Do* I like candy, sir?' If I say yes, you say…" He held his hands open.

"Yes."

"And if I say 'Hell no, you don't like it.' You say…"

Sevan's nostrils flared. "Fuck no."

"I think you're confused. I sense a little bit of attitude."

"Really? Imagine that. I'm happy as a pig in shit down in the tropics, and you have me dragged back here to talk about what candy you like?"

Beckett winked. "I don't think you were all that happy, despite the fabulous weather where you were hiding out. And understand, just because I haven't killed you doesn't mean I won't. A self-preserving little asshole like you needs to know you're powerless right now. Powerless. And damn near worthless at this point. You broke, baby?"

Sevan raised his chin a bit in challenge.

"Thought so. Knew so. I know so much about you right now, I could rattle off your DNA code from memory." Beckett stood. "The only reason I have you here is that I might have a job for you. And it has to be you, otherwise Shark would have drowned you before he screwed your girlfriend in your beloved tropics."

Sevan went to stand as well, Beckett pushed hard on his chest so he was forced to sit back down. "All you need to know right now is that I'm your boss, and I'm always right."

Sevan shook his head before sighing and nodding.

"And don't think I don't know you're scheming. Right now you're planning shit. Stop it."

Beckett pulled out his phone and fired off a text.

Eve sat on the bed watching Shark. He was quiet, just looking out the window in Beckett's guest room. He was more tan than he should've been in December.

She hadn't wanted to take him to Beckett's room. She could blame it on being tactical, not wanting a man she barely trusted to know the house's interior layout — though he could probably figure it out. But mostly she didn't want work colliding with personal. And that bedroom was personal now. At night she slept there in Beckett's arms, G snoring at their feet on the bed. With the alarm set and two guns under the pillows, she felt safe, like she could be unguarded. Like she could laugh. And despite her annoying need for healing, his concern and attention just made her love him more.

Beckett had a lot of layers. She used to hate herself for falling in love with him, but now she felt like she might be the only one qualified to do so. He was such a bull, a convincing boss. Alpha dog bullshit. But under that, and not too damn far under, he was a family guy. His love for his brothers was so touching. And now he wanted to change how crime was done, maybe even give some sad-sack people other options in the process. Damned if his plan wasn't using evil to do good.

It'd fail, though. He expected too much to go as planned, and no one could control that much. Not even him. But when his eyes had sparkled with hope, she'd realized she would live this delusion with him. She could make herself hard enough to keep him alive, to keep his brothers and their families safe. Eve wanted to protect everything about him, even his dreams.

She might not be so rational either. Crap, Cole and Livia had been kidnapped. She'd been shot. Maybe it was all smoke and mirrors. Christ, she was still tender right now.

Her phone buzzed. She pulled it out.

Th4is bitchis sipper

She translated Becky's horrible texting: This bitch is slippery. She responded:

K.

"How's Micki?" she asked the form across the room.

Shark started a bit at her words, but turned to face her. "She's good. Out of that business for now." He looked back at his phone.

She knew he meant prostitution. Shark had never discussed why the woman in Mary Ellen's employ was important to him, but Mouse's files on Shark did not include a mother for his daughter, Mackenzie. The fact that she knew the girl existed was a miracle.

"So you in for this?" Eve nodded toward the door.

"Dealing with Harmon? No. He's a dick bag. Worthless one at that. With Taylor? Yeah. Grudgingly. Mostly I trust him because he's got you. You wouldn't be two tits in this situation if it wasn't kosher."

Eve nodded. "I'm here till it ends. If that's ten minutes or fifty years, I'm not going anywhere."

She heard Beckett raise his voice downstairs and decided it was time to welcome Sevan personally. Nodding to Shark, she left the room and went to the office. After digging around for a while, she found the gun and a handful of tracker chips, plus alcohol wipes and a Band-Aid. Mouse had been fascinated by the technology when he was alive, and Eve had bought the whole set a few months back. Tracking people would always come in handy. Plus, these little bitches could be programmed to explode, not just poison their hosts, in an emergency. When she went back into the hall, Shark was waiting. He looked at her armload of stuff and stepped to the side.

She came down the stairs and watched Sevan light up a bit at the sight of her. He was a player, and it was an expected response. His gaze dropped to her chest, then to her arms. Alarm registered when he saw what she was holding.

"Hey, killer. You going all Dr. Frankenstein on me?" Beckett asked.

Eve just smiled. "I told you about this little toy," she said. They'd had a good laugh the other day about the ability to make bad guys into mobile bombs.

But no one was laughing now. She loaded the impact gun and checked that it was properly lined up. She hadn't used it yet, but Sevan seemed like a great test subject.

"Hold him." He started to struggle, but Beckett and Shark immobilized him almost immediately. Oh, how he'd fallen since being the man who conquered Mary Ellen Vitullo.

She looked from one handsome face to the next. It was a rush to have this much manpower under her command. She set the gun on the coffee table and opened Sevan's shirt wider.

"What is this? What are you doing?" he asked, eyes wild.

It was as if he hadn't spoken at all. She wiped his skin with the alcohol. Next she thought for a few seconds about the best placement. The neck wasn't recommended, but limbs could be cut off. Feeling his tendons under her fingers, she found the small gap she was looking for. After lining up the gun, she pulled the trigger with no hesitation. Sevan yelped. Shark and Beckett let him go.

"Fuck this." Sevan held his neck as snatched the Band-Aid out of her hand.

Beckett stepped in front of the man and grabbed his face. He slapped Sevan over and over until his eyes rolled in his sockets. He finished it off by punching him in the groin. The man crumpled.

"You say, 'Thank you, pretty lady.' That's what you say to her. Now."

Sevan grunted out the demanded words around groans of pain.

Once he was upright again, Eve explained the situation. "You now have a cutting-edge, non-FDA-approved tracker in your neck. I can find you anywhere. This is for your safety and ours. If you attempt to remove the tracker, the barbs will engage and release a neurotoxin that will kill you instantly. It's a horrific way to go. Every single blood vessel it touches explodes."

Sevan took his hands away from his penis and placed them back on his neck. "How? What? I can't…Does it need batteries? Will it kill me when the batteries die?"

Eve shook her head. "Nope. It's powered by the motion of your body. And don't think laying still will hide you. As long as your heart beats, there's enough movement to keep it going. At least that's what the instructions say."

Beckett slapped Sevan again before straightening his collar. "I own you now. Shark, can you take him to the apartment in beautiful NYC I told you about? I'll be out there in a few hours."

"That's it? What am I supposed to do there?" Sevan asked. "How are you keeping me alive?"

Shark nodded and went to the door.

Beckett pulled Eve into his arms. "Right now? I'm keeping you alive by not killing you. Say thank you, Sevan."

"Thank you, Sevan," the insolent bastard sassed before walking out the door.

"He's a pecker plug." Beckett tilted Eve's chin up and kissed her fiercely as the door slammed.

She moaned. "Seeing you rough him up was hot."

"And seeing you terrify him made me hard."

"I can tell." She bit her lip.

"Let's go handle that situation. I promise I'll be as gentle as a priest."

"You're evil."

"Every chance I can get."

Eve pushed away from him and gathered her tracker gun and accessories as he lightly slapped her ass.

8

JUST MARRIED

Just a few days before Christmas, Ryan sat across the police station conference room table from Capt. John McHugh, who was shaking his head. The man was frustrated.

"I expected to be ankle deep in blood by now. After this latest thing with Eve, I just knew I'd get enough to put Taylor away. How could he resist retaliation? But instead, the crime rate is pretty low. I've been working in this town for over twenty years. Right now it's like the tide is slipping out and staying out and we're all like, 'Look how big our beach is!' But the tsunami is coming."

Ryan nodded.

"How is Eve?"

"She's getting stronger. She's pissed that she's had to slow down." Ryan pictured the determination in her face as she'd tried to walk faster on their last outing. She kept at it a whole two blocks before he made her stop.

"I'm seeing new faces—people I don't trust."

"Boss, I agree. Lots of abandoned property showing life."

"So far those places are getting bought legal, mostly by a couple of businesses with nondescript names. Their backgrounds are vague." McHugh stretched his arms above his head and locked his fingers behind his neck.

Ryan copied the motion while they thought in tandem.

"You could ask…" McHugh began.

Ryan shook his head. "Eve won't tell me shit if I nose around. I'm better off staying on her good side." *There isn't a side of her that's not good. Mmm…*

"Yeah, I figured. I guess the best we've got right now is observation. I don't trust this. And I don't like it." McHugh slapped the table with both hands as he stood.

Ryan followed and offered his boss a handshake. It wasn't exactly a bromance, and maybe Ryan did have daddy issues, but he respected the crap out of this man.

As he walked out, Ryan made some small talk with Kathy. She was a welcoming, efficient respite in the busy station house. He wanted to get over to Taylor's for Eve's walk, but he would be hours early if he left now. It was stupid cold out, but he knew she'd go no matter what. He should have stayed and worked on his paperwork, but he decided to go to the gym instead.

He hopped in his truck and threw it in reverse just as a loud clanging forced him to stomp on the brakes. He was out in a flash, slamming the door behind him as he rounded the vehicle to the tailgate. Dangling from his bumper were long strings with cans attached.

He exhaled loudly. "Goddamn it, Trish."

The sign looked celebratory, but it proudly proclaimed: Morales Just Married His Left Hand!

"Smile!"

Four officers had their phones at the ready. He gave them all the finger as their flashes went off.

"You screw some batshit-crazy chicks, man."

"Your hand does look pretty."

"You want some alone time?"

"Fuck you all very much. And yes, she's insane." Ryan tried ripping off the first string, but it was way stronger than it looked.

He pulled out his pocket knife and began sawing. "Didn't you all see her doing this?"

"No. Maybe she's a ninja."

It took longer than it should have to free his truck from Trish's psychosis. She'd threaded the string in and out of his muffler. The bitch must have crawled underneath too. The sign was super-glued on. Damned if she hadn't done two thousand dollars in damage over the last year.

He drove to the local Best Buy instead of the gym and bought two dashboard cameras. He set one up facing the hood and the second out over his truck bed. He was, frankly, sick of this shit.

Eve walked slowly to the courthouse. Normally she'd wear a suit and heels, but today it was loose jeans and sweater. She was unarmed, so she scanned the area with extra caution as she went through the metal detectors. The douchebags assigned to her waited in a Suburban in the parking lot. Beckett had done as much legal fact checking as he could. Now she was hitting up her secret weapons.

Midian and Tashika, who worked at the courthouse, were contacts from back in the Mouse days. She had a sneaking suspicion that when the knitting badass had introduced her to these ladies, he'd been trying to find her friends.

He had good taste. Midian was small with dark, thick hair and brown eyes. Her figure would make an hourglass jealous. She was like a firework. At first she'd seemed sweet and innocent, but she was known for filling the quiet with accented curse words, which made her more adorable. And her talent for remembering every questionable transaction that came through her hands as a courthouse clerk made her indispensable.

Midian waved her elaborately manicured nails as she approached from the other end of the hallway. Eve tried not to pay too much attention to all the little things she did differently to accommodate her fingernail length. She took the hug from Midian with a gentle pat.

"How are you feeling, girl?" Midian asked. "You look pale, but strong. Bitch, don't you ever get shot again." She sat on the bench in the hall. This was where they met. No cameras, easy to see who was coming and going.

"I feel like a caveman's balls. Dragging. This recovery is going to drive me to drink."

Midian checked her texts, fingernails clacking on the screen. "That sucks. This must be important for you to come all the way here today, then. Or did you just need to get out of the house? Wanted to wish me merry Christmas in person?"

Eve looked around for Tashika, who came around the corner in workout gear. She apologized profusely for being a few minutes late.

Eve nodded as the woman sat next to her. Tashika was gorgeous enough to be a model, but instead she was a bail bondsman. Eve had always known the woman was ripped, but normally she kept her ridiculous physique covered. Today, however, between the skin-tight compression pants and tank top, there was no doubt this woman could crack a walnut with any part of her body she wanted to.

Tashika unwrapped her jacket from around her waist and tucked her iPod and headphones into her pocket.

Midian laughed. "Seriously? Your body's so intense. Can I just feel a gun?"

Tashika rolled her eyes before making the demanded muscle.

Midian reached over Eve to squeeze. "You're so freaking hot."

This was how it went. Periodically the three would catch each other up on little tidbits of information that might be helpful to someone. Years had provided the trust Eve had in these ladies.

"I need to know who owns these properties and any contact info you have." Eve passed the list to Midian discreetly.

She clicked her tongue. "I recognize a few of these. This one the man went bat shit. Refuses to sell. Claims the devil lives in the basement."

"Can you help?" Eve kept watch in the hallway.

"Of course. I'll have it to you before the day ends. Can I ask why we care about this?"

Eve nodded. "I'm staying in the area, and I'm interested in renovating and flipping."

Tashika gave her a hard look. "That sounds tame for a girl with a gunshot wound."

Eve appreciated Tashika's ability to cut to the chase. "I'm staying here in Poughkeepsie. I want to know who lives where. No more surprises. I'm putting eyes everywhere. But on top of that, it's going to be as legit as possible—giving people a chance who need one. That's where you come in."

She turned to face her confidantes. "If you got people you know who are in the shitter, but deserve a chance, I want to know where they are."

"What do you mean?" Tashika adjusted her ponytail and canvassed the hallway.

"Like, say you got a kid who shouldn't really be in trouble, who's a good guy? Just needs some direction? I want to give him a job on a crew flipping a house. Then we're going to rent that house to a low-income mom." Eve shrugged.

"What are the strings?" Tashika pulled out her phone and scrolled through her contacts.

"They have to work hard, stay clean, stay loyal, and be willing to try to make the experience into something worthwhile. And there might be a dog or two involved."

"You're shitting me? Really? Girl, what the hell is this? Did you knock your head?" Midian patted Eve's face.

Eve laughed. "No, for real."

"You with Taylor for good now?" Tashika stomped her feet and stretched out her calves.

Eve answered hesitantly. "Yes."

"Damn you. I was going to pick up every single gorgeous piece of that man after you left him." Midian pouted comically before smiling.

"And he's into this?" Tashika still looked apprehensive.

"Yeah. He is. It's our new thing. And it'll probably blow up in our faces. But we're two tits into it now." Eve made sure to look Tashika in the eye. "No pressure for you to be involved, and I understand if this isn't your game."

Tashika shook her head. "You know I owe you."

"No, you don't. You've helped me a ton. You helped Mouse a bunch. This is just if you want to."

Midian was already researching the addresses on her phone. "I'm in. I'll get you a few names of good kids. But if they get screwed up by this, I'll find Taylor."

"I think that's fair." Eve nodded before leaving the women. Being with them made her long for Mouse. She'd learned that missing him wasn't going to get any easier as the years piled on.

Still, even if it couldn't be him, having people in on her and Beckett's plan made it seem a little less insane.

Looking down on his family, Cole tucked the blanket around JB and kissed Kyle on the mouth, aiming carefully as she rocked the baby back and forth in his room with the hopes of an afternoon nap. "I'll bring food on my way home. Should be back in time for it to be dinner."

She nodded. He set the house alarm on his way out and blinked at the sunshine, feeling like he hadn't seen it in a very long while. His nervous system was numb. It was like baby boot camp in there. He pulled his gloves out of his pocket and got in his car, which took a bit to warm up in the cold so there was no use waiting. And anyway, he was excited to see his brothers. They were meeting at a house a few blocks from Blake's. As far as he knew, it was for sale.

He stopped at Blake's house and found him already waiting outside.

"We could just walk over?" Blake closed the passenger door behind him.

"I like to have a getaway vehicle whenever Becky's involved." Cole backed the huge car down the driveway.

"Sound reasonable." Blake buckled his seatbelt. "So how much life does this old beast have in it?"

Once the car was going straight down the street, Cole offered Blake his arm for the brothers' shake.

"Well, it still runs just fine, but Kyle wants a nice brand-new minivan too. She says she wants enough airbags to blow herself to Hell. Which is a great idea, considering the baby."

"How's my nephew?" Blake smiled.

"So, so amazing. And small. Goes through diapers like a champ. Remind me, I have to pick up a package on the way home." Cole put on his blinker and waited at the stop sign.

"No problem. And by *no problem* I mean I won't think of it until you're dropping me off later, if you're lucky." Blake waited as Cole finished their brief drive and parked. "This place has been abandoned for at least a year."

Construction debris littered the yard.

"Wonder if you're getting a new neighbor?" Cole knocked on the slightly open front door.

"Come in, you sexy bitches!" Beckett's voice echoed off the walls of the empty house.

Cole walked in and shot a look around. This was a home in transition.

Beckett stomped into the living room, wiping his hands on his jeans. "Brothers."

They met in the middle and wrapped arms while patting each other on the back.

"One of my favorite fucking things," Beckett said.

"Me too." Blake grinned.

"For me as well." Cole rocked back on his heels. "You get this place cheap, I hope?"

"Dirt cheap." Beckett gave an appraising glance around. "Still needs lots done, but I think it'll get there." He motioned to two upside-down cement buckets and a pallet of flooring. "Come into my office."

They each took a seat. After a leisurely update on both of the families and Eve, Beckett nodded at Cole and Blake. "I brought you here for a reason."

Cole's stomach turned. It was always a secret fear of his that Beckett would ask them to be a part of something illegal. It was stupid, though. He knew Beckett liked them both *out* of his business.

Beckett pointed at each of the four corners of the house. "This is one of six houses in Poughkeepsie I'm working on right now—all previously foreclosed or abandoned. Basically, I want these kinds of places fixed up and under my direction."

The brothers waited for Beckett to continue.

"I've got my guys on them now, rebuilding, working with some construction crews. The houses close to you and Livia and you and Kyle" —he pointed as he described— "are basically safe houses. I'm going to have people there for your protection. You can have my guys, you can have cops, whatever you want, whatever you're comfortable with—if you want to stay in Poughkeepsie."

He held up his hands, halting the questions he must have seen forming on their faces.

"And I know you *do* want to stay, I get that. I just want you to know as much as you need to make an informed decision. You all keep having kids and being married and whatnot, so my circle of protection must get wider. It's got to have schools and shops and roads for your wives to travel, your kids to be on. I'm still sorting out what I need to do to keep Eve safe, but I don't want to go in guns blazing anymore."

Blake stood and paced. "I'm confused."

"I know. Just give me a bit of room to run with this, and I promise you'll walk out that door with everything you need to know."

Blake sat back down.

"Well, this will ruin the Christmas surprise, but I've bought houses for you guys, and for John and Kathy, in Hawaii. It's an out. I can set it up like the most secure commune ever. You will be safe there. But…"

Beckett stood now. "In case either or both of you decides to stay in town, I'm implementing a plan. It's the best I can do, and I hope it will eventually benefit not just you guys but the whole town. But I can't promise absolute safety. There are too many variables, too many players in the game."

Cole inhaled and exhaled. Maybe his fear would be actualized after all. "What game are we playing?"

Beckett closed his eyes. "I'm looking to give Poughkeepsie a second chance. I want to be a force here. But since my time in Maryland, I've realized there's something more important than fear. Loyalty matters. And you get loyalty by being fucking decent, giving people a choice that doesn't twist their nuts in a vice. Then, when you ask them to keep watch on a street? They take that job seriously. Because you respected them, they respect you back."

He popped his blue eyes open again, then sat down and kicked out his legs, crossing them at the ankles before continuing.

"There are holes in this. Sometimes you give people a shot, and they fall back in their ways — they're shitheads, or whatever. But the ones you reach? You can't beat that loyalty into people. You can threaten people's loved ones, but they'll still turn on you when they can. Rightfully so. But after all this time, I think I found something that works better. So I'm building relationships, as cheesy as that sounds, and recruiting some new guys, treating them all right."

Beckett paused to take a breath, and Cole knew he should say something, but he couldn't find the words. Before he'd formulated something encouraging to say, Beck was off again.

"These houses? This abandoned shit no one is using? I want to let single moms live in them. I want people like my friend Vere to have a place to stay. I think if we train up some people, they can help each other, bound by loyalty. My new tactic for Poughkeepsie is defense, and we'll do it by having a strong community. Some of the lowest people on the totem pole will never get out of that fucking hole without help. They can work their jobs, earn minimum wage, and still never have anything they get to call their own. I want them to get their heads above water, if they have a desire to do so."

Beckett stood again and put his hand to the wall. He smoothed it over the light blue paint. "I sound like an insane hippy. This is stupid, right?" Blake shifted on his seat and looked at his feet. Cole smiled. He'd just watched this man in front of him give himself over to a beautiful dream. This time he found his words. "It's an amazing plan. I'm so proud of you."

Beckett looked at Cole with a skeptical gaze. "But—"

"No. Just flat-out perfection. You're a force to be reckoned with. You're so damn smart. And you have a power inside of you that's unstoppable. You—" Cole stood and walked with purpose to stand right in front of his brother "—have been put on this earth for a reason. And I do believe you've found it."

Beckett threw his arm around Cole and turned to look at Blake. "This is all well and good, but I don't want to ask either of you to rough this one out. Go home, talk about it together. Bake Christmas cookies and crap. Then tell me what you want to happen. Know that I'm yours. My loyalty, my soul is yours no matter what you decide. Crap, you can shoot me in the back, and I'll never want anything but to be around you hookers."

Blake stood and shook his head. "Nah, I don't need time. I appreciate the place in Hawaii, and it would be great to go to—maybe for a vacation sometime? But I'm here. I'm not leaving you. You're my family."

Beckett ran a hand down his face and nodded.

Cole had never been on board with a murderous bloodbath, but he could get behind trying to help the community. He was so relieved that he could finally side with his brother on this. "You know, you've helped Blake and me any chance you got," he said, "even when it meant leaving Poughkeepsie for years. This is something we can help you with."

Beckett bit his bottom lip. "I can't think of anything better." He added his arm to their handshake.

9

CASSEROLE

Cole rocked his son as he stood in the kitchen on Christmas morning. He could see the chair where he'd first told Kyle about this baby who had become JB. He could see it, but he certainly couldn't sit in it. There was an elaborate pattern of walking and standing that JB preferred. The baby opened his eyes and blinked a few times before seeming to focus on his father's face.

"Hey, buddy. Let's let Mommy sleep," Cole told him. "Good morning."

The responding cooing sounds spoke straight to Cole's soul. This child was his to keep safe. The thought covered his spine with metal and determination as he bounced out a rhythm.

He'd been thinking so much lately of his own upbringing—how much of it wasn't his fault. Stupid, common-sense stuff. But he'd been small, and the path he'd been forced to take wasn't fair. Yet he'd come out the other side willing to look for love. That was his own personal affirmation that God existed.

After a few minutes he heard Kyle stomp into the bathroom upstairs. He did his best to juggle the baby and pop the pod in the coffee maker. After descending the stairs, his beautiful bride, sexy in satin pajamas that skimmed her slim dancer's figure, glared at him and the baby before finishing the rest of the coffee-making production for him.

"Merry Christmas, sunshine." He winked at her as she rolled her eyes and gave him the finger. They were silent while she waited for her coffee. Within a minute she had the full cup in her hand, and she swallowed the steaming liquid with a sigh.

Her voice was still scratchy with sleep, her short hair wild. "Merry Christmas to you and my baby boy." She kissed him, and her lips were warm and tasted of her coffee. Then she brushed her lips on JB's forehead, careful to keep the hot cup far from the baby. "How long have you been up?"

"About two hours."

"You want to head upstairs and get a few extra minutes?"

"Of sleep?" He wiggled his eyebrows.

"You have a dirty mind on Christ's birthday." She slapped him hard on the butt.

"Nah, thanks, though. You know our niece and nephew have to be chomping at the bit." Cole transferred JB to his bouncy seat.

"Did we leave any presents here?" Kyle rubbed her eyes and tried to comb her hair with her fingers.

The coffee was doing wonders for her mood, judging from her smile.

"All the ones we need right now are over there under the tree." He took her cup away and wrapped her in his arms. "Merry Christmas, baby."

She touched his cheeks. "Merry Christmas. You and our son are the best presents ever."

They kissed deeply, but she pushed him away when he started to get grabby. "No, seriously, let me get a shower. My vagina smells like a set of nuts."

"Awesome." Cole laughed.

"So I'll go first, then get the baby fed and pack his bag, and after you shower, I'll get ready. We can't forget the breakfast casserole or my sister will shit a cow."

He stopped her by grabbing her hand. "Your mouth."

"Ah, shit." Kyle covered her offending lips with her other hand.

"You're filthy." He spanked her butt in return. "We need some sort of swear jar up in this joint."

She shook her head but refused to talk.

"Or more like a swear water tower or landfill."

Kyle stomped her feet and gave him a hard look.

"Your anger makes you cuter. So have at it." He let go of her other hand and rested against the counter, crossing his arms.

She backed up and, when she was out of sight of the baby, pulled up her top to flash her boobs at him before turning and going up the stairs.

Cole's phone buzzed, and he ignored it while she watched his wife, hoping for more nudity, but the water turned on upstairs. He answered his brother's call.

"Hey, hot stuff. You on your way? I hear Blake's kids are jumping out of their skin." Beckett sounded like he was in the car.

"You already headed over?"

"It's seven thirty a.m., and I hear that's fucking late for presents. I wouldn't know."

"Me neither."

"Time to start some new traditions then," Beckett said. "I'm not gonna be late even if I have to park in the driveway for an hour. Holidays were hard without anyone while I was gone."

"We felt your loss every time. You'll enjoy the chaos. Speaking of which, did he mention if he got our package?"

"Chaos? Yeah. He texted me a pic of the present you guys sent. That was real thoughtful."

"It was Kyle."

"I figured. I got something in the car from them to JB. You want me to bring it in?"

Cole picked up the baby and cuddled him close, propping the phone against his shoulder.

"Sure. I'm figuring we'll be there in forty-five minutes. I suck at ETA with the little guy here, though. Tough to get out the door with everything we need."

"I'm sure it is. We're pulling up now, and Blake is headed at me and Eve with coffee."

"We'll see you there. Merry Christmas."

Cole went ahead and fed JB while Kyle showered. When she came down in her robe, she saw that breakfast was already happening and turned tail to get dressed. Then they did the hand-off, and Cole showered in the warm, moist bathroom.

After they were all clothed and had received about twenty texts from siblings urging them on—including pouting pictures of Emme and Kellan—they made it to the car. Of course then they had to turn around to get the casserole.

Finally pulling into Blake and Livia's neighborhood felt like finishing a marathon.

Blake plopped Kellan in Eve's lap. His son had always gravitated to the pretty blonde, and she lit up as she positioned the baby so they could chat. Blake needed help monitoring the crazy kids upstairs while they waited for Cole's group and Livia put the finishing touches on the tree downstairs. Emme watched Christmas cartoons in between asking "How much longer?"

"Cole said they're about five minutes away."

Eve nodded to show she'd heard Blake but continued to listen to Kellan's story, which sounded like an anthology of every word he'd ever heard.

Beckett knocked on the door frame lightly, and Blake rose to stand next to his brother. "If my kids can get through the wait, this is going to be an epic morning."

Beckett smiled. "Yeah. She looks good with a kid, right?"

Blake followed his brother's gaze as Eve gave Kellan a kiss on the cheek.

"Like a different person. She healing up?"

Beckett nodded. "She's tough. My job is to make sure she doesn't overdo it."

Eve glanced out the window and set Kellan on the floor.

Beckett reacted quickly, stepping in front of the kids to stand by her side. Blake knew Eve was likely at least a little armed, and he watched as his brother went for a gun and came up empty-handed. Livia's rule was no guns. She was adamant. They made her nervous.

All at once Eve and Beckett relaxed their postures. Beckett turned and shook his head. "Your neighbor has company. Nothing to worry about."

"Is that how it always is?"

Blake watched as Eve settled on the floor next to Kellan to go back to their game.

"We can leave, if you need us to."

"I think the entire family feels better when you're here than when you're not." Blake patted his brother on the back as Beckett stood a little taller.

"They're here! Get the kids ready!" Livia's voice came bouncing up the stairwell. She sounded as excited as the kids.

Blake turned off the TV and revved the little ones up as Eve and Beckett slipped out. When they had the go-ahead, Blake and the kids went to the top of the stairs. Livia had taped wrapping paper over the doorway at the bottom. The computer in the living room began playing "We Are the Champions" by Queen.

Beckett's laugh was infectious, and the kids worked together to burst from the stairway like a conquering football team. On the other side of the paper stood a huge stack of presents under their just-a-little-bit-too-tall Christmas tree.

Phones were out to video the kids' reactions. Kyle brought JB over, and Blake noticed he was wearing the same pajamas as Emme and Kellan. The house smelled like cinnamon and pine. After the entrance song, the computer transitioned to softly playing Christmas songs.

After taking it all in, the kids started with their stockings, and the brothers found themselves separated around the living room. There would be a peace sign if someone took the time to draw a line on the floor connecting them.

Blake knew this was his and his brothers' wildest dream. Each of their women held a baby. They could almost choke on all the love in the room—the normal, what they'd never had. Beckett looked at his feet. Cole exhaled and stuffed his hands in his pockets. They were having the same thoughts.

He motioned for them to step into the kitchen. He pulled three glasses from the cabinet as Beckett saw where this was headed and went to Blake's pantry. He smiled at the bourbon he pulled out. Cole nodded. It was too early to be drinking, but they had to do it. There had to be a way to consecrate this moment. Beckett poured stupidly generous amounts of the amber liquid.

He held up his glass after setting down the bottle. His brothers matched his movement. "To family."

"To family."

"To family."

They touched their glasses and made eye contact. Each made sure to drain his entire helping of the bourbon.

Blake laughed at the burn and slapped his glass down on the counter.

"And that's how the baby Jesus would want us to celebrate." Beckett held up his arm.

They'd seen each other so much recently, it was a smooth connection. The brother's handshake.

Kyle walked into the kitchen. "You girls done having your panty-swap party yet? Because these kids have some presents to open."

It didn't take long to get through the rest of everything. Blake handed Beckett a screwdriver and a sheet of stickers for Emme's new toy horse corral. Cole worked on a new mobile for JB, and soon Blake was knee-deep in batteries for a pile of toys. The laughter and jokes flew around the room fast. The bourbon was revisited twice.

John and Kathy walked in with another armful of gifts shortly after the kids finished the first round. John shook hands with Blake and Cole and gave Beckett a hard stare.

Blake watched as Livia took her father aside and had some stern words, but the man didn't seem to relax. Perhaps sensing this, Beckett and Eve were ready to go just after breakfast. If John had been a little more welcoming, Blake bet they would have stayed longer.

He and Cole walked them out, and Beckett hugged them both. Blake pulled two envelopes out of his pocket and handed one to Beckett and the other to Cole. "This is for you guys."

He watched as his brothers each pulled out three tickets. Cole had a set for all of them to a hockey game and Beckett a set to a baseball game.

"Contractually obligated memories. That's all I'm saying," Blake explained. "And yes, I checked with the women on the dates."

Beckett shook his head and looked at Eve. She shrugged. He trotted to the car and reached into the glove compartment. He came back with a stack of envelopes.

"You already knew about this, but here are the deeds." He handed out the crumpled envelopes. Between Blake and Cole there were three deeds to houses in Hawaii.

"I thought we were staying?" Cole looked slightly worried.

"No, you're good. I hope you are. I just…I bought them and I thought, shit, I might as well hand them out. There's plenty of room to build around those houses too. I bought up the land. At the very least they can be part of the kids' inheritance. Maybe you can vacation there, and God forbid, if shit turns to a shitstorm, you all have a place to go. I got a place for Chery, Vere, and Chaos too, but it's across town."

He stuck his hands in his pocket. "And there's a place for John and Kathy." He motioned to the extra envelope in Blake's hand. "You know, just up and go if things ever make you skittish. I need to have a safe place for you to land."

Blake nodded before hugging it out with Beckett. "We don't want to leave, but I appreciate the gesture."

Cole also thanked Beckett, adding, "Well, I didn't get you guys jack. I'm lucky I'm wearing clean underwear."

Beckett laughed. "You sure about that, baby?"

"Okay, fine. I'm not even entirely sure about that." Cole swiped under his chin in Beckett's direction.

"Awww, priest man's getting feisty now." Beckett faux punched both his brothers.

Blake tried one last time. "Seriously, you can stay. John will…"

He trailed off as the screen door squeaked behind them. "It's him isn't it?"

John cleared his throat loudly. "Can I get a minute?"

Blake and Cole shook hands before leaving Beckett leaning against his Challenger. Eve slipped slowly behind the steering wheel and slammed the door.

Blake hated that Beckett still had an illegal air to him. He really just wanted the man safe, settled, and in his life for good.

Beckett waited as Capt. John McHugh approached. The man looked tense, but he always did. "Listen, I have to talk to you," he announced. "Is she still in on all your stuff?" He nodded in Eve's direction.

Nice of him to ask, but since Morales' involvement, Beckett was fairly certain there were very few secrets anymore as far as Eve was concerned. He played along and nodded.

"Can you follow me a few roads down?" McHugh didn't wait for an answer and headed for his car.

Beckett got in the passenger's side of the Challenger. His buzz had dried up. He'd wanted to spend Christmas with his family and then cuddled up with Eve at his house. Now this.

"We following him?" She already had the car in reverse.

"Yeah. Not sure what we're going into."

McHugh pulled over in the parking lot of a gas station, threading around to the back of the store. Eve parked in a way that didn't hem them in, but it was too little too late as Ryan's douchebag truck pulled in right behind them. Beckett sighed.

Eve threw it in park and got out — always a tiger, ready to attack. Beckett got out more slowly, more pissed that his Christmas now included Morales than anything else. They met in front of the car, and he didn't miss Eve's nod acknowledging Morales.

"Too drunk to drive, assbag?" Morales gave Beckett the finger and shook hands with McHugh.

Beckett didn't bother responding, just folded his arms and leaned on the warm hood of his car with Eve. It was freezing outside.

McHugh rubbed his temples. "Listen, I'll just get to it. What I need to know is if you're buying up properties to help Vitullo move in here. I know there continues to be something going on with the two of you."

Morales looked only at Eve.

Beckett would have a long discussion with her at home about what sorts of things she was sharing. He gave her the side eye, silently asking *What the fuck?*

She widened her eyes in anger. She responded just as silently, *Seriously? Do you think this is amateur hour?*

"I am investing in the area," Beckett said, meeting McHugh's gaze. "But not on anyone else's behalf, and that's not against the law." He turned to give Morales a hard look.

He smiled widely.

"Son, you need to understand that every step you take in this town is because I allow it. You're not a law-abiding citizen, no matter how you think you're acting. You're a criminal and a murderer. I deal with you only as it benefits me and my town. So do not act like a goddamn punk. We're both too old for that shit." McHugh assumed a very authoritative stance.

Beckett knew the conversation they were about to have was a necessary one. It had to happen. But he was pissed that it had to be now, when he was still freaking glowing from one of the best family experiences in his life. It had been storybook bullshit this morning. He'd loved it. Only thing missing had been a baby in Eve's arms.

Beckett gave an exasperated sigh. "Sir, my brothers live here, married to your daughters, having their kids. I'm in Poughkeepsie to ensure their safety as best I can. They're my family. And Rodolfo Vitullo remains a wild card. That's not a secret. As I'm sure you know, he was behind the recent abduction attempt on Eve, and he's expressed interest in illegal trafficking through this town. We don't want his kind here, and we don't need it, so I'm doing my best to find a way to neutralize that threat. Cole and Blake won't leave — or at least they don't want to — so my only choice is to make this a place they can stay. But I'm trying to do it differently than I would have in the past."

McHugh shook his head. "What did you drag my town into?"

"You were already headed down the drain. Since Mary Ellen Vitullo stirred things up, their sights have been on the back of your head. The shadier side of Vitullo Weapons wants this place, especially now that Sevan Harmon seems to have faded from the scene. They want to open up his trade lines using the river and the train, as well as the roads. If they get their way, there won't be a business or a cop that doesn't belong to them. You won't get anybody convicted for shit. They're bigger than me and into weapons and drugs on such a level — we're not even a crumb of shit on their shoes."

McHugh folded his arms. "I can't help but think you being here is a bad thing. Like tying up a dying goat to bring a hungry bear around."

"I'm taking them apart from the inside," Beckett countered. "The old man and I have been in touch, and he knows I'm not interested in working with him. But I'm going to strengthen our walls by winning the loyalty of his men. It's the only thing I've found that gives me an advantage. You'll also see me scooping up prostitutes, druggies from rehab, and homeless people, and giving them a break. I'm getting skid row to become our eyes and ears." Beckett kicked a rock. It sounded even less badass out loud than it did in his head.

Morales scoffed.

Beckett narrowed his eyes at the cop.

"You're delusional," he added.

"I don't know what the hell you were up to for the last five years or so, but you have no idea what's going on. You're scary," McHugh said while looking toward the sky.

"He does know what he's doing," Eve interjected, breaking her silence. "I've known men to take a bullet for him. None of Vitullo's men care about anything but the money in their pockets right now, but Beckett can make them understand that they aren't dispensable. On top of that, what he's leaving in his wake will improve this place, give people at the bottom a chance. I think it's a great idea. And it's worth trying. What's your plan, McHugh, if Vitullo wants your town?"

She'd hardly moved, but Beckett could see that having her on his side benefited him in the cops' eyes.

"I'd approach it as I do anything." He looked her dead in the face. "By the book, following the laws we have."

"And that's exactly what makes Rodolfo so successful. He assumes good men have good morals. And in this case he'd be right. He expects you to take down Beckett, and while you're doing so, he'll buy his way to the courts and set the policy as he sees fit. Does he expect you two to work together? Hell no. Does he anticipate your department and Taylor's defense to align? Never. Just like he'll never see that we're taking his guys by treating them like humans instead of just manpower. Is it perfect? Of course not. I think we should all just pack up and leave—let the assholes fight it out. But Beckett refuses to move your daughters if they want to stay. And this town is home for all of us. He'll change the way everything has ever been done to keep them safe and in the home they know."

She pushed off of the car. "Beckett has enough money to be gone. He doesn't have to be here. But he is. He does things for a lot of the same reasons you do."

The men were quiet as her rationale found its mark.

"Let it be a two-way street," she continued. "Open the lines of communication with us. We'll make sure you know if anyone gets an offer they can't refuse. You send us the people you think need a boost up in the vicious fucking cycle of being poor, or even just misunderstood. I know this: if we don't work together, we'll both fail. And there's too much on the line for all of us."

Beckett slid his gaze to her profile. She was so smart, and persuasive, and right. She'd said it far better than he would have. This mess could only benefit from estrogen.

McHugh shook his head. "I got to think about this. I don't want to get in bed with him." He pointed at Beckett with his pinkie.

Beckett bit his lips. "You take your time, grandpa. The longer you wait, the deeper Rodolfo's claws sink into your throat."

McHugh nodded at Morales. "Merry Christmas, Morales. You good? I'm leaving."

"I'm good, boss. Merry to you and yours." Morales slid his sunglasses to the top of his head as they all watched McHugh leave.

"Well, that was awesome." Beckett rubbed his hand over his face. McHugh was a man stuck in the old ways.

"He'll come around." Eve shrugged.

"You read minds now?" Morales tried flirting with her right in front of him.

"You are testing my last goddamn nerve, Morales." Beckett smiled so his dimples would show.

"Your song and dance is filled with hot air. Now you're the freaking president of the Poughkeepsie Peace Corps? I don't believe it. I think it's shit and full of lies." Morales inhaled and puffed up his chest.

Eve stepped into his personal space. "Do you think I'm a liar?"

Beckett watched as the cop deflated a bit. "I didn't say that."

"Well, I'm in this with him. And I'm letting you be involved here too. Would I base that on lies? Do you think I'm that cavalier with your life? Your job? Merry fucking Christmas, Ryan." She turned on her heel and headed for the driver's side door.

"Wait, Eve. I'm sorry. No, I don't think you'd lie to me." He held out his hands in earnestness. "But come on? Really? Druggies are going to somehow be loyal if you give them money? Surely you know they'll be injecting your funds."

She shook her head. "We're not giving druggies money. We're going to give people coming out of rehab a chance to be recognized as human beings. They can work at the properties, earn fucking food and a warm place to stay. And that's what we call a start. Will most of them screw it up? Hell yes. But for the few who can stick it out, we will have helped them, and they can help restore a property. Then a single mom or someone else who needs it will have a home she can afford. Does it really sound that stupid to you? I thought you were a good guy." She tapped her booted foot.

Beckett leaned back on the Challenger and watched his lady chew out the cop.

"Never confuse me with the good guy," Morales shot back. "You know far too much about me for that. I didn't join the force to save the world, remember?" He put his sunglasses on. "But if you're doing this? I'm all in. Every time. No, I don't think you're a liar. I just think this plan has more holes than a county road and he clouds your judgment. Merry Christmas, Eve. Die in a hole, Taylor." Morales returned to his truck.

Beckett figured that was not the way Morales had wanted to end things on Christmas, and that left him with a smirk. Eve was furious as she started the car. She gave Beckett an angry glance, and Morales tapped on the window, holding an envelope.

She rolled it down, but refused to look at him.

"This is yours," was all he said before trotting back to the truck.

Eve slid the envelope between the driver's side door and her seat.

"Really? Are you afraid I'm going to look at what the lovesick fool gave you?" Beckett taunted.

Morales backed up, and Eve was finally able to put the car in gear. She whipped it around like a stunt driver, squealing the tires and passing Morales on a double yellow.

Beckett said nothing when she responded with silence, but he kind of loved watching her go straight through the red light while holding her middle finger up high enough for Morales to see.

God, he loved her.

And if he thought seriously about it, the conversation had actually gone well. He was able to get McHugh to listen to his (okay, Eve's) explanation, and the man had said he'd think about it. Until he had some concrete results to show, that was about all Beckett could ask anyone to do.

Eve let up on the gas pedal, because although she was pissed, she didn't really want to start a war with Ryan.

Beckett filled the passenger seat with such a presence. She could feel his eyes on her as he slumped down.

"Did you have a nice Christmas so far?" He was pretending he didn't want to see what Ryan had given her, so she played the same game.

"It was great until the sheriff showed up." She drove to Beckett's place to drop him off, then she would go see her father. Although leaving him in this mood seemed a bit insane.

"I still have to go see Dad." She glanced at him. He chewed on a toothpick.

"I know. I'll take G out and be here when you get back." He winked at her.

"I don't like leaving you today, especially after that. Maybe you should come." She put the blinker on and made her way to his street.

"Naw, let's not stress your dad out too much." He leaned over to give her a kiss as she parked in the driveway.

She caught his throat as his arm snaked around her waist. "No." She clenched her fist, red nails pressing against his windpipe.

He smiled and pushed closer, reaching farther behind her. She adjusted her hip to catch his arm.

His lips were nearly on hers, the scent of the bourbon tinting his hot breath.

"Don't," she breathed.

"Don't what?"

The hand that wasn't trapped trailed up her side until it cupped her breast.

"Try to take the envelope."

He bit her bottom lip and held it between his teeth.

She teased him into kissing her by touching her tongue to his upper lip.

He deepened the kiss, seeming to forget the original goal of his espionage.

"How you feeling, killer?"

"You're playing with fire, Taylor. And that's not fair 'cause you know how I like it." She got a fistful of his pec with her next kiss to let him know she missed him and this crazy, deadly way they played.

"Don't like it when I go slow?" Beckett pulled his hand away and held out the envelope he'd snatched.

"You tramp." She took it from his hand.

"Don't think you know every trick I have, baby. I got ways. You got needs. Let's meet in the middle." Beckett put his hands on her face and kissed her gently, temptingly, over and over until she mourned the loss of him as he got out of the car.

"Tell Pops I said hi. And give me a chance tonight." He slammed the door and didn't turn around to wave.

She sighed. Recovering sucked. Gunshots sucked. And later, she hoped Beckett would suck.

The drive to her father's was uncomplicated, and she parked right in front of the apartment building. But before she could get out of the car, Ryan's truck pulled up behind her. She shook her head. He had a bit of a swagger as he exited his truck, and she had her middle finger pressed against the glass, waiting for him. He tried the handle, and of course it was locked.

"Come on, Eve."

She didn't look at him, but instead opened the envelope. Inside was a banal Christmas card, signed by Ryan, and pooled at the corner of the card was a gold chain. She pulled it up and found a tiny compass swinging from it. The arrow swung around until it pointed north.

She unlocked the passenger door, and he walked around to the other side.

"Jewelry always gets the door unlocked," he informed her as he sat.

"Relationship advice? Really?" She almost smiled.

"Touché. You don't need to wear it or anything. I just saw it and thought it'd be a good fit."

"Thank you. And by the way, are you stalking me, copper?" Eve took the necklace and put it on. Honestly, it was lovely.

"A little. I know I'm a shit, but you told me you'd be visiting your dad, and I just wanted to spend a few minutes with you. I was at my mom's all morning."

"So I'm guessing you're not hungry?"

"I could always eat." He smiled from ear to ear.

Her soft spot for this man was a weakness. Part of it had to do with who he was, but the other part was that she liked to see the fire in Beckett's eyes when he was jealous. It was stupid.

"Let's go have some ham, and if Trish shows up, I blame you," she told him.

10

CLICK

Ryan knew better. He knew cocker spaniels that knew better. She was so, so not his. She'd said it a million times. She was living with the man she was pledged to.

But her hair was down today. She wore it that way when she was relaxed, and she tossed it off her shoulder from time to time. If he didn't see that exact sight in his every daydream, maybe he could stay away. Eve was the worst decision his balls had ever made. As if it was a choice. Damn her eyes, looking around like a seasoned cop, assessing exits.

He followed her into her father's building, careful not to hold the door for her. They weren't dating, and he wanted to be a friend — a friend to keep her safe. A friend for her when Taylor broke her heart, because it was bound to happen. That man was a stick of lit dynamite sitting on top of a propane tank.

After knocking on her dad's door twice, she flicked her hair again, and he could see the slender gold chain around her neck as she unlocked the door. It gave him stupid pride to have something on her body that he'd picked out. Damned if Taylor would let her wear it, though. But he wanted to be her true north. Subtle. Or maybe not so at all.

"Dad?" She entered the apartment shouting. After the first holler, she canvassed the place, always suspicious. Ryan nodded at her eye contact and slipped into the job, clearing each room visually.

Neither he nor she pulled their weapons—they weren't that scared. He spotted a note on the counter in the kitchen.

"Hey! He's got a note for you here." He read it without really meaning to:

Dear Eve,
So very sorry but the hospital was short staffed for a car accident
The ham is in the oven, just set the temp to 350 for a few minutes.
Merry Christmas,
Love Dad

"Wow. That's a first," she said, shaking her head.

"Whaddya mean?" He felt the oven, and it was still hot. "He must've just left."

"He's never missed a Christmas." She picked up the note and traced the words with her fingers. Disappointment played for a few seconds in her eyes before she shook it off.

Gladiator.

"Want me to call the hospital?" He wanted to offer her something.

"No, I'm good." She opened and shut various appliances in the kitchen and declared dinner ready.

They worked together to set a quick table. It reminded him so very much of when she'd spent time at his place. He turned on music with his phone. He knew she hated to hear chewing while eating. A quirk. He wondered if Taylor knew.

She was quiet as they ate, so he added the color commentary. "Your dad can cook his ass off."

She nodded before getting up to go to the fridge. "It wasn't always that way." She slapped a beer in front of him and took a long pull of her own before sitting back down. "For the first few years after my mom left, Dad and I ate every meal out. We'd stop for breakfast on the way to school. And he'd either get takeout or delivery for dinner. Then he got some blood work done and hated the results, so that's when he started to cook. I'd help him, but I sucked then."

"You still suck now." He toasted her with his beer.

She closed one eye and almost smiled. "One wonky fried egg and I'm the worst?"

He nodded. "I've never seen anyone light an egg on fire."

"That pan was defective." She kicked at him under the table.

"Yes. That five-year-old pan that cooked my damn eggs every day was defective. It was not operator error. Totally the pan." He stretched his back and put his hands behind his head.

"Ungrateful. And how many more times did I make you breakfast after that?" She pushed her plate away.

"It was only the once. The neighbors are still thanking me for breaking up with you." He winked. *If only.*

"You told them you dumped me?"

"Does it matter how the fallacy ends?"

She took a drink and ignored the question. "Let me make Dad a plate."

Ryan stood and helped her clear the table, making the kitchen as orderly as possible.

"He even had dessert set up." She went to the drawer filled with junk by the phone and jotted down a note. She set it on the cake's plastic wrap in the fridge:

We'll share this tomorrow.
Missed you.

Ryan set the covered plate of dinner on the shelf beneath the cake. He didn't like it. This made no sense. He didn't have any glimpse into the inner workings of Dr. Ted Hartt's life, but he couldn't imagine a man changing something as traditional as Christmas dinner with his only daughter. Surely there'd been calls that he'd farmed out or arranged to have covered in previous years.

Eve closed the fridge and faced him. The space between them was too small. It couldn't fit all his overwhelming feelings. He wanted to pull her against him.

"Sorry he wasn't here." He looked at her feet. Okay, really he looked at her tits while pretending to look at her feet.

"Thanks for filling in." She patted the center of his chest.

He couldn't help it—he put his hand on top of hers. Stupid, because she was vulnerable. Her hand was small compared to his huge paw, and soft. The fact that she'd killed God knew how many people with it gave him an inappropriate hard-on.

She sighed. "Ryan."

It was admonishment. He knew what was coming and gave her the words before she had a chance to say them. "Ryan, this isn't going to happen. I want to be friends, but if you're going to turn everything into something more…I know. I know what you're going to say."

She patted his chest again beneath his hand. When he found her eyes, they had sympathy and a hint of a smile.

"You saved me," she told him. "And I don't have many friends. But I don't want to be the queen of your friend zone. You tell me what you need." She didn't take her hand back. She just waited.

"I need to be part of your life. And I'm not going to lie about my feelings for you. I think there will be a time when I need to distance myself. But that's not yet. Not for me."

She finally did pull her hand away, but stepped in for a hug. He gratefully accepted her and rested his chin on her head.

"At least you're my guilty pleasure," she mumbled into his chest.

If his hard-on had been running the show, she'd be the pinwheel petals and his dick would be the peg spinning her around. "And you're my pleasure that I wish had more guilt about," he told her with a sigh. He patted her back and then stepped away so as to not turn it into a horribly timed sexual advance. "Let's lock up — unless you want to open the presents under the tree?"

"No, I couldn't do it without Dad. But wait." She led him to the living room and knelt in front of the tree. While she dug around underneath it, he checked out her ass, then looked at the ornaments. There were the regular array of balls and lights, but in between were some distinctly handmade ones. A little girl named EVE in all caps had framed pictures and cut out felt shapes. Obviously Ted had cherished the ornaments and kept them in good condition over the years. There were even two tiny clay-sculpted people holding hands. The man had a stethoscope, and the girl held a flower. She rose from her knees, and Ryan cast her in a thousand porno movies featuring him and her.

He was such a dog in his mind. He reached out and touched a set of glittery walnuts with a piece of yarn hot-glued to serve as the ornament hanger.

"Did you make that set of sparkly nuts for your dad?" He pointed to the center of the tree.

She slapped his arm. "Never once have those been a dirty thing before."

"Sorry. Thought it was the obvious joke." He cupped the nuts and wiggled his eyebrows at her.

She burst out laughing. He took them off the tree and held them at the correct height to become improvisational testicles. She laughed so hard she crouched.

He loved her laugher. He wanted to bury his dick in it. He added a song to his new bouncing nuts, singing "Silver Balls, Silver Balls" in his best Nat King Cole impression. She swatted at him, wiping tears from her eyes.

He hung them back on the tree and jammed his hands in his pockets.

When she caught her breath, she admonished him, "Now you've ruined a childhood memory for me."

"You're welcome."

She held out a small wrapped package. "I left it here because…"

He nodded. He knew why. "You didn't have to do that."

"It's nothing, really." She shrugged.

He nodded and opened the wrapping, crumpling it in his fist as it came undone, so as not to make a mess. It was a wallet. It made him laugh because he needed one desperately.

"It's just a wallet. I just thought…" She trailed off again.

He opened it and tucked in the billfold was a small picture, a printed version of the selfie they'd taken on her phone in front of a sunset when they'd been "dating" while she infiltrated the Vitullo organization.

On the back she'd written "For my friend."

He nodded. "This is great. I really needed it." He meant the picture, but he motioned toward the wallet.

"Great. I was figuring you'd finally remembered to get a new one two days ago."

"Nope. You know me, I only think of it for the second I'm paying for something and no other times. This rocks." In his truck he had three other wallets, all brand new from this morning: one from his mom, one from a neighbor, and the other from Trish. He was half expecting the Trish one to explode.

He looked at the ceiling as she bent down to rearrange the presents she'd disrupted. Dangling from the ceiling fan was a clump of mistletoe. He gave it the finger, and quickly replaced it with his pointer finger when she stood up.

He had to say something and lamely offered, "Your dad like kissing himself?" *Shoot me.*

"Uh, no. When I was younger my Barbie dolls and Ken dolls loved playing under the tree and with the ornaments. We actually had a little manger, so then the baby Jesus was involved. It got crazy. Anyway, I was pretending that a little cutting from the tree was mistletoe so the Kens had to kiss the Barbies, and Dad got me the real thing. He'd do it every year for me — guess he still does. I think it's his way of trying to make me his little girl again."

Ryan exhaled, and Eve stood right underneath to look up at it.

"I think it's fake actually, or some sort of cemented, laminated nonsense." She put her hand on his shoulder and went to her tiptoes to take a closer look. "It's lived forever."

Ryan thought his balls might sprout opposable thumbs and try to hitchhike their way into her pants if she brushed him with her breasts one more time.

"Nope. It looks fresh," she reported.

He reached up and touched it gently, using his height to answer her question. "It's fresh. He must buy it new each year."

He looked down at her. She was just a few mistakes away from his lips, so close that he actually watched as her love for her father passed over her face. She was usually such a fucking panther. Making her laugh and seeing her love made his resolve so weak.

"He's a great guy." She took her hand from his shoulder and parted her lips as she looked at his.

He pulled her to him gently, allowing her every opportunity to push back. His lips touched her forehead as he inhaled the scent of her hair.

"He raised an amazing lady. Merry Christmas, Eve. Damn, your name is spot-on for the season." He stepped away from her and got her jacket.

She looked so happy that he'd not made a pass at her. Remaining under the mistletoe she asked, "We're really going to be able to be friends?"

"Were you testing me, January?" he asked, lapsing back to her pseudonym.

"A little." After turning off the tree lights, she nodded. "Okay, fine. A lot. I just don't want to give you up, but I don't want to hurt you."

"Same here. Let's Harry and Hermione this shit then."

She laughed again as he held the door open for her. "That's amazing." Locking the door quickly, she slipped her arm in his as they walked to their cars.

"Text me when you get home?" He nodded at Taylor's car.

"Sure. You do the same." Eve got in her car while already texting someone else.

Ryan knew who. He watched her leave and then got in his truck. He had no plans for the rest of the night, and if he was being honest, he'd hoped he'd be going home with company.

Once Eve was out of his field of vision, his cop instinct rumbled up from his subconscious. A man who bought fresh mistletoe every year wouldn't miss dinner with his daughter. Traditions mattered. Tapping on the steering wheel, he considered the possibility that maybe Ted was angry with Eve for living with Taylor. Or maybe some other perceived slight. But it didn't click. He didn't like it.

Dr. Ted Hartt knew where he sat was remote. Or at least soundproof. His eyes were covered, and he tried to assess his injuries but a strong wave of nausea interrupted his process. With his hands tied, it was difficult to figure it out anyway. The pain reminded him that this wasn't a bad dream, but he held on to the hope that Eve was untouched by the zealous fervor of this insane person.

He'd expected her when the knock on the door had halted his Christmas preparations.

Forgot her keys was all he'd had time to think before the doorway was filled with an unfamiliar man. He'd been well dressed. Impeccably even.

"Pardon me, sir. Do you own this apartment building?"

It had never occurred to him to deny it, and he doubted whatever else he'd thought to say would have changed the outcome.

"Yes. Ted Hartt." He held out his hand to the man. "Is there an issue?"

"I'm so sorry to trouble you on the holiday." The British accent made the man's outfit seem even more expensive. He slid off his glove and completed the handshake. "I'm Nicholas Rodgers. Pleasure to meet you. I'm in the area visiting family, and this plot of land adjoins their property. Have you ever considered selling?"

Ted invited the man inside. He'd actually considered selling a few times, and his mind had begun to turn. But instead of worrying about his safety, he'd been calculating how many people in the building would have difficulty if the property changed hands.

After the door closed, Nicholas's English accent fell away.

"Dr. Hartt, I'm going to need you to do three things for me."

He'd stared at the man in front of him, suddenly remembering his beat down not quite a year before.

"No, you're going to leave." Ted had stood tall. The man certainly hadn't looked like a thug.

"You will help me." Nicholas had smiled. "Because your daughter is on her way over, is she not? It's tradition? Your special dinner with your girl? Smells lovely in here."

Ted had said nothing as Nicholas put his gloves back on.

"The first thing I want you to do is call work. You're going to tell them to clear your schedule for the next week. Claim it as personal time. Don't explain." Nicholas lifted Ted's cell phone from the side table where it was charging like he knew ahead of time it would be there.

"And here's a script." Nicholas had handed Ted a piece of paper with the typed message. "I'll have it on speaker, so I can listen. Just know that if you sound any alarm, Eve will be here before the cops. And I will do my worst on her. While you watch. And I will leave and never be caught. This is what I do for my employer."

He had dialed Ted's phone and held it out. "Toni Lynn will be answering. She's astute—so be convincing."

Ted had told the sweet hospital receptionist exactly what he was supposed to.

Nicholas had never even shown him a weapon, he realized now. But he'd had too much information for Ted to risk Eve. In that moment he'd decided to follow the man's orders as long as he could.

Nicholas had turned off the oven and the heat under the pots. "Next, you're going to write this exact note to your daughter." He'd held out a sheet of lined yellow paper, just like Ted took all his notes on, and a pen.

The man had watched patiently as he penned the note.

"Very good," Nicholas had said, nodding. "And last, we need to leave. Quickly now, I've a report that your daughter is only four blocks away. Your car has been removed from the garage below." Nicholas had slipped off his large overcoat and handed it to Ted, who put it on. He took the hat from his head and released a fall of red hair from under it, completing the disguise. "Look down," he'd instructed. "And let's go."

After taking a seat in the back of the man's long, black Lincoln, he'd been blindfolded.

He should've done things differently. Now he was at Nicholas's mercy.

Ted had felt the air chill as a sliding door was opened. Then it was shut tight and locked, judging from the noises. Finally his blindfold was carefully removed, and Nicholas waited as Ted's pupils adjusted to the light. The room was indeed padded, and the sliding door looked very industrial.

"Dr. Hartt? I apologize for bringing you here today. I tried every method I could to avoid this unfortunate event, but apparently, you're the only one in possession of the information I need. I've a healthy respect for a man of medicine, so I'll make this brief."

Nicholas went to the table in the corner and opened what looked like a tackle box. He pulled out a syringe, tapping the bubbles out of the already-loaded delivery system. "This is a bastardized version of scopolamine, so the truth doesn't have to hurt. Right?"

Ted knew the old-fashioned "truth serum" was illegal and wildly dangerous. But it was pointless to struggle, as his hands were bound behind him, and his knees and feet were pulled together as well.

Nicholas seemed to relish acting as a professional with the injection, wiping the skin with an alcohol swab first, wearing gloves.

The needle barely pinched as it slid under his skin, and the burning of the drug being administered was the least of Ted's concerns.

Before it could take effect, he tried to find out some truth of his own, seeing that Nicholas seemed so good at chatting.

"You're good at that," Ted noted.

Nicholas beamed. "My mother would have loved it had I gotten my doctorate."

"Actually, my nurses are far better at injections than I." Ted smirked. Nicholas didn't need to know that was actually a compliment. He watched as the man's demeanor hardened. "What of Eve?" Ted asked next.

"Your daughter? She's safe for now. Rodolfo has plans for her, but that's none of your concern."

Ted's lips and the tip of his tongue were going a bit numb. Soon enough the words out of his mouth would not obey his need for discretion. Though what Nicholas wanted, he couldn't imagine.

"So, years ago your daughter was involved in a car accident," Nicholas began. "How did that make you feel?" He pulled a chair up in front of Ted.

It took a few blinks to focus now, and when he did he stared at the little red light across from him. He was being recorded. "Sad. Worried. I did not want my baby to die." His words fell heavy from his lips.

"Your baby? You mean Eve's baby, right? Got anything salacious to confess?" Nicholas raised an eyebrow.

"Eve's my baby girl. She always will be. Twice I've seen her on a gurney. It's two times too many." *Stop talking. Say no more.*

"That's right, twice. I'm thinking about that first time. Her records state that she miscarried. And needed a hysterectomy, am I correct?"

"Confidential. Patient confidentiality." He was wildly thirsty.

"Okay, I understand, but you can tell me anything now, can't you, Ted?" Nicholas frowned.

Ted's eyes closed almost completely, and the racing of his panicked heart had slowed. He was as calm as if he were just about to fall asleep. *Nothing about Eve. Say nothing about Eve.* "Fuck you." He felt some saliva slip from his bottom lip.

"Don't drift off on me, Ted. Then I'll be forced to encourage you in more unpleasant ways."

"Scopolamine is a pain killer, so you'll have to do double the work," Ted said. It was like Nicholas kept waking him up for school when he was a kid. He just wanted to sleep.

"You know what I think? I think you need a little more." Nicholas readied another syringe.

"Already had more than a milliliter. Any more and you'll kill me." Ted's chin touched his chest.

"I just need some truth, Ted. That's my ultimate goal." Nicholas came and went so fast, or maybe it was just that Ted's reflexes were slow. "Where did you store the tissue you extracted from your unconscious, nineteen-year-old daughter, Ted?"

Shame should have flooded him, like it did every other time he'd thought of that night. But emotions seemed too heavy now. He couldn't even form the thoughts. "A favor. It was a favor."

"Was it? Your daughter doesn't know about her ovary, does she?"

"She's never needed it yet. Only if she needed it. Got married, happy. I'd have a possibility for her." *No, say nothing. Say nothing.*

"That's some sick shit, my friend. But luckily for you, you're going to have grandchildren someday. And that'll be nice."

"I love Eve. Should have told her."

"You should have, but because you haven't, my job just got so, so much easier. So I'll thank you for that. Now tell me, who extracted the ovary?"

Nicholas's voice kept waking him up. He wanted him to just go away. The words made him quiet for a second. For a minute. For an hour. "I did. My friend did me a favor. She was against it at first." *No more.* Ted bit his tongue, but felt no pain even though he tasted blood.

"Where is Eve's ovary, Ted?"

Was it the first time he'd asked? Tenth? The answer was so clear in his mind, and he was losing the danger signals his brain usually gave him. It was the drug's effect. Ted knew that.

The moments passed in a blur. He wasn't sure what he said out loud and what he kept a secret.

After forcing his eyes to open, he watched Nicholas inject him with still more scopolamine. *It's over. And this is how I go.* Ted prayed right then—out loud or internally, he wasn't sure. *Let me keep her safe with my words.*

11

ПORMAL

Beckett hung up the phone. Since his merry Christmas vibe was already in the shitter, he'd decided to have a productive day and he now had in place what he thought was a good goddamn situation. The assholes and douchebags were working together fairly well, and even Sevan had been slightly useful, helping Shark identify the men in Rodolfo's organization who would be most likely to leave, based on his previous dealings with them. The two guards from his trip to the old fart's compound were now on their way to finding themselves under Beckett's umbrella. As soon as one had wandered away from his post, the other was ringing Shark's phone, asking for information.

Shark and Sevan would continue to recruit and keep tabs on things from the apartment in New York City (with Shark keeping tabs on Sevan most especially), and Beckett hoped soon he'd have quite a reliable stable of men assembled. Then he could move Sevan on to his next job: detailing the trafficking routes he'd once used through Poughkeepsie, so they could be dismantled.

In addition to being Christmas, today marked one month since Eve was shot—one month since she'd been stuffed into a car with every intention of taking her away from him. Beckett sighed. She and he had been running things or hiding out nearly the whole time they'd been together—healing or causing pain. This past summer had been their first chance for a normal relationship, a normal life, normal problems, and even so, they were definitely the weirdest "normal" couple he could think of. But he wanted that to change. He wanted lots of things to change. His brothers knew the deal and supported him, and Beckett had wanted to talk to Eve's father to ask his permission for old-fashioned reasons, but the man pretty much hated him.

Then she came walking through the door, home from her dad's place, shedding winter clothes along the way. She touched his dimples as he smiled, and he pretended to bite her fingers.

"Merry Christmas, baby. Can I give you my present yet?" He was nervous. Stupid nervous.

"I guess." She sat on the couch. "You know we don't have to do this kind of shit."

"A flowers and candy kind of girl, that's what I got here." Beckett walked over and caught her hand, pulling her toward the edge of the couch. "Can I ask you something?"

She nodded.

"I've thought of a million different ways to ask you, but not know-ing how the hell you'll respond takes the wind out of a guy's sails."

She was beautiful with her skeptical blue eyes. He loved her, he knew that. And maybe this was too soon, but with all the changes he was making, he wanted one more. He took to his knee and glanced up. She looked a little disgusted. His stomach dropped.

He'd written poems in his head—elaborate ones about her strength, her beauty, how worried he'd been while she was in the hospital. But her less-than-thrilled posture made him jump ahead. He pulled the trigger on his question like it was a gun: "Will you marry me?"

He slipped his hand in his pocket and hooked his finger on the ring there. He held it out to her, finally connecting with her gaze. She looked about as thrilled as she would have if he were holding a dead bug instead of a two-karat diamond.

He could only wait. There was no taking this back. It was what it was. Maybe a mistake.

She pulled her hand free, stood and turned her back on him. Beckett waited forever before interrupting her silence and asking her back, "Well?"

She turned again, and he was off his knee by the time he saw that her eyes were filled with tears. He put the ring back in his pocket. Answer received. "Okay, I'm going to run out to the gas station and find you a different gift." He was almost to the door when she stopped him with his name.

"Come back. Don't be a dick." Eve now leaned back into the couch, legs crossed and arms hugging her middle. A complete knot.

"Listen, I don't want it to be awkward. Let me go, and we can have the air settle…"

She shook her head and patted the cushion next to her. "No."

He walked over and sat down close to her. "I just thought maybe—"

She put her finger over his mouth to silence him. "I want to say yes. Okay?"

He nodded, but slowly because she certainly didn't sound joyful.

"I won't be with anyone else for the rest of my life. If you screw up, I'm going full hermit. But married? Us? Really? I can't even wear rings, you know that. They get in the way of what we do."

He shrugged. "Everybody in my life has their match. I just want you to be mine. It was stupid."

Eve gently straddled him. It seemed to take her a while to come up with her words. His beast, this deadly woman, was so out of place talking about her feelings. "When I picture being married, it's a picket fence. It's a grocery list and a minivan and a baby." She exhaled, trying to push the pain in her chest out of her body, he was guessing. "I don't get to have those things." She was exasperated.

He hugged her then, her whole body. Together they stayed until he felt a calm in the center of his soul. *This woman.*

"I don't get those things either," he told her. "I want 'em, though. I'm so proud of you, of who you are — that you stand anywhere near me. You shouldn't. I should have been in the grave a decade now. But I want a second to be your guy — like, open doors for you and hold your hand with my ring on it. Even if it's not supposed to be that way. I want to tell the world and our expectations to fuck off. I want to marry you, Eve. Let the world burn around us."

He touched her cheeks, then her lips before putting his big hands around her neck briefly. "Marry me, Eve." He pulled her sweater over her head, then easily unclasped her bra and slid it off. "Marry me." Beckett lifted his arms as she took off his shirt. He put his hand in the center of her chest. "We can," he told her. "We're the only ones saying we can't. Marry me."

She looked like she wanted to. He shifted under her, pressing his now-erect manhood against her jeans as he dug for the ring in his pocket. After pulling it out and shining it up, he grabbed her hand.

"I dare you, Eve Hartt. I dare you to marry me." He held the ring at the tip of her finger, risking a smile at her scared face.

Her head raced with all the reasons she couldn't marry him. And the worst reason was one she'd never tell him: marrying someone else was betraying David. Beckett was for certain the love of her life, but David was her first love. Her child's father. She hated letting go of any part of them, even if was guilt.

He read her mind. "He'd want you to be happy. You know that."

She was ready to run topless out into the street, but when she realized why — just to stop herself from doing what she wanted to do: seek happiness — she stayed put.

"Nothing's stopping you except you, killer."

Hearing her nickname from his kissable, plump lips was sin. She looked at her finger, the one threatening to make her happy, and she threw all her cares away in a giant waterfall of grief and hope and illicit love for this man.

"Yes." She said it once, and he heard her.

The smile on his face became wider and his eyes lit up. "Put it on then." He bit his lip even though his grin threatened to break his grasp.

She'd shot guns, launched rockets, and thrown knives, but this certainly felt like the most dangerous thing she'd ever done with her hands. Eve pushed her finger through the ring and grabbed his face, kissing him while laughing.

"Beckett Taylor, do you always get what you want?" He kissed her back while he lifted her from the couch.

"Tonight I do." She stayed wrapped around him as he walked her up the stairs. Gandhi had to be shooed from the room, and he lazily complied. Beckett closed their door and set her down on the bed gently.

"Listen, fiancée, I totally know how we do—with the blood and the biting and all of that. And I plan on it. But tonight, right now, I want you to take what I have to give you without a fight."

She pouted and then smiled from where she lay on the bed. She took a second to admire her ring, like a real girl should. It was gorgeous.

"Do you like it?" he asked, like a real boy would.

"I love it." It was so sparkly in the dim light of the bedroom. Beckett shed the rest of his clothing before getting to work on her jeans. She pretended to ignore him, focusing only on her ring.

He caught her attention when he kissed the inside of her thigh. He slowly made his way up her body, ignoring all the parts she was desperate for him to touch by the time he got to her neck. When his kisses stopped there, she remembered Ryan's gift.

She slid the pendant behind her neck, fully intending to take it off and set it aside.

Beckett moved to her side as he pulled on the chain with his finger. When he was finally was able to see the gold compass, his look went from loving to angry.

"So I'm not the only asshole giving you jewelry tonight, huh?"

His jealousy was a ridiculous turn-on. He was so murderous instantly.

"And you tried to hide it? Is that it?"

She tensed her jaw. It was easy to defend, but she wanted to test him. Take him too far.

"Well, he was there at dinner so…"

Beckett's eyes went wild. "Really?" His nostrils flared as put both hands on the necklace, yanking it free from her neck.

"So you had dinner with your father and the guy who's in love with you on the same day I ask you to marry me?"

The heat of his anger forced her to squirm. Now she would just make it worse on purpose. "Actually, my father wasn't there."

Beckett tossed the necklace across the room. "That's fucking fantastic. I'm going to kill him."

He was already in his pants and headed out when she stepped in front of the door. She put her ringed hand on his crotch as he looked down his nose at her.

She licked her teeth. "What was I supposed to do? I was alone, and there was the mistletoe?" She batted her eyes at him.

He raised his eyebrow, finally cluing in on the fact that she was egging him on. "Did you fuck him?" He stepped forward, dropping his shirt and caging her in his arms against the door.

She knew how to be sexy, but instead she took it to the next level. "Would that make you angry?"

His pants were on the floor because of her quick fingers by the time he'd grabbed a handful of her hair. He hissed his answer, "Yes."

"Would you say a woman who's been as careless as I would deserve a punishment?"

"Did you or didn't you? Tell me. Now." When he advanced, she turned and put her hands against the door.

"You're going to have to earn that answer, fiancé." She licked her own shoulder.

He reached around and inserted two fingers inside her. With his other hand he spanked her firmly on the bottom. He was in her ear again, demanding that she answer his question. Panting, she could barely stand between the pleasure and pain he was so skilled at delivering. Between the spanking and the friction he provided, Eve was near undone when he stopped.

"Answer me."

She turned and faced him. "Do you think anyone could ever do to me what you do? Ever? Like, has that thought crossed your mind?" Serious now, she watched as he fully understood he'd been played.

"That jewelry really was from him?"

"Yes. He's a friend. You're my love."

"You like it when I'm all fired up and jealous?"

"It's so fucking sexy I can't take it."

"Maybe I need to remind you who you belong to."

She nodded her assent. "Please."

Beckett put her against the door by her throat, not enough to deprive her of oxygen, but enough to hold her still as he worked her over. She fought him, but he was true to his promise of punishment. He brought her to the brink time and time again, taking her back to the bed and combining his mouth and hands until she slapped at his head.

Finally he crawled up her hyper-sensitive body. "You okay?"

She shook her head. "Can't finish."

"I'll finish you." He smirked as he held her down and screwed her senseless.

He pulled her close when they could finally move. "You almost killed your friend tonight. Can you imagine what that dinner did to him?"

"That should bother me. But it doesn't. Look at my pretty ring!" She leaned over and kissed him. "It's just you, Becky. You know that."

"Just make sure he knows that," Beckett growled.

Nicholas took off his blue rubber gloves like a surgeon. He'd handled the execution and clean up, and it was thrilling. Every aspect of the process spoke to him, and right now he still had the buzz. The crash would be phenomenal, but he wouldn't think about that now. Two cases in two months was an escalation—a beautiful symphony.

He looked over the room one last time. Not a single mark. It was as if Dr. Ted Hartt had never existed. He sighed before carrying the trash bag downstairs to the incinerator for "business papers," which had been a tax write-off for Rodolfo. Nicholas stood and waited, making sure every bit was consumed by the flames. All the evidence was up in smoke now. Easy. And that's what made him an artist: the attention to detail. He licked his lips and adjusted his glasses.

After consulting his expensive watch, Nicholas realized it was time for Rodolfo's pill. It was also time for the results of his interrogation to come to light.

When he entered the upstairs study, the old man was already awake, waiting. Rodolfo took his pill and sat back, expectant.

"Dr. Hartt proved helpful," Nicholas began. He nodded and sat when Rodolfo extended his good hand toward the empty chair.

"How so?"

"I have a name." Nicholas tried not to fidget. The doctor had been exceptionally tough to break in the end, a contrast to the willingness he'd shown in coming with him originally. The daughter's talents were latent in this man—not a recessive gene from her mother for sure.

"Don't make me force the information out of you, Nicholas. We have an end point here." Rodolfo's bottom lip listed to the left.

"Of course, sir. I chose to medically interrogate the doctor, in keeping with his profession. I find chemicals are better interrogators than I am for some personalities. He provided the name of the fertility specialist we're looking for, so that is a success. Unfortunately, after a brief Internet search, I found that the woman in question is no longer in the business of reproduction. She married and left her work soon after the extraction of Ms. Hartt's tissue. So, I'll need to give this fact-finding mission a more hands-on approach as well." Nicholas crossed his legs.

"So where is this ovary?" Rodolfo began to open and close his right hand.

"That's my sole focus from this point forward, as the research doctor we've discussed will arrive in just a few days to continue his studies stateside. It'll be no problem." Nicholas did his best to keep a confident smile on his face.

"I hate the words, *no problem*. The universe doesn't hear the negative qualifier and sends you what you ask for." Rodolfo's thick eyes narrowed. "I expected to know exactly the time we'd be ready for fertilization. Now you're going on a vacation?"

"I need us both to be realistic in our timeline expectations, sir. Focus on the victory here: the ovary was harvested. The doctor we need to make it useful has agreed to come on board." Nicholas clenched his hands together. He needed to set Rodolfo on a new path. He was fixated on the actual eggs. "What about the host? Do you have a female host available?" Nicholas asked.

"That's not your concern. But yes. I have a stable of females who've had health screenings," Rodolfo said. "I'll work with the doctor to find the best match." He paused for a moment, but soon returned to his previous train of thought. "So when will we have these eggs? I want to meet my children. Nine months feels like forever at my age."

"I'm leaving right now, sir. I will find Sonia Kore as soon as possible and determine the storage location. By the time the doctor arrives from Belgium, we'll be prepared to get underway. Will there be anything else?" Nicholas stood. The old man was certainly ruining his buzz, and he was probably doing it on purpose. Rodolfo thought he had the monster under control.

But Nicholas swallowed a smile. The monster inside him ran the show. Rodolfo just provided the platform. The reason. And without the reason to commit his works of art, well…Nicholas would just be a murderer.

Rodolfo nodded. "Go. Be quick."

Nicholas was really loving this Christmas.

12

PRETEND FUTURE

"Right now?" Eve stood in their closet in just a pair of panties.

"Yes." Beckett smiled to himself as he pulled a few more things out of his side — casual stuff, easy to wear.

"And I'm not allowed to pack?"

The engagement ring looked so odd on her finger. He'd found himself looking at it over and over again while they'd loved, slept, and ate their way through this day after Christmas. It was just so beautiful, making her his.

"No." He zipped up his suitcase.

"There so many reasons we can't do this. You don't even know." She crossed her arms under her breasts.

Beckett stopped what he was doing to pay some attention to them. She was moaning for him soon enough. He looked at his watch as he picked her up and put her against the wall.

"We don't have time for this. The plane is waiting."

She convinced him with her lips that the plane would wait, and it was totally okay to have sex in the closet. By the time he was done, half his suits were on the floor, and he had a hanger lodged on his arm. She laughed at him.

"Get dressed and stop tempting my stupid ass," he told her.

She shook her head.

Finally he found a set of pajama bottoms and a sweatshirt and forced her to put them on.

"We have to leave. Come on. Don't make a pussy out of all my plans." He tugged on her hand.

"I can't wear this." She looked at her body skeptically.

"You can. And you will. Now march, or I'm picking you up and carrying you, and I know you hate that shit." He grabbed his suitcase.

"We really can't leave. What about the houses? The assholes? The douchebags? Your brothers? I haven't even seen my dad for Christmas yet."

"We will be gone four days—just a long weekend. I've set up everything with the assholes and the douchebags. My brothers know we are leaving. I'll have my cell and a private plane, and we can come back if Armageddon happens. I bought them houses to flee to, for fuck's sake. We can FaceTime your dad. *Let's go.*" He emphasized his last words.

"Where are we going?"

He was relieved to see her follow him out the bedroom door. "Surprise. And you're a hard chick to surprise, just saying." He pulled her down the stairs.

"What about G?" She pointed at the dog.

"He's coming with us. Right, boy?" Beckett clipped the dog's leash to his harness.

"We're really doing this?"

Beckett smiled. "Yes, stubborn bitch. Remember? I'm taking you to a place with water as blue as your fucking eyes." He restated his promise from years ago. The night Blake was shot, the evening Mouse died, Beckett had promised her the trip he was about to take her on.

"Okay. Fine. I'll go. Give me five minutes to pack some shit." She stepped back up the stairs, and he put down his suitcase to tap his watch.

"I already packed for you. Everything's covered."

"Private plane. I need to be armed. Where's my hair knife?" She gave him a hard look.

"Fine. Go. Quickly. And if it's heavy, I'll carry it." Beckett opened the front door and took his dog and his suitcase to the waiting town car.

Eve was behind him, with a duffle bag and wearing a normal outfit, by the time he'd let G pee and put him in the car. "All set."

He put the bag in the trunk, slammed the car door, and they were off to the airport in the middle of the night. Hilarious that taking Eve on a vacation felt like the most illegal thing he'd ever done. He kissed her lips, and she rested her head against his shoulder.

"What the hell inspired this?" she asked. "It's like you're possessed tonight."

He petted his dog with one hand and put the other on her hip. "You. I want to be selfish with you. Life is short and all that shit."

She nodded. When they arrived at the airport, she shook her head and rolled her eyes. The path to the plane was lit with white luminaria bags filled with sand and a candle each. It was very Christmas romantic.

"Did you kidnap Martha Stewart for this?" She turned to look at him.

"Not yet."

She was out the door before he had a chance to open it for her. Jazz played just loud enough to hear, and the plane looked warm and inviting.

The driver grabbed their bags as Beckett led his lady and his dog to the plane for four days of bliss — days to celebrate each other and pretend they had an amazing future together that didn't involve any of the crap it most certainly would.

Inside, the plane was scattered with rose petals. G ran around sniffing them before jumping on the leather couch. Eve rolled her eyes at Beckett, but smiled as she sat in one of the captain's chairs. He sat down next to her, and they both buckled up.

"Whose plane is this?" Eve ran a hand over the buttery fabric on the chair.

"Someone who owes me a favor." Beckett lifted her hand with the diamond on it to his lips.

"I think it would be easier to find someone who didn't owe you a favor."

The pilot came over the speakers, basically just saying hello.

"Can I know where we're headed?" Eve asked when he'd finished.

"You'll see. Just a couple of hours if everything goes as planned."

The plane took off smoothly, and the low music resumed.

"Nice clear night, fiancée." He unbuckled his seatbelt. "How you feeling?"

She undid her belt as well. "Good. Stupidly optimistic."

"That's what I'm going for. Come sit in my lap, killer." He patted his thigh.

She shook her head, but complied. "This has been a long day."

"Shall we?" He motioned to the couch.

It took some maneuvering, but soon enough they were cuddled there with G at their feet. She watched him for a few minutes before letting her eyes close.

Beckett smiled to himself. They were headed to Florida. After some research and nosing around, he'd found out one of the most beautiful beaches in the world was on the Gulf Coast. Or at least that's when he'd stopped searching. The woman who owned the plane had a friend with a house along the beach, so that's where Beckett decided to engagement-moon.

He was still smiling as he dozed off to sleep with Eve in his arms and G snoring on his feet.

The plane began to make different noises that woke Eve just in time for Beckett's smile. "Killer, we got to get up and buckle up. You ready?"

She nodded and reminded herself to get off the couch like an old person. Beckett touched her arm for just a moment to make sure she was steady. She gave him a hard look. She sat in her captain's chair and buckled her seatbelt, looking out the window for a hint at the direction the plane had taken while she napped. But the landscape was cloaked in darkness, except for the runway lights.

G waddled his way over to Beckett and jumped up and down on his back legs until Beckett scooped him up and kept him in his lap.

Eve reached over to pet the dog's head and scratch his chin. "Glad we could bring him."

"Me too. The spoiled brat." Beckett kissed G's head.

The plane landed smoothly, and Eve gave a sigh of relief.

"Our destination is only a few miles away." Beckett nodded at the Land Rover parked at the end of the runway. The pilot's assistant helped expedite the deplaning, and Eve took G for a quick walk in the grass. By the time she got into the car with the dog, the bags were secured.

"So Florida, huh?" She put her feet on the dashboard.

"How'd ya know?"

"Smells like Florida. We here for any business?" She helped G get settled in the back seat, and Beckett cracked the back window so he could get a muzzle full of the fresh air.

"Nope. Pleasure only. Lots of pleasure." He found the defogger and set it on high, as the moist pre-morning air had put a foggy mist on the interior of the windshield.

He wasn't kidding about the place being close. Within ten minutes he was plugging a security code into a panel on a formidable-looking gate. The doors complied, admitting the Land Rover and sliding closed behind them.

The beach house was beautiful: whites, tans, and floor-to-ceiling glass, still lit by spotlights in the early-morning hours.

"This all ours for four days," Beckett told her. "I've dismissed the staff." He seemed to be watching for her reaction.

"This feels special." She nodded at him.

"I'll grab the bags in a minute. Let's go in." Beckett entered another code on the keypad next to the doors, and they unlocked and opened in tandem.

"Fancy."

Beckett held out his hand, and when she put her left one in his, he lifted it to his lips and kissed it right under the brand new ring. Her heart fluttered. She felt princess tingles like a real girl, and it made her blush. She could feel the heat on her cheeks. "You're turning me into a pussy."

He didn't answer, just led her through the entryway. Opulence mixed expertly with a shabby beach feel. The moon was bright over the horizon, and from their vantage point, the gentle, long stretch of white beach looked like a rumpled down comforter.

Beckett lifted a huge remote control off the sofa table and pecked in some orders with his big fingers. "Well, either this will open shit up or launch us to the goddamn moon."

The glass walls closest to the beach slid open, letting the sound of the waves crashing followed by the scent of the sea, fill the huge rooms.

"Wow."

"Come upstairs." When she headed for the staircase, he pulled her closer. "No, baby. We gots an elevator to lift our asses places, like fucking kings." He pressed a button mounted discreetly on the wall, and the door to the hidden feature slid open.

They stepped inside, and G trotted in like he used elevators every day—until the thing started moving. Then he was in Beckett's arms, whining.

They comforted him while laughing as the doors swooshed open on the second floor. The entire bedroom was white.

"Are you crazy?" She laughed. There was a huge round bed, and pillows—so inviting—piled high. G barked at the glass balcony and growled at the hot tub. "This is just...too much." She wrinkled her nose at Beckett. "I'm not sure what we should use first."

She shivered a bit from a stiff breeze. He grabbed a white throw and wrapped it around her shoulders.

"Want to see the view?" They walked together out onto the balcony.

"This is just fantastic. How long have you been planning this?"

"Since the day you woke from the surgery," he said. "You worried me. Made me face some facts..." Beckett pulled her to him using the blanket. He rubbed her arms through the fabric when she shivered again. G hopped up on the huge bed, hurrumphed twice, and then settled into a little ball of dog.

"Thank you. This has been a hell of a night." She put her hand on his throat before kissing him.

"Come, get in bed with me. We have a few hours before morning is officially here."

Eve expected some more carnal expressions of love, but instead, Beckett slid off his shoes and pants and got in the bed. His dimples were in full effect as he spread his arms wide for her. She crawled in and settled her head on his chest. He tucked the blankets all around her.

"Want me to close the wall?"

She shook her head. The sound of the surf was womb-like. She inhaled deeply and let herself fall asleep in his arms. It felt like minutes later when he kissed her awake.

"Wake up for just a few minutes," he practically shouted. "Look!"

Eve noted that the bags from the car were in the bedroom now, and she was surprised he'd managed to get in and out without her knowing.

He read the direction of her gaze. "I've got skills, baby. Shh." He hushed her even though she'd said nothing, knowing they could argue without a sound.

He pointed at the horizon, so she cuddled back into his arms and waited. The quiet was full of promise. The glass balcony allowed her a stunning view of the climbing sun, like a honeyed coin, slowly painting the morning with light orange and dim pink. The moving water became a canvas for the hope of the new day. Gulls squawked to alert the beach of the changes. She had no words.

Boaters were parked, facing the dawn, gently swaying. She looked up at him then, the soft light taking the pain from the light lines on his face. He looked from the sunrise to her, and her eyes filled with tears. He tilted his head slightly to ask her what was wrong.

She shook her head. Nothing was wrong. Everything was right.

He kissed her, his skin glowing as the sun came up, taking orange and warmth from the star of the show.

She finally stopped him, her hand on his lips. "I really do want to marry you."

He kissed her fingers. "I know."

In silence they watched the sun pull itself higher. Beckett motioned to another remote by the bed, asking with his motion if she wanted the window shaded.

She didn't. She turned away from him, forcing him to spoon her. With the morning light daring the whites in the bedroom to ignite with brightness, she cuddled into the best sleep of her life. The tension left her body, all of her concern seeping out, and then she was just a girl in love with a boy—wrapped in his arms.

Nicholas was neat. About his life, he was orderly. Everything had a place. The suitcase he unzipped in this Virginia hotel room looked like it was packed as a prop for a commercial. Things had their place, and once they were set he could breathe easier.

He checked his suit. Impeccable. Still, he used a lint remover on the shoulders. He left the hotel room and got in his car.

Sonia Kore was easy enough to track. The woman updated her Facebook page with the regularity of an advertiser. She was getting a slightly belated Christmas present of a tattoo (her first) with some girlfriends tonight. Afterward, she'd be stopping at a bar. Even though Nicholas had numerous friendly-seeming Facebook profiles for just these sorts of occasions, her page was public, so he watched her updates freely.

She'd just uploaded the picture of the new tattoo on her foot. It was a flamingo in a Santa hat. She'd regret that decision later in life. Well, someone else with that tattoo might. Sonia's foot didn't have much life left. Nicholas almost giggled out loud.

Her phone pinged her exact location every fifteen minutes and updated her profile. It was so easy to follow a woman who relied on social media as her hobby. He knew where she went to the gym, her favorite grocery store, and her license plate number from various hints in her pictures. He looked up from his phone just as Sonia drove by him with three other women in her car.

Nicholas pulled into traffic behind her. The bar the women chose to celebrate their new tattoos was a chain. They laughed and giggled, and he watched from the parking lot as Sonia passed her keys to the redhead. After some surfing on the Internet, he identified Sonia's designated driver for the evening as Daisy. Daisy had broken her foot, so, according to her comments, she wasn't taking any chances with alcohol.

Nicholas waited about ten minutes before entering the bar. He was on surveillance only tonight, he reminded himself. He ordered a beer and sat, doing his best to look like a weary businessman. No taking her tonight. No matter how much he wanted to. No matter how perfect the set up was. No taking her. Too many surveillance cameras.

No taking her.

No taking her.

No taking her.

He opened his phone and took some video, watching it back immediately. Sonia was laughing, and her friends seemed flushed with excitement. His balls felt like they were vibrating. Despite his best intentions, he thought it through. He imagined taking her in her yellow dress. He guessed at where the fabric would be damp when she began to sweat from fear. He hoped she was a screamer.

The bartender placed another beer in front of him. "You all right?"

He nodded. He used the phone's camera to see himself. He was pale, his pupils dilated. Arousal on him looked a lot like panic. He'd already broken a few rules. The bartender had noticed him, asked if he was all right.

But maybe it *could* be now.

And that snap, that thought unclipped the leash that held the monster inside of him. He pictured his pale skin turning green and scaly, his tongue lengthening and flicking out to smell.

He drank the rest of his beer and slapped a twenty on the bar.

All wrong. It was all wrong. Now it would have consequences. But he could take her. He could feel the yellow fabric between his forefinger and his thumb after it was moist with her sweat.

He left the bar. The spot next to her car was open, so he moved his car next to it. He used his rearview and side mirrors to look for security cameras. He didn't see any, but his vision was tunneling.

He opened his car door and slammed it hard into her car. Predictably, the car alarm went off. He nodded, congratulating himself for his research. He needed all the information in advance, and when he was high like this, it came back to him in torrents. It was like he was a prescient being. Omnipotent. She would hear the alarm, or someone would alert her. Sonia would take the keys from Daisy, not wanting to make her friend walk to the parking lot on her broken foot. She would have to get in the car and put the key in the ignition to stop the noise. The alarm. The screaming, bleating alarm.

All his senses were on alert. He heard footsteps approaching over the racket. He had super hearing now. And he was super strong. Every motion was perfect. Every instinct would be obeyed. Was she sweating yet? Maybe she perspired when she drank. He slipped on his gloves and pulled out a ball cap.

As she inserted the key, he was out of his vehicle. God, he wanted the struggle. He wanted the dress to rub against him as she fought.

But his instinct was necessary.

She would be drugged. Boneless. Quiet. The dress would move because he could make it, but until she was awake, he wouldn't feel it. These promises were necessary.

When she stepped back out of the vehicle, he was there, open arms. God bless women, they were such proper creatures. Her first impulse was to apologize for bumping into him.

He thanked her in a high-pitched voice, strung tight with his mental illness, before he covered her nose and mouth with the cloth. In an instant she was boneless, eyes rolling into her head. He nodded at a couple headed into the bar before pretending to nuzzle her neck.

Another mistake. It was okay; he'd come back. He'd kill them all. He'd burn down the building. He'd kill all her friends. Everyone would forget Sonia was gone. No one would care. No one would look. He was powerless to stop what he'd begun.

He slid her into his backseat, tucking her legs into the vehicle.

After reversing the car out of the parking spot, he was on the road headed to the storage building before he knew it. He freed himself from his pants and used his teeth to pull off his glove, the taste burning his lips.

Mistakes. He was making mistakes. He growled at his reflection in the mirror before taking the hem of her yellow dress in his hand. It wasn't moist. He was at a stoplight when he was able to fully grasp himself to masturbate, touching the yellow dress at the same time.

But it was too soon. It wouldn't work. She needed to be awake. He cursed and looked to his right as a truck pulled even with his car.

So many things were wrong.

After another family-gathering dinner, Livia sat with Kyle and their father in her darkened living room. Little JB slept in his car seat, and Kathy watched a video with the other kids in Emme's room. Blake and Cole were in the basement, still putting together Emme's new bike two days after she'd received it. Only Beckett and Eve were missing, having left for a vacation, of all things, which struck everyone else as long overdue.

Livia couldn't remember the last time it had been just the three of them. Her father nodded at the Christmas tree like it was a man in the room before he broke the silence.

"Girls, I think you should move." He looked from Kyle to Livia.

"No." Kyle shook her head. "I think I know where this is heading, and the answer is no."

Livia began to play with her hair as she looked from her father to her sister. This was how it always used to be. Kyle digging her heels in before she'd even heard their father out. Livia was always the peacekeeper.

"Listen for a second." She tried to convince her sister with the intensity of her gaze.

Kyle sat back on the sofa and crossed her legs.

Their father put one hand up and seemed to want to use it to pluck the right words from the air. "Taylor's here. And even he's concerned. Somehow this place, this city has come to the attention of some pretty bad people."

Their father put his searching hand in his hair. "It's getting to the point, with all that's happened in the past, that I want you both to have some distance from this situation."

Kyle began shaking her head.

He watched Kyle as he spoke his next words. "You're mothers. You have to think about the kids now."

Kyle continued to ramp up. This conversation was poorly timed. Livia knew her dad just wanted to take advantage of this moment when they were all together, but between the newness of Kyle's motherhood and the poignancy of Christmastime, it was not a great situation.

She spoke quickly, hoping to cut off a hot-headed answer from her sister. "Dad, I appreciate your opinion. We both do. But the option of moving away isn't sitting great with Kyle or me. She and I have talked about it, of course."

Kyle nodded.

"This place is where we have our memories. This very house. We created a family worth fighting for with you, and now we're making it bigger. We want this to be where we keep our roots. And if we moved? Would you be able to come?"

He shook his head. "I've got five more years until I can retire. I have to stay here."

"So that settles it. Mom left you, but we certainly aren't going to. And the kids would miss you and Kathy so much. Unless we have to — I mean, we aren't going to be unreasonable, but we're staying. And as far as Beckett's enemies? They can find us anywhere. They do that for a living. Don't you agree?"

"I don't agree that they can find you anywhere. Not as easily anyway, but I hear what you're saying, and I respect it." He stood and rubbed his hands on his pants. "That said, if I continue to feel uneasy, we'll have this conversation again." He looked back at the tree for a moment. "Whelp, Kathy and I best be going."

Kyle stood as well. "Thank you, Dad. Because of you we always know how important it is to put the kids first."

Their father nodded once and opened his arms. Kyle and Livia stepped into the three-person hug like it was a command. A flash startled them all, and they turned to see Cole checking the picture he'd just snapped.

"Looks good."

Kathy came quietly down the stairs with her finger to her lips. Livia smiled as Blake came up from the basement, whispering, "They're out?"

Kathy nodded and winked. "Big day! Another in a long line of them, right?"

Livia smiled. As quietly as possible, the company packed their things and wished each other the good tidings of the holidays.

Livia finally closed the door, and Blake switched the lock in place before setting the alarm.

"It's only nine o'clock, but it feels so much later." Livia snuggled into his arms. "Were you drinking downstairs?"

"Yes. A few times." He pulled her into a dance position. The Christmas music softly playing on the computer seemed louder now in the quiet of the house.

He began to sway, humming the melody. They watched as the dog walked through the living room, gave them both a dirty look, and headed upstairs to bed.

"He disapproves of this rowdy behavior." Blake tsked.

"Oh, hell yes, he does. We're out of control." Livia's words turned to giggles as Blake dipped her in front of the tree.

"Are you ready for the tradition, my bride?"

"Sexmas? I can't wait." Livia wrapped her arms around Blake's neck and kissed him deeply.

During every Christmastime, sometime while the tree was up, they had a date. They'd find room on the living room floor and make love in the splashes of colored light from the tree.

Blake cleared space and sprinted upstairs to get their end of the baby monitor. Livia met him back under the tree with a bottle of chilled wine and a glass.

He set up the monitor before meeting her picnic style on the floor.

"Only a few more years before this tradition gets too risky," she told him with a raised eyebrow.

"Don't you mean risqué? Only one glass?" Blake took the bottle and opened it with a quiet pop.

"The rest are dirty."

"I'm going to show you dirty in a minute." He handed her a full glass before toasting her with the bottle.

Livia sighed. "The wooing has fallen so far, Mr. Hartt. It used to be all smile counts and poetry. Now we just call sex 'the dirty.'"

"Not enough romance for you, Mrs. Hartt? I'd like you to know I took the trash out and walked the dog before bringing all my game to this carpet." Blake took a long gulp from the bottle.

"You're going to have a hangover tomorrow." Livia let him have her glass, and he set it on the coffee table.

"I'm not worried about tomorrow. I'm worried about right now, with you, under this Christmas tree." Blake supported her neck as he laid her on the floor.

Livia turned her head. "You'd better convince me. So far you've talked about the dog going to the bathroom, trash, and dirtiness."

Blake kissed her jaw and turned her head gently, kissing her mouth as she bit her lips together.

"Can't I just convince you with my manly ways?" He wiggled his eyebrows.

He could, of course, do just that—but she shook her head. She loved the playful sparkle in his green eyes. His five o'clock shadow just made him more handsome, framing his kissable lips with scruff.

"Okay." He put his fingers at the bottom of her shirt, lifting it gently so he could circle her belly button with his index finger. "You're the sexiest, most beautiful woman on this planet. So sexy, in fact, that I had to have you. I had to make you bear my children because my universe and yours had to be combined. Everything I've ever been needed to be buried inside of you, so deep, so full of love that we created life. Twice."

He lifted her shirt and kissed the tops of her breasts, whispering his devotion into her skin. "And it's never enough. Unless I can hear you coming, I can't think of anything else. All day, every day. For years now. You're that powerful, Livia. This. Us. It's so intense that years of it haven't cured me. I can't stop wanting to make love to you."

"Wow." Livia smiled and pulled his face back to hers, kissing him and effectively stopping his beautiful words.

He unbuttoned her pants and slipped his hands inside. "I wasn't done."

"I hope not." Livia unbuttoned his shirt, needing to touch the center of his chest, her talisman. Finally she could feel the steady beat against her hand. As his hand found her, she worked to keep her gaze on his determined face. It was amazing to watch him. This Blake, so sexual and dominant, was only for her. She kissed him again, trying to put some skill into it, but his fingers were taking her control. His heartbeat increased even more as she started to toss.

When he pulled her pants roughly from her thighs, she forgot to be quiet. He hooked her legs on his shoulders, changing his touch from the deep, intimate strokes to a kiss. He used one hand to brace her lower back and his other to combine touch with his oral skills.

She looked down at him, his tongue buried deep inside of her but his gaze on her face. She came.

He held her steady and showed no mercy during her climax, begging her body to go further than she could even fathom. Her legs shook and she bit her wrist, trying to stifle her moans of satisfaction.

But Blake wasn't done, nor was he interested in giving her a second to breathe. She was on her knees before she could stop shuddering, and he was forceful and wild behind her, his long fingers finding her again, reminding her he was in charge. His touch felt so good it was almost pain. He increased his tempo until she needed her elbows to help her keep balance.

When he was finally spent, they lay on the floor, panting. She kissed his cheek and felt for his heartbeat again. "Merry Christmas. I love you."

He kissed her forehead between pants. "I love you right back."

13

Doom

On the Sunday after Christmas, Ryan pulled away from Ted's building. Now that he'd broken into the man's apartment, he felt even less easy than before. His trip to the hospital yesterday had given him a brief respite from his nagging cop gut feeling. The receptionist had assured him that Dr. Hartt had been in touch few times. He was a last-minute speaker at a medical conference out of town.

But when Ryan went through the apartment again picking a lock on his way, nothing had been moved. Not a single thing. The sponge was still where he'd stowed it next to the sink. The dishwasher hadn't been unloaded. The pie Eve left hadn't been touched. Dr. Hartt had clearly not been home.

It just didn't add up. He didn't like it. He drove to work, knowing what he was doing now could be conceived as reverse stalking. Trish-style weirdness. But after Ryan let himself into his office about the time he'd usually be leaving—and on a Sunday, no less—he waved to co-workers here for second shift and began to investigate.

After a few phone calls, Ryan was looking at Ted Hartt's credit card history. The man hadn't made a digital footprint since Christmas. Thanks to the cell phone company, he knew the text messages from Ted's phone were the only evidence that he was still functioning. Another call put Ryan in touch with a somebody that owed him a favor. After listening to his friend tap around on a keyboard, Ryan knew Dr. Hartt's texts to Eve had come from an untraceable computer, not a phone. After a little more prodding, the friend told Ryan that Eve was in Florida, which explained why she hadn't already scoped out her dad's place.

Ryan hung up the phone. After seeing the mistletoe, he'd known Dr. Hartt was in trouble. Now he was sure the man was in serious trouble. If there'd been a ransom or blackmail, Eve would be back from Florida—unless that was where she'd been led. This was not good. He needed to call her.

Her phone went straight to voice mail, and Ryan knew he would have to raise hell. He'd have to call every phone and shake down every scumbag until he could find Eve. He'd start with the brothers first, and he'd have to clue McHugh in next. Ugh. He'd have to admit to the stalking, the clandestine Christmas dinner, all of it.

He pulled out his wallet and looked at the picture she'd included. Despite the fact that he loved her, Eve was his friend. This was her father, and something was very wrong. But before he went crazy, he'd contact the convention where Dr. Hartt was supposed to be.

He just wished he didn't have such a feeling of doom.

Beckett laughed as they turned their chairs away from the surf and faced the beach house instead. The wine bottle was fine where it was, propped in the sand between them. G sprawled out on a towel Eve had brought down from the bathroom.

The last of the sun was peeking over the horizon, warming their faces. They were both coated in a thin, salty mist from the Gulf behind them.

He looked over his shoulder to her face. He leaned closer and lifted her sunglasses, comparing the color of the endless waves to her eyes.

"Blue as the fucking ocean. Just so you know." He leaned forward to kiss her, carefully adding his tongue to taste her salty, wine-flavored lips.

She shook her head, but snaked an arm out of the comforter she'd brought to the beach from the bed to touch his face.

Under the blanket she wore a tank top and comfy pajama bottoms. Her feet were bare with sand caught between her toes. Peaceful.

She'd been the soft Eve for hours upon hours now, and he was so in love, so thrilled he could bring her round. No kids in sight, just his big, stupid self making her take down her guard felt like winning the biggest medal in his life.

"What's for Sunday dinner?" She unfolded her legs and stuck them in the sand. She ignored her own question as she used her feet to sift through the tiny grains. "I've never seen sand like this. It's so white. I'm used to brown sand. And it's acting like Play-Doh. It's crazy."

"It's quartz. Supposedly it'll stay cool in the summer. Only beach like it. Or so says the Internet." Beckett reached down and grabbed a handful, letting it slide through his fingers. "I like the lifeguard stands."

They both glanced in the direction of the bright shacks, each a different primary color. Although he hadn't rented out the beach, it was so offseason that there were few people on the large expanse of sand. He and Eve had made love on the beach under the moonlight just last night.

"Hungry." She pointed at her mouth and made all kinds of purring noises, acting like a cartoon cat.

Playful. Damn if he didn't want to buy the house they were living in, flush the rest of the world down the toilet, and mail his brothers and their families to the surrounding houses. This was a close to heaven as Beckett felt he'd ever get.

"I've got a plan. No worries," he told her. "Actually, let's pack up and get ready."

He helped her gather all their shit, and soon enough they were trekking back into the house.

"I hate leaving. What's in the fridge?"

"Shut it, crazy woman. I brought you a dress and shoes and crap. We are going to dinner together. Then we can come back to paradise." He led her upstairs and opened the bathroom door. Hanging from a hook was a simple white dress. White sandals that laced up her calf sat beside the vanity, and a velvet box stood next to a tube of lipstick. "It's got everything you need in here."

She shook her head, but smiled widely. "Thought of everything, right?"

He got dressed in white pants and a linen shirt, slapping on some cologne to top off the look. He fed G and took him for a quick walk, and by the time the dog had his belly rub, Eve was coming down the stairs.

The dress skimmed her curves perfectly, and she'd shrugged on a super soft white cashmere sweater. Her sandals were perfect for walking in the sand. She wore the diamond pendant and matching earrings he'd left by her lipstick.

She could be a wife. Some lucky fuck's capable, gorgeous partner—a man who wouldn't let her be in danger.

"Thank you for my accessories. This is over the top. And not practical." She hugged him around the waist and set her head on his chest.

"Fuck practical." He tilted her face to his. "I want to decorate you with diamonds. It's sort of like peeing on my tree, 'cept more expensive."

"Let me check my phone. See if my dad can FaceTime real quick." She went to the kitchen in search of the device.

Ted had texted Eve a few times, but he hadn't answered the phone when she'd called. It was the only part of the vacation that wasn't going as planned.

"Still no answer." She returned with the phone in her hand. "I'll call again when we get back. Can you put this in your pocket? I don't want to carry a purse."

He turned his hip in her direction, and she slid the phone in his front pants pocket.

"Ready?" He held his elbow out to her, and she took it. Instead of taking the car, Beckett walked them out the back door.

They strolled along the beach for about a quarter of a mile before Beckett spotted the restaurant he'd rented. The waiters were waiting and took Eve's sweater and his sports jacket. Another of them led them to the table closest to the window, which was surrounded with candles and twinkling white lights.

"You went all out."

"Just spoiling you, killer." Beckett held her chair as she sat.

He admired her hair falling around her shoulders as he tasted the offered wine and approved it. After they both had a glass, he held his up for a toast.

"To us."

She nodded before tapping his glass. After a swallow she smiled. "This is amazing."

"I picked out all your favorites." Beckett lifted his chin in the direction of the servers, and the food was delivered to the table.

A gorgeous salad with avocados and sunflower seeds was joined by a bowl of matzo ball soup.

After sipping a bit of soup and poking around the salad, she finally figured it out, "This tastes just like the soup at Nicolatti's in Poughkeepsie. And is this the Chick-Fil-A salad?"

He nodded. "Flown in just for the occasion. Well, not the salad. They had that down the street. Don't worry, this fine establishment is handing the main course."

The way she rolled her eyes made him want to kick himself for not doing this every weekend. It was always such a war — so many lives depending on them, so much to attend to. This whole vacation felt delectably selfish.

The pasta primavera came next, and it was delicious. They shared small talk about dreams and plans of a future that would require them both to take different paths. They would buy the house they were living in, for sure. And the brothers would move, no problem.

"So, where do you want the wedding?" He thanked the waiter who refilled their wine glasses.

"I don't know. We can't really. You know this has been fun, but planning a wedding? That would have way too many contingencies. We can't even really wear rings." She touched her engagement diamond.

"Maybe we get to live in these days here like we want to, you know?" He wiped his mouth with a napkin.

Eve seemed willing to go along for now, but Beckett hoped his next surprise wouldn't fail. After dessert, he stood, shaking hands with the restaurant owner and waiters before holding his hand out to Eve.

At the front door, he helped her into her sweater and handed her a bouquet of exotic white flowers.

"What's this?"

"Come with me." He led her to the beach again, but during dinner a few people had been busy. It was now lined with an aisle of candles, and a man stood close to the breaking surf, hands crossed, waiting. Someone had used the surrounding sand as a canvas, creating a swirling pattern. Their names were part of the art.

What? She asked without a sound.

"I want you to marry me. Here. Now."

Beckett let go of her hand and strode away. When he turned around, close to the water at the end of the aisle, he hoped to hell she wasn't running in the other direction.

Eve had a million reasons to turn away from this guy standing on the beach. First, and foremost, her father should be here to walk her down the aisle. But when Beckett turned, holding out his hand to her, all she could see was his hopeful face.

It was as if the beach had gotten inside, changed how she weighed outcomes and causes. She leaned down and took her sandals off. This sand, so soft and white, was now her favorite pair of shoes. Normally, she could come up with a list as long as her arm why this wasn't going to happen. But not tonight. She smiled and decided right then. Her cautiousness snapped.

She stepped toward him and watched as his face changed the second he realized she was coming to him, not running away. He was so in love, and this could make his dream come true. She picked up the hem of her dress and ran the rest of the way. He caught her in a swinging hug of triumph, murmuring tales of her beauty in her ear.

The ocean was loud tonight. The waves crashed like a stadium full of fans cheering. The officiate opened what looked like a Bible and began to speak, but she couldn't hear a word the man was saying. Instead of stepping away from Beckett, she stayed in his arms. He held her face in his hands.

"Do you want to marry me?" He touched his forehead to hers.

"I do." She wanted to tell him more, but couldn't think of how to word it. He was her accomplice, her boss, her opponent.

"I know." He could see it in her eyes, as only he could do.

The officiate kept on, the droning words harmonizing with the waves. Mist from the ocean sprinkled over them.

"Where there's you, there's always gonna be me. As long as I breathe," Beckett told her.

She touched his lips with her fingertips. "I know."

The next words came in with another wave. "I now pronounce you husband and wife. Congratulations, Mr. and Mrs. Taylor."

Beckett pulled her close and twirled her into a dip. Not waiting for permission, he kissed his bride.

14

EVERYTHING

Blake took the Monday morning phone call from his father-in-law in the basement, where he'd been holed up with his piano, trying to compose. He'd been surprised to see John's number pop up on the contact screen, but assumed Livia had left her phone in her purse.

"No, Blake, I'm calling to talk to you," he said. "This is sort of outside procedure, but anything with Taylor is."

"Is he okay?" Blake always expected a call regarding Beckett, and fear filled his chest.

"As far as we know, he's fine. We're actually looking to talk to Eve specifically. Sergeant Morales has some concerns as to the whereabouts of Dr. Hartt." He sounded like he was doing three things at once.

"Eve's dad? My uncle? He's missing?" Blake stood from the piano bench and began to pace.

"One and the same. Turns out Ted wasn't at home on Christmas Day and hasn't been there since. We're not one hundred percent sure where he is right now. So I really need to speak with Eve, and she's not answering the number we have for her. Is there any way you could get to Taylor and see if he knows where to find her? It's highly probable that this is just a misunderstanding." McHugh began to shout orders at someone else.

"Sure, Dad. Want her to call you at this number?"

"Only if she can't reach Morales first. He's running point on this situation. I really appreciate it, Blake. Hope I didn't wake anyone."

"Of course not, that would require someone here to be sleeping. Give my best to Kathy." Blake listened as John told him to do the same at his house.

Livia pounded down the stairs with a laundry basket, whizzing by him quickly, obviously intent on getting the wash started. Blake came up behind her and put his hands around her waist, nuzzling her neck which was exposed by her high ponytail.

"Mmmm…good morning, handsome. Was that my dad?" She dumped the clothes in the washer and twisted the knob into the right position before slamming the lid and facing him.

"It was. You look wonderful this morning. Did you put on that perfume to kill me?" He kissed her soft lips.

"I did." She hugged him hard, and they stood like that for a few minutes, not saying anything. The heart to heart ritual was a sacred moment for them. They were grateful, even after all this time together.

"So what'd Dad need?" Livia broke the quiet.

"Turns out Dr. Hartt might be missing. Could just be a communication problem, but he wanted me to call Beck or Eve and get them to return Ryan Morales' phone call."

Concern clouded Livia's face. "Missing as in kidnapped?"

He pulled her closer, the word giving him a moment of panic as he remembered when she was taken. "No, he didn't say that. Just needs him to call in."

She nodded. "Let me run back upstairs, check on the kids. Can you pull the clothes out of the dryer for me when it buzzes? I'll say a little prayer for Dr. Hartt. And Eve."

With that she was trotting back up the stairs.

Blake tried Eve first, and her phone went straight to voice mail. He didn't bother with a message, figuring Morales had done that already. He tried Beckett's phone, and just before the voice mail could kick in, his brother answered in a scratchy voice.

He started with an apology before telling his brother the news that had John concerned. Beckett's voice went from lazy and happy to cautious.

"Killer, you check your phone?" he called to Eve.

Her voice was audible. "No. You put it in your pocket, and I've been busy, if you remember."

There was a smack, the sound of a hand hitting bare skin. "I remember."

"No, dude," Beckett said, returning his focus to Blake. "Let me go see if I can find it. Maybe her dad called." Beckett's voice came in and out as he traipsed through what had to be a huge space, based on the echoes. "Got to get my pants, which are outside. First I have to open the wall."

Blake gave the phone a confused scowl. "Bro, are you drunk?"

His brother laughed. "Not any more. But I kind of wish I was, based on this phone call. I don't like the sound of it. Here's my pants."

He heard the back and forth between Eve and Beckett as they located her charger and plugged the phone in. In a moment his cousin was on the line.

"Phone's charging up. What's going on?" Eve was all business.

Blake told her everything John had brought up. She didn't respond, and soon Beckett was back on the phone.

"She's calling Morales."

Beckett and Blake listened to her end of the conversation.

"What is it?"

"What do you mean? Gone since when? He's been texting me."

"And the hospital said?"

"Did you pull up his credit card? No, I'm not mad."

"I don't like it either. Let me try calling him."

Eve said nothing for a bit, then she was on the phone with Morales again. "You find everything you can. Dust his place, everything. You do *everything*. I'll be there in, like, three hours. Be ready. You can meet us at the airport."

Eve was clearly addressing Beckett when she said, "My father's in trouble."

Barely an hour later, Eve sat in her captain's chair and looked at her new rings: a wedding band and a shiny engagement ring. Her hand looked like it belonged to another person.

She made eye contact with Beckett. He clearly knew what she was thinking.

"Not your fault," he said. "Having a moment for you is not evil."

She looked out the small window, nothing but sky and clouds. There would be no peace in her mind until she knew where her father was. She slid down in her seat and ran her hand through her hair, willing the plane to fly faster. The list of things she needed to do to find her father ran through her head like an endless ticker.

Beckett stood and pulled her to her feet. G moved over on the couch to allow his people to sit.

"It's not a coincidence," she said. "It's not going to be okay. Morales is a good cop. McHugh can do his job. This is Vitullo." She swallowed as her emotion became palpable in her throat.

"You want a pole vault, or can you jump to these conclusions without one?" Beckett ran his knuckles across her jaw.

She ignored his attempt at soothing and sat, twirling her rings.

He sighed. "I've got everyone out looking for your dad."

Eve wanted to throw up. She stood and shook out her hands before making fists. "I need to find him. I'll do what I have to."

He was quiet for a while before he answered, sitting next to her. "I know you will. Can we at least acknowledge that we're better when we work together?"

"I want Sevan at the airport. I'll trade him for my dad. You know Rodolfo's behind this. He wanted me, and then gave up. Do you think he ever gives up? I don't. We're about to find out why I haven't been approached again since the car accident." Eve couldn't decide where to put her hands. G whined in her direction, probably sensing her unease.

She looked at Beckett, and he held her gaze for a long time. She saw it there—what she already knew: there'd been no ransom requested. No proof of life to send Beckett and Eve in a spiral of demands from Vitullo.

"He's dead. You think he's dead." Eve willed away the tears that blurred her vision.

"I didn't say that." Beckett stood again.

"You don't have to. Jesus." She turned to nearest door and began to punch and kick as if it was attacking her.

He grabbed her by the top of her arms from behind. "Stop."

She could see him in the reflection of the window in the door. *Sympathy.* Eve turned her head so she could look at him. "I'm going to kill everyone." Her words were her promise. She was grenade with the pin pulled, a bomb with the fuse lit.

"We don't bury anyone until we know. Shit, I thought Chery was dead, and she wasn't. Everything in me told me she was gone. We don't get to go full mental. Your father needs us to be sure before we go nuclear. I refuse to be wrong about something this important. And I can't have you fucking up anything that can help him because you're too screwed up to think straight. Your father was able to operate on you. This is how you have to operate for him."

She turned quickly, with every intention of punching him.

"You wanna hit me? Be my fucking guest. But we're not pulling amateur bullshit and getting caught in something that's designed to bring us down." He let go of her arms and held his hands palm up, inviting her to do her worst.

She punched her own hand before sinking to her knees. She pounded on the plush airplane carpet.

Beckett kneeled with her. "You're my wife. Your father is my father."

She looked at his deep blue eyes. He was so serious and probably thinking more clearly than she was. "Was that marriage even legal?"

"We're worried about legal now?" Beckett raised his eyebrow. "Did it count for you?"

She nodded.

"Then that's what matters. Now, let's plan it out. You want Sevan there, which is fine. But I doubt he'd be a suitable swap for your dad, if he's indeed with Rodolfo."

"Sevan knows too much shit anyway," Eve said with a sigh. "I'm going to shake him down until I know everything he does about Rodolfo."

"Okay."

They looked at each other, close and on their knees.

"There's only one suitable swap for my dad: me." Eve stood.

Beckett pulled himself to his feet as well. "Actually, there's two."

By ten thirty in the morning the day after he'd acquired the necessary information, Nicholas had the liquid nitrogen storage tank sitting next to him in the car, buckled in like a passenger. He exhaled at the stoplight. Sonia had been delicious. Hers would be Nicholas' favorite name for a while. He remained on a high from this latest knowledge-seeking mission. The yellow dress was folded neatly in a Ziploc and stored in the glove compartment. She'd even said she forgave him before she passed. Delectable.

What a story. Really. Who knew Dr. Hartt had it in him? Maybe there was such a thing as too much knowledge when it was compressed with grief and worry.

Sonia had regretted storing the young Eve Hartt's ovary, but she'd felt such sympathy as well. Sonia had known Eve as a teenager. She'd known how desperate the girl had been for a child of her own. When Dr. Hartt had called her in, well, she'd done what she did best: preserve options, gather hope.

Now, thanks to the information Sonia supplied, Eve Hartt's legacy was in the car with Nicholas: perfectly healthy, frozen ovary tissue. The bad news was that the procedure needed to extract mature eggs was still experimental and untested in humans. But the good news was that thanks to Nicholas and his powers of persuasion — which truly knew no bounds — Rodolfo had a magician on the other end of this errand. The doctor he'd brought over from Belgium seemed fully confident, as long as the tissue had been stored properly.

Nicholas had already phoned Rodolfo, because although he would have preferred to deliver the ovaries with a lavish bow as a surprise, time was of the essence.

He'd been instructed to drive straight to the clinic they'd created. Rodolfo was at home. Anti-climactic. No in-person reward for all his efforts. As he pulled up at the house, somewhere in rural Virginia, he unbuckled the canister. Sonia had been so helpful with her instructions, telling him exactly how to enter the storage facility and transport the tissue safely. He lifted the canister and was met by the magician, Dr. Yordan, at the front door.

The doctor motioned for Nicholas to step in. "This is all cutting it close. I barely have any time to thaw and assess viability before you're bringing me the host subject tomorrow?"

He was already opening the canister to transfer the contents to a more expensive cryogenic freezer.

"Yes, tomorrow," Nicholas confirmed. "But it will be fine. This came from a high-quality facility, and the doctors who consulted on the procedure were excellent."

"Am I able to confer with these people?" the doctor asked.

"No." Nicholas answered, and he was able to prevent any further questions with just his eyes.

"Okay, so you'll be back in the morning?"

Nicholas nodded. "I'm not exactly certain of the timing, but leave everything to me. Just focus on your lab work. The rest will be handled," he said.

He watched as the magician shivered briefly and looked as if he wanted to ask more questions. But he didn't. Still, that shiver made Nicholas wonder if the doctor himself would be part of the final clean up he'd have to do on this job.

Beckett checked his email and text messages in the air while Eve changed in the tiny airplane bathroom. Gone was her soft glow of happiness. She was all business. The woman had channeled her fear and worry into battle mode as they'd packed and cleared out of the beautiful beach house.

When she emerged, she'd changed from her white sundress into jeans and a leather jacket, an outfit he knew was accessorized with her favorite weapons. He continued furiously making contact with his douchebags and assholes, but she was finally still, just sitting, staring at the door of the plane.

He took a few more calls—lining things up and finding information wasn't the easiest, though Shark had assured him they continued to make progress with flipping Vitullo's men and now had quite a group amassed on the inside. A particular coup had been a technology and surveillance expert named Spider, who was still playing coy, but was smart enough to see a good deal when it presented itself. Shark felt certain it was only a matter of time.

Beckett was grateful for this news, but he'd still not planned on moving on Rodolfo this soon. However, judging from Eve's face, she wouldn't stop until she knew where her father was, so even if it wasn't a full-scale attack, something had to happen. As the plane began to descend, Eve sat with her hands folded in her lap, waiting.

"Listen, I need you to give me a minute before we roll up into Vitullo's compound," Beckett began. "Just a few minutes. I have some things I'm working—"

She put her cold, blue gaze on his face and interrupted. "No. I wait for nothing. I'm three days behind. Maybe four."

"He's going to be expecting you. He knows you'll come to him." Beckett moved to sit next to her.

"I don't care." She didn't fidget or show her anxiousness outwardly.

"In the past we've reacted. I did Mike Simmer in a moment of planned fury. You couldn't stop me. I would never hear it. And you did Mary Ellen on an impulse, and now we're here." He stood in front of her, desperate for her to hear him.

She kept her eyes on the door, staring through him with her eyes locked on his chest. Then suddenly she stood, almost as tall as he in her killer heels. "I'm sorry I inconvenienced you. But this is my father. My *father*."

"Don't," Beckett immediately countered. "Don't talk to me like I don't know what the word *father* means because I don't have one. I have a family. I know what protection means." He would fight with her now if he had to. Play dirty, change dynamics. The most important thing was that she didn't go off half-cocked, Terminator style. Again.

There was no sympathy in her face. She was silent. The door to her humanity was closed.

"Can I tell you what I know?" Beckett asked. "That I have douche-bags on the inside? And your father hasn't been seen? Rodolfo's prime diaper-changer has been missing for as long as your father, and the old man is still in his favorite chair, watching *Wheel of* fucking *Fortune* as of a few minutes ago. Let me coordinate with Morales and McHugh. We can bring the wrath of God down on this motherfucker." He scanned her expression, hoping to see some of her calculating sureness return. She was a blank slate.

He shook his head. "I'm not gonna stop you. You want to go in Rambo-style and make the same mistakes we've made before? Go for it. Just know you won't be taking only your life in your hands."

Beckett sat and ran his hands through his hair. Eve remained standing despite the seatbelt sign illuminating. She adjusted her hair knife and only moved when the plane bounced slightly during landing. When the door opened, she was out, stepping on the stairs before they were fully extended.

Her motorcycle waited on the tarmac, as he'd promised. Morales stood next to it, the keys hooked on his index finger.

Assholes and douchebags came rolling up at the same time. An army. She took the keys from Morales without so much as a hello. He caught her hand and looked at her wedding rings. She defiantly pulled them off and turned to drop them in Beckett's hand. Her motorcycle started as his men looked to him for direction.

She was going to do it, go straight into the mouth of hell and die without even helping find her father. Beckett trotted over to his Challenger as Dildo exited the car.

"Have them sit tight. I got to go get her," Beckett told him as they traded places.

Morales opened the passenger door and slid in.

"Fuck you. Get out of my car."

"Fuck you. I'm staying." He gave Beckett the finger. "If I have to arrest her ass, I will."

There was no time to argue, as Beckett had to slam the pedal to the floor to keep up with the blond assassin in front of him.

"What's she going to do?" Morales had his handcuffs handy.

"She's going to get killed. That's what she's going to do."

"Great goddamn honeymoon, Don Juan." Ryan nodded as Eve cut the motorcycle off the main road, and Beckett barely made the turn in time, tires squealing.

"Eat a dick, fuckbag." Beckett concentrated on Eve, who despite her usually calm demeanor and excellent driving, was making mistakes. She took a rural road that was more secluded, but its turns and intersections would slow her down. Beckett chose Route 9, which was a straight shot, hopefully allowing them to intercept Eve at the train tracks.

A quick glance at the Hudson River showed a long freight train timed perfectly to piss Eve off and pull her to a stop. She'd have to wait until it cleared before getting closer to the throughway.

Three minutes later, Beckett parked the Challenger sideways and had enough time to get out and cross his arms before she pulled into view. Because she'd left her helmet off, he could see the anger flash across her face. This was quickly followed by a dawning knowledge that she'd made mistakes in her getaway. Beckett lifted a brow, and she pulled to a stop. Morales leaned against the car with him, twirling his cuffs like they'd been there together for hours.

"You got about four minutes until this train is out of your way," Beckett said.

She used her heel to throw down the kickstand and pulled out her gun. "You're not stopping me."

"*Fuuuckkk.*" Morales added four more syllables to the word than it normally had.

Beckett slapped him on the bicep. "Stop. Let me. Eve, I think your father might be dead." It was cruel. Far more damaging than punching her right in the chest.

"Dude." Morales tossed up his hands.

Eve narrowed her eyes, her nostrils flaring as she fought not to shed tears. Her gun remained steady, even.

"You know it. And I know it," Beckett continued. "There's no ransom. This might be what they're doing because they couldn't take you." His throat was dry. He hadn't wanted to say it out loud, and he still wished with everything he had to be wrong. Bringing someone back from the dead was easier on a heart than burying them for good.

The train rolled past slowly. The clacking of the wheels repetitive, like a heartbeat. They stood until the train passed completely, leaving the sounds of distant traffic and the river in its wake.

She holstered her gun. "How dare you give up on him so easy?" Her words were surrounded with knives.

Beckett bit his lip and walked toward her. He couldn't defend his accusations with anything but lack of ransom requests or other demands. He kept walking, gravel crunching under his feet. He knew she could either lock him out or fall into him. He was next to her now, so close he could reach out and touch her, but he waited. "You know I'm right."

She kicked up the stand and steadied herself on the bike. "I know that these past selfish days have left my father missing..." She stopped, anger sealing the emotion inside. "And I have to find him."

"You won't. Eve, they've got something they needed from him. They could grab you at any time. Really. You know that. This doesn't make any sense. We have to have a clear picture and a plan to beat this old fucker at his own damn game."

"You work the channels and get your clear plan. I'm going to Vitullo's and making him die. That's what's happening. I don't need you. And I don't need him." She nodded in Morales' direction.

"I love you. Don't do this." Beckett reached out and wrapped his hand around her neck, fingers digging in just enough.

She nearly ran over his toes and almost made it past Morales, who threw his handcuffs in her way. Her reflexes got the best of her, and she swerved, planting the bike on its side. Had she been going faster, it would have been an ugly accident. But she rolled like a pro out of the way.

Ryan darted in, grabbing the keys from the bike before stepping back to watch her stand. She was clearly devastated — no tears, just a vacant desperation his soul recognized. He went to her and grabbed her hand.

He pulled her to his chest, his arms holding her tightly. "It's not your fault."

She nodded against his chest.

He pulled away to look in her eyes. Broken. This broken girl had a face he'd seen too many times in his past. He watched her bury guilt as deep as it would go.

Beckett stood nearby, silent in the dust the bike had kicked up.

"I'm so sorry, sweetheart. I'm so sorry." Ryan patted Eve's back.

She shook her head and, almost like a black hole, he watched as she collapsed her sadness and energy into herself. Hardening.

Ryan knew where she was headed. Where he would've been headed in another life. "You've got to let Beckett help you. Do you think your father wants you to get revenge?"

She shook her head and looked at his feet. "That doesn't matter."

"It does. Honor his choice by living another day."

She swallowed.

"Would you want your dad to die rushing to avenge you?"

She shook her head.

"He deserves that courtesy, that respect. He earned it by loving you no matter what life you live. A man who buys fresh mistletoe every year needs to be honored by you protecting his daughter right now. You're the only one who can save her, Eve. Beckett can't stop you. I can't stop you. Just you."

"All I'm good at is killing. That's what I can do right now."

"No. Right now, you breaking? That's love. That's the love you have for your dad. You do that best."

She rolled her eyes before just giving up. The strong, beautiful Eve gave up in his arms, standing near the train tracks. He scooped her up before she could hit the ground as she cried. Her sobs barely let her breathe.

Beckett ran over, but instead of taking her from his arms, he cradled her face.

Both men held her in her human, desperate moment. She reached out and threaded a fist into each of their hair.

Morales mouthed to Taylor, "He's dead?"

Taylor shrugged, and mouthed back, "Seems like it, but I don't know. Just had to stop her."

15

Expensive Rules

Alison exhaled. Today was the day. All day, every day, this dream was what she wanted. She looked over at her sweet guy, Flint, still snoring. She turned to face him, and he woke up with a start.

"Was I snoring again?" he asked.

"Yes. I hope we can program that habit right out of this baby." She smiled.

"Designer baby? Well, I sure as hell hope she doesn't get your dagger toenails, then." He closed his eyes again and reached for her, tucking her spoon style against him.

"Dagger toenails can be a weapon. Snoring helps no one."

He parted her hair with his nose and kissed the nape of her neck.

"Actually," he murmured against her skin, "I think it was invented to scare bears away when our ancestors fell asleep in the wild."

"You're making that up. You're the biggest liar, liar pants on fire." She snuggled deeper into his arms, feeling his manhood waking as well.

"My pants are on fire, all right. You best get out of this bed, Alison. Otherwise I will break all those expensive rules we bought for your vagina."

She shimmied out of the sheets. "Today's the big day. I get knocked up after I get knocked out."

"That's right. I'm so manly my penis doesn't even need to be there to get a bun in your oven." Flint's dark brown eyes twinkled as he pointed to the implement in question with two hands shaped like guns.

"I'm going to shower." Alison gave him an elaborate sigh of exasperation. "What time should we leave?"

"In about a half an hour to be there for the appointment. I'll get dressed."

"There's gas in the car, right?"

Flint got up, naked, and let out a loud morning fart. "I got gas here."

"Quick, hurry—we need to make copies of that kind of talent so the future generations can benefit."

"That's right, woman. Now you're talking. Get in there."

She was nervous, but Flint could always make her laugh. Today was a serious day, and she needed a tension breaker. Her shower was over quickly, as she'd washed her hair and shaved her legs last night. This last one was just to get the anxiety off her skin. She brushed her long hair and met a fully dressed Flint in their master bedroom.

He held her hand until they'd parked the car at the clinic, only lifting it when he absolutely needed it to maneuver the car safely. Alison nodded, willing herself to open the door. Her job was to get up and go inside. Today was implantation day. As she stepped out of the vehicle, Flint half ran to get to her side and close the door behind her. "Ready, champ?"

She felt like crying as happiness and anxiousness combined in the most nausea-inducing way. She nodded.

A man in a suit hopped out of a van decorated with Health Department insignia. He walked purposefully toward her, his voice muffled behind a surgical mask. "Ma'am? I'm sorry, the physician insisted we meet his patients here. They've had a scare with a contaminant inside, and the fire department is on their way. They asked that anyone receiving accelerated hormone treatment stay out until the building is cleared." He paused briefly to look at each of them. "Can I ask you and your partner to sit in the van and wear a mask quickly? Just for a few moments until the building is cleared."

Alison's mind flew all over the place. The man in front of her had a pen, a clipboard, and a laminated name tag clipped to his tie.

Flint stepped forward. "I think we'll just come back later." He put his arm around Alison. Her hopes fell. She was ready now, right now. "What type of contaminant was it?" he continued. Flint was used to taking charge in situations, and as she felt her eyes well up with tears, Alison was grateful to not have to talk at the moment.

"It's actually usually very safe," the man explained. "It's a cleaning solution, but a concentrated bottle spilled near their air filters. We're just going to have the air tested. Apparently this is a very delicate time for some of the patients, yourself included." The man's eyes crinkled as if he was smiling under his mask.

"How about we wait in our car until you're all set?" Flint held her elbow, keeping her from following the man's hand gestures toward his van.

"Well, that's fine," he said. "But I just know they're going to be opening the windows in a few minutes, and my van has a filter system designed for these kinds of situations. And of course, you can also reschedule, but we do have to move along." The man pulled out a phone and glanced at it. "Yes, the secretary is saying the fire department is two minutes out. They should be able to get here and get this sorted."

She finally looked at Flint. "I don't want to reschedule. I'm already nervous."

He nodded. "Okay. Sure. Want to hang out in the van? Keep that baby carrier nice and clean?"

The man in the suit stepped out of the way. "There are two masks inside. Just sit down and slip them on."

Alison climbed in, and Flint came in after her as the van door closed firmly behind them. They looked at each other as they slipped the masks on. Alison could feel hers tangle in her hair, the rubber bands getting in her way. She looked back to Flint and watched as he seemed to fall asleep, almost boneless.

"Baby? What's wrong?" She dropped her mask on the floor and came to Flint's aid. "Hey, wake up."

She put her hands to his face, working to remove the mask.

The van door was pulled open.

"Help! Something's wrong." She looked at the Health Department official as he covered Flint's mask with his hand, keeping it in place. "What're you doing? He needs air. Get help!"

Alison had never been manhandled in her life, so when the man pushed her backward, her first thought was that he was in trouble too. It wasn't until the door had closed and he was moving toward her with her mask in his hand that it all clicked.

It wasn't the forceful way he grabbed her wrists, or even the fact that he physically slammed her into her seat, that made her scream. It was the vacant, dead look in his eyes.

When Alison came to, she was bound to a table. But her feet were free, and she began kicking. Panic flooded her, though she was blurry as to why.

The doctor easily caught her ankles and a nurse slipped on restraints. In no time, she was stuck.

"Where's Flint? Where's my husband? Where's Flint?" The fear in her voice brought her anxiety to a sharp point in her brain.

"You need to calm down, Alison. The first procedure is complete, so you need to rest." The doctor wore a mask.

"What?" She looked around the room. It was stark, sterile.

"The implantation. Correct? I mean, I do have the right lady? We want you to get pregnant, right?" He picked up an iPad and tapped on it with a stylus.

She was kidnapped. Right? It wasn't a dream—well, a nightmare. "Where's Flint?" she asked again.

The nurse patted her arm after taking her blood pressure. "He's resting, sweetheart. Just take deep breaths and think baby thoughts, okay?"

The nurse seemed to be smiling behind her mask.

Alison started to cry. "You're not making sense. Let me up. Where's my husband?"

The doctor started in with a stern voice. "Either calm yourself, young lady, or I'll have to sedate you. And I'd rather not subject you to further chemicals if I don't have to."

"I want to go home. I demand to be let up. I will file a malpractice suit against you. Who are you? Where's my doctor?" Alison managed to threaten him with tears rolling her face, into her hair.

He looked sorely disappointed as he nodded to the nurse. She prepared a needle and inserted it into Alison's IV.

The whole room was soon made of cotton. She struggled to keep her eyes open, but they fell shut. She heard a door open and another man's voice. "You want me to handle the body?"

The doctor answered, "Yes. And please don't even speak to me of it. Nothing like that was part of my agreement at all. I'm a re-searcher — a doctor!"

The cotton was invading Alison's ears, but her tears continued because she was fairly certain who the body was. Flint had to be dead. Because he'd never stop fighting for her. Never.

Beckett stood in his office dressed to the nines: his best suit, cuff-links, amazing shoes, and expensive sunglasses. Underneath he had so many weapons that a good speed bump would blow him off the face of the earth.

Eve sat on the couch, curled into herself in pajamas. They'd fought and screamed and fought and cried for hours last night. In between he'd touched base with every asshole and douchebag he was sure of.

But they still knew very little about Ted. One asshole who did nighttime rounds for Vitullo had finally reported that Nicholas had put a very large barrel in the trunk of his car a few days ago in a timeframe that worried Beckett. And no one was being held at the house, according another asshole who worked security at the New Jersey compound. Beckett's gut still told him Ted had passed on, but he'd been hoping for a miracle. Bringing home Eve's father was his greatest wish right now.

The doorbell rang, and Beckett went to let Morales in. He was the only one Beckett could use to make sure Eve stayed put. She'd never kill him. The men traded insults quietly. Despite their mutual hate, they were both committed to their common task.

She was standing when they returned to the room together. "I'm coming."

Beckett shook his head. "You're the best guy I have. But right now I need you to be Ted's daughter. I refuse to deliver you to Rodolfo. That's what he wants."

She exhaled. Clearly she knew he was right, though he knew she still wanted to kill the pain out of her heart.

"I'm going," he told her.

She nodded. No mushy embrace or tonguey kisses. She said *Come back* with her eyes.

He gave her the best interpretation of a smile he could muster. *I will.*

Morales opened his mouth and looked like he might say something, but thought better of it. Beckett nodded at him. "This has to be done. You two have a nice afternoon."

Then his ride pulled up, followed by a convoy. Every man under his command was dressed to kill, figuratively and literally. And in addition to these assholes riding with him, others were keeping gates open and guards down at the Vitullo compound. They pulled smoothly away from the curb like a fleet.

The text messages coordinating their arrival came in steady as a bloodstream. When they arrived at Rodolfo's New Jersey compound, the gates were open and the cars pulled into the driveway three wide. Beckett and his team exited the cars in one fluid motion, and like a SWAT team, his men took to the doors—thirty in all, each ready to go to war on Beckett's command.

He strolled through the house as the assholes who weren't in on his visit scrambled for cover. "Dolfy! Ol' Dolfy! Where you keepin' yourself today? We're due for another in-person meeting, don't you think?"

Beckett jogged up the stairs, his men fanning out around him. Anyone who posed a threat was disabled and tied up. By the time Beckett kicked open Rodolfo's bedroom suite door, the whole place was on lockdown.

The old man didn't even stop spooning soup into his open maw.

Beckett shook his head before collapsing in the chair across from him. His douchebags closed the door and stood guard outside.

"Tell me where Ted Hartt is," he began.

Rodolfo put down his spoon and used his right hand to help his left hold up the middle finger.

Beckett stood and grabbed the bowl of soup. He poured the hot liquid in Rodolfo's lap.

The man grimaced but made no noise.

Tough old pecker junkie. "Tell me or I'll burn this whole fucking house down."

Rodolfo narrowed his eyes and his mouth pulled a bit to one side: the bastard's version of a smirk.

Beckett produced a huge lighter and strolled over to what looked like a priceless tapestry. He used the dangling tassels like candlewicks.

The fire crept up the fabric slowly as Beckett returned. "Where is he?"

Rodolfo shook his head. "Ungrateful."

Beckett nodded and took his lighter to the couch near the bookshelves. He lit a few books while Rodolfo hit a buzzer over and over, obviously calling for help. The shelves and the books on it were going pretty good.

The man's anger caused him to slur. "This is an act of war, Taylor."

"No, this is a truth-seeking mission," Beckett explained. "But your ass is like a constipated cockroach—hard to get shit out of. I will burn you to death, Rodolfo. You took her father. Why? Did you want her here? Are you in love with her, you mostly dead moth-bait bitch?"

The two fires began to pop and crackle. He paused to look at his phone. His men reported that Ted Hartt had not been found inside. All hidey holes had been checked, assisted by turncoat assholes.

"Nothing? Nothing to say?" Beckett used his talk-to-text feature, telling his whole group at once, "Light it up, boys."

Rodolfo's hands shook with fury, and he now spit with his slur. "Burning this house does not make you a winner. This is not even the tip of my iceberg."

"Do you know that you're not dead yet?" Beckett asked. "Do you realize that? I could've sliced your throat months ago. I paid my dues, then agreed to leave you be, and you try to take her, then take her father? What on earth would make you that fucking stupid? Actually, I know you're not stupid, so you must be desperate. What do you need that you can't buy? What is it? That's my issue."

Rodolfo took a glance over his shoulder. Flames had started to lick the walls and ceiling. Alarms began going off all over the house as the fires Beckett had demanded got rolling.

"You kill me now and you'll never know," the decrepit man said. "Won't that be fun? You'll always wonder."

Beckett licked his lips. "Yeah, but you'll be dead, and I'll have your men. I'll find out what you know. They'll talk. I can be very motivating."

"You think I didn't know you were wooing my men? Promising them respect? I know. And I don't give a fuck because of what Ted Hartt gave me. His gift to me was worth more than this house, your ego, and her golden pussy. It secures my future no matter what happens." Rodolfo settled in the chair, abandoning his buzzer. "So you're really too late."

The curtains had caught now, framing the old man in fire like the devil he was.

Beckett was truly stumped. His phone vibrated again. He looked at it to learn one of the assholes had found Primo and was bringing him to the house. And that's when it hit him. *Primo. Mary Ellen.* Rodolfo's whole legacy was crap. He was the end of the line for everything he'd spent his life building.

"Your son is dead." Beckett lied to test the waters.

Rodolfo shrugged, more with his right than his left. "We all die."

Beckett's wheels were spinning now. He could feel the connections just out of his reach. "We do," he confirmed. "Imagine your whole empire being under my command. It's really going to bolster my reputation."

The floor had started to glow with the heat from the fires.

"You don't know jack shit, you pompous little ass." Rodolfo wrestled himself to an upright position in his chair. "None of this will be yours. I'll have heirs. Plenty of heirs."

"Will you, now?" Beckett got close to Rodolfo. "I'll find them, and I'll kill them."

"You'll do no such thing." Rodolfo started laughing like a madman. "That's why it's so perfect. You'll not touch a hair on their heads. Ever."

"Bullshit." Beckett grabbed the man around his throat.

"I'm giving Eve the one thing you could never give her. And I like the idea that her father blessed the union. Before he left this earth, he knew he'd be a grandfather, just like he wanted."

"You killed him." Though he'd known it was likely, the news hit Beckett like a brick wall.

Rodolfo nodded. "She'll forgive me. You wait and see."

"You're delusional—dementia or some shit. You're not even making sense."

Maybe it was the sight of his belongings going up in flames, maybe it was the desperate need to one-up an opponent—to throw the last blow even if it was only a mental one. But suddenly Rodolfo became quite forthcoming.

"Her father gave me the chance to use her as breeding stock," he said, his words choking out between coughs as smoke filled the room. "He preserved her best bits just for me. Our children will be masterpieces: the most skillful, deadly people my business will ever have met."

"Eve can't have children, you bag of assholes." Beckett began stepping backward.

"Can't she? Can't she? Technology is amazing." Rodolfo laughed with a spluttering croak. "Run, Taylor. But no matter how fast and how far, know that I will be in your life for as long as you love that woman."

Beckett thought about putting a bullet in the old man, but he decided to burn him to death instead. Let him feel the hell of his damnation. He turned and slammed the door behind him.

None of it made sense. Maybe it was the smoke inhalation. Maybe it was another damn stroke, but as Beckett called his men out to the safety of the driveway to watch the house burn, he had a horrible, horrible feeling that Vitullo had just left him a puzzle he was scared to solve.

16

HEAVEN

When Livia woke on the first morning of the new year, she opened her eyes before flopping around. The bed was full. She could feel Kellan's foot on her chin, and Emme's hand was tangled in her hair. Blake smiled—just scruff and white teeth, all the teasing he had for her kept under the veil of early morning silence that had ruled their lives since the kids were born. But she knew he'd whisper it to her later.

Sleep was a god: trying to get some, convincing the little people in their lives that they wanted it, and mostly losing it.

White ear buds plugged into Blake's phone explained the soft, barely there music she could hear. She tried to move her leg, and the dog protested with a snore. She shook her head as the mattress bounced with Blake's silent laughter. He flipped his phone around and took a picture of her predicament. She stuck her tongue out for the flash.

Saturdays were Livia's second favorite, topped only by Friday afternoons when Emme ran off the bus after kindergarten and threw her school bag in the hallway, announcing, "I'm so done with that place," or something similar. She had so much of Kyle in her. But Christmas break was like a string of Saturdays. Heaven—despite the lack of sleep, of course.

She finally found a way to slip out of the bed, and the kids and dog readjusted to seep into the space she left behind. Blake snapped a picture of that as well.

After a freshening up, she came back into the room and changed into comfy pants and a sweatshirt. They had nothing going on today. The pantry was stocked, so she figured they would play in the snow, but other than that…

Blake caught her eye. Of course he'd watched her change. She winked at him and slipped out the door, intent on starting the laundry. As she pulled out the clothes left in the dryer from last night out, she felt his hands on her hips.

She wiggled into him, finding him ready for her.

"Really?" She laughed over her shoulder when he responded by cupping her breasts.

Blake was all at once hers in the way they knew so well: the look in his eyes when he spun her to face him, the way he touched her face with devotion while his other hand followed a more carnal path. He picked her up and set her on the washing machine.

She noticed then that the door to the laundry room was closed. Locked. This was a premeditated ambush. He stepped between her legs, forcing her to spread them for him. For a minute he pulled her close — chest to chest, nose to nose — before smiling at her, his white teeth framed by his naughty lips.

This was the version of her Blake she'd first met. They reconnected with the fire that had drawn them together and still kept them together years later. For him, she would always burn. Sitting in the minivan, driving the kids to the store, just the thought of this Blake made her strong enough to fight an army, destiny, and death. Did anyone know how tremendous he was? It didn't matter, as long as he knew. She grabbed a handful of his hair, and he slid his hand into her pants.

"I love you." She was almost angry. "Do you get it? You. These kids. This life. It *is* my world."

He nodded. She knew he felt the same way, but this Blake didn't talk, he proved. He found the spot on her body that made her see white and held her until she was desperate for more. Then he reached behind her and turned on the washer.

Dirty. Filthy for her. He kissed her and added tongue, bit her neck gently while the vibrations from the machine increased.

She would come for him like this. He pushed up her shirt and pulled down her panties so he could be inside her when she was lost in the ecstasy of it, of him.

He came right after she did, and she locked him close with her legs, dragging her nails down his back as he bit his lip to stay quiet.

He kissed the top of her head in between gasps for air. He looked in her eyes before responding, "I get it."

When Beckett had finally come home, smelling like smoke after all that had transpired, Eve had been waiting. Morales was gone, most likely sent away.

She didn't say anything, but he knew the question she was asking as she stood: *Is my father dead?*

"I don't know," he told her. "We didn't find him. The assholes we have didn't have answers for us…yet."

She put her hand over her mouth and wrapped her other arm around her waist.

"I'd hoped we'd find something, find some evidence, find him," Beckett told her. "But that wasn't the case. I'm so sorry."

She walked past him and put on her jacket and gloves. His sigh asked her where she was headed without words.

"I'm going to spend time with the assholes," she said. "You've taken some from Vitullo?" She wouldn't look at him.

"I did. And then I burned his house to the ground after it was searched. Rodolfo is dead."

With that Eve had left. He'd kept tabs on her through his men, and he knew she was questioning them every which way about her father. She'd taken some long rides to check out a few possible locations for her dad as well. She had nothing to show for her efforts, though Beckett only knew this from text messages, and now her worry and fear had turned to wandering. She hadn't been home.

He knew better than to look for her when she didn't want her to be found, so today, two days after the blaze and at the start of the new year, Beckett focused on assessing their situation from his house/command center. Any man who had claimed loyalty to Rodolfo had been given a choice: come work for Beckett or die. Almost all had decided to stay alive. So now the assholes Beckett had previously converted to his new way of running shit helped explain things to the new guys, and those who'd been working for him covertly now came out in the open.

Spider, who had been Rodolfo's main tech/communications guy, had already been transitioning, but he'd seemed particularly relieved to hear his former boss no longer breathed. He was a paranoid son of a bitch, but probably not without reason. Today, as the douchebags helped the new guys settle in to work at various sites around Poughkeepsie, Spider sat in Beckett's basement.

"I can pull up the security footage," he assured his new boss. "I have it in the cloud. But are you sure Nicholas doesn't have a hard-on for me? He wasn't there when you torched the place, right?"

"Nope." Beckett looked past the man to the screen of the laptop. "But I don't see how that matters right now." Sure enough as he watched, Nicholas led Eve's father, blindfolded, into a room. After fast-forwarding through a depressing number of hours, Nicholas rolled a barrel out. It didn't take a genius to know who was in there. "Can you get me all footage you have on Nicholas?" Beckett asked. "I'm going to send you someone to help." He texted Shark to join Spider for a Nicholas-footage expedition. Sevan and Primo, their newest addition to the unhappy family, were to be left alone — to either sit still or die trying to leave. Sevan had just about exhausted his usefulness at this point anyway. And who knew if Primo had any usefulness at all.

Beckett then turned his attention to the next item on the list and went upstairs, leaving Spider to his work. He now also had a Rodolfo defector with accounting as his specialty. Perhaps he'd be willing to list out all of Rodolfo's holdings.

As he returned to the main floor, he wondered again about Eve. Only this time, as if thinking had brought her forth, she opened the front door and came toward him, dressed in leathers and wearing the hardened look he knew she'd perfected in the throes of her previous losses.

And now he had to hand her another death for sure. That's all he'd given her in their time together: his love and the death of people she'd loved. He stood in her way. She stopped and stared at him, waiting for an update.

"I'm sorry."

It was the confirmation of what she must have already known. Ted Hartt was dead. She nodded. Dry eyes.

He wished she would cry, punch him, curse.

But he knew her. She'd lost control for a moment by the train tracks, and that was it. No matter how much she was bleeding, she would pretend she wasn't now. He wanted to ask her to give him a hug, to let her know it had been his intention to fix everything, to bring her father home. His heart crumpled like ash at all he couldn't do for her.

"Nicholas did his worst," she said.

It wasn't a question. It sounded more like an answer.

"We're married now," he told her. "I need you to let me help you with this. You're my wife."

Her jaw tensed. "It wasn't legal."

He caught her shoulders as she tried to walk past him.

"You're my family."

A hint of a softening before the walls were back up. "I wouldn't say that out loud. That position is cursed. You'll end up dead." She gave him such a level stare he had to move aside for her.

"I could make you stay," he said to her back.

"You could certainly try."

She took another step back toward the front door. He stood behind her and quietly pointed out what she hadn't said. "It's not you that gets your people killed. It's me." He opened his palms.

She didn't turn around. "I can't keep you safe. I couldn't keep Mouse safe. I couldn't keep David and Anna safe. And I couldn't keep my father from being tortured and killed by Nicholas."

The word *tortured* clearly tripped her up. Beckett knew her imagination was so much greater than anyone else's because she'd been on both the receiving and delivering end before. Plus, she'd probably been on Nicholas's receiving end before. He shuddered thinking of how she'd been brutalized before he traded his freedom — at least temporarily — for hers.

"Where's the point in it? In any of it?" She walked the rest of the way to the door and grabbed her helmet.

He'd rather she killed him than walked out on him. He punched the wall four times in a row. It settled nothing. He needed to flush Nicholas out and get to him. Beckett couldn't tell Eve her father might have had a secret that would hurt her. He ran after her out the door. She had just started up the bike, helmet in place, when he grabbed her by the waist and pulled her off with one arm, grounding the motorcycle with his other hand.

She began fighting him, like he knew she would.

Manhandling this woman was like playing Russian roulette. He grabbed her by the throat and spoke to his own reflection in the shield of her helmet. "When it hurts like this? I'm here. From now on. Fuck your legal bullshit. I am yours. And I'm going to take you upstairs and fuck you until you stop crying."

She slapped his arms. Her voice was muffled, "Let go."

"I don't. I don't let go. This is the package you bought, lady. I never let go."

He wrapped her in a quick restraint, her back to his chest, and lifted her, walking back through the open front door before kicking it shut.

"Leave, assholes. Get out!" He heard the douchebags scramble before shutting the basement door.

Her curses were full of fire. He tossed her on the couch. He knew she was angry, but her helmet was still on. He held her down by her breasts. "Stop. Just stop," he asked her.

She brought her knee up hard, and he barely closed his legs in time to avoid contact.

"I know you can kill me. Just stop fighting for a goddamn second," he practically yelled. "You want to wall me out. Distance me. And I'm not going to let you. You can't get on the bike and go find Morales so you can cry to him."

She growl-sobbed from under the helmet. Beckett switched his grip from her breasts to her wrists when she started punching him.

"You can't be soft with him and hard with me. Are you safe there because you don't screw him? All of you. I married every part of you. I demand it now. This pain. This loss. We share it. You can hate me, you can hit me — but right now, as we mourn the loss of your father, *we* are together."

She stopped struggling, but her body was still tense. He unlatched her helmet and pulled it off her head.

Under its shell she was devastated. Broken. Guilty.

"You father's dead, Eve. The man who raised you. Loved you. He's gone." Her eyes filled and her nostrils flared.

He was poking a dragon with a stick. It was cruel. But it was necessary.

"He's gone. But he loved every version there was of you."

The tears spilled over onto her cheek.

"Feel that."

He kneeled on top of her.

"Feel that."

And she spiraled. The screaming was unearthly, shattering. "Nooo!" She lashed out, slapping and punching him, and he let her this time. Clenching the muscles she bruised so efficiently. Her mind was lost for a few heartbeats, eyes wild with more white than color. It was the opposite of an orgasm. Pain flooding her system, bursting the levy she'd so carefully maintained inside.

He stayed on her, accepting her pain however she had to share it with him. Physically, for now. And then she switched to words, cursing him, calling him the devil, blaming him for every loss in her life. Spitting in her anger.

Still he waited. He'd seen this kind of breakdown before. The struggle of the scared. Too many years in foster homes and juvie had taught him well. Energy had to transfer through all the seasons of torment.

Finally she was depleted. Used. Weary. She slumped against the couch, face wet from tears. She exhaled like a beaten beast. The last season. The pain would enter then, slowly incorporate into her reality — this new way of living — without her father.

He stood and pulled off her jeans. He entered her quickly. She didn't react.

He pulled her onto his lap, never letting their connection break, sitting while she straddled him.

"Feel that."

Eve finally made eye contact. "Being a monster hasn't saved anyone." She choked on her sob, gasping for air.

He pulled her into his arms, and she finally let herself be hugged.

He cradled her head, holding her tight. He didn't have words to soothe her. He just thought about how much he loved her, hoped somehow she would know.

"Revenge won't bring him back." She sobbed against him, crying anew. "Rodolfo is dead, and all we have left to do is grieve."

His shirt grew damp as his own eyes filled. "You're not feeling this alone," he told her. "I'm here. I'm inside you. I'm *inside* you."

She sat up and covered her mouth with two shaking hands. She spoke her fear around her fingers. "What if nothing stops me now?"

Beckett nodded. A monster without a leash was a dangerous thing. He couldn't fix her, but he could bring her pleasure. He started in on her body as only he knew how. He swung their intimate connection into the painful fucking she needed. He had to squeeze her tighter, slam her harder, and choke her more than ever. She wanted to be physically punished now, and his hands were the safest place to become an object to be used.

She was naked and bruised on the floor when it was over, Beckett cradling her hair knife on his chest, covered with both their blood.

"Tell me the plan," she finally said.

And with that, he knew she was at least thinking beyond the very moment they were in. She wanted to know how Beckett was going to face what had just happened as a boss. As a man. As Beckett fucking Taylor.

The text from Taylor said only this:

**H#e's dea$d. It wa4s NichWolas.
& Vitullo's wormSSFood.**

It had been two days since he'd stayed with Eve while Beckett went off, all dressed for battle. Well, stayed until she'd forced him to leave. After an hour she'd announced that his babysitting services were no longer needed. And though she was clearly a fucking mess, he'd honored her wishes after she promised not to go after him.

And now it seemed his instincts had been correct about Dr. Hartt. He hated that. The stupidest superpower on the books—all he could do was make sure people cried. In a situation like Vitullo and Taylor's, there was no real revenge, no resolution, just an endless circle of stupidity and poor choices.

The fire at the compound hadn't been a surprise, though Ryan had told himself he wasn't enabling anything by staying with Eve. At least he'd kept her safe. People had died, as was bound to happen in their sorts of business. The swirling power grab would be next. Instead of keeping Poughkeepsie safe, Taylor had the city walking the plank. For all his talk of loyalty and family, he'd swung with an iron fist.

Ryan answered the knock on his door. Capt. McHugh was on the other side, looking exhausted.

"Well, for all it's worth, I just got conformation that Vitullo's alive. One of his men, Vin something or other, showed up with the old piece of grizzle at the fire station." McHugh walked in holding a six pack of beer. "But he was treated and gone before we could organize anything."

"Thaddens does good work."

"He does, but who knows where they've gone to now." McHugh shook his head.

Lovell Thaddens had been inside the Vitullo organization since the post-Mary-Ellen rebuild, part of McHugh's pledge toward more creative thinking and better vigilance where this matter was concerned. Thaddens was a master of undercover playacting—so good that McHugh had Ryan check him out on occasion to make sure the man was still on the up and up. Tasting something over and over might just let a palate feel entitled to explore. But Thaddens always came up clean, with just a few smudges.

Ryan and his boss used the counter to open their beers.

"Surely you have better plans than cracking into a brewski with my sorry ass on New Year's Day," Ryan said as he tapped the bottleneck of McHugh's beer in toast.

"I do," said McHugh. "And you should too. This is just a quick stop. I want your impression of this whole situation off the record." He sat on the couch, and Ryan joined him.

"The Taylor debacle? Mmmm. Yeah. What are your thoughts? To be honest, I feel like I have clouded judgment." Ryan took a swig.

"Got it bad for her?"

"Can you blame me? Jesus. Beyond the looks, her way around a gun is just…" He shook his head.

They sat in a companionable silence for a few before McHugh seemed to get around to the real reason he had come.

"I can't help him turn this city into his lapdog," he said. "One devil's the same as another for me. No matter what Taylor says he's doing, this feels like a classic turf war."

"And that includes her." Ryan began picking at the label of his beer.

"It will," McHugh confirmed. "She's had enough choices and chances. She's in." He shook his head. "I like that girl. I see so much potential. Imagine if we got her on the force?"

Ryan shook his head as well, lamenting the loss of a career Eve had never mentioned wanting. "We could do so much with her." As if seeing the next question in a crystal ball, he added, "She'd never turn on him, though. They got married."

"Did they?" McHugh finished his beer.

Ryan nodded. It burned in his chest. Knowing she'd married Taylor was like watching her put a loaded gun in her mouth.

McHugh went to the fridge and opened Ryan another. "You deserve this."

He took it, but he didn't want to talk about it. "What's the plan? Let Taylor and Vitullo blow themselves to hell?"

"Right now, we play it as usual. Someone breaks the law, we haul 'em in. We'll keep Thaddens inside and see if he can work both teams against the other. And speaking of which, about Eve…" McHugh trailed off.

"If she gives me anything we can use, you'll get it. I can't get her away from him, but maybe circumstances can work in her favor, and she can still get chance at a life." Ryan took another long swallow.

"You know she's in a real dangerous situation. And she's had more than one chance out. If push comes to shove…" He trailed off again.

"She'd be on the bad guys' side. I know."

McHugh nodded before standing up to leave.

Ryan sighed. His boss's message had been delivered: Eve couldn't be protected. Which made sense. You can't protect a person who has her gun trained on you. But he'd never be able to shoot her.

He sighed again and finished his beer. He'd left last year sad and now entered the next one mad. And alone.

17

LED BY THE HEART

A week after the fire, when it seemed the dust had settled, Nicholas walked into the newly established Virginia safe house, ready for the worst. But Rodolfo looked good, considering. An oxygen tank sat next to him and one of his hands was bandaged.

"Sir, you look well, and you've only had a week of recovery. I wish I had been there for you."

"It's done?" Rodolfo looked paler than usual, but alive, and still totally focused on the project at hand, ignoring Nicholas' platitudes.

Nicholas surveyed the room before speaking. Vin sat in a chair nearby like he was entitled to it. Nicholas pointed at the man and then the door. Since he'd dragged Vitullo's tired ass out of the fire, Vin seemed to believe he was so much more than an associate of minimal importance.

Vin waited until Rodolfo nodded, approving Nicholas's direction, before he bowed curtly and ambled toward the door. "I'll be just outside, sir," he said as he left.

Once the door was closed behind him, Nicholas pulled out a folder. "So that bag of rocks had enough sense to get you out?"

"His father's a firefighter. Kid used to go to work with dad. He came straight for me." Rodolfo looked shaken.

"Taylor lit your house on fire?"

"Took seventy-five percent of my men too. This is obviously war."

Nicholas decided now was the right time to give his boss the good news. He opened the folder and set it on Rodolfo's lap.

The old man flipped through the pages. Nicholas knew some things would make sense and some wouldn't. But he gave Rodolfo the respect of waiting him out. Finally he was addressed.

"So this means?" The old man held up a picture of Alison.

"That woman has received the ovary tissue. After a few weeks and a regimen of hormones, which we've already begun, we can potentially harvest eggs."

"So she was the best candidate?"

"Yes. According to Dr. Yordan, she actually has a wonderful profile—amazing family history, and she's a great genetic match for the original source. Ideal."

"And her husband?" Rodolfo set the picture down.

All Nicholas did was nod.

"I want you to run point on this. Keep the doctor and nurse happy and scared in equal measure. There can be no mistakes, and no one can back out now. Yordan has to have realized this isn't just academic research, so be sure he's incentivized to stay. And let's extract a few extra eggs too—as many as we can get—just in case."

Nicholas nodded again. "Of course. Sir, I'd be happy to see this through, but I really don't like what happened with Taylor. Don't you think I'd be more useful here with you?"

He sat down. Playing full-time babysitter was not exactly a great way to quell his urges, but he had to play the game. The old man was closer to death than ever, and he needed to make sure there was a place for him in the empire after his demise, particularly with jokers like Vin on the move. These babies were just babies, after all. And not even actually babies yet. Someone would have to manage things for a while…

"I've got this under control. I have ways of keeping Taylor in line. Plus, I'm only two towns away from my future children." Rodolfo touched the picture of Alison. "It's going to be perfect. Everything he takes he will eventually have to repay threefold. He's led by his heart." Rodolfo coughed.

"How long until he knows?" The last thing Nicholas needed was Taylor trying to mess up the delicate process he was in charge of with the doctor. He was already pressuring the man as much as he could to keep the timeline moving forward.

"A bit. No need to rush things. He'll do a better job staying out of our way without this information, and I'll stay out of sight so there's no need for him to even go looking. He thinks I'm dead. Good for him."

Nicholas nodded, relieved. For once they were working together. "I've got to say, I'm surprised you haven't dragged Taylor's family into the woods like dogs yet." He sat and crossed his feet at the ankles.

"You would be." Rodolfo used his good arm to wipe at the salvia seeping from his mouth. "I need Taylor firmly stuck up to his neck in his own bullshit. Then I can offer to dig his balls out." Rodolfo took a deep inhale from the oxygen mask.

"You're going to lose more manpower." Nicholas reached over and closed the folder.

"Be that as it may. People make more people every day." He gestured to the door, sending Nicholas the message to leave.

"Very well. Let me know if things start moving in my direction. The host is sedated, and I don't want to have to move her in a hurry—especially during this delicate time." Nicholas opened the door, watching Rodolfo smile with half his face.

Alison opened her eyes slowly. An internal alarm somewhere reminded her to appear asleep. She used her yoga breathing to settle her racing heart, as she knew there was a monitor somewhere in the room. She remembered the few times she'd struggled, only to be sedated again.

She listened from her prone position even though she was desperate to sit up. To cry. To scream. She waited. Monitors clicked predicable patterns, telling her kidnappers she was alive, functioning. Her situation was becoming clearer in her mind.

And it was a horror movie. She could feel the needle in her arm, delivering the sedatives and cocktail of hormones. She tried peeking out of her eyelashes. It was blurry. She decided to give it a few seconds to sharpen up. Her head pounded and her breasts were so sore.

The nurse monitoring her must have been getting paid a fortune, because she immediately began talking, as if she'd just been waiting for this moment. "I can tell from your eye movements under your lids that you're awake, which is good. I need to sit you up a bit."

Alison opened her eyes the rest of the way. The nurse looked friendly. Alison knew she was anything but. The room seemed to be a regular bedroom that had been equipped with hospital furnishings.

"How are you feeling?" The nurse tapped on her iPad and added some information.

Her voice was scratchy. "Trapped."

"Let me get those straps off of you. And let me just say, real quick before we do the hard work, that beyond this door are two men with guns. And outside that window there's a woman with a very long gun. They mean business about you staying here. You leave, and they will drag you back. And they will probably shoot me too. My job is to keep you healthy. Understand?" The nurse's hand hovered over the restraint.

Alison nodded.

"No, I need you to say it out loud." She stepped back, enforcing her words.

"I understand." Alison waited.

"Please say it all. I need to make sure the medication isn't inhibiting your ability to reason. This is literally a life or death agreement." She put down her iPad.

"I understand that if I try to escape, people with guns will hurt me. And possibly kill you." She wanted to add questions like, *Why am I here? Who are you?* But her tears had started. Hearing her own voice state this nightmare out loud made it more real.

"There, there, sweetheart. We'll be okay. We'll do this together. Okay?" The nurse smiled.

Alison pictured the people on the other side of the door. Flint. Where was he? God, was he hurt? Was he really dead?

"Sweetie, I'll have to sedate you if you get upset again. Please try to keep it together." The nurse looked worried herself this time. She glanced at the door.

Alison swallowed her sobs, hiccupping them to a stop.

"Okay. That'll work. I'm going to undo your hands, and I want you to just move them real slow. Then I'm going to raise the bed, again real slow. You've been in this position for a while, so I don't want you to get a head rush. You've been getting hormones in fairly high doses, so we can address any side effects you may be experiencing."

The nurse started with the first restraint. Alison followed the instructions and rolled her wrist. Her hands had a bit of a pins-and-needles sensation. The whole process went methodically, as if this nurse had helped a ton of kidnapped people sit up before.

"I have to pee." All at once her bladder was like a basketball full of water.

"Go ahead, pumpkin. You've got a catheter."

As if the word *catheter* sent a signal to her urethra, Alison could suddenly feel the tubing. It was an awful sensation to just let go, but she had no other choice.

"Hmmm…That's a little more yellow than it needs to be. I'd better increase your saline." The nurse futzed with the bag hanging by the bed. "For now I just want you to sit. I'll bring you some cool water to sip on, okay?"

After Alison had two glasses of water, which felt like heaven on her raw throat, she attempted some questions, "Am I pregnant?"

"Not yet. But we're working toward that goal. For now we just hang out. We can watch movies, or I have books for you to read. We just have to keep you calm and healthy." The nurse plugged more information into her iPad.

"What happened? I was ready for my embryos to be implanted." Alison wished she could take back the question as she saw the nurse go pale.

"Well, I'm afraid I don't have all that information." The nurse gave her a hollow smile.

"Can't you undo my feet as well?"

"I'm afraid I have to keep you close, dear. We can't risk any complications to your health while you're in this preparatory phase. The less we have to sedate you, the better."

Alison didn't respond. It was as if she was on another planet. She had no idea what this woman was talking about. But she did know she was being held against her will, and her husband was gone. She filed that horror away for another time. This woman in front of her was the only contact she had, so she needed to play her like a fiddle. Unfortunately, Alison was the suckiest liar in the world. She could never even keep Flint's presents from him, often dragging them out from under the bed herself.

Flint.

She couldn't stop the question. It fell out of her when she thought of his face every time she ruined a surprise. He loved her for it. He was charmed by her openness.

"My husband?"

The nurse hardened a bit, her smile in direct contrast to the knowledge her eyes held. "As soon as all the things are in place, you two can be reunited."

Alison nodded and made it a point to comply with the directions the nurse had for her body: She wanted this vessel to move, eventually to eat small bits. Her heart wanted to have hope, but the sinister look in the nurse's eyes had answered her question clearly.

No one was worried about Flint.

Choking on that sob was the hardest thing she'd done since she woke.

Cole sat in front of his home computer at the end of the day, his first back at school after the winter break. It had been chaotic, as expected. Schedule and routine were so important to his students with special needs, so even something as wonderful as a holiday could wreak a lot of havoc. There had been three restraints, and two kids from his classroom spent some time in the crisis room. But they'd all survived. And in fact, for some reason, he felt insanely energized.

Rather than flopping into bed the moment JB was down, Cole was surrounded by ideas sketched out on graph paper—and he had a few matching files on his desktop. He wasn't sure if it was the lack of sleep, his own blisteringly happy heart, or his lack of a pulpit to preach from, but he felt a calling.

He had been holding his son—his beautiful, miraculous son—in the middle of the night a few days ago when it hit him like a thunderbolt: what he had wanted the most as a child was a family, a family that treated him like a person and respected his space, his body, and his place in the world. He was never held with love until Mrs. D, who came along so many years into his childhood that he was almost out of it.

No one had kissed his head and inhaled the scent of baby soap in the middle of the night. Part of what had created his brotherhood with Blake and Beckett was violence, not being in a safe place. By the time they met, all three had given up on receiving the cuddles and adoration of an adult—what they needed was safety, a promise that the day would be a tolerable one, a predicable one: homework, chores, cartoons, video games. This never came. Instead they'd kept busy covering bruises and plotting murder.

But now Cole knew it could be different, if he had his way it *would* be different for this generation of boys like they'd been. Beckett had told them he'd been buying up properties and refurbishing them. And Cole knew money was no object. He also knew there was an abandoned Catholic school at the edge of town. Father Callaghan had brought it up after mass last Sunday. Its doors had been shuttered for a little over five years—not enough time for things to get truly scary in there, but long enough that revamping the building would surely be a project.

He'd driven by it earlier today on his way to school to take pictures and stroll the grounds. He'd felt like he had a special set of glasses on that made him able to see the future layered on top of the present. He wanted to create a home, a home for teen boys—maybe girls too. A safe place for the kids who got bounced from one place to another, just waiting for time to run out and thrust them into the world. He wanted to offer them the basics, childhood's essentials: help with homework, a locking door, part-time jobs, and people who showed up to cheer them on at football games.

He leaned back in his chair, the pictures he'd taken scrolling by in the slideshow he'd created to show Beckett, as his potential investor. He'd designed the font and used Photoshop to layer the name above the door: Brothers' Legacy.

He'd also worked their tattoo into a logo—even Mouse's needles. As he looked at the image again, he had another brainstorm: mandatory knitting. They would all learn to knit. That would be a thing they had to do—make stuff. Cole sighed. He was definitely going to need some additional input on this...

Kyle made noise on purpose as she entered his office. He knew she could be silent as a ghost if she chose, her dancer's feet taking her as quietly as she wanted. He turned to greet her with a smile.

"What ya got there, handsome? Looks fancy," she said.

He pulled her into his lap and tried out his pitch on her. He showed her the slideshow, the steps toward his calling spelled out carefully with Blake's music threaded behind them. *Am I insane?* Kyle was so quiet he was nervous. His plan certainly sounded more idealistic out loud than it had in his head.

She reached out and touched the name above the door in the final picture. Then all at once she turned and kissed him so forcefully they almost tipped the chair together.

He had to put his finger on her lips to slow her enthusiasm. "What do you think?" he asked.

She licked his finger and nipped the very edge. He forgot he'd asked her a question until she answered it.

"I think it's perfect." She stood and pulled on his arm until he got up.

"It would have to be funded by —"

"Beckett. I know. He'll do it. Anything you need, he'll do it. It's about time his money did some good. Let the blood he's spilled create life." She jumped easily, wrapping herself around him so they were eye to eye. "I'm so proud of who you are — that you would go and take pictures, that you dare to hope for this. I'm all for it. JB and I can't wait to help." She kissed him again.

Cole had never been good with physical affection until her. Now his heart burned with their closeness — so much bigger and better than lust was this love. He kissed her deeply as she slid down him to put her feet on the floor. She was so flexible, it made him a better lover than he should have been. Her skirt was easy to lift, her panties sliding to the side. He could try anything with her, and she would smile and accommodate. When he asked her to put her calf on his shoulder while he dipped into her so deep, it was easy. He ran his hand from her ankle to her thigh as she shivered in response.

They used the chair, the floor, and for a few minutes the wall. When they came, it was together, but she used the strength in her legs to intensify his release.

She cuddled into him as they shuddered together. "Well, I got what I wanted."

"I feel so used," he said with a laugh.

"Good, then I did it right," she replied. "When are you going to show this to Becky?" Kyle readjusted her skirt and then his hair.

"I don't know. It seems like a tense time for him. He's already done so much for us…"

He finally noticed the baby monitor on the table behind his desk. She'd come prepared. JB slept in his bassinet.

"If the situation was reversed, would you want him to sit on this?" She pointed at the computer.

"No." But Cole felt nervous again. It was a lot to ask — not just for the property itself, but for the continued funding. Would Beckett have to kill more people to fund a charitable organization?

It was as if she'd read his mind. "He'll have to make sure the funds come from a real, legit place. No backdoor bullshit. And that seems to be what he wants, right? He and Eve are going straight."

Cole nodded. As JB woke, Kyle ran upstairs, and he began to pray about the future of his new dream.

18

WHISKEY

Eve had built the cardboard boxes and taped them together. Now she sat on the floor of the living room, under the dried-out mistletoe. The Christmas tree was plastic, but the mistletoe had been real. She drank her father's whiskey straight out of the bottle.

The past week had been a blur of doing things in a great rush and then staring at nothing. She blamed Beckett and herself in equal measure, and the pain of it all kept tripping her. She would delude herself for a little while sometimes, arguing that without her father's body, there was no loss—so much so that Spider showed her the surveillance video. Now she wasn't sleeping, picturing the video in her head over and over.

As of this minute, she'd cried herself hoarse. Now she sat, and the lights to the Christmas tree had illuminated according to their timer's instructions. The whole place smelled like her childhood. Her father, his cologne, his furniture—it all was a comfort, a love.

When she entered, she'd stepped over the notes from tenants and mail that had piled up outside his door. At some point she'd have to deal with all of it. She'd come with the idea of packing up his stuff, handling business for him, looking for clues on where Nicholas might be. But she'd succeeded only in finding his whiskey and sitting in front of her presents from her father under the tree.

At the sound of a light knock on the front door, she withdrew her pistol and watched as it swayed in her hand. She knew then she was drunk. Eve opened the door while holding the pistol behind her, against her thigh.

Ryan frowned when he saw her. "Saw the light on from the road and I wanted to check it out. Then I saw your bike. Pretty effin' cold for a bike ride."

She turned and set the gun on the end table by the sofa. She wasn't really in the right condition to be wielding a weapon. Ryan came in and shut the door.

Her spot was still warm when she collapsed on it again. She scooted back so she could lean against the couch. Ryan reached down and snagged the bottle from between her knees, taking a swig.

"That's some good shit." He sat next to her. Close, but not touching.

"He was tortured to death. I know it. It was Nicholas. Tortured. This man who wrapped presents and had them under the tree. This man who spent his entire life fixing people. He was hurt until he died." She took the bottle from Ryan and had another drink.

She was blurry enough that the tree lights had started to bleed together. Just like her life choices had bled into her father's.

"Eve, you had to know that could happen. You're too smart not to know." He didn't feed her any false hope that it wasn't her fault.

She turned and looked at him. He met her eyes as she drank again. "What's your point, Morales?"

"Get out. Get out of this now. Come with me tonight. Be better than this." He was still looking at her when she turned to face the tree again. "I'm here to tell you you're not protected anymore. McHugh can't stop the inevitable—and neither can Beckett." He reached over and turned her face with his knuckle so she had to look at him. "You're going to say you don't need protecting. And you're so goddamn tough everyone will believe it. But I don't. You do need protecting."

Eve watched him look from her lips to her eyes and back again. He was beautiful, truly. The dark hair, the broad shoulders—all that was a woman's dream. But it was the monster in him that he'd tamed which commanded her respect. He'd taken revenge and made it into something that mattered. This was a good man.

Her cell phone buzzed. She pulled away from Ryan's hand and slipped the phone from her pocket. Beckett wanted to know where she was, if she was okay.

She texted back:

I'm fine. No worries.

She wasn't fine. All she had were worries.

"I'm going to find the man who did this to my father." She took another drink before setting her phone down on the carpet next to her.

Ryan rubbed the tips of his fingers over his mouth. "Good. You should totally do that. Definitely. That's what your father would want."

He stood so quickly it made her head spin. He walked over and pulled a framed picture off the wall.

"He would want that. See this here? That's the look of a man who wants his only daughter to die." He cracked the frame over his knee and pulled out the photograph inside. He tossed it to her like a Frisbee.

She looked at it despite herself as she caught it. In the photo she sat on her father's lap, probably in kindergarten. She looked at the camera, and he looked at her.

Three more pictures landed near her in the same manner — pictures her father had framed and hung. All had him looking at her while she looked at the camera.

"Let's see what this man got you for Christmas, shall we?" Ryan asked, his voice cold.

No. No, I never want to see what's in those packages. But she didn't say it. Instead she set the pictures down and took another long pull on the bottle, surprised to find it was almost empty.

Ryan tore into a box, angrily tossing aside the brightly colored paper. Her father had sucked at wrapping, but he knew she loved the paper, the surprise. So even when present bags became a thing — an easy, man-friendly thing — he still wrapped.

"Oh look, pajamas. Surprised it's not an assault rifle? I sure as shit am." He threw the pajamas at her feet, and her heart died at the sight. They were her favorite color of blue, so soft and perfect.

"Here's another. Oh, the matching fucking slippers." He tossed those as well.

Next a bigger package was ransacked: inside, a pretty blue afghan.

It overwhelmed her that in a store, thinking of his daughter, her father's impulse had been to wrap her in softness. She finished the bottle and laid it next to the blue pile.

"And this? This is truly meant for an assassin." Ryan set a jewelry box down carefully and opened it. It played their song — the lullaby her father had sung for her, even when she was far too old for that nonsense, because it made her feel safe.

Ryan went for another present, and Eve's gaze fell on the front of a package where her name was spelled neatly in her father's handwriting. Another tradition: her presents had always had her name on them so they wouldn't get lost in Santa's big red bag. So many little things hit her like a truck.

"Enough," she announced. Standing took more work than it should have.

He picked up another present from the pile, ignoring her.

"Stop, Morales." He began to tear the paper away roughly, forcing her to face all the things that were killing her. She slapped him.

He stood stone still, aside from the vein in his temple that pulsed. Then he ripped the paper away in defiance of her wishes. It was a simple brown box, and she felt like her sanity would break if she had to see another thoughtful, hopeful gift from her dead father.

Jumping at him was the quickest way to make him stop, so she tackled him, knocking the box from his hands. As they fell together into the Christmas tree, the box flew, and whatever was inside shattered.

The glass ornaments exploded around them as the tree slumped and collapsed under their weight. Ryan grabbed her and made sure she landed on top of him, protecting her from the shards he was surely landing on for her. From her.

She hit him in the chest, but half-heartedly because she was crying so hard. Ryan's arms came around her firmly. He grabbed a fistful of her hair and held her in place, making soothing, shushing noises the whole time.

Eve was sure she'd cried forever when she finally cried herself out. His arms loosened, and she pulled herself to her knees, then picked herself up, offering him her hand. He took it, and she pulled him from the wreckage of the holiday she never got to have.

As he stood, she saw that he'd surely been impaled by glass.

She wiped her eyes. "Take your shirt off carefully. You've got glass there."

She left him in the living room to go find her father's medical bag. When she returned, he was struggling with the shirt.

"Stop. I got it." She methodically pulled out the shards that pinned the fabric to him.

When he was finally shirtless, she took her father's tweezers and began to pluck the glass from his back. She covered the small wounds with bits of antibacterial cream.

"I'm sorry I wrecked your dad's apartment. God, I'm a fuckhead." Ryan looked at the floor.

She dabbed another cut with cream. *Doesn't matter. Dad doesn't need it.*

When she had finished, Ryan shook his shirt out, bits of glass falling to the carpet like snow. She put the cream and the tweezers back in the bag. Her mood was sober, but her body was wildly intoxicated. Sitting seemed like the only option, so she picked the couch.

"What must the neighbors be thinking? Is someone going to come check out all this noise?" Ryan wondered aloud. He disappeared for a moment, then came back with a broom and dust pail.

He began a halfhearted cleanup operation, but after watching him for a few minutes, Eve had had enough. She turned her attention to her father's medical bag, the zipper pulled open. A haphazard light from the tree shone into the inside.

The glint that caught her eye was surely a zipper. But the leather bag's construction didn't appear to have any need for something metal in that spot.

She kneeled to inspect it more closely. Her rough handling of the bag had exposed a weakness in the seam on the inside. She reached in and grabbed the penlight, shining it directly on the spot.

After a moment Ryan was next to her, his interest piqued. He manipulated the bag from the outside so the mysterious bit was more exposed.

"Someone was tracking him. I assume Nicholas," she mumbled.

"Easier than a tail," Ryan agreed. "No audio from what I can tell. Don't touch it, though." He pulled his phone out and took a picture.

"Who are you sending that to?" Eve sat back, wishing she could send a picture to Mouse. He would've had an answer for her in an instant.

"I got a guy who owes me a favor. He's gonna tell me if there's a way to reverse track this thing." Morales typed out a text.

"To find Nicholas." She held her head in her hands.

"Yup." He sent the text and regarded her.

"I can't go with you," she said after a moment, hoping he remembered where their conversation had begun. "I'm staying in

Poughkeepsie, living my life. I'm finding Nicholas. That girl my father thought I was? He was right. For him I was that girl. Part of me still is. But to walk away and let what was done to him be the last word? I can't do it. He wasn't a criminal. He wouldn't hurt a soul. Even if it kills me, I will find Nicholas." She closed her eyes.

Even here, among the things her father had believed were real, she couldn't pretend she wasn't a murderer. Vengeance didn't just haunt her, it drove her to take her next breath. As a grown woman, she'd coped by hanging on to hate. David. Anna. And now her father. Stopping now wouldn't help anyone. Beckett wanted her to see things differently; Ryan wanted her to walk away. She wasn't able to do either just yet.

"I think you want it to kill you," Ryan told her. "That's your version of a samurai's death. But Eve, this whole thing is exploding. I can't promise that you won't be on one side, and I'll be on another. I have a job to do." Ryan ended his half-assed cleanup attempt.

"If it comes down to me or you?" She lifted her head and looked at him. This man wasn't her lover, he wasn't her future, but in her heart he was a friend. "You take that shot. Make it clean. And while you do that, I'll watch your back. I'll make sure no one else is taking you down."

He exhaled and looked at the floor, shaking his head. "Don't say that. Shit. Fuck. Eve, don't say that. I think this is me giving up on you. I can't do it anymore."

She nodded. "Please do that. Please give up on me." She willed him to walk away, to cease having any connection to her. It might just keep him alive. "The sooner I finish my business or get taken out, the less of an albatross I'll be to the people who care about me."

Ryan sat on the couch, and she moved to sit next to him. "I'm so drunk right now." Eve laid her head against the back of the couch.

"You staying here?"

"Naw, I can't. I feel like I'm drowning here. I have to take that tracker and do some work."

Ryan stood and shook the blue blanket out, glass falling again, before draping it over her. "You're going to have to sleep it off for a while. You do that, okay? I'll stay here until you wake up." He leaned over and kissed her forehead.

Her last thought before drifting into the whiskey-induced black was that he was still kissing her, when all she'd done was offer him violence — again.

Their Friday night dinner was over, and Blake had settled himself in Cole's office for the big presentation his brother could barely contain himself about. Beckett sprawled on the floor, drinking his beer almost upside down. Beckett was drinking for a few reasons tonight, Blake guessed. First, it was Friday and he loved Fridays, and second he was probably numbing the pain. Beckett had told Cole and Blake in hushed tones the news about Ted Hartt earlier. They all had questions—some Beckett had answers to, some he didn't. The violence was close to home. Blake had excused himself, returning with the beer to toast his uncle.

Now Cole seemed intent on making the mood a bit lighter. He pushed his chair out of the way and angled his computer to face them, smiling broadly.

"If this is a slideshow about how awesome my testicles are, I'll totally understand. You want me to make them bounce for you like a set of tennis balls?" Beckett raised his pelvis and began to pump his hips.

Blake threw a piece of popcorn at his brother, taking a peek upstairs instinctively. The kids were playing with Play-Doh, and fortunately none of their little faces graced the doorway.

Cole glanced around nervously. "Okay, this whole thing sort of came to me in a dream. So if you hate it, just say the word. I'm realizing now that I'm pretty much spending Beck's money and roping us into a ton of responsibility…"

Beckett sat up and put his elbows on his knees. "Everything I have is yours. You know that, brother."

Blake looked at his feet. And that's why Beckett was so easy to love. He trusted Cole and Blake more than himself. He took his vow of brotherhood so very seriously.

"Right," Cole said. "And it's an honor. Listen, I know you've been buying up property and stuff, and I had my eye on a place—"

"I'll buy it tomorrow." Beckett cut him off.

"Wait, it's a whole lot more than that. Just watch. Then tell me in all honesty what you think." Cole turned and hit a button on his keyboard.

Blake heard his own composition begin playing, and he smiled at Cole's thoughtfulness. He knew his brother had bought every single track on his iTunes page, and he pounded his chest gently with his fist in tribute.

Together they watched Cole's presentation unfold. He wanted to refurbish an abandoned Catholic school into a place for homeless boys to go, a place to run to when they had nowhere else, or when they weren't safe.

Chills went up Blake's spine.

A place to work, to earn money, to apprentice in a career. Blake looked at Beckett, who bit his lip and nodded with each new slide. This was Cole's best sermon in pictures and music. At the very end, Cole had superimposed a name on the old building: Brothers' Legacy, and their familiar tattoo was mounted close to the front door. The music trailed off, and Beckett took another sip of his beer—right side up this time.

The three were silent after that, and Blake got lost in his memories, wondering what, exactly, it would have felt like to have a place to go. To have looked at his two teenaged brothers and had a place to stay safe with them—a place with no beatings, unlike their last foster home.

Cole coughed. "It's awful. I'm sorry."

Beckett stood, and Cole and Blake followed. He held out his arm for their handshake, and all three arms entwined.

"I love it." Beckett was so quiet, his words were like a prayer. "But I can't be a part of it. I'll give you every dime I have to make it happen, though."

Blake put his other hand on Cole's shoulder.

Cole shook his head. "I want all three of us to be involved. Blake can teach the kids music. It's so important. And you—you can be the heavy, help me with behavior and stuff. I know we'll need professionals to help too—I'm hoping Livia and some of my partners at school can help with that—but I want so much more than your money from you. I want you legit. I want to keep you in this town. If we make you an upstanding citizen, you'll get to stay. All three or nothing at all." Cole's grip tightened.

"I'm in," was all Blake could think to add. He would follow these two men into a fire. He squeezed as well, helping Cole keep Beckett locked in their grip.

"This means so much," Beckett said, shaking his head. "It touches me deep, I'm not gonna lie. I love you fucking bastards. But putting me on that—" he pointed at the computer "—dooms it from day one. No one will trust you with kids, and the cops will have a huge hard-on for it. I can't do that to you." He shook his head sadly. "It's amazing, though. Damn, can you imagine? I woulda grabbed up those kids at Rick's and we woulda all been safe. If I could turn back time and all that. Shit." Beckett tried to pull away.

Cole put his arm on Beckett's other shoulder. "It's happening right now. There are kids desperate for a place to call home. We can give them a place—a start. We won't let them crap their pants at eighteen, wondering how to make it in the world. I think you're perfect to be involved. Bring the cops. We'll make sure we're totally on the straight side of the law. I mean, it won't make money or anything. Is that it?"

Beckett laughed. "No. Not the money. I have enough to light on fire. But I've started something that will be tough to end, even though I want to. Even though I'm trying. I still want to do things differently, but things are different than how they were even just a couple weeks ago. Eve's not going to let this thing with her dad go, and I'm not even sure that's the end of it. She's my wife now. It's my duty to see it through. It would be my duty anyway…" He trailed off, seeming overwhelmed.

Blake asked, "You still you, brother?"

"I am." Beckett sighed, obviously thinking this was a bad thing.

"Then you can do anything you damn well want to." Blake smiled. "Let's build together. If it doesn't work, then so be it. But how about we try?"

"Really?" Beckett seemed amazed. "You two still want to get mixed up with my crazy ass?"

Cole smiled back. "So much so it's inked on my skin."

Blake pounded on Beckett's shoulder in his joy.

"Dessert's almost ready!" Kyle called as she came down the stairs. "Are you fuckers having a dance-off again?" she whispered once she saw them.

All three turned and gave her the middle finger in tandem, which they then had to hide creatively when Emme followed her down the stairs. Kyle stepped in front of her niece and turned her by the shoulders. "Let's let your daddy and uncles finish playing dolls, okay?"

They laughed as Emme protested, saying she wanted to play dolls too. Then before they knew it, each of them was in charge of a Barbie doll and taking orders from Emme's favorite stuffed frog—who was also king, apparently.

Between the Barbies and dessert and looming bedtimes, Blake didn't get a chance to ask Beckett about where Eve was at the moment. But it seemed she was alone, at least for the hours Beckett had been here at Cole's. He was worried about his cousin. He'd tried to call a few times since Beckett had given him the news, but she hadn't returned his calls.

She was sorely missed. And judging from the times Beckett checked his phone, Blake knew he wasn't the only one worried about her.

Beckett arrived home that night to find her gone. He wasn't surprised, but he was disappointed. She wasn't answering her texts.

He was excited to share his brother's new plan with her, but as he looked around his office, he felt dejection set in. Maybe it was too risky. His damn brothers had never asked for anything, really. Though he'd been desperate to provide for them, they'd made their own way. That Cole wanted to do something and have Beckett's name on it gave him such pride he could barely stand it.

He sat at his desk and pulled up the property in question on the computer. After doing as much investigating as he could online, he had a sense of the surrounding properties. He already owned two. The school shuttering its doors had certainly dissuaded new buyers in the area. He could surround the school pretty well, staff it with his misfits.

During dessert at Cole's, the ideas had flown around the table fast and loose. Blake wanted McHugh involved, to get the kids working with cops—keep the communication open. Cole wanted to bring service projects in and have the kids do things in the community as well: provide lunches for the homeless, do clothing drives. Beckett had tossed out the idea of having some foster dogs and cats as well—just one giant building full of hope. Livia had some friends from school and a few professors she wanted to hit up for recommendations on hiring. Maybe she could even work there part time when the kids were old enough.

He fucking loved the ideas—all of them. But not surrounded by his brothers and their relentless optimism, he knew the dream would be squashed and the building made a target if he didn't get a good handle on the leftover Vitullo nonsense. He'd had Primo in his possession since the fire, and he was supposedly "working" for Beckett now, but no one believed him. He'd just flipped his loyalties like a coin to protect his ass. Beckett had put a tracker in the man, making him a matched set with Sevan and little more than a prisoner. Now Shark was in charge of both Sevan and Primo, which easily doubled his complaining.

To build this for his brothers, he would have to bulldoze any remnants of the Vitullo empire, at least in the northeast. He began jotting down notes. He'd need Spider and the accountant to complete the list of all Rodolfo's surrounding holdings—warehouses and shit, no doubt. Then he'd either burn them to the ground or buy them, whichever was easiest. And he could send the cops to right where they needed to be after Sevan and Rodolfo's former men enlightened him about the illegal weapons trade routes through Poughkeepsie that Vitullo's shadowy business had been using.

It might take months. But the permits and zoning and all that bullshit for Brothers' Legacy would take time too. Who knows when they'd even be able to pound one nail in the wall, let alone assemble the expert caregivers they'd need to manage the program.

But in his heart, he knew it: he and Eve could do this. Together they could be devious and smart enough to protect this haven. A home. A place to run. A place to be safe. *Scholarships.* Damn, they could help the kids by giving them scholarships to college!

He wished it wasn't so easy to dream. He could almost feel his expanding hopes being crushed by any number of circumstances that could arise. His stupid idea of refurbishing Poughkeepsie and helping fuckers had spread to his brothers. And Brothers' Legacy would be the heart—the beating heart that all his projects could flow to and from. And it would be clean. If he was really, really careful, he could keep it clean, untainted by any of his horrifying past, make it something that would outlive them all.

He had three things to handle, and they were all related: First was finding out what the hell Rodolfo was talking about concerning

Eve, which likely included finding her resolution about her father. Finding Nicholas. He couldn't let an unknown hurt his woman, and Nicholas also seemed as likely to make trouble with the remnants of Vitullo's empire as anyone. And finally, he needed to flush Vitullo Weapons out of the area completely now that the dragon was dead.

He looked at the clock and messed with his phone. Eleven p.m. now, and Eve was still not answering. He wrote her a note that he was out looking for her and left in the Challenger. He hadn't wanted to leave her alone today in the first place. But she'd insisted. She hadn't wanted to go with him to Cole's. A family event would just hurt too much. He tapped the steering wheel, trying to decide where she would go on her bike. It was titty-fucking cold, and even someone as tough as Eve wasn't immune to freezing temperatures. He drove by her favorite place at the river. No dice.

While sitting at a red light, it came to him. She would go to her father's. Of course. He drove a little too fast to get there, and sure enough, he saw her bike. Morales' truck was also parked nearby. He knew it had to be the asstrap's vehicle because of the sheer amount of vandalism, which contrasted nicely with the shiny new windshield and front end, which had been repaired after he helped Eve escape her abductors. Dammit if he wasn't grateful for that. Beckett looked harder as he walked toward the building and yup, that was a pair of panties shellacked to the tailgate. The side of the truck had a bra and another pair of panties affixed with some sort of permanent clear cement.

He turned his walk into a jog. Fucking Morales. Of course he would be here with her. Beckett hit the front door hard and jogged up the stairs. He tried the doorknob on her dad's apartment, and it was fucking locked like it fucking would be. He'd backed up, ready to kick in the door when it opened.

Morales stood there, shirtless, shaking his head. "Did ya think to knock? Were you raised in a goddamn barn? I expected your lousy ass hours ago." He stepped to the side and gestured to the couch.

Eve was covered with a blanket and passed the fuck out. Beckett took in the apartment's state of disarray. They'd had sex. No way they hadn't. Wrecking shit was Eve's goddamn sexual calling card. He looked at Morales with the red of sheer rage.

"You really think she'd cheat on you? Really? Do you even know her at all?" Morales slipped his shirt on and winced when it went over his back. "She drank her weight in whiskey. I've got to go. You got her?"

Beckett didn't humor him with a response. Instead he waved good-bye with his middle finger. "Enjoy your panty wagon, ball gobbler."

From Morales' puzzled look, he guessed the douche finger didn't know his car was wearing drawers. Fine by him. It would make sense soon enough.

As he left, Morales reached into Dr. Hartt's medical bag and pulled something out, which he took with him. Beckett didn't even have the energy to ask. He sat at Eve's feet and took in the destruction in the apartment. Presents were torn open, and the tree was flattened. He rubbed her leg under the soft blue blanket. That he'd spent the evening with his heart soaring while she was crushed could have been one of his most horrible offenses since marrying her. Well, that and telling her that her father was dead. He groaned at the circumstances, in the apartment and beyond.

Her eyes opened at the sound. "Ryan?"

"He left."

She nodded, closing her eyes again.

"I'm getting you some water and some Tylenol. You're going to feel like a deflated balloon after this bullshit passes through you." He collected supplies from the kitchen and bathroom and had to wake her when he returned to the couch.

She sat up slowly and took the pain reliever without complaint. He tucked her under his arm and rested his head on hers.

"All he wanted was a normal daughter," Eve said softly. "Look what I did to him." She stared at the tree remains despondently.

"He loves you still." Beckett kissed the top of her head.

"Of course he loved me. He was a great father. I'm the broken part. How is he not walking through that door again? You'd think I'd be used to death, but I'm not. He just always seemed so solid." She exhaled sadly.

"You opened some presents?" Beckett tucked the blanket around her shoulders. The apartment was cold.

She tossed the bottom half of her blanket over him after he shivered. "Dad turned down the heat when he was cooking. The oven heated up the place. Why did I not check the thermostat before assuming he went to the hospital? Maybe I would have put it together."

Beckett pointed at the pajamas in a heap on the floor. "Those look comfortable."

"Ryan ripped open the presents trying to get me to leave with him."

She was still drunk. No way she would have told him that sober. Beckett closed his eyes as the need to punch the fucker went from his balls to his fingertips.

"Then he tells me I'm not getting special treatment from McHugh, or anyone else for that matter. The lines are being drawn, and I'm on the outside," Eve explained with a sigh.

Beckett hugged her to him.

"I'm in rough shape right now." She snuggled in closer.

"You had a lot to drink. It happens to everyone." He tried to de-escalate the anger boiling inside him.

"No. More than that," she insisted. "Something's not right. In my head."

He reviewed how she'd been treated, first by him, forcing her to feel the pain of her father's loss and fucking the fuck out of her. Then dumbass Morales had ripped into her presents and helped or forced her to trash this apartment. No one had treated this woman the way a grieving daughter should be treated. Just because Eve was different didn't mean she didn't deserve respect as Ted Hartt's child.

He kissed her head again and laid her down on the couch. "Sleep it off, gorgeous. You're safe now."

Eve cried a little, just a gentle wash of tears before she closed her eyes, and Beckett began picking up. He gathered three trash bags of mess before he could right the tree. It was not so great at standing up straight anymore, but he rehung the ornaments that were still useable. The glass he swept up and would vacuum for the shards when she woke.

As he worked, he felt the weight of the loss of the man in his place, his daughter sleeping on the couch. Everything was so normal—remotes, lamps, newspapers. It was not nearly sad enough.

Once he had things in place, he whispered to her before he started the vacuum, because he knew it would wake her. She mumbled and rolled over against the racket, but soon enough the living room was clean. Beckett propped the pictures on a hutch, the frames too broken to fix. When he turned, she was looking at him, her eyes clearer. "Are you ready?" he asked.

"For what?"

"Christmas." Beckett handed her the new pajamas. "Put these on."

"I don't want to. I want to leave." She stood and rolled her eyes at the pain that her head must have harbored. "I think I'm going to hurl."

"Go shower, put these on, and come back. I'll get you some more water." While she trudged into the bathroom, Beckett went to the kitchen and started work on the fridge. He tossed the expired food and spoiled dairy.

He took the trash out and spoke to a few tenants on the way back into the building. He let them know Dr. Hartt had passed on and that he would be sending Blake by to attend to any building needs soon. The tenants he spoke to remembered Blake as the handyman from back in the day.

When he came back in, Eve was sitting on the couch in the new pajamas, wrapped in the blanket with the slippers peeking out from under it. Her eyes were rimmed in red. She had cried in the shower.

Beckett closed the door and sat next to her. "Talk to me."

"All that was in there was his soap and stuff. It just smells like him." She cried again. He rubbed her back and treated her like a normal goddamn person.

When she finally stopped, he moved to the presents. "I think you should open these. He wanted you to have them. That big present was a mirror. It broke, though."

"I don't want to look at me anyway, so that works out."

"Do you want to do it, or should I?" He held out a gift.

"Why are you doing this? Seriously, it's torture." Her hands blocked the present being handed to her.

"Because he was your dad. And you need to be his daughter for a few fucking minutes." Beckett shrugged. Maybe he'd been off base.

Eve reached reluctantly for the gift. And with that they opened each remaining present. She commented on all of it. Whether it was her favorite perfume or a stuffed bear, she told Beckett stories about Dr. Ted Hartt. Some made her laugh, some made her cry.

"He told me he'd failed once," she said, her eyes far away. "After David and Anna were lost. He couldn't figure out how to cheer me up. Imagine that—this guy who had no one helping him raise a child thinking he'd failed. It was the other way around." She looked at the pile of unwrapped affection.

"And what would he say now, if he heard you say that?" Beckett asked her softly.

She thought for a while before responding. "That I could be anything I wanted. That he believed I should have hope."

Standing suddenly, she was done all at once. "I need to get out of here. Please."

Beckett stood as well. She grabbed her music box, and he hit the lights, pocketed her gun, and almost locked the door with her keys.

But she stopped him. As an afterthought, she retraced her steps and checked the medical bag Beckett had set on the dining room table.

"Morales took something out of there before he left," he told her. He watched her get angry before walking out the door.

She strode out of the building still wearing pajamas and slippers, so he unlocked the Challenger's doors. They could get someone to bring home her bike. She got in the passenger side as Beckett sent a quick text to Blake explaining the situation at Dr. Hartt's building.

"Thanks."

She was so quiet he almost didn't hear her.

As he backed up, he caught a glimpse of her sitting a little taller. Underneath it all, she was just a girl who wanted the normal. How easily he forgot.

"Do we need to visit Morales?" He prayed she would say yes.

"No, it's fine."

Clearly, Eve was pissed at Ryan, and Beckett felt a little bad for how great it made him feel.

19

SERVICED

Sevan watched as Primo scratched at his neck. "I wouldn't try tearing that out if I were you. It'll kill you." Sevan was eating edamame like a monster. He'd been on a health kick since he was pretty much the prisoner of his neck tracker too. In the New York City apartment Beckett had arranged for them, Shark and Primo were constantly practicing the fine art of pissing each other—and him—off. At least Shark could come and go as he pleased. He and Primo had only enough leeway to go somewhere not far beyond the lobby before their trackers were set to poison them. And, the place was wired with cameras and boom mics like they were on a reality show. They could order food and complain, but that was pretty much it.

Primo launched into another rant. "I'm the prince of a king! This treatment is despicable. I've never been handled like this in my whole life."

Sevan could almost mouth Primo's speech now. He also knew how to distract him. "Want to play cards?"

In an instant, Primo was all in like the addict he was. They played for "money." Primo thought it was real, which was fine. Sevan had pretend amounts of money all over the world, even if he currently had only a humiliating trickle of allowance from Beckett—a percentage of which he'd unwisely bet and lost to Primo earlier in the day.

"When can we get some girls in here?" Primo had taken to chewing gum.

"I'll give you the same contact number that was given to me when I had a giant case of blue balls." Sevan read the number off of his cell phone.

"So I call this now?" Primo started dialing.

"I've haven't been willing to call it yet, because I know where it goes. But be my guest. I know how you like taking risks." Sevan shuffled the cards.

Primo hovered his index finger over the send button. "Where does it go?"

"It calls Eve. And she's the scariest chick I've ever met." Sevan started dealing.

"Sounds like she knows her way around a dick. I'm calling." Primo pressed the speaker button as the phone rang.

The female voice that answered sounded agitated. Sevan couldn't make out her exact words, but he watched as Primo stood and started bossing her around.

"I need some bitches up in this joint. You can't expect a hot-blooded man not to be serviced for this long." Primo raised his weak chin a few inches. He turned to Sevan. "Watch this."

"Primo, you sorry sack of shit. You can't take care of your own balls? Do you even know how to wipe your ass? I swear to fuck I am in such the mood to kick your taint into your nostril. Motherfucker. Drive me there now, Beckett. Son of a bitch thinks he can order girls…" The line disconnected.

Sevan widened his eyes as Primo looked surprised. "This is what happens when girls are in charge," he whined. "How can she make a decent sandwich with that attitude?"

Sevan picked up his cards. "You should tell her that when she gets here. She totally needs someone to put her in her place."

Moments later, Shark let himself in the front door. "Which one of you stupid fuckers called Eve?"

Suddenly Primo didn't seem all that excited to own up to it. Sevan set his cards down.

Shark pointed at the cameras. "Don't make me look it up on the recording."

"Well, I did," Primo finally said. "But I've never been anywhere where I couldn't get girls when I needed them. Surely Taylor is running a top-notch situation here." Primo strutted a bit in a way that must have worked for him in the past.

"Insane son of a bitch. You're lucky she can't make it here right now." Shark scanned the room and reached for a sturdy-looking golf putter that Sevan used to pass the copious amount of time he was alone. "Go stand there with your legs spread."

The indignation changed Primo's face, contorting it. He obviously believed if he protested enough, things would get better.

Shark waited, tossing the putter from one hand to the other. Then he glanced at his watch. "You're up to three now. I'd get there quick. It starts multiplying per minute—and not in a good way."

"Really? You want me to stand there with my legs spread?" Primo made a noise that started in his stomach. It was the soundtrack to entitlement. Sevan recognized it because he was great at imitating it.

"In ten seconds you'll be up to six," Shark reported. "Nine...eight..."

Primo hurried to the center of the room and spread his legs, covering his crotch.

"Move the hands. Four...three..."

Primo moved his hands slightly. Now it looked like he had a set of jazz hands around his groin.

Shark adjusted his stance as if he were actually swinging a club on a course with eighteen holes. His first swing was vicious. Primo fell over, grasping his testicles. Sevan grimaced with sympathy pain.

"Move your damn hands. I got two more." Shark kicked Primo's foot.

He pulled his hands away, shaking the whole time. The next two blows were delivered while he writhed on the floor.

Then Shark got low. "Are you listening? Can you hear me? In Taylor's organization that is how genitals get service on demand. Feel free to request it anytime."

Shark pointed the club at Sevan. "You'll get the same as he does if you ever share her cell number again." He tossed the club at Sevan, who scattered the cards in an effort to catch it.

"Brainless assholes. Of all the shit I have to do, babysitting you fools is my least favorite." Shark slammed the door on his way out.

Sevan put the club down before going to the fridge and finding frozen peas. He tossed the bag to the floor next to Primo, who flinched. He guessed the card game was over.

"I'm going for a walk," he told Primo as an afterthought. He couldn't listen to the man cry anymore.

On the sidewalk, Sevan lit a cigarette. It was hell knowing that at any moment Taylor or his bitch could throw a switch and kill him. He'd been buying the food he and Primo didn't order out at CVS because he was scared to test the boundaries of his neck bomb.

He stretched his neck, hating his invisible collar.

"You got a light?" He turned to face the voice behind him. She was pretty, so Sevan smiled.

"Allow me." He lit her cigarette while smiling.

"You got Primo in there?" She didn't look at him while she took her first deep inhale.

"In my pants? Yes. Everything in there is primo." He chuckled at his own joke. The woman gave him a hard look.

Sevan swallowed and looked around. The street was busy, and he couldn't pick out anything out of the ordinary.

"I need you to nod yes or no," she said. "I know who you are, Sevan. Is he there or isn't he?" She tapped her foot.

"Who's asking?" Sevan took his own pull on the drug.

"Someone who cares." She tossed her cig on the ground and pressed her high heel on top of it.

Sevan had so many dirty thoughts about her heels. Primo hadn't been wrong about needing some girls.

"I never know who to trust anymore," he told her. "You trustworthy, princess?" He continued to smoke. On his allowance, he had to take it down to the goddamn filter.

"If I were going to kill you, do you think you'd still be talking?" She smiled like he'd just said something nice to her.

He matched her smile. "He's here, but neither of us can leave." He gave her another glance.

"Why not?" She put her hand on his arm.

"I think that's all I'll say. If he's getting rescued, I want in. And he can't leave here or they'll know. I got to go now, otherwise you'll call attention to me." Sevan went in for a kiss, which she allowed.

He moaned.

She moaned back.

With that she was gone. Sevan stood on the sidewalk trying to figure out what had just happened. Eve could have sent her here to test him. Maybe he'd just slit his own throat and get it over with. His hand shook as he took the last possible drag.

After an extremely rough start on Friday night (for Eve, at least) the weekend had been a good bit of healing, both physical and mental. Beckett took a page from his beach playbook and spoiled her. They'd watched stupid movies, she got to verbally assault Primo's stupid ass on Saturday afternoon, and he'd slow danced with her in his living room. She talked more about her father, memories and disappointment. They'd popped by the local shooting range and let off some steam too. Eve was in a process now, and he wouldn't try to snap her out of her grief quickly. Tending to the beast in her was his default, but tenderly finding the woman took more forethought.

Nevertheless, Monday had come, like it tends to do, and Beckett had two meetings. One Eve could attend, and the other she couldn't. Spider was up first after a late-night text saying he had some useable info, and thankfully Eve had gone to the courthouse to meet with a few friends regarding the empty schoolhouse. They were approaching it carefully, because they didn't want to stir up controversy just yet.

Beckett found Spider at Starbucks. He sat a table away.

"What do you got?" Beckett took a sip of steaming coffee while glancing at Spider's screen.

"A few weeks before Dr. Hartt, there was another person in there." Spider clicked through some stills. "Our friend brought her into the same room, through the hallway. Unfortunately, we only get a profile. You recognize her?"

The lady with Nicholas was not someone Beckett had seen before, at least as far as he could tell from the still. He shook his head.

"This is the best shot," Spider said. "And I've been messing with it to get the clarity up since I found it. I've also been crossing her description with reports of missing women since that time stamp." He pointed at the screen. "So far nothing. I've branched out to international reposts, but still nothing."

Beckett studied the picture. The woman was scared, he could tell by her body language. And as Spider clicked through the other stills, he could see she had every right to be. The next clear shot was Nicholas dragging a body-shaped form from the room. He was grinning like it was Christmas morning.

"Wait, back it up. Zoom in." Becket waited while Spider complied. "Those look like scrubs to you?"

"Thought it was pajamas." Spider hit a few more keys and got a bit more detail.

"No. That's scrubs. And we still have no idea where this fucker's home base is?" Beckett pointed at Nicholas with his pinkie after Spider zoomed out.

"Not yet. He was paid in cash at the New Jersey house. His car's plates and make bring up nothing of worth. He's smart. There's a reason he was high up on Rodolfo's totem pole." Spider took a sip of his coffee as well.

"He's young. Cocky even. Somewhere he made a mistake. I need to find that. Can you send me the pictures of Nicky there and the lady?" Beckett stood.

Spider nodded.

"She's wearing scrubs. I want you to delve into the files on women who work at Poughkeepsie General. Get me a list of them all." Beckett slipped his jacket on.

"You think she was from the hospital?" Spider looked interested.

Too interested, Beckett decided. "Do your best, asshole. Don't ask questions. Deliver."

Beckett drove the rest of the way to the next meeting thinking about the woman in the video still. She might have had nothing to do with why Dr. Hartt was dragged in. But if she worked at the hospital too, that was a connection. Maybe a connection Ted Hartt hadn't known about.

Ted Hartt had been a good guy. Beckett knew he'd never do anything to hurt Eve. Not on purpose.

Eve sat down on the bench with Midian and Tashika at their usual place at the courthouse. It was colder than normal in the hallway. Or maybe Eve just couldn't get warm anymore.

Tashika started. "I'm so sorry about your father." Midian's face registered surprise. Tashika added, "Heard at the hospital he'd passed away."

Midian turned to Eve and gave her a huge hug. "I'm so sorry, baby."

Eve patted Midian's back, swallowing the emotion that flooded her throat. Kindness might just be the worst part.

"Thanks." Before the girls could ask any questions—such as *how?*—Eve continued on. She passed out two index cards. "I need find out about this property. I'd love to know about the paperwork situation, who owns it, that kind of thing. And Tashika, I'd like to know if it's on the radar for any of your clients."

"A school?" Midian tapped the card against her bosom.

"Yes, old Catholic one. You know it?" Eve waited. The small brunette had a mind like a steel trap. If something crossed her desk, she remembered.

"Just saw this the other day. Someone was putting in the paperwork to get it condemned. My cousin used to go there."

Eve nodded. "Thanks for that. We have some pretty interesting plans for the place, and they're all on the up and up. I just want to make sure it's not in the center of something I don't already know about. I would like to know if it's going to be condemned." She looked from one friend to another. "You guys got anything you need me to do?"

"Not right now. I've got a few people for you when you're ready with that project we discussed last time." Tashika scanned the hallway out of habit. "But nothing that needs action now."

"Well, none of the houses is quite ready yet, but we've got crews working, if your people need jobs," Eve said. "Text me their info and we'll get in touch."

Tashika nodded, and Eve watched as Ryan came walking around the corner, dressed in a suit. He spotted her and smiled. Tashika got up from the bench like she didn't know Eve or Midian, pretending to talk on her phone. They weren't hiding, but they tried to not make it too obvious that they were friends.

"Eve." Ryan nodded at her.

"You motherfucker." Eve stood. "Take anything that's mine lately?"

"Well, technically it wasn't yours…"

Midian was between the two of them so quickly, an earring clutched in her hand like a weapon. "You stole from her? You son of a bitch. You best hand it back right now." She pointed in his face.

Ryan looked down at her. "Slow down. You just attack people now?"

Midian was hopping mad, and Eve smiled wickedly at Ryan. "I wouldn't mess with her. She'll kick your ass."

"I don't give a crap what you took from her," Midian said. "You give it back now."

Eve watched Ryan's eyes sparkle a bit while Midian threatened his life. Her friend was a little powerhouse. She'd have to ask her if she was still dating that hot guy from the Internet. She touched the woman's shoulder. "I got it. Thanks, though. I'll sic you on him if he doesn't pay up."

Midian pointed at her own eyes and then at Ryan's face before turning to leave, putting her earring back on.

Ryan watched her go for a moment before he addressed Eve. "I've got the tracking device with my guy. He's been able to get a few things done. Right now the chip registers that it's still at your father's apartment, and he's working to find a reverse-track procedure. As soon as I have any information you need, I'll give it to you."

She crossed her arms. "Really? You're in charge of this? When did I decide I was putting that in your hands?"

"When you were toasted out of your mind on whiskey?" He looked at his watch. "I have court in less than five minutes."

"I want the chip back." Eve narrowed her eyes.

"It's good to want things." Ryan stepped past her.

"This isn't over." She scowled at him.

"I didn't think it was. But you having that chip means you have that chip. I want to be a buffer between you and that knowledge. Take that as you will. I've got someone working on it. Trust me."

He continued down the hall, and Eve noticed that he looked at the door Midian had gone through.

So Ryan wanted to be the one to check out Nicholas' whereabouts. She understood why, but it wasn't going to play out that way. She needed that information for her own purposes, which meant she needed to find out who his friend was. She had plenty of friends too. Eve waved good-bye to Tashika on her way out of the building.

That afternoon, Beckett pulled up to the meeting house late. Eve was already there, having arrived in the Audi she drove when her bike wasn't an option. He buttoned his suit jacket and pulled his laptop out of the passenger seat.

When he walked into the house, the group quieted down. He went to the table that had been set up for him in one corner of the room. Eve stood in the opposite corner, and he caught more than a few of the guys checking her out.

"Assholes. Douchebags." He opened his laptop but remained standing, tilting the screen up to face him.

"I've pulled up the work reports on the properties, and things are progressing nicely—except the place over on June Street. Which fuck-ups are on that one? Raise your hands."

Four guys put their hands in the air, hesitantly. Beckett looked them over.

"Rocky, you're dropping Evergreen Road and taking over June Street. If these jizz rags can't get their dicks to stand straight, you tell Eve."

Rocky nodded. "My crew can finish at Evergreen without me, boss."

"Spider? Can you give these bastards an overview?" Beckett waited for the pale computer genius to put his words together.

He stood with slightly trembling hands. "We're looking into acquiring three businesses in Poughkeepsie. Uh…um…A laundromat, a pawn shop, and a liquor store that used to belong to Vitullo. The employees were forced into the situation, so we're going give them the option of being on their own—no more money laundering or storing illegal weapons or drugs—or having Taylor backing as they get started fully legit. Either way, if we see any movement on these stores, we need to alert someone."

Spider projected pictures of the businesses and their employees on the blank, freshly painted walls.

Assholes and douchebags nodded, processing the information.

Beckett rubbed his forehead. "Next up, we've got three warehouses that we're burning down in the next week. I know how it's going down, but your job is to have solid alibis until at least Friday. I need you all to pay attention to your surroundings. And also, anyone who finds any information on the whereabouts of Nicholas Rodgers—Vitullo's henchman—will be rewarded."

Eve met his eyes with her cold, calculating stare. It was her thanks.

"Now, like last time, if you got people who need help, a job, or that you're worried about please see one of the five of us. We'll get that shit handled. Class dismissed."

The longest part of these meetings was always the one on ones. Eve, Shark, Spider, Rocky, and Dutch listened to concerns. Some people were getting shaken down by loan sharks, and there was a guy hanging around the rehab joint trying to sell drugs. There was a little league team without uniforms, and even a report of a dog tied to a tree in a backyard, seemingly without water.

After all the douchebags and assholes had been heard, the five brought the concerns to the center. They matched similar problems and issues, looking for patterns. It seemed like four of the problems were being caused by the same loan shark. Eve wanted that case. She wanted it so bad Beckett almost didn't give it to her. Some coordinating and bargaining resulted in a manageable task list for each person.

Next up was the largest project, burning down three warehouses, one of which was a Vitullo property.

"I think all at once," said Eve. "Same damn minute. We can have Spider hack into the cameras so we can pull anyone out before we light them up."

Shark nodded. "I've got a firecracker arsonist on speed dial. She'll get us some nice, hard-to-trace shit. Name's Bang, which is perfect."

Eve lifted her eyebrows. "Bang? I've heard of her—you sure she's legit?"

"So far." Shark shrugged. "She's freelance, but…"

Beckett nodded, closing the matter as he pulled up the map on his computer. "I have a company that's pushing a merger that will effectively reestablish these four warehouses as legitimate businesses." He pointed at the screen. "They'll be recycling products that we can utilize in our builds. But that won't be in place for at least a year. They've got to get through legal, retrofit the machines—it'll be a while. So for now we keep on keeping on. We just finalized the Certificate of Occupancy on five homes, so after the burns, Eve and I will place some people in the houses. Any questions?"

Spider cleared his throat, "What about the abandoned school?"

"That's a clean project. Still have to dilute enough cash to make that work. It'll be a charity-based operation." Beckett closed his laptop.

Shark stifled a laugh. "No, what is it really? A brothel?"

"It's legit. Shut your mouth." Eve gave him a harsh look, and he stopped his ribbing.

"Let's go." Beckett held the door open as everyone filed through before he locked the door with his huge set of keys.

Eve hung back.

He leaned in for a kiss, and she gave him her cheek.

"How'd your meeting go?" he asked.

"Good. They're solid. Midian thinks she can dig up some stuff on the school. Apparently someone's trying to get it condemned." She leaned against the car.

He leaned next to her. "I'll go to the Pope if I have to to get this done."

"I ran into Morales. I think he was into Midian a bit." She looked at her shoes.

"That make you jealous?" He wished he could take it back the second he said it. "Forget I said that. He's got great taste in women, so I'm sure she's hot."

"I think I'm doing good, and then it hits me all over again." Lacing her fingers together, Eve sighed.

"Time doesn't heal all wounds." He wrapped his arm around her. "Especially this quick."

"Yeah, I know."

They stood like that for a few before she pushed away from the car. "We got to get home to G. If I don't feed him on time, he'll give me the business."

"Meet ya there."

Beckett got in his car and watched as she pulled out. Something was wrong with his wife. Above and beyond her father's death, she was wilting as he watched.

20

THE MASTER

Weeks passed, and Beckett began to feel a bit more positive. Eve was clearly still struggling, but she'd opened herself up to helping with his projects—what he wanted to be their projects—making Poughkeepsie a better place. The process of tracking Nicholas remained agonizingly slow, so they just didn't speak of it. She went about her duties, and he went about his during the day. Then at night they worked to move forward into a life built around something other than pain and fear.

He allowed himself a small smile and a moment of optimism as he pulled up to the freshly painted house. There was a rental moving truck outside, and his new tenant, Catrina, struggled toward the front door under the weight of a large box. He hopped out of the car quickly and grabbed the other end.

"Wow. You moving in by yourself?" He took the brunt of the weight off of her.

"I'll have help in a few. My brother is getting off of work soon." She went to take a step backward.

"No, you push, I'll go in reverse!" Beckett helped her maneuver the box inside and onto the living room floor.

"So you're a landlord who does moving? This is my lucky day." She stuck her hands in her jeans.

"Where's the little one? Preschool?" Beckett looked around the interior. She'd brought a huge bunch of boxes in by herself.

"Yeah. He loves that program. I have three hours, and then I have to leave to go get him. Thanks for hooking me up with that counselor. She really knew what I was looking for." She was pretty, but looked tired. "Look at all this stuff people donated!"

As one of Beckett's new renters, Catrina had been vetted through one of the most unconventional processes ever. Tashika, Eve's friend, had mentioned that her cousin knew someone living in a car with her child. She'd been giving the kid to friends and neighbors when it was time for a job interview. Her brother was working two jobs, but between the two of them, they still couldn't save up enough for a security deposit and rent.

Beckett had driven by the car in question and got out to walk around it one night. Sure enough, a woman was curled in the back under blankets, and a small hand peeked out. She was keeping her son safe and warm as best she could in such an exposed situation. He'd called a douchebag to provide security while he made calls through the night. By morning, Ryan Morales was approaching the car, calming the panicked mom who thought he was there to take her son away. Instead, he had a number for a counselor.

The counselor, Tammy, had met with the mom and offered a new situation, which Beckett had orchestrated. After working though her disbelief and distrust, the mom had met with Beckett in a Panera. Over bagels he'd purchased, he told her his genuine story, so she would know what she was getting into, that his past was littered with things that made him an unlikely hand to hold.

He'd shown her the house they were now standing in with Eve one afternoon last week. Eve had a cool, calculated business demeanor that for sure classed up his shit show. The contracts were drawn up, and the two-bedroom rambler was now hers to live in until she was ready to move out. The rent would be ten percent of her paycheck, and for now she would be doing bookkeeping for Eve from home so she could be around her son. Her brother, who'd dabbled in petty crime, was to live in the other bedroom. It was small, but it was safe, and it would be warm.

After wishing her the best and helping with a couple more of the heaviest boxes, Beckett presented her with a fan of gift cards to local businesses and restaurants. He waved away her thanks. None was necessary. Helping her helped him. It gave him a rush, just like his work in Maryland had done. He had a fresh set of principles he was proud of.

Her brother arrived just in time for Beckett to shake his hand as his sister left to pick up her son from preschool.

"On the up and up," Beckett told him. "Or I'll know and you're out. Got it?"

The brother nodded. Beckett was satisfied with the mixture of respect and fear in the man's eyes.

Next, Beckett took a short drive across town and pulled into the counselor's parking lot. She'd given him a tip about a prospective client for the Brother's Legacy home, once it was ready, or at least a kid Beckett should get to know. Tammy was friendly and on the ball, and she had a truckload of common sense, which was his favorite. Midian and Livia both had given good references for the woman.

When her secretary signaled him, Beckett swooped into her office, taking his seat and his hat off in the same motion. "So what've we got?"

Tammy passed a photo over to him. "Well, Scottland Bell is kind of an asshole. But I think he's your kind of asshole." She tapped the teen's face with her manicured nail.

Beckett took the picture. The kid looked surly, shooting a camera a look like he didn't trust it. He was smoking and already had tattoos on his fingers and neck.

"How old?"

"Scottland is almost seventeen."

"Who took this picture?" Beckett committed the face to memory.

"It was on the Internet. I printed it to show you." She pulled up his file on her computer. "Four foster homes. Hasn't been to the latest one in three days. Also forgot to show up at school for the last week. So I'm a little worried. He's got a ton of street smarts. But he's still a kid." Tammy shrugged.

"Tell me why you think I need to be all up in his business." Beckett leaned back in his chair.

"Okay, so I went on a home visit a while back. And the foster mom? She has a heart of gold, has a bunch of special needs kids. How Scottland was placed there, I'm not sure, but she kept raving about him. And I thought, *really?* Are we talking about the same kid? I mean, he's charming, but you know he's trouble. But I get to the kitchen, and he doesn't realize I'm there, so I just watch from the doorway. He's patiently feeding one of the kids in a wheelchair, just chatting away, wiping the boy's face with such tenderness. When he saw me he threw a wall up and made a point to curse, but I saw him when he didn't have to front for anyone. That's why I think he's worth fighting for." Tammy looked back at the screen.

Beckett nodded. "So is he still in the special needs house?" He pulled out his phone and began scrolling through his contacts, trying to picture who would know where this kid might be.

"He is. It was the best fit so far," Tammy said. "The foster mother is crazy about him, and he was getting into a lot less trouble. But now he's disappeared, and she's concerned."

"They don't call him Scottland on the street, though. What do they call him? Do you know?"

Tammy shook her head. "He jokes that his nickname is 'The Master.' But he usually responds to Land."

"I'll have him back home in the next twelve hours, if he's alive." Beckett smiled at Tammy when he saw her grinning.

"I think I'm going to love this new arrangement," she said.

Beckett was already texting, putting out an APB on Scottland, as he returned to his car. When his phone chimed back at him, he was amazed at his douches' speed — until he saw the message was from Spider. He'd found something new.

Beckett changed courses and headed home immediately. When he arrived, he found Spider down in the basement, working on four computers at once. Beckett thought again about getting some sun lights installed. The dude was seriously pale. "Do you ever go in the sun or anything?" he asked. "I'm legitimately concerned that you might develop scurvy down here." He sat in a computer chair next to Spider.

The man held up an orange. "That's what this is for. Okay, so I've been hacking my face off and trying to get a bead on the scrubs lady from Nicholas' debut performance on Vitullo's security tape. And I was able to get a partial number off this here part."

Spider zoomed in on a still of the nurse walking with Nicholas into the interrogation room. What had looked like a fold in her pants was actually the very tip of an ID card.

"Okay, so she doesn't work directly for Poughkeepsie General, which explains why there hasn't been any missing persons report or delinquent employee records showing up. She works for a placement service, so they send her all over. Or at least they used to…Anyway, I've cross referenced and even created a program that compares employee numbers with the reference files and, ironically, the drug testing they're subject to, which is super hard to find—"

"I get it. It was hard. You worked. You're a computer genius. Just tell me what you found out." Beckett squinted at the computer.

"Well, this nurse has taken shifts at Poughkeepsie General on and off for more than a decade. And turns out she was on duty in the OR one night about ten years ago when Eve Hartt was admitted after a car accident."

Beckett looked over his shoulder, thinking of his woman and his role in that terrible evening.

"So I checked into the records for that night a little more closely, and Eve was in surgery a long time," Spider continued. "Turns out she had a hysterectomy—no more baby-making parts, except they left an ovary so her hormones aren't totally jacked up. It saved her life, but she must hate hospitals." Spider shook his head as he hit a few more keys.

"So this tells me nothing I didn't already know, really," Beckett said aloud, but inside his mind was whirring, feeling the pieces he needed to connect just out of reach once again.

"Well, you know that woman was there when Eve had her accident, and something about her—or about that night—was interesting to Vitullo all these years later. And you know who else was there that night? Dr. Hartt? Also in the OR. It's weird, but I think he actually did Eve's surgery."

"Yeah, he had a habit of that," Beckett said absently.

Spider pulled up a picture of a nineteen-year-old Eve posing next to David, the handsome young father of her unborn child. Beckett was haunted by the hope and happiness reflected in her eyes.

"Anyway, these are pieces to a puzzle, if there is one," Spider said. "Connections. That's what Vitullo always liked me to find when I was with him. He didn't believe in coincidences. He used to tell me, 'There is no fate, only dirty money. Look for connections,' anytime I was researching stuff—for what it's worth." Spider shrugged and resumed typing, recording facts on a beast of a timeline. "I'm trying to keep track, just to watch for patterns."

Beckett slapped the man on the back. "That's some interesting bullshit. Keep at it."

Still feeling like he needed to sit and process for a good long while, Beckett instead returned his attention to his noisy phone as he went back upstairs. A few well-placed texts had sent him reports of a teen running a scam on a pool table down in the older section of town. A quick call to Eve confirmed that the pool hall had been on Sevan's payroll back in the day, so Beckett had business there as well.

He pulled into the parking lot as dusk was starting to settle. A few assholes had also showed up, and they nodded in Beckett's direction. In addition to finding this kid, he wanted to show the owners which direction they needed to take.

As he walked in, Beckett spotted Scottland talking shit at a table in the back, surrounded by a few shitheads he wasn't fond of. Beckett ordered a whiskey and sat at the bar. The bartender brought his drink quickly and refused his money, letting Beckett know that his reputation preceded him still.

"You got a boss?" He took a sip, the whiskey wasn't the worst they probably had.

"I do. She's in back. You need her?" The bartender tripped over his words a bit.

"Yeah. Bring her out, if you don't mind." He spun his stool around to watch Scottland.

The kid was great at pool. He put a wad of cash on the table. Pointing out an impossible shot, he dared the men to match his bet. After some grumbling about easy money, the verbal deal was sealed. Scottland finally stopped posturing and focused on his shot, clear blue eyes assessing the lines. He had a multicolored Mohawk, which was a new addition since the picture Beckett had seen in Tammy's office. The boy rubbed his neck tattoo, an elaborate design Beckett couldn't quite make out, and hit the eight ball at the same time as he exhaled.

The shot went all over the table, following the impossible path the kid had predicted. When he sank the last ball, he began celebrating—very unlike a pool shark—putting his age on exhibit for the older men.

Instead of paying up, they scoffed before taking their cash off the table. "We ain't paying a baby," one of them explained. "That's some sort of scam shit."

Scotland immediately began fighting, tossing the first punch like a punk. The three men quickly schooled him and had him pinned by his neck to the table. Then one took a pool cue and began raining blows on the kid. Instead of tears, Scotland started spouting curses, making his situation even more difficult.

Beckett took a few more sips of his whiskey. The bartender and the boss lady came from the back, and he held up a hand to stop them from getting involved. He set his glass down and strolled over to the pool table, hands in his pockets. The shitheads who hadn't noticed Beckett when he walked in noticed him now. He turned and gave his assholes a brief head shake, telling them to stay out of it.

Beckett lifted his brows and looked from the shitheads to the kid and back again.

"This little pussy? You want him?" one of them asked.

Beckett shrugged, refusing to respond with anything other than a smile.

"He yours? Shit, Taylor. We don't mean nothing by it. We're done here."

Another shithead piped up, "Yeah, we're happy to leave it as it fucking is. All done. Everything's cool." He held up his hands as if Beckett were brandishing a gun.

The men stepped away from Scotland, who jumped up and straightened his jacket before shooting the shitheads the middle finger. "Yeah? How you like some of that? You basic bitches." The kid was full of himself at once.

Beckett's smile never faltered. "You know what? Go ahead and punch him one more time."

The nearest shithead happily complied, knocking Scotland right in the jaw. The kid's eyes were wide as he recoiled.

The shitheads knew enough to leave the pile of cash on the table. "So he's yours or not?" they asked again.

"Not sure yet. Either way, he made the shot, and I heard you agree, so pay the fuck up." Beckett crossed his arms in front of his chest.

The shitheads moved as quickly as they could, tossing bills on the table without complaint. Before they were all the way out the door, Beckett added, "Assume he's mine."

Scottland had no gratefulness, just fast hands. He made a quick play to grab the cash. Beckett leaned forward and placed his index finger in the center of the money.

"What?" Scottland protested. "Now you're going to fucking take it all? Fuck you, man." He proceeded to stomp around, flailing his arms angrily.

"What's it for?" Beckett waited.

The kid's eyes looked clear. He answered with the venom of a Chihuahua pissing on a Great Dane. "None of your damn business."

"Everything in here is my goddamn business right now. Answer or I will fucking take it. And don't lie. I can tell." Beckett leaned forward, finally putting the entire force of his attention on the kid.

Scottland ran his hands through his Mohawk, making it ripple. "It's for my mother. Okay? She needs it."

Beckett began stacking the money quickly. It was easily six hundred dollars.

"No. *Fuck*. No, please don't take it," Scottland said in a slightly desperate voice. "She needs it."

"You're lying."

"I'm not. Okay, listen, she's my foster mom, and one of the other kids needs this expensive computer. They think he can maybe talk with his eyes and shit. And he's in there, I fucking know it. I just want to hear what he has to say." The kid punched the table in disappointment as Beckett put the money in his pocket.

Now he was telling the truth, and it was beautiful. Beckett didn't let his face show that he was pleased with the answer. "You haven't been home or in school, Mr. Bell. Care to tell me why?" He crossed his arms again.

"You know me? What are you, a fucking narc? Shit." The kid began pacing.

"I just met you, fuckhead. And you better find yourself some respect to show 'cause I'm the furthest thing you'll ever meet from a cop. How'd you make this money?"

"Pool. You just saw."

"No, the seed money. You're wasting my time."

"I sling a little dope. Shit, it's freaking legal. What's the big deal?"

Beckett gave him a hard look. "No, that's not it. Those kids you live with, they got a lot of meds?" He watched Scottland's eyes widen. Beckett had obviously unearthed his secret. Then he started explaining in earnest.

"Listen, he needs that computer. Do you know what will happen to him when he ages out? The state ain't buying him shit. Who knows where he'll end up? He needs this fast, so we can teach him how to use it, and he can have an opinion and then speak in time for him to be an adult. Shit. It might affect his whole life. And my foster mom doesn't know she's sitting on a goldmine. The docs just replace the missing meds, and I can make money and then double it here at these tables."

"You can wind up in jail for doing that shit."

Scottland sighed. "My foster mom figured it out, so I can't go back now. Not until I have the money for the computer. And shit, so what? They put me in juvie? I've been there before. At least I'll be able to talk. Trevor needs this or else he won't." The boy shook his head as he gave up. "I swear the older people get, they just don't hear anymore. Trevor *needs* this. And I'm going to get it for him." Scottland met Beckett's eyes with a fire he recognized.

"How much is it?" Beckett asked.

"Well, he'd need a computer and then an eye-recognition program. I think we can get one for about five K." Scottland looked dejected.

"How much have you saved?"

"What you got in your pocket." Scottland motioned with his chin toward Beckett's jacket.

"You're a little light for a fancy computer."

"No shit." Trevor jammed his tattooed hands in his pockets.

"I'll tell you what, I'll talk with your foster mom and find out what he needs. You good with computers? Can you handle setting it up and that kind of bullshit?"

"Yeah, I'm good." Defiance. The very definition of it. "What do you want from me? Ain't nothing for free."

"You tell me the truth when I ask questions," Beckett said. "Don't steal any more meds. No slinging dope. Just go school." He sighed. Uphill battles sometimes with these kinds of people. It always was for the people who'd worked with him as a kid. He watched Scottland size up the situation.

"We'll see what you do. Can I have my money back?"

Beckett shook his head. "No, numbnuts, I'll give it to your foster mother. You and me, we have an understanding?" He tilted his head to the side.

"All right." Scottland approached Beckett with his hand extended. "They call me Freaky Dick."

Beckett shook the kid's hand and his head at the same time. "Dude, that's worst nickname. Stick with Land. Go home. Go to school."

Land looked like he wasn't entirely sure walking out of the pool hall without his money was the best idea, but he went anyway.

The assholes in the corner started laughing. "Shit, we didn't know we were watching an afterschool special today."

Beckett gave them the finger. "Shut your faces. One of you trail that kid and makes sure he gets home. I'm invested now."

He spun to face the bartender and the boss. Both looked guilty and worried as Beckett returned to the bar. "First, that freaking kid didn't belong in here, and you both know it." He pointed at them with his thick fingers. "Second, how deep was Sevan Harmon's dick in your asshole around here? And has someone else been sniffing around?"

The conversation that proceeded involved an elaborate detailing of the inner workings of a popular drug line through town — managed first by Sevan's people, and more recently by Vitullo's. By the end of the conversation, Beckett had decided not to offer these guys the opt-out choice. They didn't seem to have much potential, falling from one sleazy overlord to another. Instead, he assigned a few assholes and one douchebag to the pool hall and decided it might be time to meet up with McHugh, show him exactly where he should be concentrating his efforts.

A little good faith might be welcome at this point, and a few high-level drug busts would certainly make the Poughkeepsie PD look good.

21

G⊙D

Just after the one-month anniversary of Alison's arrival in his lab—something he still preferred not to think too carefully about—Dr. Yordan determined that her hormone treatments had been a success, and the implanted ovarian tissue had produced a healthy crop of mature eggs. Her follicles had reached sixteen millimeters, and he'd sedated her for the extraction.

He now evaluated the eggs as the nurse monitored her, tending to the woman's recovery process and her continued sedation—another thing he tried to avoid contemplating. Nicholas had informed him that the woman would remain under until sometime after the completed embryo transfer, which would be five days from now. This was, of course, highly irregular, but also clearly not up for negotiation, and it had become clear that more than his research funds were at risk, should he fail to follow the prescribed protocol. Setting his nagging conscience aside for the greater goals of scientific research—and self-preservation—Dr. Yordan focused on the task at hand.

The next part was his favorite. Four hours had passed, so it was time. The eggs looked wonderful under the microscope—youth was a beauty, for sure. In his sterile lab, he became God. He carefully prepared the sperm and took a steadying breath. He was about to create life. He'd chosen only the strongest specimens from the sample, which had been a process. The male donor was old enough that he had genuine concern for the virility of his biological material. But with nothing but time to work, he'd found what he needed.

Classical music played in the background. As he guided tip of the needle to the egg, the lab door slammed open. Nicholas walked in like he owned the place, not stopping to worry about the contaminant on his shoes, or the delicate process the doctor was now undertaking.

"Are they done?"

The doctor kept his hand steady and fertilized the egg. He carefully put down his equipment before addressing the man. "They aren't like your favorite breakfast order. This is science and patience and education all happening here. You're lucky I have nerves of steel, you silly twit. Your disturbance could have ruined that whole batch. So no. They aren't *done.*"

"What can I tell Rodolfo?" Nicholas took a step back, seeming to catch his error.

"You can tell him that after thawing ovarian tissue that was more than a decade old, I was able to graft it inside Alison, which is a goddamn miracle in and of itself. And not only that, but she was successfully able to produce the original source's biological eggs, which is pretty much time travel. And then, after that, with any luck at all and no thanks to you, I will have created viable embryos using his half-dead sperm. I have a few more to go, but in five days, I'll be implanting these into Alison's womb, and because I'm so amazing, I'm fairly certain she will become pregnant." The doctor paused to take a breath. Nicholas seemed to be searching for words.

"Now," he continued. "You can leave me alone, because out of all the things I do in a lab, this one is my favorite." The doctor watched him until Nicholas backed out of the door he had entered.

It was so hard to have the money and the science not collide.

Alison woke slowly in her bedroom at the prison of a house where they were keeping her. She felt like she'd been hit by a truck — and lobotomized. Absolutely nothing made sense anymore. When her eyes finally focused, the nurse was smiling at her, and the doctor looked incredibly pleased with himself.

"How long have I been under?" Her brain was foggy.

"Almost two weeks," the nurse said matter-of-factly. "But we have good news. Doctor?" The woman took her vitals.

As the doctor came forward, Nicholas stepped from behind the nurse, leering at her like he did.

"You're pregnant," the doctor announced, looking at her as if she might jump up and cheer. "We just tested you. Positive." He turned to Nicholas. "You best tell the boss the good news."

Alison felt empty, devoid of everything except her hate for them. She raged silently against each face in the room with her. To hear she was pregnant had been her dearest wish before…and now it was a horrible nightmare.

Nicholas stepped closer. "So you understand, you're only as good as the babies in your belly, so you'd best take care of them. Wipe that horror off your face. This is an honor."

The doctor stepped between Nicholas and Alison. "Keeping her calm and unthreatened is the most important part of what we have to do now," he told him. "So you might want to dial it back."

Nicholas left the room, looking as surly as always.

Alison felt like crying, but the nurse and doctor were jubilant, completely oblivious to her feelings. It was as if a gun pointed at their heads had been lowered. He smiled, she joked. Alison looked out the window as her tears welled up.

In another life, Flint would have loved this moment. She'd pictured it a million times: the positive result, twins even. But never anything like this.

As weeks went by and spring crept over the city, the puzzle Vitullo had left behind was never far from Beckett's mind. And it was definitely made worse by the fact that he wasn't sharing it with Eve. He couldn't. This sort of uncertainly just wasn't fair. He'd done enough.

He would honor her by sorting through this himself and presenting her with answers — if needed — when everything finally made sense.

But because he lacked her wise counsel, her presence as a sounding board — and because Nicholas was the slippery bastard he was — it was slow going, and he was reduced to moments like this: impossible thoughts as he walked G. While his dog took care of business, Beckett began thinking about Rodolfo's words, his promise to make Ted a grandfather. But Eve didn't have a uterus. Why torture the nurse? What possible options could there be for a woman with no remaining reproductive system? Maybe the same as those for a woman with a non-functioning reproductive system? He knew only one person who was in touch with that particular problem. And it was a person he could trust: Cole.

After giving the dog an organic chew treat, he left, shouting his good-bye to Spider. Cole was due to end his school day in less than twenty minutes, so he drove over to his house. No one was there, as he'd expected since Fairy Princess was back at work as well these days. Livia now provided what was likely the world's best daycare for little JB at her house. It made him smile thinking of the cousins growing up together. Family mattered.

A few minutes later, Cole pulled in behind him. Beckett got out and offered him an arm to shake. "All good things, just have a question," Beckett quickly announced in response to the worry on Cole's face.

"Sure. Any time. Need a drink?" Cole opened the door and held it wide for Beckett as he disarmed the alarm.

"Was it a bad day at school?" Beckett joked as Cole brought his messenger bag into the kitchen.

"Water, brother. That's what I've got for you. It's three thirty in the afternoon."

"JB with Whitebread?" Beckett accepted a bottle of water from Cole.

"Yep. He's doing great. Been at it a couple weeks now, and Kyle and I are finally settling in, not climbing the walls. She was complaining that Mode had fallen to crap without her, so I know she's glad to be back, but it's just hard to be away." Cole sat at the kitchen table with a sigh that sounded like he was happy to be off his feet.

"How are all those crazy kids at school doing?" Beckett sat down as well, taking a huge gulp of water.

"Good. Testing me as usual. I got this one kid—he reminds me so much of you. Son of a bitch will punch his way out of anything. Good kid. Horrible impulses." Cole put a hand through his hair.

"Sounds about right. Hey, can I ask you a weird, slightly personal question and rely on your Jesus ways to keep it private?" Beckett closed one eye and held his hands out palms up.

"Of course. Fire away." Cole put his feet up on one of the empty chairs.

"Okay, so let's say a woman can't have kids—no inner apparatus and all that—could she still somehow have a baby? Like, scientifically?" Beckett put his hands behind his head and tried to ignore the feeling that he was telling secrets.

Even after a long day, Cole could slide into confidante mode. "Is this about Eve?"

"It could be. I just know you've probably done some research in this area." Beckett waited to see what Cole would deduce.

"As far as I know, from what Kyle shared, Eve has a total hysterectomy. So apart from cloning, which is way down the road and has dicey ethics, it's not possible." Cole pressed his hands together and rested them against his lips.

"So there have to be eggs, right?" Beckett asked. "Can you just like pluck those from a lady at any time? I'm picturing a young Eve right after her accident." His mind filled with the image of Eve and David he'd seen.

"I'm going to say no. I mean, from what I learned, the body needs to be prepped. We had to give Kyle a bunch of fertility drugs to stimulate her egg-making process."

"Okay. That's what I thought." It was clear he was grasping at straws. Rodolfo had been spouting nonsense.

"But, wait a minute," Cole said after a moment. "I mean, if we're talking theoretically…At one point I was reaching, really reaching, reading everything I could find online about fertility studies. I remember a study in Belgium that was sort of mythical—and still just in animal trials when I was reading."

Cole stood and signaled Beckett to follow as he went downstairs to his computer. He fired it up and plugged a few keywords into a search engine.

"Here it is. This doctor published a paper on his results in mice. He was able to reactivate frozen ovarian tissue to produce viable eggs.

I pretty much just read it and moved on, as that wasn't really our issue. Besides, ultimately our infertility brought us JB, and neither of us would change that for the world."

"I completely agree," Beckett said with a smile. "But can you click on the researcher's name there? It's a link."

The doctor's home page featured a number of other articles about his work, as well as a notice that he'd left Belgium a few months ago after receiving a generous stipend to continue his research in — oddly enough — the United States.

No coincidences. Spider's voice echoed in Beckett's head. *Just dirty money.*

22

CLOSER

Alison wanted to scream. She'd now spent almost five months staring at the walls of this stupid room, and at the moment she was really tired of hearing all about the panel of tests the doctor was busy administering. Wouldn't want the little million-dollar babies to want for anything. And of course, if they weren't genetically superior and in perfect health, she could totally picture the smiling doctor terminating the pregnancy, considering the fetuses nothing more than a failed science experiment. He had the worst combination of overly friendly bedside manner and mad scientist that honestly gave her the creeps.

"We'll get these results shortly, but I'm expecting perfection," he told her. "You're doing wonderfully, Alison. I'm very pleased." He tapped a few more notes into his iPad as the nurse removed the rubber tourniquet and bandaged the small wound in Alison's arm from the needle. This was surreal. The doctor and the nurse focused exclusively on the minutiae of her pregnancy, ignoring the larger questions like, *Where's Flint? What will happen to these babies? What will happen to me?*

However, she'd found she learned more when she kept her mouth shut. The doctor seemed to find silence uncomfortable and would fill it with chatter. His go-to subject was always science and, more specifically, the science of creating life. If Alison was quiet enough, he would really drop his guard.

It was through this technique that Alison had learned the eggs used for her embryos weren't hers — though evidently they'd been cultivated inside her body. The doctor had gone on and on about donated ovarian tissue and the special way he thawed and implanted it successfully — just like in a mouse! — when he'd suddenly remembered himself and clamped his lips shut. It was like she'd watched him realize she was listening to his words.

Then another time the nurse had let it slip that she thought the man funding the babies was involved in weapons. Alison made sure not to show any reaction to *that* news. They needed her docile so they would continue to confide in her. Also, the more she listened, the more the doctor and nurse would project the feelings they wanted her to have, like excitement and happiness. And she wanted them to believe she felt everything they thought she should, because she was plotting the whole time.

She had to have a plan because the second these babies were born, Sir Resting Bitchface, aka Nicholas, would kill her like she was betting he'd killed Flint. Whenever he was lurking in her room, the tension ratcheted up a million notches. And of course, Nicholas always made a point to be there for her internal exams. She was certain it was just to make her uncomfortable, keep her mentally off balance.

She hated to admit how much it worked, yet she refused to believe he was smarter than her, or more dedicated to keeping her than she was to escaping him. All of them. And she *would* escape. And find these babies a good home. That's the purpose she hung on to.

"Next up will be your glucose test at twenty-four weeks." The doctor tried to make it sound like fun.

"Of course," she responded, nodding complacently.

The door of the van slammed, and Blake could hear Livia's feet crunch on the stray pebbles of the driveway. Quickly, he clipped a beautiful white tulip from the garden, the snap audible. She padded over into his line of sight as he stripped the extra leaves from the tulip with the sheers.

The May sunlight masked her features. "The kids were happy to spend a few hours with Dad and Kathy," she said.

He stood as she stepped into the shade of a tree. The slight incline made her taller, the garden a distance between them. He smiled at her as she looked suddenly flustered and fixed her hair, which swirled around her in the spring breeze. He locked his eyes on hers and placed a kiss on the bud he'd chosen for her.

She bit her bottom lip. He maintained eye contact as he carefully tossed the tulip to her. She caught it with a laugh. And when she looked back at him, she was running her tongue across her top teeth. Aroused. He could tell she liked the gesture. A blush crept up her neck and touched her cheeks.

"We are supposed to be painting," she said. "I'm leaving right now for Lowe's." She tucked the tulip into her hair, and her breasts strained against her dress a bit, her lower back curving as she set her hair in a quick bun and added the flower.

Gray eyes, brown hair, a slight sunburn on her shoulders. All she needed was minutes in a sleeveless dress to have her skin react. Blake tossed down the shears and bounded over the distance between them. He pulled her to him, her lips dry against his moist ones. He took a glove and tapped the end of her nose.

"But you're so filthy," he teased.

He ran the stubble from his jaw along her cheek, adding the soft touch of tongue against her earlobe, gently outlining the metal stud earring there. She sighed. He smoothed his palms down her body, over the sides of her breasts, feeling the curve of her hips, pulling the loose fabric tight across her stomach. Her breath quickened.

He bent his head and her rapid breath moved a few strands of his hair. Her hands ran up his back, and the plaid shirt he wore pulled up, revealing a strip of skin above the back pockets of his jeans and the waistband of his boxer briefs.

A bird in the distance flew closer, the flap of his wings in time with the blinking of her eyes when he looked at her again. The blue sky etched around her, highlighting the small hints of the same color in her eyes, in her dress.

His voice was low, quiet, for her. "Now?"

She nodded and slipped a hand underneath the shirt she'd lifted, running her finger across the waistband. He pulled her hand to his and kissed the back of it before leading her back to their house.

The screen door squeaked as he held it open for her, finally letting her hand go and finding the small of her back with the tips of his fingers.

She placed her hand on the wall and turned, her hastily rendered bun unraveling. Her hair spilled over her shoulder and tickled the top of his hand. The tulip tumbled as well. He closed the door behind her and touched her chin, then let his palm cover her cheek and put his thumb against her bottom lip. He came closer, running his nose from her cheekbone to the tip of her nose, the dirt there now shared between the two.

Her shoes landed sole up as she kicked them off. He tripped slightly over one, then laughed as she fisted her hands in his shirt, steadying him. He used one foot to step on the heel of the other so his sneakers were left to lie with hers. He put his hands on her hips and turned her completely to him, pressing her against the entryway wall.

Her dress caught on the uneven woodwork, gentle pops of fabric losing the fight between friction and passion. Her hands rested against the wall, back arching again, the sunlight streaming from the window, glinting behind her lower back. His long fingers created a shadow puppet before he tucked his whole forearm behind her, eliminating the rough feel of the wood.

The kissing started slowly, gentle nips and tastes before he initiated the deeper movement. In sync their heads moved. He pulled up the side of her long dress, using one hand to protect her, the other to reveal her.

The kissing continued, gentle, and finally, the searching hand found the gap, the soft skin of her hip blocked only by the white panties with the edge of lace—his favorite pair. His kisses continued, but there were breaks for the wide grin that took a moment here and there. His hand found the warmth between her legs, and she sighed, breaking their kiss to exhale warm breath on his neck.

"Here?" she asked.

He didn't answer, instead letting his hand work harder. He kissed her again before freeing his other arm and sliding to his knees. He disappeared under her dress. Soon the white panties were at her ankles. She bent her knees as the fabric of her dress moved rhythmically with his ministrations. The clock struck the hour. In the house somewhere a TV was on. The dryer shouted a quick alarm, alerting them to chores undone.

She leaned forward as he freed one leg from the panties that bound her, and her stance widened to accommodate him. He kept a hand on her upper thigh, holding her steady.

"It's good. God, it's so good. Blake, don't stop. God!"

As her orgasm took her, he imagined her tossing her head, her hair and the sun from the window a brief, elegant latticework, the tips of it almost reaching his hand as she gasped for more air. In a flurry, he moved up and out of her dress, dipping her almost like a dancer and placing her on the floor. She fought him briefly, unzipping his jeans before taking him in her mouth.

He struggled to stay standing, knees shaking as she worked. One hand rested on her head while his other was caught at the wrist by his teeth, His deep, guttural moans rolled from his chest. His jeans slipped lower, his elbow held his shirt above his stomach. His eyes traced a path down to where her lips were busy.

Their sounds were fervent, active, quick. She moaned as well, a soft noise of appreciation as his hand grasped her hair harder, his knuckles going white.

"Stop." He stepped away from her mouth. "God, I love you."

He knelt finally as she laid back. He wrapped his hands around her calves and pulled her closer. His hips and hers moved together—a dance with years of experience.

An email tone sounded, and a cell phone began to ring.

She panted, her lips tinted a deep red from her passion. Her pupils widened, darkened. He knew his matched hers.

"Harder," she commanded.

He accommodated. The look between them was only for each other.

Intense.

In love.

Determined.

A bead of sweat slipped from his temple.

Both were gasping. He moved the neckline of her dress to free her breast, the sight of it causing his tempo to increase. They both tensed, muscles clenching, and shouts of ecstasy echoed in the foyer. The dog barked from the backyard.

He laid next to her and kissed her forehead.

"There's not enough air in this room," she said.

Her hair was in knots now, tangled on her shoulders. Her free breast heaved as she caught her breath.

He smiled at her. Satisfied. "What you do to me? It's not legal," he breathed.

The sunlight caught tiny bits of dust in suspension, as if the air was actually thicker for a moment. She shimmied her dress down, covering her bare bottom. The harsh sound of denim rustled as he put his jeans back in order.

"I love you, too," she told him, the sentiment not lost during their exertions.

His lips placed one last kiss on the tip of her pert nipple, and her giggle spilled forth.

As summer began in earnest, Kyle lay on the bed with Cole, watching the miracle of nearly seven-month-old JB sitting on his own. The baby, surrounded by pillows, looked from one parent to the other with his gummy smile.

Cole reached out and touched his toe. The baby giggled again. Kyle's iPad was almost out of space for the video, but she couldn't bring herself to stop. This was her baby laughing. Life was a miracle.

About the time JB finally tuckered himself out and crawled into Cole's arms, Kyle's iPad gave up as well. She set it aside as Cole bounced a bit on the bed, watching his son begin to fall asleep. JB put his fingers in Cole's mouth, and Kyle smiled as Cole pretended to eat them. JB let out one last giggle. They were forty-five minutes late for his nap, which explained the tired giggles they'd recorded.

"So how'd the meeting go with my dad today?" She'd derailed his recounting when he'd arrived home by directing him to watch the show JB was putting on.

"Okay." Cole shrugged. "You know anything with Beck's name on it is going to be tough to swallow. I showed him around, showed him the business plan."

"And?" She rolled over on her back and put her hand on his leg.

"I think he sees what I'm angling at. I explained the role we want law enforcement to play. We want these kids to have a nice relationship with the authorities, some friends on the force before they're out in the community full time. And I didn't mention it to him, but I want the cops to recognize these kids' faces, you know?" His bouncing slowed. "I think he's warming up to the idea a little."

"I think it's great he heard you out," Kyle said softly. "That alone means you have a shot. If he's not interested, he says so up front."

"If Beckett wasn't involved, it would have been a raging success." Cole leaned down and kissed JB's head.

"I'm sorry." She turned to look him in the eyes.

"Don't be. I get where he's coming from, but I refuse to edge Beckett out of this. I know he'd step aside in a hot minute, but I want him to feel the movement of us as a brotherhood. You know there are times when he puts Blake and me on a pedestal he doesn't think he should share."

"I agree. He totally treats himself like a weapon for your destiny—that kind of bullshit." Kyle sat up and turned to look at her husband and son.

"Yeah, that's a good way of putting it." Cole nodded. "I want him to be equal in this, not just behind the scenes. He's doing so much good nowadays. I want that rewarded." Cole started to scooch off the bed.

Kyle skipped ahead and readied the crib in JB's room. They worked together to get him transferred to the mattress and adjust all the things to his liking: the fan turned on, the soft blanket over his feet. Cole took all the stuffed animals out of the crib where Kyle had put them earlier. They tiptoed out to the hallway and down the stairs to where they could see the monitor.

"That is one spoiled baby," Kyle said as she hopped up on the kitchen counter. "You know I've watched Livia vacuum with one hand and hold a sleeping Kellan with the other."

"You want a water?" Cole dug into the fridge and returned with two bottles when she nodded.

"That's the second kid for you. I bet we'll be more calm with our next one, too." She smiled.

He opened her water and handed it to her. "Second? You ready to adopt again?"

"Not exactly." She touched her stomach.

"What?" He set down the water and put his hands around hers.

She whispered then. "This morning. I'm only a day late, but my schedule was off…"

"Are you telling me you're pregnant?" Cole's mouth opened in disbelief.

"According to the test I am. Barely. And I don't want to get all excited like last time—as best we can." She watched as he did the math.

"JB will be..."

"Sixteen months," they said together.

"If, and that's a huge if," Kyle warned. "We know our track record. And if this one isn't meant to be, I want to figure out a way to stop the whole process from happening over and over again. I feel like JB makes it a bit easier to take, but still."

"We'll do whatever you want," Cole said. "And if we're meant to have this one, we'll be very busy." He leaned in to kiss her.

"Let's just try not to focus on it. I'll do all the normal stuff, but I want to just...be. Like, I don't want to tell anyone until I'm showing." She twisted her bottle top on and off nervously.

"It's okay. I get it. And whatever happens, we'll take it as it comes," Cole promised. "I love you. I love JB. And he and I will always be here for you." He hugged her to his chest, and Kyle smiled, excitement rising in spite of herself.

The rest of the summer passed beautifully, and almost every weekend either Cole or Blake manned the barbecue. The tradition became setting up a tent, catching fireflies, and roasting marshmallows on the fire. Sometimes there were huddles around Cole's iPad as everyone added ideas for Brother's Legacy and what it could be, and Livia offered a few names of potential staff members. Eve was at first reluctant to come to these gatherings, but soon enough she began to join them, kicking back with a glass of wine and her feet in Beckett's lap. And when she finally wore her rings, Livia, Kyle, and Emme fussed over them.

Beckett made time to get his branded scar from Vitullo tatted over, and then of course Blake and Cole got matching protection charm tattoos as well. (Beckett figured a little extra protection couldn't hurt any of them.) New man in town Hayden had to take the place of Chaos as the artist, because the latter was doing well with Chery and Vere in Maryland, and no one wanted to travel that far for the work. Further adding to Beckett's joy, Ryan Morales had backed the fuck up off of Eve a few months back. After he'd told her he needed some time, some space to breathe (which mainly seemed to mean he stopped just dropping by), Eve got an excited phone call from Midian. The cop had asked her out, and from the squealing Beckett had heard through the phone, Midian thought the guy was a catch. Cheers to her.

Of course fall came before anyone was ready. Blake and Livia began preparing Emme for the wonders of first grade, and Cole readied himself to offer endless patience and compassion to the troubled kids he knew he'd find in his class. Every day Kyle's secret grew a little bigger and more possible under her baggy shirts, and though Beckett's search for Nicholas continued to return very little, Eve's smile came out to play a bit more each weekend, and they learned to focus their attention on the things they could change: the people they could house, the troubled souls they could offer a different path.

As September began, Beckett announced—to anyone who would listen—that it had been the best summer of his life.

23

Air

Alison rubbed her large belly dry. The sonogram had required a sticky jelly.

The doctor seemed pleased as usual. "Development is spot on," he told her. "You're doing great work."

She smiled and resisted rolling her eyes. The most important thing she had to do was make sure the people around her thought she was amenable to this situation. After her appointments, she would go on and on about the miracle of birth to whomever was sitting with her that day — the nurse, the doctor, or the worst, Nicholas.

Today the doctor was going to hang around and run some blood tests — yet again. The man was truly obsessed. He excused himself from the room to make a phone call before they began, and as soon as he shut the door, she was up and had her hand cupped, closing her eyes to listen as best she could.

"Yes, sir. The twins are healthy. Yes. Of course."

The doctor paused and listened. "Well, these are your children as well, and in just three more months they'll be yours to hold. The girl is calm and seems almost happy. I think she's just happy to be pregnant. Of course. I'll send you the sonograms now. And a picture of her belly. Great. I'll be in touch."

Alison scurried over to the sonogram pictures, touching one for added effect. "So do we know?" She tried her best to look pleased as the doctor returned to the room.

"The genders?" After taking the pictures from her, the doctor used the back of his pen to point. "Fetus A is clearly a girl, and her… brother looks great as well."

"One of each. Flint will be so pleased." She watched his face when she said Flint's name.

The doctor sucked in his bottom lip and nodded — his tell for lying. He only did it when she asked something that compromised his sense of professionalism.

Then she hit him with her request while he felt guilty. "I'd love to go for a walk today."

"Well, Nicholas will be here soon. I don't want to make him wait." The doctor pulled out a camera and motioned for her to reveal her stomach again.

She turned to show him her profile and chomped down on her revulsion. Son of a bitch made her feel like a science project.

"It's better for the babies if I get exercise in fresh air," she added.

He nodded after he'd checked the pictures. "Okay. Get your shoes on, but I need to draw your blood as soon as we get back."

She tried not to whoop. The doctor was the only one who took her out. The nurse was too scared, and Nicholas was a creep. She got ready quickly, braiding her hair behind her.

"All right, missy, let's go. You know the rules: no running or yelling." He smiled and held the door.

Her hope soared. "Of course."

These strolls allowed her to see the house from the outside. It was remote. Super remote. But on the last walk she'd thought she heard a bit of traffic in the backyard, way off by the trees.

She took a deep breath and sped up a bit. It felt amazing to be out of that god-forsaken room. She could finally think clearly.

It had been nearly nine months since she'd been taken. Time was easy to keep track of with the close monitoring of the twins. Like a puzzle, she gathered pieces and tried to make them fit. As far as she could tell she was the only pregnant woman they were monitoring, and she was fairly certain she was alone in the house with her captors.

She had a deep sense that the babies in her belly were not related to her or Flint at all. It was the way the nurse acted, and the way the doctor had pontificated about all of his science. Plus, they never referred to her as the twins' mother. It almost seemed ingrained in them. Little bits of conversation and information she'd earned with her compliance and silence painted a fairly clear picture.

Fall was coming. She saw a few early leaves littering the dry ground of the side lawn. She listened for vehicles again, tuning out the doctor's voice as he went on about the beauty of the changing seasons. The steady white noise of a road close by was definitely there. She hadn't imagined it. When she escaped, she would run this way, straight through the woods as the crow flies.

After escaping, she didn't have any plans. The babies she carried meant a great deal to someone—someone evil. And they were her only protection. As soon as they could safely live outside her womb, she was as good as dead.

She surveyed the landscape once again: a slight hill, a small bump, and then woods. The back door looked like it had seen little use, and it might stay stuck shut if she tried to open it in a rush. It would be a plan B or C escape route at best. There was no garage, and her bedroom was on the second story.

"Why do I feel like you're not listening, Alison?" The doctor stopped walking.

"Sorry. I just get overwhelmed at being outside. I miss it. You were saying?" She nodded and continued their walk.

"I was telling you that with multiples, we have to really make sure our lines of communications are open. You have to tell me if you have any cramps, bleeding, or pains. This will be a delicate time."

He grabbed her arm quickly when she faked a stumble. He was an older man, but still had good reflexes. She had to escape when the doctor was in charge.

"Careful," he admonished. "It's time to go back inside." He kept his hand firmly on her arm as he guided her back to the front door.

Just then Nicholas pulled up in the long driveway too quickly. He was out of the car in an instant, barely having taken the time to stop the engine. "You have her out?"

"It's good for her and the babies." The doctor looked pale. "Please don't tell him. I'm really just trying to keep her healthy."

"Get your things and leave." His accent was clipped.

Alison hated when Nicholas had his eyes on her. He was a predator. Her motherly instinct made her want to cuddle her belly. She stood still, scarcely breathing as she waited, savoring the last moments of fresh air on her skin. The doctor was up and out in less than five minutes with not a parting a word, the blood tests forgotten.

"You're obviously interested in seeing the old doctor part ways with his head." Nicholas pointed to the door.

"I wanted to walk, not hurt anyone." She wanted to slap the smug look off his face.

As she walked up the stairs to her room, she wished he wasn't right behind her. As soon as the door to her room closed behind them, he pulled her by her neck against his chest. A surprised gasp passed from her lips.

The knife flashed before her quickly and was under her throat. "You will not ask that old man to take you out of here again. Do you understand?"

She kept trying to make a noise, but failed. He was aroused. With a knife to her throat he was sexual. It was sickening.

"As soon as you're done with these babies, you're mine. And don't think for a second I won't cut them out of you. I practiced on a few creatures growing up. I know how to do it."

Nicholas was the kind of human that made her believe in the devil. He moved the knife lower, outlining her breast with it before holding it to her stomach.

She played the only card she had. Her Oscar-worthy cry of pain would alert a neighbor if they had any. "I'm cramping! Jesus. I'm having a contraction. I know it."

He let her go and pointed at her while slipping the knife back into the holster he had at his hip. "You're lying."

"No, I think my water is breaking." She went to her knees and reached between her legs. "Oh, God. They're coming!"

Her hand was bone dry, but he was already on his phone, barking for the doctor to turn around and come back.

Fifteen minutes later, Nicholas stood at the foot of the bed while the doctor examined her. She waited to hear him confirm that she was indeed a liar.

"How'd you get that laceration?" The doctor pointed to her neck.

"Nicholas was threatening to kill me." She writhed a bit on the bed.

The doctor looked her in the eyes before he bit his bottom lip. "She's having early-term labor. Call the nurse. I'm hoping it will pass if we put her on fluids and keep her very still."

She almost cried with relief when she realized what he'd done.

The doctor stood, and although he was shorter than Nicholas, he presented his opinion with a regal demeanor. "Stress-induced early labor. You better pray to God that we're able to get this under control. Are you an animal, sir? Did it ever occur to you that putting a knife to her neck would endanger the babies? I'm going to have to call Vitullo myself and tell him we need a new caretaker." The doctor went for his phone.

The knife was out immediately. "You'll do no such thing. This is my detail. I can find your family in Belgium, don't you worry."

Alison began to moan and toss in the bed. "The babies. The babies. I think you better take me to the hospital. We need an NICU. Doctor, can they even make it this soon?"

"No, I'm sorry. They will likely not be viable at this stage." The doctor bit his lip again, slightly, as he spoke. "Our best bet is to keep you here. And keep you calm."

Nicholas snarled before putting the knife away, like a guard dog denied a steak. "I'll get the nurse." He stomped out of the room.

Alison met the doctor's eyes. He shook his head no. No, they shouldn't talk about the lie they'd entered into together.

She might have an ally after all.

Beckett surveyed the progress on the restoration of the school. The red tape involved with getting to this moment had been hilarious — ridiculously frustrating, but hilarious. There were meetings, zoning laws, certificates applied for. There were times Beckett had really doubted it would happen. And yet it was.

For two weeks now his crew had been had at work, tearing down anything that wouldn't work with the new design. Everything had to be up to code and fresh and clean. It would take a while.

Cole was there after school as usual, blueprint rolled out on a sawhorse while he spoke to Rocky. Beckett waved as he left, confident the two would continue to work well together. Both were quiet, powerful forces. Both of them set on the same goal had to equal success.

On his way home, he drove past a few of the houses they'd renovated and rented. The first stop was one of his favorites. Blake had known a couple who'd both lost their jobs and had three kids to support. The house was in a great school district, the neighborhood chock full of other kids. And after he'd gifted the kids a trampoline, their yard was instantly the best place on the block.

He waved to the mom, who sat on her porch watching the jumping beans throwing themselves around. She knew his cell and could call if she needed help. Right now, while the kids were in school she worked at the laundromat Beckett had purchased during the day, and her husband put in the afternoons and one late night a week. They paid one hundred dollars a month in rent, and Eve tripled the money and socked it away in a college fund for the kids.

The second renovated house Beckett passed was home for two male roommates. They'd met in rehab and seemed to be good for each other. Right now they were completing their landscaping, with the hopes of moving on to more landscaping projects together. Hard, manual work was what they needed.

The last item of business was at a house not owned by Beckett. Yet it still seemed to be a bit of a project. A few months back he'd had Eve drop by to talk with the homeowner about the treatment of a dog in the yard, which had been chained to a tree for most of its life. They'd had a very enlightening conversation. And since then, all his previous drive-bys had been good. The dog liked to lie on the back of the couch in the living room, so Beckett could see he was inside and happy.

But tonight the dog was out on a chain again. Beckett pulled into the drive and was half out of the car when the homeowner came running out the side door.

"I'm so sorry! My new girlfriend is allergic to the dog. I had to put him somewhere."

Beckett just stood there shaking his head.

"No? No to the girlfriend?" The man unclipped the dog, who jumped around happily. He lifted his eyebrows. "What if the dog's only out when she's here, and I'll make sure she only stays a few hours at a time?"

Beckett cracked his neck one way, then the other.

"I'll break up with her. Right." He pulled out his phone and told his girlfriend he was done.

Beckett headed back to his car.

"I'm sorry!" the man called. "I'll never have sex again. Just me and the dog. We're best friends. Please don't send that blond woman back over!" He rushed the dog inside.

If only all Beckett's issues could be solved that quickly. Next he drove over to the house where Spider was staying, because he supposedly had an update. Beckett parked on the lawn because fuck driveways and opened the door without knocking. Spider was at his computer.

"Whatcha got for me?" Beckett asked.

Spider looked up briefly, unfazed by Beckett's entrance. "Well, I accessed another batch of Nicholas footage—this one more recent than Dr. Hartt but stored in a totally different location. I think they must have reorganized their servers after the fire and maybe since some of their staff was leaving and—"

Beckett cleared his throat.

"Sorry." Spider got to the point. "It's yet another woman, and since we had luck with hospital employees before, I started there this time. This doctor is a specialist in private practice—or at least she was—but she had privileges at Poughkeepsie General. And like everyone else who's had a turn in Nicholas's room lately, she was at the hospital the night of Eve's crash."

Spider paused, seeming to wait for Beckett to say something. When only silence ensued, he shrugged and continued. "Her specialty? Fertility. Or else it used to be. She got married, then divorced, and was living on her own. Somewhere in there she left her fertility practice, so I followed her trail. These days she's been in real estate, rather than baby-making, but turns out she left the firm she worked for without so much as a two-weeks' notice a little over nine months ago. She hasn't been heard from since—no parents looking for her because they're both dead. And no kids. Apparently one of her friends filed a missing person's, but not much came of it. There was nothing to go on. They were totally wasted the last time they were together, so her story was a little hazy."

Beckett looked at the image on Spider's screen. It was now a key component of his worst nightmare: another sign that Rodolfo had possibly been telling the truth. "Okay," he finally said. "I want you to look at fertility clinics in and out of the country with any connection to that woman — in the timeframe of Eve's accident and now. Tell me if you find anything out of the ordinary. And I need to talk to Eve."

His mind raced as he went back out to his car. What could have happened that would benefit Rodolfo, even beyond the grave? Had Eve had some sort of treatment and never told him? Did she even know? He did not look forward to this conversation. Not one bit.

24

ĮПSAПE

After more than a year back in town, and despite all the tragedies that had happened since, Eve realized one day that she'd found a bit of peace in Poughkeepsie. With Beckett by her side, she found even pain easier to bear. And partnering with him to rehab the rougher parts of Poughkeepsie had been surprisingly satisfying. She hadn't killed anyone in…God, she didn't even remember. Convincing and attitude adjustment was still in her repertoire, but there had been less blood.

She'd spent this sunny Saturday afternoon checking progress on another of the soon-to-be rentals and had been pleased with the team's progress. Didn't even have to raise her voice. Following Beckett's lead, they really were doing things a new way—a way she'd doubted she could ever exist.

But she was still haunted by the image of Nicholas rolling the barrel out of the interrogation room, which is why she answered the call from Ryan on practically the first ring as she got into the Audi. He'd been a whole lot easier to deal with since he started dating Midian about five months ago, and though that meant she spent a lot less time with her friend, it was worth it to see him happy and moving forward. Plus, she loved how Midian teased the ever-living fuck out of him. He needed someone with sharp wit and a sense of humor.

"Yes?" She waited, but didn't hear her friend's fast-paced chatter in the background.

"So I got a hit on your dad's tracker."

"You got a hit on the tracker."

"Yeah, I found where it was being traced from. Well, actually the guy who owes me a favor did. Anyway, I was about to go check the place out, and I want to do it alone. I don't want to involve you. But now I'm calling your crazy ass. Because I want you to have peace." He sighed.

Despite his speech all those months ago about her being on the outside and him having to take the shot, he had still been finding ways of touching base with her. Midian must have been working on his soft side.

"Let's bounce," she told him. "You want me to pick you up?"

"Yeah. You better. My truck isn't really awesome camouflage right now."

"Trish?"

"Yup. This time involved some neon wallpaper and quotes about men's failures."

"I'll be there in ten."

She armed herself and was on her way over in four minutes. When she arrived, Ryan met her in the parking lot. A blue tarp covered what had to be his truck.

"That bad?"

"Worse. She's insane. Creative, but insane." Ryan smiled as he got into the car.

He smelled good and looked amazing—happy, and without any secret pining for her.

"How far away?" she asked.

"You got a full tank? About two hours. New Jersey." He waggled his eyebrows, then looked at his phone and responded to a text. When he saw her watching he smiled. "She's at her cousin's birthday. Figures."

"Family means the world to her." Eve navigated the back roads before merging onto the thruway.

"Yup. I've noticed that. Just take this until we get to Twenty west. Then we sit on that for a while." He put his phone away. "I have some ground rules: You cannot go in. You cannot initiate contact if we see Nicholas. My guy says this place hasn't shown movement or body heat for the last three days."

"That's some friend." She put on the cruise control as soon as she got up to speed.

"That's why I took the chip to him. He's got mad access to a lot of bullshit, but this kind of stuff takes a load of time."

"You clearly cashed in a large favor. I appreciate it. But there's no way in hell I'm staying in the car." She adjusted her rearview mirror.

"I figured as much."

Her phone buzzed. When she took it out to read the text, Ryan swiped it.

"No texting and driving. Taylor wants to know where you are. He was expecting you home. Can I tell him we're naked together?"

"Go ahead. I'd love to see what Midian does to your testicles in return. And have no doubt, that chick finds out about *everything*." She took her phone from his hand. "I'll leave it be for a few. He'll be okay." She changed lanes to go around a slower driver. "So what else do I need to know, Morales?"

"Well, as you know, it's likely this guy works for Vitullo. By crawling into the enemy's nest, we might be poking the hive."

Eve drove faster. "I've been waiting to poke the hive for quite some time now," she said.

They made the two-hour drive in ninety minutes. They parked down the street and held hands like lovers on a stroll as they ambled past the house—a very tidy small rambler. There were lights on inside.

"They're on a timer," Ryan commented as they passed. "So my guy says, anyway. The alarm will be disabled. Can you still pick a lock or should I?"

"Do all your ex-girlfriends wear a straightjacket for fun?"

"That's low." He handed her the slim tools she'd need as they crossed the street and followed her to the back door.

She went in quickly, almost as fast as if she'd had a key. And as promised, the alarm was disabled. Ryan set down a small device that emitted a high-pitched noise.

"Disrupts any radio frequencies and webcams," he explained.

"Good enough for me." Eve began sweeping the place, taking pictures of anything out of the ordinary as Ryan headed down the hall. The inhabitant, presumably Nicholas, was obviously a neat freak.

"Always in the bedroom. Fucking freak." Ryan's voice sounded disgusted from farther back in the house.

When she entered the room, he'd found a false cover on the footboard of the bed. He had on rubber gloves and was moving the items inside around with a pen. They mostly looked like scraps of fabric with probably dried blood on them. Souvenirs. Trophies.

Eve felt her world implode as she saw her father's watch among the treasures. Without thinking, she reached for it. Ryan went to stop her, but pulled back when she looked him in the eyes.

She pulled out the watch and held it up. Inscribed on the back was her message to him: *Love always, Your Girl.* She held it to her chest, close to her heart.

Ryan photographed the remaining items and put them all back where he'd gotten them. "I'll have the place buttoned down tonight, and after we get a warrant, we'll get forensics in to find out what we're looking at here."

Eve saw that the ridge that held the glass in place over the watch's face had a deep brown stain in it. She put the watch on and silently dared Ryan to tell her to take it off.

He shook his head. "You keep that. That's okay."

It wasn't okay, but she got that he was breaking a rule for her now. Waiting in the entry, she watched him search the rest of the apartment, which was neat and together. That terrified her even more. Only a mind this set on organization could be so well-versed in torture. Experiencing that first hand was the last thing she and her father had in common. This had to be Nicholas. She'd felt his particular talent before. Her right hand shook a bit. It might be forever impossible to think of her father without shuddering as she remembered his end.

"I need some air." She left the way they'd come in and went to the front porch. Stupid. She was making a spectacle of herself, or at least that's how it felt.

The mailbox was nailed to the house by the front door. She lifted the lid and saw junk mail. After sorting through it quickly, noting that it was all addressed to Nicholas Rodgers or Occupant, she was about to set it back inside when an envelope fell out from between the flyers. It was from the DMV. She quickly folded it over twice and stuck it in the back pocket of her jeans.

Just then Ryan signaled to her from the shrubs between this property and the next. "You okay?" He gave her a harsh look.

"No." But she left the porch to take his arm, and they continued their evening as lovers on a stroll.

"We'll get information from this place," he told her as they returned to the car. "I'm sure of it."

Nodding, she unlocked the doors, but she was quiet all the way home. She dropped Ryan off without so much as a good-bye.

By the time she got to her house she had a text from him:

I'm going to need that watch after all.
I'll make sure you get it back.

Sitting in the car in the driveway, she typed back:.

Why

Sent the locals there to watch the house,
and they recognized the address.
4-alarm fire in progress.
It's all going to be gone.

I'll bag this in a zip
and get it to you tomorrow.

Keep it clean. It's our only chance now.

K

She walked slowly up to the house, but Beckett opened the door before she could get her key in. G stood next to him, barking his butt off. She moved past them both and put the watch as carefully as she could into a Ziploc bag. After handing the bag to Beckett, she reached down and picked up G. He finally settled after licking her face.

"Where'd you get this?" Beckett asked.

She told him the story and then asked what she had to: "Was that one you?"

"The house? No. We haven't had need for a burn in over a month. Someone was either onto you or it was a wild coincidence." He set the bag down and pulled her and his dog to his chest. "The pictures will be inadmissible, and probably this too. But maybe it will be enough to help them give some people closure."

"What is it?" Eve felt like he wasn't telling her something.

"Nothing. I just hate that you went without me," he said. "Take me next time. I'm worth shit, you know." He kissed her lips.

She nodded. The envelope in her back pocket felt like it was screaming at her.

"Let's go upstairs. You want a shower?" he asked as he took G out of her hands. He dug out a chew bone for him and handed her the bagged watch before they all went up.

The pants went in the laundry with all of her other clothes as she let Beckett's hands do their best to take her pain away. After the shower and the inevitable sex, plus a late-night dash to the kitchen for sandwiches, she followed him into bed, but couldn't sleep.

"Why you tossing around so damn much, baby? You need to talk?" Beckett propped up on his elbow.

His chest was rippled with the muscles that kept his heart safe, and gunshot wounds testifying to his lifestyle. She got out of bed and fished the envelope out of her pants.

"You got a bill for that service, killer?" Beckett sat up completely, running a hand over his face.

She clicked on the lamp by the bed and sat crisscross on the comforter. "I was going to handle this on my own. But I want to tell you."

She opened the envelope and looked at the contents before passing it to Beckett. "I got this out of Nicholas's house before it burned down. Actually, it was in his mailbox."

"So it's a registration expiration reminder in a different name. This could be helpful." Beckett nodded. "Give me a few." He left the room and trotted downstairs.

Eve twisted the blanket in her hand, wondering if this had been the right move. She'd just laid down when he was in front of her again. "I got Spider on this," he promised. "He'll work all night. For now, let's try to get some rest, okay?"

She nodded, reluctantly, and focused her eyes on the watch in the Ziploc bag as she waited for sleep to come.

Though Eve felt like she'd laid awake all night, she must have dozed, because now Beckett was shaking her awake.

"You wanna get in the car?" he asked. "Spider sent a lead on someone who might have more information."

"Did he find Nicholas?"

"Not yet, but he's running a digital footprint on the car registered to Nicholas's other name. He thinks he can triangulate the car's GPS with Google Earth and satellite information and to come up with a pattern of its regular locations. But he had no estimate as to how long that might take, so this seems like our best bet in the meantime."

"Yeah. Let's go." This felt like a step in the right direction. She ran her fingers over her father's watch on the nightstand. She'd get it to Ryan as soon as she got back.

25

CRAPPY

Rodolfo didn't like the safe house. Virginia was such a crappy little state. He missed his luxuries, the things he had earned. Maintaining the illusion of being dead for nearly nine months was tiresome. What good was a life without his favorite chair? And now Nicholas stood in front of him, fuming and interrupting his reading.

"My house burned down last night. Why would you do that to me?" The man was spitting, he was so angry. Rodolfo had never seen him this off kilter.

"We did what had to be done," he explained calmly. "Someone went to your property last night."

"That's impossible. I have it alarmed and wired." He ran his hand through his messy hair.

Nicholas had never been askew before, even after he'd killed people.

"Well, like I always say, newfangled stuff doesn't trump a good old-fashioned pair of eyes living in the house across the street. Mrs. Rio has lived in that house for over forty years. She knows when something's not right." Rodolfo squeezed his hand exerciser.

"My things were there. *My things*." Nicholas's tone was bordering on disrespectful. "And if you weren't so busy hiding and letting Taylor give it to you up the ass, maybe it would all still be there."

Rodolfo stopped squeezing his hand. "Mind yourself and your place."

Nicholas tried to fix his hair. "I apologize. It's just that the reason I can be so good at what I do was in that house."

"Do I need to replace you? Is this a weakness?"

"No. Nothing like that."

"Tell me about my children then. Do you have pictures?"

Nicholas paced a bit before producing the envelope. "Here's the latest sonogram. One girl. One boy, as you know. Healthy."

Rodolfo reached out with his bad hand on purpose, forcing himself to use it even though it took twice as long. The gratification was worth it. He touched the children's profiles. Beautiful. They would have their mother's nose.

"And the host?" he asked. He couldn't take his eyes off of his offspring, who looked more like people than ever before.

"A bit restless. We're having her take it easy." Nicholas sat down on the loveseat.

"Restless how?" He finally shuffled to the last picture, in which the host woman stood with her shirt up, her belly distended with children. His genetically superior children.

"She wants to go for walks. I told her it wasn't a great idea, and she went into a bit of distress. Luckily I was able to get the doctor there in time. She's settled now." Nicholas crossed his ankles, seeming to get a hold of himself.

"That's best. It's still too early for them to enter the world. Every day is important *in utero*. Good work, Nicholas." He set the pictures down and picked up his exerciser again.

"So do you have a job for me?" Nicholas asked. "Is it time to move on Taylor? Or are we readying more hosts? I figured you might want to get started with some more eggs." He began tapping one foot.

"I'd like to wait," Rodolfo countered. "Let's get these two into existence first. But thank you for your exuberance." He didn't care for this side of his man. "As far as Taylor, I want him all puffed up with his own success. He thinks I'm dead, and as far as I'm concerned, that keeps my children safer. Why else would I stay in this ridiculously under-appointed safe house?"

"He has Primo. Doesn't that count for anything?" Nicolas seemed to want to call some of the shots.

"How are you so certain I'm not letting him keep Primo for my own purposes? Have you been out of the loop so long you need an adjustment?" Rodolfo pursed his lips.

"It's all fine. Sir, you know I trust and respect your decisions. I know how important the children are to you. Everything will work out." Nicholas's foot stopped tapping. "Anything else, sir?"

Rodolfo knew the man needed a release. "Actually, there's a friend who's been putting up missing posters for that fertility doctor who was so helpful to us a while back. It would good if she stopped doing that, don't you think?"

Nicholas took a quick inhale before his breathy response. "Yes, sir."

It felt like an almost sexual exchange; it clearly gave the man so much pleasure.

"She needs to stop doing this permanently?" Nicholas asked, his eyes growing vacant.

"Yes. That would be best," Rodolfo said. "And soon."

Nicholas stood, not waiting to be dismissed.

Rodolfo had to put up his good hand to stop him. "And please see Vin on the way out. We have a new safe house that is to be yours in the interim while you find a new home. I know you like to have your own space."

"Thank you, Mr. Vitullo. You are too kind. Thank you so much. Her name?"

Rodolfo dragged an envelope out from under the book he'd been reading. "It's all here."

Nicholas put the envelope to his nose and inhaled like it was an expensive wine. "Thank you so much, sir."

Eve and Beckett were in Virginia before lunch on what should have been a lazy Sunday. She was anxious to meet the woman Beckett, via Spider, claimed might have information on Nicholas' current whereabouts. He'd explained that this woman's friend had gone missing a while back and seemed to have come to a similar fate as her father, probably by the same evil hands. Treats and Spider had provided them with an exact location, and they pulled into the driveway of the house without the benefit of its occupant having a warning.

Eve led the charge from the vehicle and knocked on the door. It took three rounds of knocking before it finally cracked open. "Hi. You were a friend of Sonia Kore?" she asked politely when a face appeared.

"Was? I am. I *am* a friend of Sonia's. Unless you know something I don't."

"According to your posters, she was wearing a yellow dress the night she went missing. Is that correct?" Eve pulled out her phone and brought up the picture Ryan had sent her of the shard of dress he'd seen at Nicholas's place.

"Are you with the police department?" The friend pulled her robe closer and gave Eve a skeptical once over.

"No. I've recently lost someone. And I think my someone and your someone might have had the same killer." Eve showed the woman the picture. She knew her name was Carly Logan, but didn't want to freak her out by using it.

Carly peered at it before shaking her head. "I need to get my glasses. Give me a second." She shut the door for a moment before opening it again, this time wearing glasses.

As Carly took a moment to decide if the bloodstained yellow dress piece was possibly Sonia's, a glint of metal caught Eve's eye. She focused on the window above the kitchen sink, visible off to the left, and then the entire window shattered.

Eve pushed the woman to the ground and drew her weapon in one motion, going low. She knew Beckett would be circling around back. She tried to get a bead on where the attack had come from. She looked at Carly's head and saw a laser dot right at the nosepiece of her reading glasses. She took a blind shot with her gun pointed in what seemed to be the general direction of the attacker.

The dot fell away just as Carly got over her shock enough to start screaming. Eve shook her head no, but the woman was in a panic. She jabbed the woman in the windpipe just hard enough to quiet her. Carly's eyes bugged out.

Eve pulled her hard by the arm into the hall, where there were no windows. She whispered quickly, "That's the man who killed Sonia. You're supposed to be next. But stay quiet, and you'll stay alive."

The woman nodded. Eve pointed to the floor, and Carly crouched.

Eve kept her gun leveled at the doorframe as a man's silhouette took shape. She aimed for the neck before she recognized Beckett.

"He ran," Beckett told her. "She okay?"

Eve nodded and helped Carly off the floor.

The woman had to clear her throat a few times before she could speak. "That was Sonia's dress," she confirmed. "At least it was the same type she was wearing. I recognize the little bit of lace she added to make the cap sleeves. I can't imagine many people do that to a store-bought dress. Does that mean…what you said? Is she dead?"

Eve looked away, and Beckett stepped up. "I'm pretty close to positive she was killed," he told her. "I'm so very sorry."

Carly lost her shit, right there in the hallway. "I knew she took too long. But there was a cute guy, and he was winking at me. I shouldn't have let her go alone. Oh, God. And now he wants to kill me? Oh no."

She sat down again on the floor, sobbing.

Eve headed out the door to see if she could track what seemed to be Nicholas trying to tidy up his messes. She could hear Beckett speaking soothing words to the distraught woman as she left.

Once outside, Eve dialed Ryan.

"'Sup?"

"You got a second?"

"Yes. I'm taking Midian on a picnic today, but I don't have to leave for, like, eight minutes."

"I need you to call the police station in Fallom, Virginia, and tell them we're bringing in a woman named Carly Logan who needs to be protected. Can you do that? Is there, like, some courtesy bullshit you can do without explaining much?"

"I can try. When you bringing her by?"

"Actually, can you have them pick her up on Route 35? By the Wawa? We have to follow Nicholas. He just tried to kill this chick."

Beckett widened his eyes at her as he walked Carly to the Challenger.

"Sure," Ryan said. "I'll call you right back."

Eve widened her eyes back at him as she put away her phone. Message received. Try not to freak out the freaking-out girl. She followed them to the car.

Beckett checked his texts while she told him to head for the Wawa they'd passed earlier and answered her ringing phone. He took off like a drag racer, and Carly gasped from the back, still in her pajamas and robe.

"What's going on down there?" Ryan was on high alert.

"We're getting closer to that reunion with Nicholas. Listen, I gotta go."

"Eve." He sounded serious. She expected the "be careful" warning.

"I have to tell you something. It's classified, and I can't tell you how I know either." He sounded reluctant.

"Just a minute," she told him.

The Wawa convenience store was only a three-minute drive away, and a police cruiser was already there when they arrived. The cop must have been gassing up or getting donuts, whatever. Beckett pulled around to the side and sent Carly through the doors so she would meet up with the cops on the other side of the store. She promised not mention them or anything that had happened that morning, though whether she'd keep her word only time would tell. Beckett told her to say a domestic dispute was the reason she needed protection.

"Okay, spit it out, Morales," Eve commanded once the woman had left the car.

"Well, again, this is really not something I'm at liberty to share."

Beckett looked at his texts again and shook his head. "We got something from the car info Spider was tracking. Two places that vehicle has been quite a bit."

"Eve, I'm sorry, but Rodolfo is still alive. The last intel we had put him in a safe house in Virginia. Tell me where you are. We need to know, if you've spotted Nicholas."

Are you fucking kidding me? "Do you know the address?" she asked.

"No, I don't."

"Thanks for your help. Tell Midian I said hi." Eve hung up and sent Ryan's next three calls to her voice mail.

He would probably start tracking her cell phone immediately. She sighed and threw it out the window, watching it smash in the rearview window. The sun made it almost difficult to watch.

"Rodolfo is alive—so says the Poughkeepsie Police department." She turned to her husband.

"I find that pretty fucking hard to believe, being that I lit his ass on fire," Beckett countered.

"Did you, though? Did you really light *him* on fire?"

"No. I wanted him to see it coming. So I guess there's a wild chance in hell that someone got him out. I doubt it, though. My guys were all over that old turd's house."

"Well, okay. I guess we'll know if we see him. Anyway, you have two places for Nicholas? Let me see." After taking his phone from him, she scrolled through the addresses and information Spider had sent. "He can't determine which one Nicholas has spent more time at yet," she reported. "Still working on it." She looked at the two addresses on a map. One seemed more remote than the other. "I think we should assume Rodolfo is at one of these spots and Nicholas at the other. Eenie meenie?"

Beckett thought for a few before asking her to navigate to the one close to the main road.

"I would go for the other," she said. "Why this one?" She scrolled through the map as Beckett put the pedal to the floor, letting the Challenger's engine have its head.

"Gut feeling. We go there."

Alison adjusted her gown and watched the doctor as he recorded the heart rates in the babies' chart.

"How are they?" she asked.

He gave her a grandfatherly smile. "Beautiful. You're doing a great job." As he turned he added, mostly to himself, "It's always amazing to see a theory come to fruition. We're almost there!"

Alison pounced. "The surrogate theory? That's been around for years. No big deal, right?"

The doctor put down his clipboard and helped her sit up in the bed. "Well, actually, it's more than that in this case. You're quite an amazing specimen and the direct result of tremendously cutting-edge fertility science."

"I figured as much," Alison said, nodding. "You certainly seem like you're meant for more than monitoring only one lady's twins." She hoped the praise would keep him talking.

"You're not 'only' anything. You were chosen from a very wide pool of women because you're a very close match to the original ovary tissue." He clamped his lips shut after that.

"I'm fascinated. Please, tell me more." She smiled, working to make herself the most non-threatening person to share information with.

And with that, he went professor on her, seeming to relish telling someone what miracles he'd worked. "Well, the ovarian tissue was taken from a young woman who lost her pregnancy in an accident and was about to lose her uterus. A forward-thinking specialist was called in, and the father of the woman was open to trying anything to preserve his daughter's fertility. So the tissue was cryogenically preserved and kept for years. In my home country I've been working on this sort of procedure — getting frozen ovarian tissue to begin maturing eggs again — and an investor here in the U.S. contacted me last year. When I received the opportunity to not only move into a human trial, but fertilize, implant, and track the results, I knew it would be a tremendous experience. I had to come."

He shook his head at the magnitude of the whole thing. "I don't mind telling you that developing eggs from this girl's ovarian tissue was quite a chore. To wind up with seven viable eggs is mind-blowing. Such a huge moment. And look at you! Twins. Healthy twins. The findings here can help millions of women." He flipped through his notes and consulted his iPad, a genius lost in his own thoughts.

"So let me get this straight," Alison cut in. "You harvested eggs? From someone else's ovarian tissue? So these babies aren't mine. And I'm guessing not related to Flint either?" Anger raised her blood pressure, and the monitor on her fingertip recorded the spike.

"Whoa. Take a few deep breaths." The doctor took both her wrists in his hands and checked her pupils.

"No, I will not. Answer me. Are these babies even related to me?"

"Technically, they are not biologically related, but you are their home. They need you, and you are creating life. It's incredibly important."

"To who? Vitullo? I've heard you mention his name." She yanked her wrists from the doctor's grasp.

"Yes," said the doctor, looking decidedly nervous now. "He's the man funding this study, allowing my research to go forward." He crossed his arms on his chest, watching her.

"You took me from my life, from my husband. Where is my husband anyway? Wait, don't tell me — they killed him. Someone killed him. And I'm next. You know it, and still you stand here, doing their bidding. What kind of doctor are you? I thought you were supposed to do no harm."

"That phrase is actually a myth, though its meaning is implied." The doctor couldn't seem to stop himself from offering more of his knowledge.

"You know what I mean," Alison snapped. "And I know you care, at least a little. You lied to protect me from Nicholas just last week. Or was it to keep your precious research safe? What are you? How can you see value in helping millions of women yet fail to see that you can save the one in front of you?" She bit the inside of her cheeks, not wanting to cry but losing the battle.

"How about a walk? Would you like to take a walk?" The doctor went to the door.

"Those aren't allowed." She wiped the tears from her cheeks.

"No, they aren't. But let's go." He opened her door for her.

She knew he was trying to give her something — anything to make up for the fact that he was a mad scientist, and she was his lab rat. She went with him anyway, because the air sounded good.

These babies weren't even hers. Weren't even Flint's. She wrapped her arms around her middle, and the twins kicked in response. Whose babies were these going to be? And for what purpose? Who was going to raise them? Would they live in a room like she had, desperate for a breath of fresh air?

She had to get out of here. Get these babies out of here. Walking slowly across the backyard, Alison could once again pick out the car noise from the road, but it seemed clearer than last time, maybe because they walked in silence. It was on her right, for sure. Through the woods.

"Do you have children?" she asked the doctor.

"No. Never got the chance. I had prostate cancer when I was younger." He touched her elbow.

"Do you at least acknowledge that this is wrong? Or are you too involved in the science of it?" She pulled her elbow away.

"I was tempted by being granted a human trial so quickly. Usually there are so many hoops to jump through. You're the first human subject, and the first not related in any way to the ovarian tissue." He finally looked at her and seemed to really see her, not just check her pupils for once. "But this is too much pain," he added, looking down. "It's wrong."

Her heart quickened, and she felt almost afraid.

"I will help you. I will help you get out of here." His nostrils flared and his accent thickened with the adrenaline boost he too must have been feeling.

Alison began to look around, but they both stopped still when they heard a car tearing up the gravel in the driveway.

"It's him," she gasped, no doubt stating the obvious. "He must be angry we went outside. But how would he know?"

"The nurse might have texted him. Let's just stay here for a minute." The doctor took her hands. "Breathe in, and slowly breathe out."

A roar from came from inside the house, followed by stomping, and then the little-used back door flung open. "What the fuck do you think you're doing?"

Nicholas's eyes were wild, and he held his upper arm, blood seeping out around his fingers and staining his white dress shirt.

"She seemed to be having some pregnancy-related asthma, and in lieu of an inhaler, I wanted the patient to take a more natural course of action first. It appears you have a wound that needs to be attended. Shall we?"

"Yes. Get in here and bring her." Nicholas stepped backward, blood dripping from the crook of his elbow.

"She needs to remain out here for a few more minutes until I'm happy with her respirations. The nurse will stay with her. Let's get you up to Alison's room. That's where I have what we need to examine that wound."

Nicholas shouted for the nurse.

Alison stood frozen as the doctor turned to face her and mouthed his true intentions: "Run." He looked pointedly in the direction of the car noise.

As the doctor and the nurse passed each other in the doorway, he grasped the nurse's arm. "Do you have an inhaler for Alison? Make sure you have that; we don't want her in distress, in case the fresh air isn't enough. It's in the sitting room downstairs."

As soon as everyone disappeared from sight, Alison tried to run as best she could, straight for the woods.

26

BE CAREFUL

Beckett was relieved that Eve hadn't scrolled through his other messages before handing the phone back. He hadn't told her about the possibilities, like the fact that her father might have taken something from her. Or the possibility that he knew she had frozen her chances at having a future without mentioning it to him.

Nicholas bouncing between two houses was just the beginning. Beckett had taken a call from Treats while Eve was talking to Carly, and a hunch he'd had worked out in the worst possible way. Treats had done an investigation on recently missing women to see if any were of childbearing age and perhaps under the care of a fertility doctor.

He'd confirmed one who fit the profile—an Alison Wexford. She was last seen driving to her fertility appointment with her husband almost nine months ago, and neither of them had been heard from since. Add that up with the old bastard's taunting words, and Beckett began to fear Rodolfo might have found a way to Frankenstein together a baby with his and Eve's DNA. It made him sick to his stomach to even imagine it.

But if some woman were carrying Eve's child, his tactical brain told him she'd be near a main road and close to a hospital in case things went wrong—hence his choice of address to visit first. As they neared the location, Beckett pulled over on the road running behind it, and they decided to go in on foot through the woods at the back of the house.

"Be ready," he told Eve as the house came into view. "Make sure to confirm before the kill. We might have friendlies."

Just as the words left his mouth, they heard pops of gunfire in the distance—first one, and after a moment, another.

Eve looked around wildly at the woods before announcing, "Call nine-one-one now. I'm not letting anyone die who doesn't have to."

"But we don't even know—" Beckett began.

"Doesn't matter," she said firmly. "Think of Mouse, think of Livia pounding Blake's chest in the forest. They needed help sooner."

Beckett nodded silently, handed her his phone, and waited as she made the call. Once she nodded, they proceeded steadily, but quietly, diving for cover when the sounds of someone moving hurriedly through the foliage drew near. They both prepared their weapons.

Beckett took a quick look, and Eve copied him from behind her tree. A woman came into view, and she seemed to be running for her life. Beckett took a step out and waved his hands to catch her attention.

Another gunshot rang out, and the woman fell. Eve focused on the echo, and Beckett followed her eyes to see Nicholas leaping over a fallen tree trunk. He had a snow-white bandage half-wrapped around his upper arm. It snagged a small tree and stopped his forward motion for a moment.

While he was distracted, Beckett dove toward the woman and covered her with his body, which put him in the worst position ever. Eve stepped out from behind her tree and leveled her pistol at Nicholas. She shouted so he'd look at her. But he stood where he was and trained his gun on Beckett. She shouted again and Nicholas looked her way, a horrifying smile blooming on his face. Eve took her shot and was off in Beckett's direction before Nicholas hit the forest floor.

Beckett sat up to assess the woman, who was heavily pregnant. "Are there more coming?" He nodded toward the house while putting pressure on the woman's chest.

"Not that I see. I'll go check on the house."

"No, stay here. I'll go." Beckett and Eve swapped places.

Beckett walked toward the house, past Nicholas, silently hating even his dead body. Eve's bullet had gone in right between his eyes. He hoped it brought Eve a measure of peace.

Up at the house, the backdoor was agape, and Beckett proceeded carefully, noting a woman shot execution style in the living room, and upstairs, in a surprisingly complete hospital room setup, an older man dead as well.

He'd picked up a pile of folders and an iPad before the gravel in the driveway announced an incoming vehicle with pops and crunches. He saw four men getting out of a black Suburban just before he slipped out the back door, and he could hear sirens in the distance. He jogged the rest of the way back out to where Eve waited with the injured woman, and together they carried her out to the Challenger, settling her into the backseat.

"They had me. They kept me. These babies...not mine." Alison's eyes rolled in her head.

Beckett put the files and iPad in the glove box and jogged back out to the road to flag down the ambulance.

The EMTs were efficient and calm, but it was serious for Alison. As serious as it gets.

"She said babies, so maybe it's twins she's carrying," Eve told Beckett as he pulled her aside.

"Stay with her, and no matter what, the babies are important," he said.

Eve made a face. "So is she."

"I know. I just...keep track of everything." Beckett pushed her toward the departing gurney. "You're her cousin as of right now."

"Where are you going?" She slipped some of her more obvious weapons to him. "The second address? I'm coming."

"No. She's more important. I'll tell you later. I promise." Beckett pointed at the ambulance before getting into the driver's seat.

Eve climbed in to the emergency vehicle and gave him one last glance. *Be careful.* She didn't need to say it. He felt it.

Ryan held still as Midian wiped her lipstick off his cheek and from around his lips. This was among the best post-picnic desserts of all time.

"I'm leaving it on your dick though." She smiled. "Marking my territory and all."

"It's all yours anytime you want it, kitten." Ryan pushed her thick hair behind her ear. He loved when it peeked out and he could see the lobe. He leaned in and nibbled it while she purred. When she was really excited, she spoke Spanish, and it killed him in the very best way.

"Come here." He grabbed her and pulled her onto his lap. They'd parked along the river, the truck hidden from view by the thick underbrush.

"Again? *Sabes? Hay una razón por la que eres mi número uno. Eres un dios del sexo. Ahora, muéstrame el cielo.*" She tossed her hair, and it covered the steering wheel.

"Tell me what that means." Ryan touched her lips as she translated.

"You know? There's a reason you're my number one. You're a sex god. Now, show me heaven." She smiled against his fingers. "Seriously, considering your heritage you should be fluent."

"As long as you give the lessons naked, I will be." Ryan freed himself, already tinted to match her lips, and it was easy to find her under her skirt. Soon they were rocking the truck and fogging the windows. She was so much woman. Her curves called to his hands, her tan skin and his complementing each other. They laughed a few times when they set off his horn, but they still finished within strokes of each other.

He helped her tuck her delicious breasts back into her dress, then challenged himself to kiss her lipstick completely off. Eventually she held his happy face, smiling.

He touched the scar on her forearm, rendered almost invisible by the tattoo there:

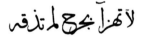

"When will you tell me what this means?" He brushed her hair away from her face.

"When you earn it." She adjusted herself to sit on his lap instead of straddling it. She drew a heart with the tip of her finger in the fog on the window.

He put his initials above the heart and hers below. "I'll earn it again right now if you're ready to go." He tickled her until she smacked him.

"All right, fine. It says 'Do not mock a wound you haven't tested.' It's Arabic." She shrugged.

He noted the location on her forearm and raised his eyebrow in concern. He'd seen cuts like that before.

"No. Not like that. I'm a fighter, baby." She touched the scar, seeming to remember for a moment. "It's from when I was in high school."

He held his breath a little. Waiting.

"We were on a school trip," she began. "I was fifteen and our bus was first on the scene of an accident. A car was nearly totally crushed. Everyone was trying to help. The three adults had already passed, but there was a baby. She was less than a year old. No one could figure out how to get her out, but I broke the glass and got her. And that's when I cut myself."

He kissed her. "That's amazing. You're amazing. Why wouldn't you be screaming that from the rooftops? You're a hero."

She sighed. "I still talk to the little girl's grandmother from time to time. It was the worst day of her life. The whole course of her future changed, even though she doesn't remember it. It was an honor to pull her out."

Ryan shook his head. "You are exceptional."

She rolled her eyes. "You just like the boobs."

"Those are wonderful. We both know that. But you, you're something else."

They spent far too much time laughing and making out, and only Ryan's police training gave him the presence of mind to look for his phone when it started to buzz.

Midian found it on the floor mat and read the text. "It's Eve," she reported. "She's using Beckett's phone. Says she might need a cop's help."

"Ahh…okay…That's all it says?" Ryan asked, praying silently that Midian wouldn't read anything into this.

"Yep. But you should text her back. If she's asking for help, she likely needs it."

"Thanks, baby. I know you're right," Ryan said, in awe of her all over again. He typed for a moment, and almost instantly, Eve responded. "Ahh, this could be a mess…" he said as he read.

"Come on, get me home," Midian said. "I still have to iron my bullshit for work tomorrow, anyway."

Ryan reluctantly drove back to the center of Poughkeepsie where Midian shared an apartment with her sister. "I wasn't even close to finished with you," he said as she climbed up onto the truck's running board to give him a kiss through the window.

"You'll get your chance," she promised. "Keep me posted on Eve." She winked, and he watched her walk up the steps.

Before he left, he called the local deli and arranged for a dinner delivery for Midian and her sister. Then he texted Eve that he was on his way and set off for Virginia.

Ryan then got on the phone with the Fallom police department, hoping they'd be a bit more forthcoming with details than Eve had been. They were happy to talk, but didn't have much information, so they put Carly Logan—the woman they had in protective custody at his request—on the line. She unloaded everything she could think of to him on speakerphone while he drove. She explained that a man and woman had come calling that morning, asking about her friend who'd gone missing. Her friend Sonia's specialty had been fertility before she changed careers, and she recounted a tipsy evening the two had spent together where they'd discussed their greatest regrets.

"I think that's why she left the profession," Carly said. "What she'd done felt wrong. But it was years and years ago. A young woman had been in a car crash and lost her baby, lost her husband or boyfriend or whatever, and she still hadn't regained consciousness. Sonia said she'd had the hugest crush on the surgeon involved with the case. So when she found him struggling to hold onto his decorum in the break room, when he'd shared his fears with her, she went out of her way to help him."

Ryan paid the toll quickly, trying to get the window back up to block out the road noise.

"God, that night is a little fuzzy, but I remember she was still torn up about it, so many years later. I kind of thought it had been a brave choice."

"What do you mean?" Ryan tried to move the conversation along.

"Apparently, the girl in the accident was his daughter. And her uterus was badly damaged, so she wasn't going to be able to have kids anymore. It had to come out. The surgeon was asking her what could be done, and Sonia finally suggested freezing some ovary tissue. She wasn't even certain anything could be done with it, but it was their best shot so that someday, if the girl chose to, she could still have babies. The surgeon wanted to give his daughter the chance, so Sonia guided him through what to do while the girl was still unconscious. Sonia had been storing the tissue for the doctor all this time, even though she was living here. A few years ago she told me a doctor in Belgium had successfully extracted mature eggs from a previously frozen ovary. She'd wondered about calling the surgeon to tell him. Don't know if she ever did."

Jesus. "Did she tell you the surgeon's name?" Ryan held his breath as he listened.

"She just called him Ted. Anyway, that's all I know about her worst secrets. I feel awful sharing them with you." Carly sounded scared.

"You know what? Consider me your priest right now. The information you just provided might help someone else." He found a piece of gum in the cup holder, unwrapped it, and popped it in his mouth. "Do you know where she was keeping the tissue?"

"Well, she never said. But there's only one place in town. That's where she worked before she moved on to real estate." Carly spoke to someone else in the room, then to Ryan. "When can I go home?"

"Soon. I just have to double-check that the person who came to your house is under control," he told her. "Everything's going to be okay." Ryan was about to hang up when Carly dropped her voice to a whisper.

"The woman, Eve, she really protected me."

"She's good at what she does," Ryan conceded.

"Is she okay?"

"Well, she might be one of the people your information is helping. Thank you for being so forthcoming. I'll get back with you soon." He ended the call and voice-commanded his phone contact Beckett's phone next. But the call was sent to voice mail. "Cue me in when you get this," he told Eve. "Text...whatever." He hung up again and had a short conversation with Midian, still driving as fast as he could to Virginia while she got started researching fertility clinics in Fallom, Virginia.

What the hell kind of mess had Eve's father created? And what new mess had been left by Eve and Taylor this morning?

Rodolfo didn't like how fast Vin drove. And the boy kept humming. It was taking everything in him not to hit the kid in the back of the head to get him to stop. He looked out the window. He could see his own reflection as they bounced to another safe house in another state. One code red alert after another. What the fuck had happened this time? What the fuck had his life become?

Vin also looked at his goddamn phone while he was driving—and then he was all over the freaking road.

"Drive!" Rodolfo roared.

"Sorry, sir. Things have gone to shit. Bonds just checked it out to confirm. Nicholas is dead. The doctor. The nurse. The girl is gone. He's headed to the hospital to see what he can see."

"Well, what the hell happened?" Rodolfo could feel his left side locking up again.

"Shoot out. Someone found 'em. Sorry." Vin put his phone away.

"Tell the crew down there to clean that scene. And until I know where my babies are, no one sleeps. Damn it!" Rodolfo steadied himself with his right hand. If he had to take the babies out of the damn woman himself, he was getting those children. "Have them do a sweep at the clinic too. I want the rest of the damn eggs."

He wanted the babies. If this batch had been ruined there'd be hell to pay, but he'd better damn well still have additional chances. He needed a whole new setup now that Nicholas was dead. That stupid sycophant had been a crafty bastard. And giving him little "presents" along the way had kept him tied in place and loyal like a dog on a leash.

This was the worst possible way for things to go. He should've taken Taylor down right after the fire. He'd just thought staying under the radar was the best way to get the babies born. But now this disaster, plus he was down a good portion of his men, and Taylor had made quite a bit of progress screwing up the drug-running lines he'd helped himself to. I mean, really, those were the least that prick Sevan Harmon owed him.

The minute he was back in Jersey again, he was putting Pough-keepsie under attack, old school. But first, he needed that pregnant girl under his control again.

27

BABİES

Eve stood outside the operating room, waiting. She'd passed herself off as Alison's cousin, as Beckett suggested, so she'd been allowed to stay. Spider forwarded her information on the missing person he believed this injured woman might be. Her name and description matched, and apparently her husband, Flint, had been married before. Based on letters found at their home, police believed he was avoiding alimony payments to an ex-wife by simply disappearing. Eve rolled her eyes at that one. Letters left behind? How convenient. Vitullo's organization was home to at least a couple master forgers.

But what was the end game here? What could Rodolfo have wanted with this poor woman and her babies? *Fuck him.* Eve felt herself harden, but she channeled her energy toward doing what needed to be done right now. There was family to be notified.

A nurse came out to speak with Eve. "Did you get a hold of your family? We do need those answers as soon as possible."

"Still waiting on them," Eve lied. The hospital needed to know if Alison was allergic to anything, if she was on any medicine.

"I have some really unfortunate news," the nurse continued. "Despite our every effort, the mom's vitals aren't looking great. Do you know what life-sustaining measures she would be comfortable with in circumstance such as this?" The nurse touched Eve's arm. "We'll take her into surgery soon, though, so don't give up hope."

"The babies?" Eve had a horrible flashback to asking about her child so many years ago.

"As far as we can tell, they're okay. Heart rates are good, and they're moving around. For now we are stabilizing Mom. But she's not responding well. It's very important that we have her immediate family here as soon as possible." The nurse nodded at the phone in Eve's hand.

"Of course. I'll try again and tell them it's urgent." Eve looked at Beckett's phone as a text rolled in from…Beckett. He always kept a disposable phone in his glove box.

Oth#er Hou?se emptyp

Okay

Ho3ws Alison&?

This woman's fate was out of their hands. Eve could picture herself in a similar bed. She knew how important it had been to have her father there making decisions for her.

**I'm calling her family.
She might not make it.**

Just wait for me, please?

The whole thing was spelled correctly, which meant he was concentrating.

She texted back:

How long?

5 min

**I'll find the names and numbers,
and if you aren't here soon, I'm calling them.
Or if something goes wrong.
I really want to get in touch with them.
It's important.**

He didn't respond. They had tracks to cover. This girl could get police protection. Eve didn't have to be standing here. As much as it sucked, their staying around would create problems left and right. Yet she couldn't have it any other way. Not this time.

After a bit of Google searching, she jotted down the home number for the woman's parents. She'd moved backward in time until she found Flint and Alison's wedding announcement in the local paper.

She had the parents' last digit already dialed and was ready to hit send when Beckett put his hand over the phone.

"Let me tell you this," he said. "Just quick—then we'll do whatever you want."

"They might miss the chance to say good-bye to their daughter." She didn't have to tell him she'd missed that chance with her dad.

He sat next to her and held her hand. "Eve…"

He was using her name. She braced herself for bad news, though she couldn't imagine what it might be.

"Those babies, there might be a chance—a chance that—"

"That they're Vitullo's grandchildren," Eve finished for him. "I figured that out already." She looked at her phone.

He cradled her face in his hands. "Children. They could be his children."

She had a little shiver. The idea that he was still spouting DNA was totally disgusting. He was old enough to be a grandfather's grandfather.

Beckett took a deep breath. "Sweetheart, your father wanted to give you a gift. He made a choice when you were unconscious after your first accident."

The life-changing accident. The one that took her from potential mom to killer. The waiting room was desolate—a bland place that could be in any hospital in the world.

She waited.

He swallowed and looked wrecked. Torn.

She inhaled twice in a row.

"I have reason to believe your father had some of your ovary tissue frozen. Did you know about this?"

She knew he was speaking English but his words didn't make sense.

"I'm guessing no." He kissed her forehead. Tender. Unlike him.

And then it clicked. Rodolfo's children. Her father being tortured. Alison being kidnapped. She was a surrogate.

"Mine?" She dropped her phone and pointed toward the hospital room where Alison lay. "Mine with…him?"

"I'm not a hundred percent sure," Beckett told her. "I'm not. But I have a suspicion. There's a lot of information in that stuff I collected at the house where Alison was. I'm still sorting through it. He was trying to hurt me. He wanted you. It's why he didn't need to take you again. He must have figured out that you couldn't, well, have babies. But she could. If it worked, she could."

Tears of anger caused his face to go out of focus. "Mine?" This seemed to be the only word her mind or her mouth could form.

With that, two policemen approached.

"I'm sorry, I'm sure this is a bad time, but we have some questions about the gunshot wound your...cousin, is it?...acquired."

She heard them, but couldn't stop looking at Beckett, searching his face for answers. Her father had betrayed her. Rodolfo had used her. Beckett knew and didn't tell her. She stood and shook her head, knocking away his searching hand.

"I'll speak to you in a moment," she told the officer. "Right now I have to tell someone to call her parents. They have to get to the hospital and say good-bye to their daughter."

She went to nurse's station and showed them the number on her phone, explaining what she knew in a soft voice. The nurse in charge began to dial, taking the situation in stride.

Eve watched as Beckett's face fell. He understood what she was doing, and the danger and trouble it would cause them both.

The worry for Bill Landstone and his wife, Cindy, never stopped. For eight months and twenty-two days Alison had been gone, Flint had been gone. If the pair had followed through with their plans to have Alison implanted at that fertility clinic, there would a grandchild out there for them somewhere, maybe. But Alison's doctor had said he never saw them that day.

It was like the world didn't hear them when they screamed their concern. Cindy had spoken to Alison every day for her whole life except when it was totally impossible. The letters they'd found in the house made no sense. That wasn't the Flint they knew.

He knew Cindy was still expecting a phone call. Someday. From Alison, her beautiful daughter. They prayed at church, lit candles, wore ribbons in her favorite color of lavender—the color she had asked for her room to be painted at fourteen, the color of her prom dress. Her wedding had all been shades lavender, and she wanted to name her baby Lavender, if it was a girl.

He missed the everyday happy words that should be in their hearts. He sometimes caught himself with his mouth open, desperately forcing his lungs to breathe around the pain. Not finding her was their failure, and they continued to try. They walked the streets by her house, they visited the fertility clinic where she was last seen. Cindy went to psychics regularly, and he'd finally stopped complaining about the visits. It still made him angry to hear the latest "update": she's by a windmill, by the sand, wearing green. He always told her it was all bullshit. But it gave her something to believe in.

Today they were eating grilled cheese sandwiches for dinner because they had to eat, no matter how insulting it felt to carry on when they didn't know where she was. Bill made a point to complete this ritual with Cindy every day. It was the only way he could be sure she would eat—or that he would eat, for that matter.

The phone rang.

They locked eyes, and a shot of adrenaline coursed through his system. They rushed, of course. Of course they rushed to the phone. Before it was done with the second ring, the receiver was in Cindy's hand.

The caller ID took a beat to catch up. When the hospital's number appeared, he felt Cindy go rigid next to him.

The call was prayer answered—any time the phone rang it was a split-second of hope. To see it wasn't a friend meant more prayers answered. And lastly, to be from the hospital…to be from the hospital was the worst and best dream come true.

Maybe an answer.

Bill held Cindy around the waist to keep them both standing. She placed the phone on her shoulder and tilted it a bit so he could hear too. "Hello?"

"Mrs. Landstone, we have a woman matching your daughter's description here at the hospital. Could you possibly drive carefully down to see her?"

Cindy made a noise, but it wasn't a word.

"Is she alive?" he interjected, taking the phone.

Cindy went to the floor as if she were melting. He cradled the phone and made sure she stayed sitting, not hitting her head.

"Yes, but she's seriously injured," the voice confirmed. "Will you be able to make the drive? I'm going to have to insist it's soon." Sterile. Comforting. The person on the other end was used to making these phone calls. "I'm calling from Fallom County Hospital. Do you know how to get here?"

"I do. Do I need to bring her anything?"

He didn't hear the answer because Cindy started screaming, clawing at his pant leg. He knew it was because he had an answer and she didn't.

He hung up the phone. "She's alive, Cindy. She's alive. But she's hurt, and we need to go. Go now."

They ran out of the house, leaving the front door open. The only reason Bill had the keys to the truck when he got to it was because he always had them in his pocket. For this moment. For this second. Wherever he was. In case they needed to race.

He looked at Cindy's wide eyes, her knuckles white as she spoke the first two sentences of the Our Father over and over because that's all she had. That's all she could comprehend.

When Alison was born, so many years ago yet it seemed like yesterday, they'd taken this same route. And then years later they'd taken it again, but with both his girls in the backseat this time—Cindy holding Alison carefully as his little girl cried. Broken arm. She'd had a hot pink cast, which she hated, but with her big blue eyes she'd conned them into getting her a cat. That stupid cat took a dump in his left work boot four times a year until it died.

Died. The word *died* made his vision blurry. He fought. He had to be a man. Be her father. She was at the hospital, and he was going to take her home. Take her home.

His girls.

He pulled into the ambulance bay and ignored the signs warning him against that very thing. Cindy was right between running and falling when he caught her. They proceeded forward like a frantic sack race.

The nurse behind the desk in the emergency room didn't know about a phone call. Didn't know about Alison. Cindy started calling out, calling her daughter's name. He tried to hush her, and also get an answer.

A blond woman touched his shoulder. "This way, sir."

"Are you a nurse?"

"No, sir. But just come this way and the nurses will tell you everything."

She was pretty. Could have almost been a sister to Alison. About the same age. Maybe she'd once had a pink cast. *I have to bring the girls home. Cindy's unbalanced. Hold Cindy up.*

The girl pointed out a nurse who began to speak. He couldn't hear her. The word gunshot was too loud. The blond girl began talking to police officers.

"Are you ready, sir? She's been through a lot. Please, this way."

Of course he would come. *Help Cindy. Cindy is shaking. Cindy is cold. No, Cindy is scared.* The pink cast was the worst because he'd had to hold Alison while they rebroke her arm. She begged him to make it stop, but he couldn't stop it. Cindy was crying but trying to be strong. Years fade. Today and yesterday are the same.

The door swung open, and at first he was relieved. It wasn't Alison because Alison's not pregnant. Cindy knew, though. She knew immediately.

"My baby! My baby!" she cried, pulling away from him, kissing her Alison. "I'm here. Shh. I'm here. I love you."

Then it was his turn to lose steam. He fell into the chair next to his daughter. *His daughter.* Tubes everywhere. Cindy fixed Alison's hair. She's so pale. So many monitors.

Stop it. Stop it. I can't do it. I need to take my girls home. Please. Stop it.

"I'm here, sweetheart. No one's going to hurt you. I'm here," Cindy said.

In an instant his screaming wife, who couldn't balance her own body fourteen steps ago, had become a pillar. His wife. Her mother. Clear. Firm. Not crying.

She looked to him. "Come. Kiss her. Tell her you love her, Bill. She needs us now."

The room was swarming with people in white coats, reading things. Knives, scissors.

No.

He was a loving father, but he did his loving in private. Quietly, he would tell his daughter to drive safely. On her wedding day, when he walked her down the aisle, he'd whispered the words to her. But today, above the noise, he would have to shout it. He closed his eyes for a moment. "I love you, Alison!" he boomed. "You're the best daughter a man could ha…" His words were choked off by fear.

Then they were wheeling her away, fast. So fast he jogged to keep up, his keys jangling. He kissed her cheek, his bottom lip hitting the oxygen mask.

He looked to the pair of eyes next to him. Because there were masks, he could see no complete faces. "I want to stay with her. I love her," he gasped.

And then it was Cindy holding him back. It was her grabbing him so he wouldn't follow the bed. And then Alison was gone around a corner.

He looked at his wife. "What's happening?"

She nodded and covered her mouth, pulling him hard against her. "She's dying, Bill. They're trying to save the baby."

I want to bring her home. My girl.

28

WAITING

Although they were in different waiting rooms, Beckett could see Alison's parents from where he waited with Eve, sitting one seat away from her, allowing some space. She hadn't said much, but watched the parents carefully.

Morales had arrived and was in deep conversation with the local police. Eve had confirmed with him that Carly was likely safe now that Nicholas no longer breathed. And while she kept him busy, Beckett had called for backup via Treats and Shark. The scene at the house needed cleaning. It was awful that it had sat as long as it had.

Morales waltzed back into the waiting area rolling his eyes. "I just fed them so much bureaucratic bullshit they will hate the fuck out of me forever. And I don't know how much time I bought you—or if you should even have time. What the hell is going on?"

"Turns out my father liberated one of my ovaries years ago," Eve said flatly. "He never told me. But Rodolfo knew. He tortured that information out of my father and killed his way to find the frozen part of my body. Then used it to extract my eggs, which he fertilized and implanted in this poor woman. So there's a good chance the girl in surgery is pregnant with mine and Rodolfo's monster spawn." She put her elbows on her thighs, holding her head.

Ryan sat down hard next to her. "No shit? That's some crazy bullshit."

Beckett leaned forward so he could see Ryan. "And that means that girl and those babies are in a lot of danger. I'll do what I can to find out what I can, but Eve's called the girl's parents. They're here, and they know we were involved on some level."

"How involved were you?" Ryan asked.

Beckett shook his head, his mouth shut tight. He wasn't telling this nut nugget shit.

Eve had other plans. "I shot Nicholas," she confessed. "It was split-second choice. He tried to kill Alison." She sat back in her chair. "He may have succeeded."

Morales shook his head. "If they still have a person to work on in there, you did all right. Should have taken the cops from the Wawa with you. Didn't that occur to you?"

"Nicholas was mine." She leveled a stare at him before standing up. "They're telling the parents something. Shit. Shit!"

Ryan stood as well. "I'll see what I can hear." He sauntered toward the other waiting room, looking official.

Beckett stood behind her and put one hand around her waist. She watched Ryan eavesdrop with everything she had.

There was crying, more breaking down from the girl's poor bastard parents. He felt Eve swoon a bit before replanting her feet. She looked at his face, and he could see her fear.

Not again.

Morales double-timed it back to where they were standing. "The babies were delivered by emergency Caesarean. They went to the NICU. They're alive, but pretty early. The mother died shortly after their birth. They think those babies are their grandchildren, by the way." Ryan shrugged and put his hands in his pockets.

Eve turned from Ryan and buried her face in Beckett's chest. He held her close and knew she was delicate. PDA was never her go-to for comfort. Morales took the cue and left the scene.

Beckett pulled her back into her chair as he sat, wrapping his arms around her.

"We'll figure something out. Okay? We'll get something worked out."

Eve's eyes were red, weary. She covered her heart with both hands, as if she was feeling it beat for the first time. "I've got to know. I have to know if they're mine." The hands over her heart started to shake.

"I'll find a way." He put one hand over both of hers and promised.

His phone vibrated, and he looked at the text from Shark:

**It's all gone. Someone was here.
Burned to the ground, charcoaled bodies.**

"Fucking Rodolfo. He's definitely still alive."

Eve looked from his phone to his face. "What?"

"Scene's toast, everything burned including the bodies, according to Shark. I called him and Treats in to clean up anything that needed it."

She shook her head, blond hair framing her shoulders. She never failed to amaze him. The contrast of her here, having chosen to reveal them both so Alison's parents could say good-bye, with the fact that he knew her brain was running a mile a minute reviewing murder scenes—she was so much more complicated than her pretty face revealed.

"We have to stay here," she said. "Those babies. How are we going to do that?" She took a step toward the grandparents' waiting room.

"They just lost their daughter. They need time to process this." He touched her arm, trying to remind her of her place. "Let them have a little space. There's plenty of security around."

She wrestled her fingers into a complicated knot. "We have to get Rodolfo. Soon. Now."

"We will," he assured her. "But first we have to get the hell out of here. They probably like us for this whole mess. And as soon as Morales stops seeming trustworthy, we're going to be out of options on how to handle this." He stood and offered her his hand. She took it, which she rarely did.

He pulled her to him and whispered into her ear. "I want you to go first, then I'll act like I'm going to the vending machine. Okay?"

She nodded and pulled away from him, tucking her hands in her pockets and heading for the main exit door. She was out, and now it was his turn. He left to pretend to go to the vending machines in the opposite direction. He would to count to one hundred, then meet her in the parking lot. It wasn't the first time they'd left a place all sneaky like.

Ryan watched their split and escape maneuver from his spot in the hallway with the other cops. When Taylor took off, he excused himself from his conversation with a local cop and traced Eve's steps out of the building.

Her blond hair was a beacon under the huge parking lot lights, giving the dusk more clarity. She was nearing Taylor's Challenger.

He'd almost caught up to her when she spun on her heel and pointed her gun at his head. And then they had the moment he'd dreaded. He'd believed in her, yet she was ultimately ready to kill him despite their friendship.

She was fast. She took in his stunned face and fired. He felt the bullet skim the air close to his cheek as he went to one knee. He'd taken aim at her heart, ready to return fire, when he noticed her gaze was just behind him and now, a bit over his head. With every explosion from her gun, she stepped forward until she was standing over him.

Eve crouched so her body was against his back. And then he heard her growl — a protective growl.

He yanked his leg out from under her, but the return gunfire kept him crouching. He assessed the scene. Four gunmen, possibly five. They were surrounded.

"Stay down," she told him. "I've got this." After bending even lower, she aimed under the cars to the left, obviously hitting someone by the sound of the scream.

The cops in the hospital now ran out, shooting.

Eve's face paled.

"What?" Ryan returned fire to the right.

"It's a distraction. Jesus. I've got to get back inside." Eve stood as if the decision itself would keep her safe.

He karate-chopped her behind her knees, forcing her to sit hard on her ass. The place where she'd been standing lit up with gunfire, and a machine gun cut into the metal around them.

"Taylor's still inside." Ryan checked his ammo. "I'm good for a few more. They've got to be sending backup. This is some suicide bullshit."

The foyer of the hospital exploded in front of them, and he pulled Eve to him, covering her with his body. She grabbed and covered his neck.

When the shards of glass cleared, the gunfire resumed. "This was planned!" she screamed. "They want my babies, and now I'm *useless!*"

Ryan closed his eyes against the anguish in her voice.

Beckett stood in front of the vending machine, counting in his head and thinking. If Rodolfo had already cleaned up the scene, his people were here. And the babies were in even more danger than just their delicate internal organs.

He was trotting back to the spot where he'd last seen Morales to tell the locals they needed round-the-clock on the kids when he heard gunfire in the parking lot. One shooter, two shooters, a machine gun. *Shit.* The cops he intended to speak to turned tail and ran for the parking lot. Every single one of them.

Every single one.

Someone had to stay behind. He had to have faith that Eve would stay alive, stay smart out there. Beckett found the stairs and took them two and three at a time until he could get to the NICU. While they'd been waiting for hours and hours, he'd looked at the hospital map a few damn times. Know your exits and all that bullshit. This was why. He ran full-out as the building rocked with an explosion, and as soon as he could steady his feet, he ran again. Alarms and buzzers sounded as the fire sprinklers kicked in.

Oh, this was a set-up all right. Jesus.

He skidded into the NICU and helped a few nurses to their feet. "Where are the twins who were just delivered? Are they okay?"

As the nurse started to point at the nursery, three men carrying guns and duffle bags entered the hallway with the look of people who knew what the hell was going on. There were two sets of doors to the nursery, and Beckett ran through the second ones and grabbed a scalpel, an old faithful friend, off a cart by the nurse's station.

The room was packed with nurses and some doctors, all carrying on like nothing was out of the ordinary. He was at the other entrance seconds before the hit men. He suspected Rodolfo had given strict instructions for how the kids should be taken: Avoid gunfire near his babies, and take a nurse and doctor with you. At least that's what he would do. He warned the others around him. "About to be gunfire in this room. Take precautions."

As if this were a direction they were used to handling, the staff began to move. They wheeled incubators out of the center of the room, shielding them behind machines. Those that had nothing to use for cover draped their bodies over the little plastic cribs, still checking stats the whole time.

Heroes. They were all heroes.

The door yanked open, and Beckett went low, swinging the scissors into the knee of the lead man. The second got a left hook to the jaw, the sound of his teeth cracking together audible. The third aimed his gun at Beckett, and he grabbed the barrel. He pushed the weapon back so it collided with the man's nose, giving a sickening crunch. The gun fired past his ear. Beckett then proceeded to beat the living piss out of each man in a round-robin version of ass kicking.

Two of the nurses joined him, and one of the doctors was swinging an oxygen tank. Beckett focused on getting the guns and duffle bags out of reach, sliding them to some of the other nurses with his foot. Not a single one swooned or screamed. These people were unflappable. When all three men were disarmed and lying on their stomachs, another nurse came over with three prepped needles. "These will keep those fuckers down until we get the cops here."

Beckett nodded. Perfect solution. "Are the babies okay?" If it wasn't Armageddon outside right now, he knew they would have forced him to leave. Instead they turned back to their business.

Once the men were snoring on the floor, they called the babies out by their mothers' names, doing a count and a condition update.

"Smith, Victoria."

"One. Accounted for and stable."

"Wexford, Alison."

Beckett held his breath.

"Two accounted for. Stable."

Oh, thank fuck.

Morales and Eve ran into the room and gave a scan before holstering their guns. Morales kicked the bastards on the floor.

"The babies are fine," Beckett reported. "You're good. It's okay." He held out a hand to her.

The assessment of tiny patients continued, and Ryan immediately handcuffed one of the perps. His official demeanor and a flash of his badge commanded all the attention and gave Beckett and Eve a second. He pulled her over to the incubator where the twins had been counted off.

He held her shoulders and stood behind her as she looked at the babies for the first time. Her whole back shook with her shaky intake of air.

"They're so beautiful," she said softly. "They're okay?"

The nurse met her eyes. "Yes. And you are?" She looked at Eve's wrists to see if she was the unlikely, un-pre-oped mom.

"A friend. I'm a friend." With that she turned, eyes closed.

Beckett pulled out his phone and snapped a few pictures before following her out the door.

Morales stood just outside in the hall. "It's a fucking nuthouse downstairs," he reported. "And in the parking lot. They are evac-ing everyone. They have to stabilize the area. NICU is always the first to be transferred out back in Poughkeepsie, but not sure they do it the same way here."

Eve looked at Ryan and spoke quietly. "Vitullo likely knows that. He's done his research."

Beckett opened the duffle bags Vitullo's men had brought in to check for bombs. Instead they held everything someone might need to handle a medical situation. Firefighters filled in the hallway. They seemed to know that the adults in the NICU would never leave their little patients alone for a second.

Beckett put a call in to Dildo, who quickly confirmed that the evac procedure was easily found on the hospital's website. Nurses and various personnel began putting on orange vests and unpacking carrying cases. Eve stared at the little clear crib with a mixture of shock and desire.

Beckett looked at Morales. "Can we get a private ambulance to take these kids to a different hospital?"

"Do we know how Alison's parents are? Where are they?" Eve turned to face them.

"I'm assuming they were downstairs," Ryan said. "Maybe visiting with...their daughter."

Eve gave a look that told Beckett to watch the babies as she ran from the room.

Eve had to put her shirt over her mouth because the smoke was so thick. The firefighters intercepted her and pointed her toward the side parking lot. She exited the building and finally took a deep breath.

Babies. The babies were so tiny. Part of her was scared they were really hers. And part of her was terrified they weren't. Her loyalty to the woman who carried these children was off the charts. She had a ton of emotions to feel, but now wasn't the moment. She spotted Alison's dad first, then her mom was sitting on the curb. Both looked shaken, but not hurt.

She approached them slowly. They were dazed, and the whole morning seemed lit more by sirens and shouts than the sun that was beginning to rise.

"The babies are still okay," Eve said. It was all she could think of by way of greeting.

They both nodded and spoke simultaneously. Eve got the impression they had been married a long time. "Good. That's good," they told her.

"I'm sorry about Alison." And she was. So much. So sorry.

The pain on their faces was everyone's worst nightmare.

"I wanted to give you an update," Eve continued. "The babies are going to have to be moved."

Cindy stood. "That can't be good. They must be small."

"They are. But the hospital is not very well equipped any more, and the man who kept Alison, he's still around. There's no telling what he'll do next." She looked around, watching for any new attackers.

Bill spoke. "Who are you again, young lady?"

Eve ignored the question. "We're going to need you to stay with the babies at the new hospital," she told them instead.

"But Alison is still in there." Cindy looked back at the simmering lobby and covered her mouth for a new round of sobs.

Eve's heart clutched. "Where would Alison want you to be?"

It was a low card, but she felt certain the woman would want her babies protected.

Cindy nodded. "With them. Which hospital are they going to?"

Eve motioned to them. "Come this way. We'll discuss all of it."

"My car? Should we take my car?" Bill asked. "Oh, wait."

Eve watched as his gaze found what had to be his vehicle. It was covered in debris from the explosion.

"Well, I guess that won't work." He looked confused again.

These people were in as much shock as she was, or more so. So much more. "Just come with me," Eve said. "The sooner we move, the better."

She walked to the loading dock of the hospital in time to see two unmarked ambulances back into parking spots. A convoy of people in orange wheeled machines out. Beckett walked alongside, scanning the area. He spotted her with the parents as they drew near and raised an eyebrow.

She responded by shrugging. *Couldn't leave them.*

They loaded the ambulance quickly: first with the babies, then two nurses and two EMTs, and finally more equipment. One of the EMTs assumed Eve was the mother and banded her arm. How Beckett had arranged this on such short notice, she didn't know.

He smiled at her and answered her internal question as Ryan pulled around in the Challenger. "Money talks, baby."

Bill held Cindy's arm. "We need to make sure Alison's cared for. Just tell us the hospital you're going to."

"They probably don't know just yet," Ryan explained as he joined the group. "How about I take you where you need to go as soon as things are settled?"

Eve got into the Challenger as Ryan held the driver's door open. "I think you're our best eyes on the babies right now," he told her. "I'm going to try and fix as much bullshit as I can down here. Then I'll head up. I'll watch these two as well." He tilted his head toward Alison's parents.

Eve kissed his cheek. "Thank you. I'll call Midian if you want?"

He nodded.

"Where's your ride?" she called to Beckett.

"I got something, no worries," he assured her. "I'll call you in a minute."

And with that, they all parted. Eve stayed close to the ambulance, and watched the back doors like they contained her future. She gave Midian a brief rundown on speakerphone, and then forty minutes into the trip she had a call from Beckett.

"Watching out for them on your own might be a lot for you." Beckett's voice filled the car from her speakerphone.

She swiveled in her seat, checking her surroundings while driving. "Yep, it's already a lot. But until I know different, they get treated like family."

"Noted." Beckett was quiet on his end.

"I feel so angry and hopeful right now. I think my brain is going to snap." She ran a hand through her hair. "And how long did you know about this? Like, did you know before tonight?"

He exhaled deeply into the phone, the sign of his truth. "I had a guess about it after Rodolfo's fire. He said a few things about your father, but nothing concrete. It's come together over time, but the documents I found today are what really spell it out."

She was quiet for miles before responding. "That's a long damn time."

"It was. And I doubted keeping it from you every damn day. But how could I put this on you without proof? And maybe you knew about your father and the ovary and all that, and you just didn't want to use it with me. Not that I'd blame you." He was obviously in a car now, the noises giving him away.

"I didn't know," she said softly. "And it's beyond creepy, but also loving. I mean, I had no idea, and yet he was thinking of my future. This is a lot to process. It feels like a nightmare. Or a dream. What's the destination of these ambulances?"

"The babies are only a few hours old and premature. We needed a hospital. And we can't pick the one in Poughkeepsie. Not now. So I decided on Maryland. We've got Chery, Vere, and Chaos nearby. It could work. They have an amazing hospital there."

Eve followed the ambulances as they exited the highway.

"This whole thing could be seen from cameras and triangulated through satellite," Beckett said. "Spider will be busy covering our tracks."

Eve touched the window where it was fogging up, running her fingers through the mist. "Is that where you're headed too?"

"No. Morales has a ton of crap to handle down here in lovely Fallom, and our pictures are on all of it. I'm going to call Spider and see if he can erase some things, but I should stay local. I'm here for as long as you need me, though," he assured her.

They were quiet for a long time, despite all they had to say. The drive to Maryland was about two hours.

"So where'd you get the car?" she asked nearly an hour later. "Because I know you're not still at the hospital."

He laughed a little. "There was a whole parking lot full of them, killer. I'm safe. Nearby, but safe."

She got a text from Ryan as the ambulances pulled onto the local road.

More of RV's people arrived on the scene.
Were subdued. Stay gone for now.
Bill and Cindy in a hotel.
Can't risk someone following them to you.

She relayed the information to Beckett.

"Dolfo wants those kids bad," he commented.

"I want to know if they're mine." She'd been quiet about it, but this was really what she thought of most. "And his. Do we need to get his DNA?" She bit her bottom lip, thinking.

"We've got Primo," Beckett offered. "I bet he could work in a pinch. And I'm sure they've pulled some blood from those poor babies. I'll have someone get on it."

The ambulances pulled into the ER dock, and Eve noticed the security cameras. She texted Spider. They'd need him to wipe her presence here too.

Unloading the babies from the ambulance took much longer because of all the equipment. The moving ECMO was particularly impressive. Eve parked and walked up next to an EMT.

"How'd they do?" she asked.

"The girl's heart rate dropped twice, but we're here," he said, rubbing his face.

Eve walked alongside the crib. She couldn't get too close because of all the personnel around them, but she saw a flash of a little hand. Her desire to cover the tiny bodies with a blanket was overwhelming. After putting the phone back to her ear, she spoke to Beckett, who had stayed on the line. "What now?" she asked.

"Well, I've warned the home front that things went south quickly down here, and told them to beef up security in Poughkeepsie. I'll get some of our guys running security up there for the little ones and here for Bill and Cindy. I think you should stay there. But whatever you need."

"We need to get him out of the picture," she countered.

"I know. But for now I've got to get things squared away here. Stay put and do your thing. I love you."

"I love you too."

Her wristband allowed her to stay near the twins after they entered the building, and she didn't protest when the nurse in charge replaced the baby's bands with ankle monitors that matched the new band they gave her.

The boy's alarm went off, and soon they were using an air bag with a pump on it to give him a tiny version of rescue breaths. A man standing near her smiled. She had her eyes glued on the boy.

"Did you name them yet?" he asked.

"What?"

"Did you name the babies yet? I'm sorry, I'm the chaplain for this hospital, Timothy Rowe. I was told to report here in case you needed me." He smiled. "I understand the hospital where you gave birth had to be evacuated. Do you need to sit down? Do we need to get you to a doctor?"

"They were born via surrogate, but she passed." Eve looked at her shoes. It sounded like a lie in her head, but was probably closer to the truth than she was able to admit.

"You've had quite a morning. Would you like to pray? I'm here if you need that."

Eve thought of Cole. He'd pray. What good it did she didn't know.

"Okay." She bowed her head as the chaplain ran through some pleasant-sounding prayers. When she looked up again, both babies were being attended to feverishly. Tears filled her eyes.

"How about names? That might be good right now." The chaplain touched her hand. The children might not make it. As small as they were, she knew he was right.

She wondered if she should call Bill and Cindy. But they didn't know how complicated this situation truly was. And from the looks of the frenzy, there might not be time. "For the girl, Mouse Anna Taylor."

"Very good." He took out a pen and paper. "Like this?"

"Looks good. Yes." Never in a million years would she have guessed she'd be naming babies today. Never.

"And the boy?" The chaplain waited patiently.

"Theodore Beckett Taylor." She hugged herself and watched the activity in the nursery.

She approved the spelling, and he had one more question. It was more loaded than he could ever know.

"And the father? Do we leave it blank?"

Eve stepped closer to the window now separating her from the babies.

"No, the father is Beckett Taylor. No middle name."

29

SHITSTORM

That night, after the shitstorm had subsided somewhat, Beckett met Morales in a dark parking lot four businesses over from the fertility clinic in Fallom. They were both wearing black.

"This is our best guess. It's the only facility within driving distance of the house where they were keeping that pregnant girl," Beckett explained.

"Let's go then. The worst part is we have to look for labels. And this feels like a mythological beast—maybe it's here, maybe it isn't," Morales replied.

As they walked over, keeping to the shadows, Beckett had to ask. "How'd you get away from that scene at the hospital? That was nuts."

"Well, I don't actually work for the local police, so once they had it under control I was able to bail. It'll all come back to bite you in your fluffy ass anyway." Morales looked up and put up his hand to stop Beckett.

He pointed to the front door of the clinic, where two figures dressed all in black were letting themselves in, sketchy as shit.

"What is this? A fucking ninja convention?" Beckett hissed.

"Well, that'll make finding the right eggs easier—and the beast is real." As he spoke, Morales elbowed Beckett and pointed out a car waiting down by the road. The engine was still running, but it was quiet.

"Morales, you might want to make yourself scarce. I can't promise I'll keep them alive like the last batch of assholes. And I got to move. That fucking stealthy-ass Prius is mine. Later." Beckett took off in the direction of the car, using shrubs and landscaping to creep up alongside the driver.

Beckett looked in the side-view mirror and watched as the get-away car driver spotted him. Before the guy could get over his shock, Beckett had the door open and was stepping on his throat. Morales' boot appeared out of nowhere to kick the gun away from the driver's hand, and in no time the man's hands were bound by PlastiCuffs. Beckett finished the job by tying a wrap from his pocket around the guy's mouth. Then Morales opened the back door to the Prius and together they lifted and tossed him inside.

He'd started kicking and making a racket when Beckett hammered him with a fist to the carotid artery. The man went slack. Morales rolled his eyes in disgust. Beckett shrugged. He took the driver's place and used the man's discarded gun as his own. Morales took cover in the backseat, readying his own firearm.

Beckett whispered out the side of his mouth, "We're on."

The two figures now carried a miniature metal barrel between them, which they treated very gingerly. They opened the car's passenger door and set the barrel inside, never once looking at Beckett, they were so intent on their purpose.

As soon as they stepped back, he gunned the engine, holding the canister with one hand as the door closed with the force of his acceleration. "So long, suckers."

Morales took to the back window as the empty-handed ninjas fired at their retreating car. The men began to run after them.

"Shoot them, for shit's sake!" Beckett slapped the steering wheel.

Morales shook his head and took a few shots, which seemed really wild—even for him. *Friggin' Boy Scout*. Beckett looped around a bit in the parking lots of other stores before returning to his Challenger. After a thorough search yielded no sign of the would-be burglars, Morales helped him transfer the canister to the backseat. He buckled it in like a person before returning to the front seat.

"So these are Eve's eggs? This whole thing is getting weird." Morales made a face.

"Yep. They're *hers*. Not up for trade on the open market. Dolfo wants them, therefore he cannot have them. Where are you parked?"

Beckett put the car in gear, and they found Ryan's truck parked by the woods. As he dropped Morales off, he turned and unbuckled the canister. "I'm a target," he explained. "They know my car, and this is too important to take risks with. Can you find a good place for this?" Beckett looked at the cop. He still hated him, but now that Morales was dating the little ball of fire from the courthouse, he might be a little fucking bit less annoying.

Ryan lifted the container. "Yeah. I can find something."

"And don't tell anyone where it is, okay? Unless she asks for it. Not even me. The fewer people who know the location, the better. Just don't add your own baby batter to it." Beckett hated watching Eve's potential for a family walk away. But for now she needed to focus on the twins, and he needed to focus on exterminating Rodolfo.

He called her as soon as Ryan was out and he was rolling on the road. "How are things?"

"The twins are stable," she said. "But that status changes quite a bit. It's a little scary."

"Any visitors?" He pulled onto the highway, focused on making sure no one was following him.

"Not yet."

"You exhausted?" He just wanted to hear her voice.

"I guess. I hadn't thought about it. I've just been sitting with the babies. I'm wrist-banded as their mother."

He shook his head that she had to endure this alone. So few people in this world would understand how much wearing that band hurt her, being responsible for two little babies born way too young.

"You're a great pinch hitter, gorgeous. I know you can do this. Listen, I hate to do this on the phone, but I need to tell you something."

She was silent on the other end, but he knew she was listening.

"It turns out Rodolfo extracted more eggs from your ovaries than he's had a chance to use. The others are frozen. I'm not sure how many, and they've been traveling a few times, so I don't know. But Morales and I just got them, and now he's going to store them somewhere safe."

He waited as he handed her hope. After all the death he'd forced upon her, now he could offer her life.

"Wow," was all she had to say.

"So use those things—even if I don't get out of here clean—if you want. I just didn't want any more secrets, okay?" He wished he could see her.

"I can't even think about that now. Just stay safe. Sort out what you need to do in Fallom, and then let's get Rodolfo—for good this time."

"I'll do my goddamn best. You know I will. And the douches are already on it." He hung up. He just had to stop Rodolfo's resurrection and get a handle on Poughkeepsie once and for all.

Just two hours later, Ryan found a place to keep Eve's eggs safe: at the Maryland BioResearch Labs. His roommate from college had a giant brain and was now a practicing microbiologist there, plus their bro-code had allowed the late-night call. Seth had hugged Ryan hard and transferred Eve's eggs into cryostorage in his lab in the middle of the night. He hadn't even asked too many questions.

As Ryan drove away, noting the time as two a.m., he texted Taylor that the goods were safe. Now he needed to get back to the home office and maybe grab a few hours' sleep before he'd have to start fielding the emails he'd been watching roll in on his phone from the Fallom PD. The small town was seriously overwhelmed by the breadth of destruction they'd accumulated. But true as Taylor's ass pointed to the ground, wherever he went, things fell to shit. However, as he drove, the insanity of the last twenty-four hours began to take its toll. The center line seemed wavy, and when it finally became nonexistent, Ryan knew it was time to stop. He pulled over at the next hotel he saw, texted Midian, and promised himself he'd just take a couple hours to rest.

After months of ridiculousness, Rodolfo had finally settled himself in more appropriate accommodations in Rhinebeck, New York. The house was a huge rental. A president's daughter was married here. The works. Because fuck hiding. Maybe he wasn't quite bold enough to go back to one of his known properties (the ones not burned to the ground, that is), but Taylor had to know he was still alive after the disaster in Fallom. So it was only a matter of time until their next showdown. Why not at least be comfortable in the meantime? Christ, he couldn't even buy green bananas anymore. Now was not the time of his life to live like a pauper.

Vin and a handful of other guys were on hand to attend to his needs, including his morning coffee, which they'd just delivered. He had index cards out in front of him, outlining his holdings that had been compromised. Anything taken and still standing was marked with a T.

When a phone was thrust into his circle of thinking cards, he was annoyed.

"Just got a text. You should see it, boss." Vin raised the phone into Rodolfo's line of vision.

He gave the boy a death stare until he moved it. "Read it to me." Training this kid was like teaching a box of rocks to fly.

"Okay. 'Girl died. Babies missing. Eggs gone.' Does that mean something to you? That seems like some sad shit." He slipped the phone back in his pocket.

Rodolfo took four of the cards in his good hand and crumpled them so hard they sliced him with paper cuts. "I'm going to be downstairs. Have everyone there. I will eviscerate Taylor. Now. Today."

The sight of a cop car in the driveway should have caused Blake a little more concern, but he was walking the dog with blurry eyes—it had been a long night—so instead, the cop was out of the squad car before he had a chance to get anxious.

The uniformed officer looked around as he approached, but when he stopped to pet the dog, which jumped up to greet him,

Blake recognized him as Melvin Forcola, a guy who'd been on their security detail before.

"Hey, Blake," he called in greeting. "Everyone inside?"

"Uh, yeah, they are. Everything okay? Is Dad all right?" Blake pulled the dog to his side.

"Yeah, Capt. McHugh is fine. He's the one who sent me over. Would it be possible for you guys to pack a quick bag and get the kids? I need you to come with me."

Blake held open the door for the officer. He felt self-conscious about his flannel pajama pants and sleeveless tee standing next Melvin in his full uniform. "We're leaving?"

"That's what he's requested. We just want to move you guys for a little while."

"Cole, too?" Blake went into the kitchen to grab his phone off the charger.

"Yeah. Cole, Kyle, and the baby will meet up with you."

Livia entered the front room, tying her robe in a bow, her hair messy but her eyes clear—always good in a crisis. "How much time do we have and for how long?"

"As soon as possible, and maybe a day or two. It's just a precaution." Melvin excused himself when his radio sounded, alerting him to a fire in town.

Livia put her hands on Blake's arms. "Okay, I'll throw a few things in a bag and grab the kids. You pack snacks and dog food, and just keep Marx on the leash. We'll meet back in the living room."

She kissed him on the lips and took off up the stairs.

Blake put juice boxes, graham crackers, and dog food in a bag and met Livia in the living room. She tossed three duffle bags at his feet. "Gotta get the kids."

Melvin signed off on the radio and looked even more rushed than before. "I've got these bags. Go with her and grab the kids. We're leaving now." The police officer grabbed the duffles and shopping bag.

Livia gave Blake a look that said she wasn't liking this one damn bit. They took the stairs two at a time and without consulting each other, Blake went for Emme and Livia went for Kellan.

As they came back downstairs, each with a sleepy bundle cuddled on their chest, Melvin had Marx's leash. "I've got the car seats in the trunk, but get in," he told them.

The backdoors were open. Marx jumped in the passenger seat, and Livia and Blake cuddled the kids as they shut the doors. He met her eyes as she mouthed, "Beckett?"

He shrugged, then nodded. What else would it be? They both took time to kiss the kids' heads.

Cole waited at the window of the hotel room. "What did your dad say?" he asked Kyle.

Kyle wore yoga pants and a shirt she usually worked out in, which had been where she was headed when the officers arrived. She rubbed JB's back as he slept in the center of the bed, peacefully. "He said it's all a precaution. A few bad guys are getting pissed at each other, and he wanted us out of the equation. I thought this place was closed." She gave the hotel room's interior a side eye.

"I'm thinking it should be. I guess we're in your father's version of the witness protection program." Cole nodded as a squad car pulled up. "Here they are. Let me go see if they need help. Yup. They've got the dog." Cole opened the door, but the police officer on the other side blocked his exit.

"Captain would prefer you stay here. Their room will adjoin yours, so you can go ahead and open the door in between." He pointed at the metal door.

"They've got two kids, a dog, and knowing my sister-in-law, a pile of bags. Going up two flights of stairs without an elevator is a punishment."

"Look, here they are." The officer stepped to the side, and sure enough Melvin had Marx by the leash. Blake had Kellen in his arms, and Livia held a sleepy-looking Emme's hand. Cole took the dog from Melvin while the cop gave them some ground rules.

"First, we're sorry this place sucks. The windows have a sun guard on them, so no one can see inside. The building's made of concrete, so that's good too. No matter what, if you see anything you don't like, tell me. Joe has to go, but my assignment is right here, making sure you guys are comfortable."

"I'm taking the patrol car," announced the departing officer. "Melvin here has an unmarked. I'll put the bags in the lobby?"

Melvin nodded as Blake walked into Cole's room and placed Kellan down next to his cousin. Emme crawled into Kyle's arms, falling asleep with her head on her aunt's chest, mumbling about vending machines and how much she loved hotels. Cole followed Blake into the adjoining room.

"So how much have we put together?" Blake sat on the hotel bed.

"Just that shit's going down, and we have to wait to see how it pans out. Sometimes I feel like I've been waiting years for this to happen." Cole touched his *Sorry* tattoo.

Blake exhaled. "I know what you mean."

Ryan's alarm failed to wake him—or maybe he'd failed to set it in his delirium—but a text from McHugh at nine forty-five the next morning sure as shit got his ass moving.

The text inquired as to where he was and let him know that Lovell, their man on the inside with Vitullo, had reported that shit was going down today. Vitullo was spitting mad about the loss of his creepy breeding program and was ready to take it out on Beckett via Poughkeepsie.

Ryan looked at the clock and texted his boss that he could be there in about five hours because he was in Maryland. Within moments, McHugh told him to just go back to Fallom—and fortunately he didn't ask why Ryan had wandered into another state. He said he'd had quite a few calls from Fallom as well, and Morales should be there to handle complaints and questions and coordinate any needed future action.

Ryan acknowledged receipt of the message. Though he couldn't imagine being anywhere other than Poughkeepsie with this level of crap about to explode, he decided perhaps he shouldn't push his luck. He'd been a bit off the straight and narrow lately, and McHugh did appreciate a man who could follow orders. So, boring-ass Fallom it was.

And then he had a choice: warn Taylor and let him get a little bit of a defense going, or leave him in the darkness—just tell Midian to find a safe place and let nature take its course. He knew Eve was somewhere else. It was almost like the universe was telling him to let it go.

But the more he thought about it, the less he liked the possible outcome Between the two devils, Taylor was the better. So he called.

"What?" Beckett answered in his endearing way.

"Rodolfo knows he's been bested. And he's doing the only thing he can." Ryan put his truck into gear as he spoke.

"Poughkeepsie."

"That's what I'm thinking," Ryan said. "He's vindictive right now. Ready to strike. I'd be on my way, but I've been ordered to manage things in Fallom."

"Well, let's see what my assholes and douchebags can get done," Beckett said, a smile in his voice. "Any idea where he's going to start?"

"No idea. But he wants to bring you to your knees."

"That's comforting." Beckett sighed. "Does McHugh know about this?"

"Yeah, he's the one who told me."

"Okay. You stay classy, Morales. I'll call Eve and tell her to stay put."

Later that morning, once the hour was reasonable and the kids had been fed, Livia listened as Blake and Cole talked to Beckett, who was evidently on his way back to Poughkeepsie.

Not content with what she could glean from half the conversation, she pulled out her iPad and went online, determined to piece it together herself. The local forums were alive with random fires and a few explosions. Some people speculated terrorism and a few the end of times. She was worried for her father, because despite his level-headed approach to anything his job could throw at him, the reports seemed to be coming with increasing intensity.

"Turn on the police channel," Kyle called. She was keeping track of all the children on one bed. Emme looked at her usual books while Kellan and JB played with a rainbow of blocks.

Livia tapped on an app that broadcast the local police chatter. Both she and Kyle had the translation skills to make sense of a lot of the fast talking and lingo. Their father had had a police radio in the kitchen when they were growing up and sometimes told them what was going on. They'd learned to identify what was serious based on the times he'd called a sitter instead of finishing his dinner.

Kyle flashed her phone at Livia, showing Google maps, and came to kneel next to her after determining the kids were fully engrossed in their activities. She tapped a flag on the map every time a new crisis was announced. From time to time they heard their father barking orders, but mostly it was quick updates from other officers. Kyle popped a flag on the hotel where they were staying, and after a half an hour, a pattern emerged: the flags—representing reports of loud bangs, flash fires and sporadic gunfire—circled a radius around and spiraled closer to where they now sat.

"You think anyone else is seeing this?" Kyle pointed at the map.

"I'm not sure," Livia said. "Let me call Dad."

She dialed his number as the men stood in the adjoining door-way, their phone call with Beckett complete. Her father knew she would never call unless it was important, and she prayed he'd have a moment to answer.

"Livia." His familiar voice made her chest tighten.

She got right to the point. "We've been tracking the events. They're spiraling closer to this hotel. Did you notice that? It might be nothing. It's probably nothing."

"Hold on." He kept the line open. "Okay, I see that. It's possible." He was obviously addressing someone else as he said, "These latest incidents, within the last forty minutes or so, are all within proximity of previously safe locations. Someone's got inside information. Anyone check on Lovell?"

"What should we do?" She took another look at the kids on the bed.

"Sit tight, and tell Melvin. But stay there." Her father hung up.

Livia watched as Cole took position by the hotel's window, scanning the street with his gaze.

Rodolfo had the benefit of a head start, but as Beckett pulled into Poughkeepsie around noon, he was getting reports on his phone, catching up as quickly as he could. Two, no three explosions had already rocked Poughkeepsie, plus a variety of smaller pops and bangs, and there were currently four working structure fires as well.

Rodolfo was literally fighting fire with fire.

He pulled up to his house, parking across the street, and watched as the roof was engulfed in flames. *Gandhi.* It had seemed so convenient to have the dog spa to drop him back off at home in anticipation of his arrival.

Beckett could see the dog waiting for him at the front window, barking his ass off. He ran to his door and opened it with his keys and a shaking hand. As he stumbled in, covering his mouth with his shirt, G ran at him like a cannonball. He caught his dog and turned to run back out. As he stepped onto the lawn, the roof slid from the house, the flaming wood almost clipping the back of his heel.

He busted into an all-out run until they were a safe distance from the fire, then tried to check the wiggling dog for damage. G tried to lick him even though he couldn't reach.

"That fucker." Beckett shook his head as he put his dog in the car and called Spider. "I need to know where Rodolfo is right now. Don't give me shit. Right now. Use every contact you still have. He tried to kill my dog."

Spider had bad news. "The answer is Rodolfo is everywhere. This just escalated like crazy. Reports are pouring in from assholes that they're seeing Vitullo's guys everywhere. Some of them must be flipping back."

"Fuck. You still with me?" Beckett rolled down his window to listen as he drove closer to downtown.

"Yeah, boss. Of course. What you want to do? Police and fire departments are getting spread thin."

Beckett heard Spider clicking on a keyboard or two. Vitullo had a pattern, or so it seemed. It was half brilliant, half pure evil. The old fart had planned violence and crime in far-flung locations, keeping everyone off balance and no one able to concentrate on any one situation with enough force. The acts of terrorism would then slip around the conventional defenses in place to keep the community safe.

Beckett felt swamped with desperation, thinking of all the families and people he was now vested in. A new text from Spider offered a running ticker of 9-1-1 calls in the area. He clenched his teeth together and pounded the steering wheel. He could find Rodolfo and kill him for good this time, but chopping off the old fart's head didn't protect his town in this very moment when he needed to defend it from so many licks of flame.

Sirens wailed as two cop cars flew by, and G howled in response. Then a fire truck rushed by, lit up, the firemen inside already covered in soot.

Beckett spotted a newscaster braving the street to deliver a report, her cameraman looking over his shoulder for danger as often as he was peering through the lens.

"Boss?" Spider checked to see if they were still connected. "The guys are reporting paid mercenaries in the area. They recognize them from other jobs. Looks like Vitullo bought himself some loyalty."

Then it finally hit him: this was too big for him alone, or even for his men to handle. But loyalty—he could drum that up. In his head he pictured the wall of maps in his now-smoldering house. He had people scattered throughout Poughkeepsie who would maybe do him a favor. Maybe.

He executed a perfectly illegal U turn and parked behind the newscaster. "Spider, turn on the Channel Five news and record what I'm about to do. Send it to every friendly contact on my grid. Got it?"

"Ten-four. Let it rip."

Beckett pulled off his sunglasses and exited his car, carrying an overexcited G with him.

The blonde delivered ominous news: "Reports are sketchy right now, but we've been advised to encourage all citizens to stay indoors. It's a very dangerous time for—"

Beckett smiled and took the microphone right out of the blonde's hands, all Kanye West style. She couldn't help but smile back.

"Thanks, sweetheart," he told her. "You're doing great. Are we live?"

She nodded, shocked.

He turned to the camera. "Good. My people—and you moth- erfuckers know who you are—right now, in this moment, we are being attacked. This is not random violence, but a planned terror attack intended to bring this city to our fucking knees. Our police force and firefighters are heroes and are totally overwhelmed right now. So that leaves us. Me and you bastards. I'm asking you not to hide inside. Do not turn into pants-crapping cowards. I want you to stand with me. Use whatever skills you have at your disposal if you see shit going down that you can stop." G licked Beckett. "I'm ask- ing you to step up and help me. Right now, help our motherfucking town. Our goal is this and only this: Saving Poughkeepsie."

He handed the microphone back to the newscaster, followed by an armful of G. "Please take care of my dog for a while, would you?"

Stunned, she nodded and turned back to the camera, where she began apologizing for the cursing.

Beckett trotted back to the car and heard gunshots coming from a street that had never had that issue. He fired up the Challenger and turned toward the direction he thought it was coming from. Sure enough, a commando-styled guy he didn't recognize was reloading. He was preparing to run the guy over when a group of his construc- tion guys came out of the apartment building, armed with hammers. They attacked so quickly that the commando was overwhelmed, so Beckett just backed up, rolling down his window again to listen. The construction workers were pissed.

"Nobody takes our city. Fuck you!"

He called Spider again. "How we doing?"

"I made that speech a video, looped it, and sent it to everyone on our contact list. Plus I slapped it all over the Internet. Hashtag SavingPoughkeepsie is trending in the northeast. People are digging the we-don't-take-shit-in-Poughkeepsie vibe."

As Beckett rolled through the streets, he saw the people taking the town back. They were putting out fires with garden hoses, step- ping on the necks of Vitullo's men, and helping protect businesses from looters.

"The nine-one-one channel is firing away. You need to see it," Spider said as he sent the rolling information to Beckett's heads up display.

Every other call was to report a citizen's arrest.

Beckett smiled, chills running up his spine. It was his hope, and maybe a stupid one, that the kindness he'd enforced lately was more important, more powerful than the violence he'd used in the past. And all these bottom-dwellers, society's cast offs, had street smarts and skills they were happy to use to protect what they felt was theirs.

"Boss, I got a report of a girl who looks a whole lot like Bang downtown."

"Try and get me real-time reports on that," Beckett said. "She's the shit. A real deal arsonist. And she's not working for us right now." He pictured the hospital lobby exploding in Virginia. That explosion had looked like a sparkler compared to what Bang could do.

"On it. You might want to get away from that area though. She goes big so no one else can go home." Spider disconnected the phone but kept the feed running to the Challenger.

Beckett dialed and put Blake on speakerphone. "So tell me, you're where now?"

Before Blake could respond, Beckett heard Emme's sweet voice ring out, "Look! It's Uncle Becky! They're using a lot of bleeps. He's on TV!"

"Okay, so you're asking Poughkeepsie to fight for you?" Blake said. "What's really going on?"

"Listen, I don't have time to talk, but you guys stay in your houses. Disregard those other instructions." Beckett was distracted by the feed on his dashboard as he slowly rolled through the downtown streets. Traffic was stop and start due to the random accidents and fires blocking the usual pathways. But the closer to the center he got, the more predictable the destruction became—a calling card, if you will. There were only a couple people he could think of who could cause this much destruction without an army, and one of them was currently guarding a set of twins. That pretty much left one other option.

Blake finally got through to him. "Beck? You there? We've been moved to a hotel, but we're all together."

"Which hotel? You in Rhinebeck or Kingston?" Beckett finally gave up trying to move the Challenger and pulled it to the side of the road.

"No, we're at the Starlight Motel. Downtown."

Beckett's stomach dropped as he got out of the car, still talking on his phone, eyes searching. "Get safe. Get away from the windows. Prepare for a blast. Jesus fucking Christ, why do you guys have to be here, right now?" He could see nothing. No one unusual. Bang was amazing at fitting in. She reminded him of fucking Merkin from back in the day. "Cole got his piece on him?" After a moment Blake reported that he did. "Tell McHugh we have a bomber in the area. Watch for a female…" Then Beckett slipped his phone into his pocket instead of finishing his sentence.

He made eye contact with Bang as the slight female stepped to the side of a restaurant across the street. Bang, freelance arsonist extraordinaire, was dressed like a typical college freshman — jeans and a T-shirt. No one would point her out in a crowd, which made her the least likely to be identified as an explosives expert in a lineup. She could always get away with the most brazen shit. Hell, she'd done some brazen shit for him.

He took off running immediately, as fast as he could. As he came for her, she ran straight for an ugly cement building. Of course. Of *fucking* course the sign proclaimed it the Starlight Motel. It was such an eyesore, Beckett had forgotten it was even on this goddamn street. He hit the lobby doors just as the door to the stairs slammed against the dirty wallpapered wall.

He bet she'd had a silencer on the weapon she'd used to kill the clerk, who was slumped over her desk with fixed, unblinking eyes and a hole in her forehead, as he hadn't heard the shot. He took he stairs two at a time, using the handrail to propel him faster. Fear added to his adrenaline when he realized he didn't know what floor his family was on. *Oh my God.*

He heard the door a flight above him click into place, so Beckett had to take a chance that the third floor was correct. He pulled the door open and blazed through with the names of his brothers pounding in his ears instead of common sense. He heard a pop and looked up in time to see the officer fall to the floor, victim of the same sort of attack that had killed the clerk. The door on the opposite end of the hallway clicked shut.

Bang's backpack lay next to the officer. A bomb. Beckett didn't stop to think, only knowing he had a minute, maybe just seconds, before Bang released the plunger on the remote device she favored. He sprinted down the hall and grabbed the bag, throwing it over his shoulder. As he raced by, Cole opened the door.

At least the cop would be assessed by his brothers, and Livia knew CPR. If he could be saved, she would help. All he knew was the bomb was not going to take his brothers' lives — literally or figuratively. Beckett never stopped. He just hit the pane of glass at the end of the hallway like a running back, glass exploding around his shoulders as he fell.

He closed his eyes, expecting to be annihilated by the bomb, or to die upon impact from the three-story fall. But instead he had the breath knocked out of him, gravel embedded in his elbow. He'd hit his head, and the shoulder that cracked the glass now throbbed under his weight, but he was definitely alive. Disoriented, he sat up. When he looked back, the window he'd come from was about ten feet up. He'd landed on the roof of the building next door.

Mere seconds, if he had any, were left, so he stood, thrilled that his legs would carry him, the pain making him howl. Blake's voice followed him.

"Beckett!"

He yelled to his brother as he hit the nearest staircase, "Get down! Bomb!"

His voice carried through the echoing outdoor stairwell, and when Beckett got to the sidewalk, people were already screaming.

He scanned the area for Bang. She had to be close, because the bomb still existed on his back. He felt sick looking at the sheer number of people on the streets, all potential victims.

He saw her again, just a block away. This told him the bomb must be as big as a fucking war in a bottle, or she would have let it go already. She needed some serious distance before she could detonate it. Second, he'd never make it to her in time. And then he saw it: the most gorgeous rainbow Mohawk in the world.

Beckett whistled hard and loud and friggin' Scotland was so heads up, his eyes found Beckett immediately.

"Grab her!" Beckett yelled, pointing to Bang, who was just passing to the kid's left.

Somehow the kid put it together and tackled Bang. Beckett ran as fast as he could, nursing his elbow and shoulder, knowing the closer he got to Bang, the less likely she'd be to set off the bomb on his back.

Scotland had her pinned, but had big eyes for the weapon in her hand. Bang was smart and sneaky, but she wasn't strong.

"Hey, Bang. You've met my new friend?" Beckett asked as he jogged up. "Let go of the gun."

She did as she was told. Any other day in Poughkeepsie two men tackling a woman might be cause for concern, but with so much pandemonium, anything that wasn't on fire was just not that exciting.

"So here's what's happening," he told them. "You, me, and my friend Land here are going to sit in my car. Got that?"

Land got off of her and pocketed her gun.

"Put the safety on, pup," Beckett offered. "You know how to drive yet?"

Land gave him a slow smile and a nod. "No license though." He shrugged.

Beckett shook his head. "See that Challenger? That's my ride. I might need a wheelman today. Got that?"

"Sure." The loyalty in Land's eyes was as close to worship as it got. The computer must have arrived for Trevor.

Beckett slipped into the backseat as Land pushed a surly Bang into the passenger seat. His shoulder throbbed, and the adrenaline that had kept him functioning was tapering off. It might be dislocated.

"So, Bang. First things first," Beckett said. "I know you protect your own ass like it's your religion, so that's why you and this bomb are super good friends until I have the answers I need."

Land gasped at the word *bomb* and covered his mouth. "Shit. Shit. Damn, son."

"Shut it." Beckett would have slapped him in the back of the head, but he wasn't moving his arms for anything right now. "Start the car."

Land twisted the keys dangling in the ignition.

"Are you the only one bombing shit up here in Poughkeepsie today?" Beckett demanded.

The woman nodded.

"Remember not to fucking lie to me. If someone so much as has a smoky fart here in town after this, you are chopped meat," he snarled.

"He wanted it varied today. I'm the only bomber." Bang started to look shifty. "That's the way I prefer to work."

"Did you tell him my brothers were at the hotel?" Beckett asked.

Land interrupted, looking in the rearview mirror past Beckett. "Damn, here comes, like, the entire New York police force."

Beckett looked up at the hotel window where his brothers should be, then he looked at the heads-up display. Spider reported the arrival of backup from surrounding counties. And he could see that his brothers had called 9-1-1 and reported an officer down.

"Where'd you hit the cop?" Beckett rested his painful elbow on his knee and used one hand to pull out and open the tracker-gun case he'd kept in his pocket. He palmed the air-pressure gun he had loaded with a tracker.

"I hit him in the armpit, trying for the sweet spot in his vest," she relayed calmly. This was just a job.

Land was horrified. "Bitch."

"Let me guess, he wanted you to kill my brothers?" Beckett asked. "That old bastard is a rat."

Bang said nothing, neither confirming or denying, and kept staring out the window.

"I'm going to offer my advice," he continued. "I'm going to dismantle Rodolfo's whole goddamn empire. You're part of that at the moment, while you're working for him, so I'm afraid I can't let you go without a new commitment." After he fired, a small puncture wound marked Bang's neck, a tiny trickle of blood trailing from the origin point. "That was a Grade four-sixty-five tracker chip."

She whirled around, her calm façade cracking.

"And I can tell by your eyes you know that means you're no longer protected, no matter where you are. Your contract with Dolfy just expired."

Her eyes narrowed.

"You're obviously thinking," Beckett continued. "And that would be a poor choice right now. Just so we're clear, no less than five people have the code to end your life. You can now have your heart stopped while you're walking to the CVS." He let her process that for a moment. "Care to dismantle your bullshit and then we can talk?" Beckett slid the device to her over the seat.

They watched, with Land's eyes on and off the road as he rolled around the block, as Bang went through a series of motions to disconnect the bomb's external trigger along with the remote in her pocket.

She threw the backpack down beside her when things were finally safe. "How dare you?" She held her neck and looked like she wanted to slap Beckett.

"Don't you think it's poetic justice?" he asked. "Bang ends with a bang—just an internal one."

He was rewarded with a shudder.

"What are your conditions?"

Beckett could hear a touch of an accent now. Maybe a former Southern Belle? "My conditions are simple: Leave. Go use your talents for something worthwhile—work in construction, or as a fireworks specialist, some shit like that."

"Fine. I will do that. But first you take this thing out of my neck. I don't want to be tracked like a dog." She moved her hair and pointed to the offending device.

"Nope. No can do. Just review in your mind how that thing is made and let me know when you figure it out."

Beckett tapped his foot and spoke to Land, who had thankfully pulled the car to a stop. "Type out a message on that display and send it to Spider. Tell him to send Dildo here to pick up Bang and help her dispose of this fucking bomb." He turned his attention back to the woman.

"Hmm…yes, poison, barbs, I get it," she assured him. "But how do I know you won't light me up when you're high as a kite sometime?"

"Because when my brain is intoxicated, all I want to do is fuck. And I'm off drugs, so it's your lucky fucking day. In the past I would've killed you so hard right now—and part of me still really wants to. My fucking brothers? Really?" He stopped for a second and let the hate flow through him, his protective instincts washing in like a tide. "But I'm taking a new approach now. Know this, though: I own you, Bang. I own your mind, your talents, and every fucking thing you know." He smiled.

"Okay. I will do this," Bang said, nodding. "I will leave. But if I find out how to remove this thing, I will." She turned and looked at Beckett as if she knew this moment of mercy was an act for the kid sitting in front of him.

"You mess with it, it kills you—which also makes me warm and fuzzy. So have at it." He shrugged. "I have a friend who's going to pick you up on this corner. I'll need you to hang with my people for a while, you got me? Remember the tracker." Bang got out of the car and Beckett called after her when she failed to take the backpack. "You have a memory problem? I said this backpack was your new best friend. It's on you."

Dildo pulled up behind Beckett and waited.

"That's your ride." Beckett nodded toward Dildo.

Bang leaned in and grabbed her pack. When she'd pulled away with his man, Beckett had Land type new orders for Spider into the car display: have Dildo bring the bomb to Treats.

Land was all jazzed up, clearly thrilled to see Beckett Taylor in action. "I think you need a doctor," he said, turning to look in the backseat. "Just guessing, but I'm pretty sure that tore-up shoulder is disgusting." He made a face.

Beckett glanced down and saw that the fabric on his jacket and shirt was worn away. The road rash beneath was bright red and bleeding. "I got to get to my brothers. You cool? You can leave. You should be home, by the fucking way." Beckett opened the back door. The motel was now swarming with cops.

"No way. You wanted people enforcing shit. I was on it. Helped a crowd stop a guy with a gun, and now this sick bitch? This is a rush. I want to work for you!" Land bounced in his seat.

"Just keep the car running for now. You're not working for me, pup." Beckett stepped out and made his way — much more slowly than the first time — toward the motel. His brothers must have been watching for him, because in an instant they were both in front of him on the sidewalk.

"Everybody all right?" Beckett felt relief washing through him.

"Melvin's still with us, and the family is fine," Blake reported. "Thought we lost *you* for a second, though." He put his hand on Beckett's un-mangled shoulder.

"Back at you both, and I'm thrilled to see you, but you need to get inside. I don't need you as bait on the street." Beckett pointed to the motel's side entrance, and one of the cops there let them stand inside.

The arm he usually committed the brothers' handshake with was too painful to move, so they all just half hugged quickly.

Blake leaned in. "So, the woman, you want the cops to pick her up?"

Beckett shook his head. He had plans for Bang he had no intention of sharing with his brothers.

Just then John McHugh's voice carried as he stepped into the vestibule where the brothers stood. "Why don't you ask Taylor?" he yelled over his shoulder. "That's why we're here, right?" The older man stepped up to the toes of Beckett's shoes and poked him in the chest. "Taylor, you waste of skin. What did you bring into my city? How dare you issue a call to arms on television? An officer here is *down!*" he said, seething.

As Livia rushed in and stepped between them, Beckett had flashbacks to her wedding day. Her father only moved because she was there. He was a man on the edge.

"Dad, please, he's hurt," she said.

McHugh took the smallest of steps back.

"I need you to treat these guys as if they're under fire," Beckett told him. "I will handle Vitullo."

McHugh glared as he was called away by another officer. He didn't even acknowledge Beckett's words.

Beckett looked at Livia as her father retreated down the hallway. "Can I get you to watch G? He's with the local Channel Five newscaster. I'll have a kid named Scottland with a rainbow Mohawk bring him over."

She nodded, and Beckett hugged her with his good arm, waving away her concern over his wound. He turned to his brothers. "Stay here. This is a great place to stay safe now."

He slipped out before McHugh could return and remember he was looking for his head. He had Scottland drive him a few blocks over so he could watch the ticker on the display. The 9-1-1 calls reporting crimes were down, and the reports of citizen's arrests and fires under control were dominating. Satisfied that the city had pulled itself back from the brink, Beckett gave Scottland the new job of getting G to Livia and handed him a wad of cash for taxis or whatever he'd need.

Then he eased himself back into the driver's seat and headed to the home of one of his tenants. She just happened to be a nurse.

30

PARLAY

As his nurse/tenant finished up on his shoulder, Beckett used his good arm to text:

Me4et at Firefly Par#k in on1e hour$.

He sent the message to Spider to have it relayed to all his people. This feud was as personal as it got.

He thanked her profusely and promised to see a doctor when the smoke cleared. He returned to the Challenger and called Dutch. "Did you take Primo and Sevan to the doctor and get their blood drawn, cheeks swabbed for DNA, and all that stuff?...And you have the results? Sweet. Hold that crap in a safe place and bring it to the meet. Thanks."

He rolled up into Firefly to see most of his douches hanging around, with a few stragglers still trickling in. When he had a good crowd, he began to speak:

"I tried to do this painlessly, in a way that protected each and every one of you. But today things changed. Rodolfo Vitullo lived through the house fire we helped him have, and after months of lying low, he decided it was time to fire back. What he wasn't expecting, and could never imagine, is that you guys would defend Poughkeepsie. Together. And I want to fucking thank you for that." He took a second to swallow his thankfulness. "We're going to split up and make sure no more crap blows up and no more people get rowdy."

The crowd started to clap, slowly, but eventually it rolled into a full-out shouting session. They'd saved Poughkeepsie, impossibly, by being an army all of their own.

Beckett clapped as well. But he had more to handle. The man that had orchestrated this terrorism was still sucking on air, and that needed to stop. He had his people break into teams, continuing the good work of kicking any ass they needed to. When the meeting dispersed, Beckett turned to see Shark, Primo, and Sevan walking with Dutch from his car to the meeting site.

"Okay," he announced as they arrived. "We're taking ourselves to Rodolfo."

Primo's mouth opened. "I thought Father was dead!" he gasped.

Beckett gave a brief head shake, and Shark punched Primo in the face.

"I'm going to take these two fuckers to Rodolfo to see if he wants to trade," Beckett told Shark and Dutch. "I'll be alone. If things go haywire, you know what to do." He pointed to his prisoners and then toward the Challenger.

Once he'd stuffed Primo and Sevan in the backseat, Beckett called Dutch over. "You've got the DNA stuff, right?"

The man nodded.

Beckett reached into the car and grabbed an envelope from the glove box and Eve's motorcycle helmet from the floor. "These are the remaining pieces of the puzzle you should need. Do what you have to do to check for a familial match among these ASAP. As soon as you know, I know, got it?"

Dutch nodded again.

Beckett nodded in return — seemed like the thing to do — and began the drive to Rhinebeck, where a terrified Bang had told Spider Rodolfo was camping out. She'd become very chatty after he showed her the app he had to engage her tracker's neurochemicals.

When they arrived, less than an hour later, three men stood at attention at the front entrance of Rodolfo's new estate. Their eyes widened when they saw Beckett get out of the car. Sevan and Primo refused to come out.

"Fine, fuckers. Stay here." Beckett held up his phone and showed them the buttons he had on the screen. "Lest you forget, I own you.

And if I don't call by a certain time, Eve will press the buttons from where she is." Beckett put the phone in his pocket. "And if you tell anyone about the thing in your necks, I'll kill you. Plus, Spider's watching from the heads-up display. Smile!" He gave them a big smile before turning to address the doormen. "I want to parlay with Vitullo."

It was an old-school trick: two bosses would meet with the promise of leaving alive. It had fallen out of favor because there was no honor among thieves, but Beckett figured if anyone would appreciate an old-school reference, it was the cryptkeeper himself. The men spoke into a walkie.

After a pat down and a few minutes' wait, Beckett was approved. He walked into the living room to find Rodolfo with index cards spread out on a dining-room-table-sized coffee table. A man in the corner had his gun trained on Beckett.

"A little late to parlay, Taylor. You fucked with my ultimate plan. Now nothing will stop me from making Poughkeepsie a crater in the ground that no one would even stop to take a shit on. And soon." Rodolfo crossed out the contents of one index card with a giant red X.

"So poetic." Beckett shook his head. "You seemed relaxed. Must have had a good dose of fiber." He rocked back and forth on his feet, hands in his pockets. "I'm here for a trade. I have two bitches you might want."

"Let me guess: Primo and Sevan?" Rodolfo smiled. "I do not care one flying fart what you do with them."

"Tsk-tsk. Primo will be so sad to hear you say that," Beckett countered. "Also, I have the eggs."

"Better yet, tell me what happened to the babies. Then we can talk trade." Rodolfo shuffled another stack like they were playing cards.

"They didn't make it. Too fragile. Too soon. You had to know that, though. Just as I'm sure you know your beloved Nicholas shot Alison." Beckett shrugged. "So much for trust, right?"

Just then one of Rodolfo's minions led Primo and Sevan into the room. Rodolfo looked up. "Your bargaining chips? They're now mine."

The minion then took Sevan out with a silent bullet to the neck. Beckett worked not to flinch.

"Vin, clean up that mess," Rodolfo barked.

Sevan's lifeless body required both Vin and the gunman to drag it out of the room. They had to stop and adjust a few times.

"Now I have my son, and one of my most despicable enemies is dead. Things are looking up," Rodolfo said. "Now, the eggs you mentioned. Let's talk about that."

Beckett whistled. "Seriously? Why would I tell you shit? Look how you treat the son you have. He's totally expendable to you, no?"

Primo's holier-than-thou act fell off like a dead foreskin. "Dad, Jesus! I've been kept for the longest time by this asshole. Please tell me you tried to get me out? His stupid girlfriend had people golf-club my balls. My *balls*." His hands shook.

"Son, do need I remind you I didn't let them kill you when there were thirty laser sights trained on your face? Of course you matter. I just didn't know what had happened to you, and I was desperately trying to replace you in some way."

Primo looked a little confused, but nodded. "Thanks, Dad. That means a lot."

"Give him a nice, big hug so I know you mean it, and then we can deal with you forcing your decrepit sperm on my wife," Beckett suggested from across the room.

Rodolfo made a face like he'd stepped in dog shit. "I don't have to do this. I don't have to do anything you say. I can make you give me the answers I need."

"One little hug, Rodolfo. What's it going to do, kill ya?" Beckett stepped backward and invited Primo in with a sweep of his arm. "Say hello to Papa. I'm sure he's missed you, like he said. Maybe you'll even get to borrow the car!"

Primo looked wary, but walked past Beckett, eyes hopeful as they turned toward his father. As Primo stepped in and embraced a stiff Rodolfo, Beckett slipped his hand in his pocket and tapped his screen twice.

The effect was instantaneous: Primo's neck and head exploded. And as his body slipped to the ground, Beckett noticed Rodolfo was also missing some vital parts of his head.

Behind him in the hallway, partially down the stairs, Sevan's body had also worked as a bomb. Both Vin and the gunman lay slain.

Beckett pulled out his phone and took a picture of Rodolfo with Primo at his feet. Next he grabbed the gunman's weapon out of his bloody hands. He then slid down the handrail of the stairs, taking aim at Rodolfo's men wherever they popped up. He hit the ground running and made sure the men standing outside also had a bellyful of lead before he left.

As he drove away from Rhinebeck, Beckett sent the picture of Rodolfo to his whole crew with the accompanying message:

This is how we thank assholes
for messing with Poughkeepsie.

Eve was startled awake by the phone that vibrated in her hands. She opened the picture, and it took her a minute to figure out what the hell she was looking at. When she finally figured it out, she was grateful she hadn't eaten in God knew how long because if there were anything in her stomach, she would surely want to vomit.

She stood and looked into the nursery, where she found a much more pleasant scene. The babies were in the same crib again, pressed together like they were still in the womb.

A nurse touched her shoulder. "Hey, want to wash up and come get a closer look?"

No. Yes. No. Yes. Please God, yes. Don't get attached, Eve. They might not be yours. Eve smiled and washed her hands carefully as the nurse watched.

"Okay, Mama, let's go."

When Eve walked into the NICU, it was as if her heart was leading the way. They were so tiny, a lump together. It was hard to see their faces through all the tubes.

She felt a lump in her throat.

"Go ahead—see this?" The nurse pointed to a gap in the crib. "Reach in there and stroke their skin. They like it."

Eve had a desperate need for Beckett right then. He needed to be here with her, not presiding over dead bodies. The pink of little Theodore was closest, so small and delicate that you could see his veins—almost a transparent version of a baby. His skin was soft when she stroked him. The nurse fed her details.

"Theodore here is just over three pounds, and he's doing fairly well. He's a fighter, that's for sure."

Eve looked at his tiny face. Tape and tubes cluttered his beautiful body which was dressed only in a diaper. He turned his head a bit toward her.

"That's right. He knows his mommy!" The nurse walked quietly to the other side of the crib. "How about little Mouse? Come on over." She smiled, which seemed out of place here, surrounded by the tiniest of babies. When Eve didn't move, the woman touched her shoulder. "It's okay to be happy. You're a new mom. I know this looks scary, but these are your babies. Love them for the moment you're in. And know that you're in a good moment."

Eve nodded and reached in to touch little Mouse. She ran her finger up her desperately small chest. The baby took a shuddering breath.

I love them.

It was tripping and falling. The walls inside her tumbled down. And she didn't know how long she had with them. She didn't know if they were really hers. Maybe it didn't matter. Teddy and Mouse. Everything else fell away.

She reluctantly removed her finger from where she could feel Mouse's heartbeat like butterfly wings. And she took her phone out and took a picture. Then a little video. Then another picture. And then she washed her hands again, and until shift change, she went from one twin to the other, stroking them and talking softly.

Ryan kissed Midian again. He'd just stopped in to see her on his way back into Poughkeepsie after he'd finally been able to leave Fallom, and she'd been *very* happy to see him. He was a bit pissed that he'd missed all the insanely crazy action on the home front, but Midian seemed to feel just fine about the fact that he'd been far away from danger all day.

Now he kept trying to leave to help the station do the ridiculous amount of paperwork required to explain and document the crazy-assed day they'd had, but then he'd spin on his heel to taste her another "one last time." The knowing look in her eyes drove him crazy, and her accent was brain meltingly sexy.

"You leaving, Chuck Norris? I've still got a little time for you." She traced his chest with her manicured finger.

"Mmmm...so much of Poughkeepsie has just finished burning right now," he said, struggling to form coherent thoughts.

"I know a few things here that are extremely hot. You may need to attend to them." After that she initiated a kiss, her grip on his neck promising that her words were true.

Finally, moments later, she pushed him out, shutting the door so he would go back to work. Ryan shook his head as he headed for his truck. That woman was better than Viagra dipped in tequila for his penis. She could make fun of him, yet still keep him feeling super-duper manly — her words.

They'd been coming out of a restaurant after dinner a few weeks ago when she'd first told him that. "You know I love a man who carries a piece," she'd said nonchalantly.

He remembered the burst of pride he felt when she'd noticed he was wearing it. "Part of the job."

"It's a sexy part, Chuck Norris."

His male ego had exploded all over the place, and he'd just smiled, unable to form actual words for a moment.

"Hey, what's that bitch doing to your truck?" Midian had asked a moment later as they crossed the parking lot.

He'd shaken his head at his pyscho ex. "That's Trish. She's insane."

"Oh, the chick that keeps putting all that crap on your truck?"

"Uh, yeah. She seems to still be pissed we aren't dating anymore."

"Well, shoot her," Midian had said, as if the solution were perfectly obvious. For a moment Ryan had felt like he was talking to Beckett. Trish still hadn't noticed them. She was busy toilet-papering the truck as if it were a mummy.

"I can't. I wish I could. She's wrecked my stuff a ton."

"That's bullshit. No way, *cariño*." In an instant, Midian had slipped off her heels and pulled off her earrings. "This bitch will have a very nice conversation with my fist in a minute."

He'd held out his hand and accepted her jewelry, thinking surely she was kidding.

"Hey, slutron, back up off my boyfriend's truck!" Midian called. She moved so quickly, Ryan had to jog to catch up.

Trish had her wild eyes on. "Boyfriend? He was my fiancé, my soul mate. How about you back up off my future?"

Trish had stood a good foot taller than Midian, but she didn't seem to notice.

"Hit me," Midian dared. "Hit me once, baby. Make it good, though. It's the only shot you'll get in."

Trish had bared her teeth in a way that meant she was on her second bottle of wine and she thought she was making a smile. "Fine, bitch." She'd stepped up.

"Ladies, please, no need to fight over me," Ryan had said. But an evil voice in his head contradicted him. *Go for it, ladies. Fight for me. I need popcorn and a little alone time in the bathroom.*

Trish pushed hard on Midian's forehead with her index finger. Midian had used her boobs to begin, bouncing them off Trish's torso. And Trish had snapped. Ryan had stopped fantasizing when she slapped Midian across the face, then grabbed a handful of her hair.

Instead of returning the slap or grabbing Trish's hair in retaliation, Midian had reached up and grabbed the hand Trish had put in her hair. She then gave her a right uppercut to the jaw that surely resulted in whiplash. Trish tried to pull her hand back, but now Midian used it as a way to keep her close. She punched Trish in the eye and then again. The last time she hit her, Trish had covered her face with her other hand.

At that point Ryan had finally stepped in and lifted Midian in the air. "Whoa, spitfire. I don't want you to kill her."

He'd then realized a crowd had gathered, which grew his man card another two sizes. And the cop part of his brain liked them all as witnesses for Midian. Everyone had seen that Trish instigated the physical part of the confrontation.

That date with Midian had next included a trip to jail for Trish—finally his truck-cam footage had paid off as a record of her vandalism—and Midian twisted up like a pretzel, screaming his name at her apartment. Yet another time he'd been reluctant to leave.

As he pulled into the parking lot at the police station, he contemplated turning around yet again. She could fight, she had an accent, and his mother was freaking crazy about her. "*That girl, she looks at you like you're her future,*" Mom had told him. "*You be good to that one.*" And that was his plan. If Midian stayed in love with him, he was going to let her know he had every intention of marrying her. Difficult as it had been, he was now thankful for Eve's presence in his life, because she'd made him realize he wanted love. He needed it, and more importantly, he deserved it.

He texted Beckett to check in, still smiling to himself as he walked into the building. Beckett texted back almost immediately and asked to meet—quite politely, actually—and also asked Ryan to bring McHugh along.

No wonder he'd been so polite. Perhaps Ryan was just in a charitable mood, but it did seem to make sense for them to work together at this point. He took a deep breath and texted his boss as well.

Beckett sat on the hood of his Challenger and tried to ignore the pain in his shoulder while he waited for Morales to arrive. He pulled into Firefly Park about twenty minutes later, just as dusk gave way to full darkness.

"Penis chunk." He said in greeting.

"Vagina flap," Beckett replied.

Morales came around his infamous truck to stand in front of him. "Eve okay?"

"So far. She sent me pictures of the kids. Doing the DNA testing, so we'll see."

Ryan looked at his shoes. "You going to be with her soon?"

"As soon as I tie up a few loose ends." Beckett nodded in the direction of the parking lot entrance. "Company's here."

McHugh parked his car and got out with a look of supreme disapproval. He shook Ryan's hand and ignored Beckett. "I see no point in us talking. Actions speak louder than words, and I know you almost got my girls, my grandchildren, killed today." McHugh pointed at Beckett's face.

"But they're just fine, aren't they? I'm not suggesting that was a good thing to have happen. I hated it," Beckett said. "But since then I've been able to stop additional fires and explosions. And also,

Vitullo's dead," he added after a moment. "And his son. I'm positive. No resurrecting this time."

"Is that supposed to help? Because Vitullo's been in business for years. Hell, since I was a little kid, and never have any of his dealings blown up a building in my town." McHugh's veins were popping out in his neck.

"No, but his daughter did kidnap Livia to impress her papa," Beckett countered. He noticed Morales giving a small nod.

"And my son-in-law found her," McHugh shot back. "And he brought her back to me. He has a lot going for him, but getting mixed up with the likes of you is not one of his strengths in my estimation. You are a rabble rouser and damn near had anarchy in Poughkeepsie."

"I'm not trying to take credit for Blake's heroism," Beckett said calmly. "My brother did good. I'm inspired by him, just like you are, and as I've said, I'm making changes. You guys had your hands full, and I'm not saying I'm blameless, but as much as I love my brothers, I needed to make the people of this city safe as best I could. That's what I had. I could ask them to defend what's theirs. And they were proud to do it too. I don't deserve it, but I wish you'd give me a shot. We've already started giving people a chance to go straight and get on their feet. And we're trying to make a place to help foster kids' transition into life. Can you see the intention there?"

"I've seen the places you and your crew are fixing up. I'm aware. But don't you see, I have to assume these places are for your own gain. 'Cause I remember you from back in the day, when you were a drug dealing, thieving pimp with a chip on his shoulder. I remember that guy real well. You weren't the one on the other end of testimony for years dealing with the outcomes of your 'leadership.' I'm going to have to see a lot more than freshly painted drywall to put a halo on your goddamn head."

McHugh crossed his arms in front of his chest. "One of the ones who comes to mind now is Eve. How's she doing? Did she live through your little escapade? How about her father? Dr. Hartt's been missing for months. No funeral. No explanation. Those are the kinds of telltale signs that, for me as a policeman? That raises a few flags."

Beckett chewed on his bottom lip. He didn't deny any of it. "Time will tell, then. I know nothing I say means anything to you. You'll have to see success, and I'll give you that. Just like you guys had help when you needed it."

"You're assuming I'll let you stay in town, Taylor. And I've never agreed to that."

"I'd like to offer my crews to aid in clean up from today's mess," Beckett said. "They work fast, and they deliver top-notch construction."

"I'm not taking anything from you, except your freedom one fine day. Walk the straight and narrow, Taylor. The minute you spit gum on the sidewalk, I'll have your ass in jail. You need to drop to your goddamn knees and thank the Lord that my two girls love you as much as they do. They don't see what I see, and they're the only reason I'm not pulling you in right now."

McHugh got in his police car and sped off.

"That went well." Morales snapped his gum.

"I thought so, Sargent Sarcasm. He didn't arrest me on the spot, so I'll take what I can get. I'm serious about my guys helping out. Each house has a site leader and a nice little crew of hard workers, and they went out into the streets with hammers in hand this afternoon. You get in a pinch, call me." Beckett pushed away from his car. "I'm just glad the worst of it seems to be over."

"You going to see Eve?" Ryan took steps toward his truck. "She's going to need you. Alison Wexford's parents intend to try for custody of the babies. They don't understand why Eve is 'posing' — their word — as the babies' mother. They want a DNA sample from her."

"Yeah. I'm waiting on those very DNA results right now — need to have some answers for her before I bring it up again. But I'll get in touch with her right now." Beckett got in the driver's side and nodded at Morales as he walked away.

Once the truck had left the parking lot, he dialed Eve and couldn't believe how great he felt when he heard her sleepy voice on the other end of the line.

"Hey, killer! How you doin'?"

"I'm just fine. How are *you?*" she asked. "Spider won't tell me much, but I can see from the news that some serious shit went down in Poughkeepsie today."

"Yeah, sort of Rodolfo's last stand, but baby, you'd be so proud of the work we've done. Our people really came together today, and we beat him. We saved this town — something none of us could have done on our own."

She was silent on the other end of the line.

"I know I sound like a crazy person, some drugged-out hippy, so I'll shut up," he said. "Tell me about those babies. I can't wait to come see them."

"No, no. I'm just amazed," she finally managed. "I'm overwhelmed by everything at this point, but if everyone's safe and you feel good, I'm really, really glad."

He could hear her taking a deep breath.

"Listen, visiting hours will be over by the time you could get here, and I'm going to get some sleep as soon as they make me leave," she said. "If things were as crazy as they seem to have been, why don't you sleep for a while and come in the morning?"

Always so practical. Beckett decided this wasn't the time to tell her their house had burned to the ground, or that he wasn't quite sure where his brothers were staying at the moment. "I think you're probably right," he told her. "I'll keep tabs around here for a few more hours, get some rest, and then be there first thing tomorrow."

"Okay, see you then," she said. "Love you."

Beckett hung up and decided a quick trip to urgent care would probably be in his best interest. And he didn't want any leftover Vitullo idiots flaring up either. He looked down and silently willed his phone to bring him a message from Dildo. He needed that DNA info. He needed to not break his promise to Eve.

31

FIGHTERS

The next morning, with a few hours of sleep in the front seat of the Challenger under his belt—just like the old days—and a last-minute delivery from Dildo in his pocket, Beckett strolled into the NICU in Maryland with a nurse by his side. He was busy charming her, like he always would. She watched carefully as he washed his hands.

Eve had taken a hotel room next to the hospital, running there for a quick shower and a power nap when there were shift changes, but she was here right now, keeping her vigil.

He kissed the top of her head, standing behind her chair. "How are they?"

"Good. They're fighters. This is Teddy, and that's Mouse."

Beckett smiled and shook his head as he went to the opposite side of the crib and reached his big hand in to gently touch her. "They both are loving that, you know? Wherever they are, they love it."

Eve just smiled. Teddy had his little hand curled around her pinkie finger. She winced as she shifted positions.

"You okay, killer?" he asked.

She smiled. "My back is seizing up a little, but I'm not letting go until he does."

A nurse pulled a second chair over, and Beckett thanked her as he sat.

He smiled at Eve. "I would expect nothing less, but you haven't slept in a while. You need a break?"

Eve shook her head. "They never take a break. Not for a minute. They fight every second."

Mouse curled her free hand around Beckett's index finger. "They are so tiny," he marveled. "Perfect too."

She nodded.

"I've got some news for you."

She met his gaze. "Okay."

"You are their mother."

She dropped her gaze from him to the babies. Even he could hardly believe it: the precious, tiny ones were hers.

"Oh. Wow."

She was silent after that, so controlled. Beckett didn't notice she was crying until one of her tears splashed on the plastic crib.

"Wow," she said again, looking up to smile at him.

He nodded, smiling back. "Congratulations."

Then she asked with her eyes the question he knew she didn't want to voice. His face went from happy to resigned to the truth.

"So he's the father," she said softly.

Beckett shrugged. "Doesn't change the fact that these kids are yours and they're perfect."

She rocked back in forth in her seat. "My dad would have loved this day."

"He's loving it, baby, just like I said. You know he is." Beckett removed his hand from the incubator reverently before coming to stand next to her. He held his arms open, and she pulled him down to her, hugging him hard. Little Teddy wiggled and freed her finger. Eve let Beckett pull her into a standing hug.

After a moment she sighed and looked at the clock. "Shift time. We got to get out."

She blew kisses to the babies. *Her* babies. And left the NICU with Beckett as the nurses started their change procedures. As they walked in the hallway, he held her and she allowed it.

"Now the bad news." Beckett stopped and turned her by the shoulders to face him again. "Ryan says Bill and Cindy are starting the process of attempting to get custody of the babies. They've asked for a DNA sample from you."

Eve closed her eyes for a moment. "I guess I should have called them back. I know they left messages with the nurses here. This must be so painful for them." Eve reached into the pocket of her jeans and looked at the note. "I'll fix it now."

"What do you want to do?" Beckett asked.

"I'm going to talk to them. Tell them the truth."

Beckett followed her to the sidewalk where she dialed the number on the note and hit speaker.

"I have a message from you," she said when he answered. "This is Eve."

"Well, as soon as I get the courts involved you're willing to call," he snapped.

"I'd like to meet with you," Eve continued, her voice even. "When's good for you?"

"How about now? We're staying at the Hilton. Because as soon as the papers go through, we want to see the babies. Just because the hospital thinks you're their mother doesn't make it true."

"I'll meet you in the lobby now," she continued smoothly, un-ruffled. "That's my hotel too." Eve disconnected the call.

"I can have lawyers handle this," Beckett offered. "You're exhaust-ed. And they're raw from the loss of their daughter and son-in-law." He held her hand again.

"I'm doing it now. Coming?" Eve walked to the back of the parking lot. The Hilton was connected to the hospital by a dirt path made by all those who'd cut through before.

Bill and Cindy were already waiting when they walked in. Bill gestured to the two sofas in the lobby like he owned them. Eve sat, and Beckett took the spot next to her.

Bill had just opened his mouth to speak when Eve turned to Beckett.

"Can I have the results?" she asked.

He pulled a folded paper from his back pocket and handed it to her.

Eve was exhausted—physically and emotionally—but she knew these parents' pain was just beginning. It infused her with patience and compassion rather than the irritation and anger she might have expected.

"We did a DNA test," she told them calmly, handing them the paper. "I'm the biological mother. But know that I'll take as many of those tests as you want me to. Whatever you need. The biological father is dead, and I can bring you proof of that as well."

Cindy slumped into Bill, as if the hope of grandchildren had kept her upright and now she had nothing to stand for.

"I'd like to tell you that your daughter was forced into this situation," Eve said, struggling to help them understand. "It was not her choice. She was kidnapped. And she could have done anything she wanted to those babies, but she kept them safe. Even in her death, she held on to give those babies a chance. I'm so thankful for that."

Eve covered her mouth briefly to compose herself.

"I'm not sure how this pans out. I feel like we've got a lot of ground to cover, but I lost my dad earlier this year, and my mother hasn't been a part of my life for a long time. These two babies could really use a set of grandparents. I know that might not be what you need or want right now, but it's my goal to stay in contact with you. And at some point, God willing, those babies will consider you family. They'll know that your daughter saved their lives."

Eve sat back, and Beckett took her hand again.

Bill set the paper down and rubbed Cindy's back. She began to sob, and Bill wrapped her in his arms.

"I'm so very sorry for your loss," Eve said after a moment. "Your phone now has my phone number, and I will always answer your calls from this point forward. I'm also adding you to the approved list to see the babies. Please feel free to go whenever you'd like."

Eve stood, and Beckett followed her back across the lobby.

"Wait," came a voice from behind them. "We'll see the babies."

She turned to see Bill still rubbing Cindy's back, but looking at her. She nodded. "The next visitation begins in two hours. That's when we can see them."

She and Beckett continued to the elevators, and as soon as the doors closed, he pulled her into a hug. "You know you're amazing, right?"

She hugged him back, the steel walls of the elevator reflecting them. "I can't believe they're mine...What are we going to do?"

"That has to be a mind trip," Beckett agreed. "You're probably in shock."

When the elevator opened on her floor, she let go of Beckett and showed him to her room. "It's crazy," she said as she unlocked the door. "And they are so, so tiny. I feel like I can't breathe when I'm not looking at them. Anything can happen." She put the card key on the dresser. "I've got two hours before I can head back."

"They'll be great. Their mother is stubborn and a fighter. You wait and see." Beckett sat on her disheveled bed.

"But they're partly their father's. I can't believe I'm tied to that man. It's such a violation." She felt her insides squirm.

"He's dead. And those children will be like you. You're going to raise them."

She sat next to him. "I killed their aunt."

Beckett shrugged. "I used their half-brother to blow up their father. I think we should stay away from that family tree."

"Does anyone else have a claim on these children? I don't want his family crawling out of the woodwork." Eve kicked off her shoes.

"I don't think there's much of that family left, and unless you put him down on the birth certificates, there shouldn't be much way to trace." Beckett kicked off his own shoes.

"I put you." She turned to face him. "As their father, I put you."

Beckett's jaw fell open a bit. "Me?"

"Yeah. You." Eve crossed her arms in front of her, watching his reaction.

His face softened. "Me."

In an instant he was off the bed and kissing her face, then her lips. She couldn't even get her arms around him. They were pinned to her chest.

"I thought maybe you wouldn't…want me as the dad. For a dad. You know what I mean?" He grabbed a handful of her ass and freed her hands with the same motion.

"We're married. Of course it's you," she said. "Teddy's middle name is Beckett. And Mouse's is Anna," she added softly.

He held her for a moment, scarcely breathing.

But after a moment, she looked up with a broad smile. "You ready for instant kids?" She put her hands on his chest.

"No. But are you? Is anyone ready for kids? I fucking doubt it. And baby, wait until you see — I'm making Poughkeepsie so goddamn safe God himself could take a shit with the door open on Main Street." He spread his arms wide.

"You should put that on the town sign." Eve kissed his now-frowning lips.

"Seriously? You want to be a wise ass? I have ways to deal with that." Beckett pulled her to him using the button on her jeans. As soon as they were undone, he yanked them down her legs, kissing her once she was bare.

"Is this a bad time?" He looked up at her from his knees.

She pulled one foot from the jeans that were like ankle handcuffs and set it on the bed behind him. "No. It's just what I need. Now."

With that she pushed his face between her legs. His laughter tickled as he took his time with her, using his fingers in wicked places and his tongue that knew just where to be. Soon she was whispering his name over and over. When she was at the very tippy edge of that wave of release she craved, he stood.

He wasn't laughing now. He was a predator, deadly. Her favorite man to fuck. He tossed her on the bed and before she could laugh, he entered her. He took her roughly and usually she was able to push back, but this time he held her down. She was close, so close she saw white, when he pulled out again.

She growled with anger and the loss of him.

"On your knees. Quick," he commanded.

Evidently she wasn't moving fast enough, because he grabbed her hips and flipped her, pulling her into a kneeling position. And then he was fury. With her hair in one hand, he used his other to alternate between spanking her ass and grabbing her breast, pinching the nipple hard. He was a warrior for her. When she came it was tension, then release.

She'd barely finished when he repositioned her again, this time on her back. He licked her, adding three fingers, deep and knowledgeable. What he could do with his mouth had her arching her back, toes curling until she came again.

And she knew he wasn't done. She kicked his shoulder until he stumbled backward, landing on his back. She was off the bed and standing over him in no time.

"Hang on," she told him. She landed on him hard and used every muscle she had to become a vice for him. She spun and rocked backward so he could see her ass while she grabbed a handful of him, rocketing him to his orgasm.

He sat up, and she slithered off of him, taking his dick in her mouth, still pulsing with ecstasy. She traced him with her lips and pinched his nipple to match.

He grabbed the back of her neck. "Fuck! Damn it, Eve. Jesus, that was so good."

She kept him in her hand as she finally put her head on his shoulder. His fingers went between her legs as well. They lay together, just breathing on the floor of the hotel.

"I was supposed to let you nap." He kissed her forehead.

"I needed that more. You have no idea. Best stress reliever ever."

She sat up and he followed suit, eventually helping her to her feet.

"I brought some clothes for you," he told her.

"You are my freaking favorite right now." Eve walked to the bathroom naked. When she looked over her shoulder, Beckett was biting his lip.

"You'd do the world a favor if you stopped wearing them all together," he said. "Let me run to the car and get your stuff. Get started, and I'll meet you in there."

Halfway through her second shampoo, he got into the shower behind her. They took turns washing each other's backs with the hotel washrags, and then he turned the water off and held the curtain open for her like a door.

"So, Ryan has the eggs, or what?" She got dressed quickly, all business again.

"Yeah. He's storing them somewhere for you. But keep your expectations low—all the transfers and stuff can't be good." Beckett pulled his shirt over his head.

"I can be back in there with them in ten minutes," she said, looking at the clock. "We got to roll." Eve put her shoes on but then looked up at Beckett. "Thank you."

"Thank you for giving me a chance," he said. "For not killing me when you wanted to. For treating my brothers as your own. For being the best mother those babies could have. For being my partner when we get to Poughkeepsie." He took her hand and pulled her in for another deep kiss.

A few days after the most exciting day Poughkeepsie had seen in quite a while, Livia and Kyle sat on the floor at Livia's house, building with monster-sized Legos. Mode had been mercifully untouched by the destruction, so Kyle was just back from work to pick up her son. And as it did on most days, her arrival turned into a visit. She had propped JB up between her legs, and Livia watched as Kellan kept busy with his own tower. Emme had her nose buried in a book, surrounded by stuffed animals.

"You know, we're thinking of moving," Kyle announced as she clicked a red block into place and smoothed a hand across JB's head.

Livia was immediately sad. "Really? The other night was just too much? Are you going to use the house Beckett got in Hawaii? I mean, I totally understand but —"

"Yeah, across the street from you, the Andersons are moving," Kyle interrupted. "So I was thinking, you know…"

"Oh. Oh! That would be fantastic. Holy shmoely. We could be sister wives!" Livia reached over and hugged Kyle around the neck.

"That's just disgusting. Jesus," Kyle said. "We're sisters, and that's enough. Keep your wifely parts in your pants." But she did hug her sister back.

"The cousins will be right across from each other. It'll be great!" Livia said. "Oh, now I went and moved you in in my head. What if the Andersons are being fickle like last time? I'll start being the worst neighbor ever so they have to leave." Livia smiled at her sister, which seemed to loosen something inside of her.

Kyle's next revelation sort of bubbled out. "I'm pregnant. Again."

Livia felt her mouth drop open. "No way! Congratulations. That's the best ever. Wow! Are you nervous?" She hugged her sister again.

"Of course. That's why I'm not going to tell you for a few more weeks." Kyle rolled her eyes. "Except I seem to have stopped being able to keep the secret. What if I jinxed it?" She went pale.

Livia shook her head. "That wasn't bad luck, sweetheart. It was biology. And we don't believe in jinx stuff here. You know that."

JB whimpered and Kyle picked him up, standing and starting to rock in one motion.

Livia stood as well. "You're a natural."

Kyle smiled. "That's because you keep popping out vagina fruit."

"The miracle of birth." Livia tilted her head in Emme's direction. "I'm sorry. I forgot."

Emme piped up, "My mommy say *vagina* is the name for girl parts, and they are very special."

Livia closed one eye, afraid of what her sister would say next.

"Mommy has a very special vagina," Kyle agreed. "I'm not surprised that she's so proud of it."

"Put my nephew down so I can slap you." Livia readied her hand.

"I will not." Kyle used JB as a shield, and he started laughing every time Livia pretended she was coming with a slap.

Soon Emme was mimicking her mother, and Kellan did his best as well. The whole room giggled, then held their breath, waiting for JB to laugh again with his little dimples showing. They must have played this game for almost ten minutes. Livia got a brief snippet on video to send to the guys.

Then as quickly as it began it was over, and JB began making sad noises instead of happy. Kyle took him into Livia's kitchen and popped him in the high chair as the whole crew followed, the older children suddenly needing a snack as well.

Livia opened the cabinet and pointed Kyle toward an assortment of jars as she moved to find something for her own children. She shopped for JB like he lived there too.

In a moment, JB was happy again with his prunes, Kyle moving quickly to keep up with his searching mouth, and Emme and Kellan had settled at the table to trade goldfish back and forth.

Livia touched her sister's arm. "It's going to be okay. I'll always be here for you. I hope this will be wonderful, but you'll never feel pain alone."

Kyle's eyes filled up. "Who said we needed a mom to know how it's done anyway?" She pulled her sister in for another hug.

EPILOGUE

SEVEN MONTHS LATER

Beckett held Mouse while watching Teddy toss all of his food on the floor. Gandhi ate it quickly, wagging his little stump the whole time.

He rubbed his hand over his face and sighed. "Dude, at least you're helping," he told the dog.

Teddy started laughing as Gandhi jumped up to see if Teddy had any more food on his highchair tray. Beckett held Mouse more tightly as she started laughing at the dog too. When Eve came in from the grocery store, the twins were still giggling.

A smile appeared on her face as soon as she heard them. "What's Daddy doing in here? And that stinky dog?" She unbuckled Teddy and lifted him from the chair.

"That dog is a goddamn hero. I would have been crying real tears if he hadn't just cleaned up all of Teddy's food." Beckett puckered up as Eve came in for kiss. She also kissed Mouse, who squealed.

"Crying? How far we've fallen, Mr. Taylor." Eve was soft. God, she was gorgeous. They were both exhausted—like boot-camp crazy stupid exhausted. The laughing was far less prevalent than the crying. These days, it felt like something was always crying. Sometimes he really wanted it to be him.

"No way. Running an empire is far easier than keeping these two happy." Beckett positioned Mouse in her bouncy chair and pointed it at Teddy. He trotted out to the driveway and grabbed the bags of groceries, handing them off to Eve who unpacked while he went to get more. When the car was finally empty, his phone buzzed. Cole was texting.

You coming for the final walk through?

S^ure t2#hin5g

He double-checked with Eve, who nodded at the calendar hanging on the newly painted wall. The rebuild from the fire had been fairly swift. The crews from Beckett's organization had put extra zeal into making things right for the boss and his new family.

"I know," she said. "Tomorrow the twins have their checkup, but today is your date with your favorite girlfriends." She winked at him when he growled at her teasing. "I drove past a few of the properties on the way home. The latest two renters look good—kids playing in the yard. It was great. Shark checked in too. His daughter is settled in school."

"More of the dream clicking into place. That's great." Beckett spanked her hard on the ass, which made Mouse laugh. "They've been hitting the sauce or something," he said. "Can't stop cracking up."

Eve bent over a little so he could smack her again, making the kids giggle. "They're overtired. If only I could explain the importance of naps in a way they'd understand. Next up they'll start throwing stuff."

He gave her one last smack. "You sure this is okay?"

"Yes. Go. You're already late. I got this."

He kissed her one more time before locking the door and heading over to Brothers' Legacy.

When he arrived, Cole and Blake were leaning against their respective cars, waiting for him. He got out, smiling because it was broad daylight and he was meeting his brothers. He missed Mouse right that second, and wished his lumbering form was here. He belonged. But still, life was good: no one shot at him, Cole didn't look like he'd been praying for Beckett's soul all night, and Blake was standing in the fucking sunshine.

"Look at this!" he yelled as he approached. "You beautiful bitches."

They pounded each other on the back, and Blake reached over and looped his finger around the pacifier ribbon Beckett had mistakenly left clipped to his shirt.

"Hardcore criminal no longer."

Beckett winked before popping it in his mouth. "I'm never afraid of a little prosthetic nipple."

Cole jangled the keys. "Are we ready? Let's see what all this hard work and ball busting got us."

"Father Bridge, your language!" Beckett taunted his brother in a high-pitched voice around the pacifier.

Blake put an arm around each brother as they walked to the entrance. "Oh, how the tables have turned."

They paused to take a selfie in front of the sign: one with Beckett's pacifier, one without.

"I feel like I should be carrying you brides over the fucking threshold," Beckett told them, laughing as Cole and Blake pretended to jump into his arms. But when they finally made their way in the foyer, they quieted.

There were still a few things that needed to happen, a few more curtains, and the molding was missing in a few places, but other than that it was a goddamn dream come true. In an instant, Beckett had chills. The interior had everything it needed to run a professional facility, but it was homey. The door clicked into place behind them, and the air was thick with possibilities. They strolled down the corridors, looking at the rooms, touching doorframes and light switches. Classrooms and offices were off a main hallway, giving the kids separate space from their living quarters. It was here that they'd learn a skill, learn how to apply for a job, how to dress for an interview, maybe knit.

Beckett finally stopped and pounded his chest with one fist. "I feel like I should have found this for us then. Back then I should have packed you guys up and found a place like this for us."

Blake nodded and put his hands in his pocket. "I feel the same way. Like if I'd been able to be in the sun, I could have found this for us."

Cole looked from one face to another. "We were kids. We did the best with what we were given. And because we were failed, we learned what was needed." He stepped into one of the offices and shuffled through a few folders on the desk. "Here it is. So I was at work, right? And I get a call from McHugh. He asked me to come down to the station, where I find a punk kid in one of the interrogation rooms looking surly."

Cole showed them both a mug shot: Bastian Reed.

"This kid was caught stealing food last week," he continued. "McHugh and Morales sensed something was off. He's supposed to be at home with his parents, but it turns out the parents left him to go score drugs in the city. This kid is homeless, and he was stealing food for two other kids who were living with him in an abandoned house. All three of them are coming here next week. He'll never have to steal food again."

Beckett nodded at the picture, recognizing the defiance in Bastian Reed's eyes. "I got a little fucker named Scotland I have in mind for one of those bedrooms too." He pointed at the hall.

Blake grabbed Beckett's shoulder. "Brotherhood."

Beckett had no words, he just held up his fist. Blake and Cole wrapped their arms around his, tattoos touching.

Once the brothers had given everything their seal of approval—they'd found just a few cosmetic things still in need of fixing before opening day—Blake and Beckett hurried off, but Cole stayed behind. He had one more appointment this afternoon.

Mrs. D was so short that he didn't see her at first, but when he laid eyes on her, bobbing her way through the parking lot and up the stairs, his whole body relaxed. His time in the Evergreen Home for Children was punctuated with her kindness and insight. She'd refused to see only the angry, disagreeable child he was, insisting on investing her time and praise until he was able to stand proud. The sight of her was a journey back to his awakening as a person of worth.

And once she got close enough for him to see it, her expectant smile let him know that her being that type of talisman for him was not only okay, it was expected.

He stepped up to her and enveloped her in a hug.

"Cole Bridge, what have you gotten yourself into?" she asked.

"We've made this place for kids, and it's going to be like a home and—"

She kissed his cheek and hugged him again. "What did I tell you? All those years ago? Great things, my dear. Great things."

"Come inside. Let me show you around," Cole said, opening the door.

"Wonderful. And don't you have a little one? I heard around town that your family had grown."

"Yes, it has," Cole said. "Our son, JB, is seventeen months, and our daughter will arrive any day, so there's lots happening in our lives right now." He beamed with pride.

"Another? Won't you be blessed. They'll be the best of friends. I had my three boys close together."

"Three? I was pretty sure you had two," Cole said. "Was I not paying attention?" He stepped closer to her, her familiar perfume still a scent that meant safety to him.

"I had three sons. My oldest passed away when he was four. Alex even got to name his brother." It was stated as a fact, but the entire experience was in her eyes.

"I'm so sorry. I didn't know." Cole put his hand on her shoulder, realizing she'd found the courage to not only love her other sons, whose pictures she'd had decorating her office back in the day, but also find room in what had to be a bruised heart to love him as well. She was stunning.

"Don't be sorry. Even pain can't diminish the exquisite love Alex brought into this world, or my soul." She rubbed Cole's arm as she spoke.

Maybe because he now taught kids similar to the one he'd been with Mrs. D, he saw her technique for what it was. She was still teaching him, though she was long retired. Mrs. D once again showed him the appropriate response, the love of a mother.

"You are a wonderful mother." Cole patted her hand.

"And you are a wonderful man. And you were a wonderful boy. Let your heart help when you have choices to make. Of all the things you've been through, Cole—and trust me, I saw your pain when you would return from home visits—your heart remained pure, untouched by that woman's shortcomings." Mrs. D hugged his middle.

All the sudden he realized, like a light in the dark, that the mother God had given him was right in front of him. He almost gasped when he realized it. This woman, so eager to love him, had a space empty in her life, one for a son.

"Mrs. D?" He put his hands on her shoulders. "Can I ask you something?"

She nodded, smiling.

"My children, they only have one set of grandparents. They could use another." He waited, looking her seriously in her eyes.

A slow smiling of knowing came across her face. "Mr. D and I would love to fill that position."

Cole hugged her again and kissed the top of her head. "I'm not trying to replace Alex or anything…"

"No one could, sweetheart, but I've always had room for four. You're not a replacement. You've been mine since the day we met. Now, come, show me this new building," she said. "Let's celebrate. I'll tell you about my Alex while we walk." She looped her arm in his and smiled. "I'm so proud of you, Cole."

"My success is all because you believed I could be more." He felt his own eyes fill with moisture.

"The sky's the limit, dear. Always has been for you."

Cole made sure to mind Mrs. D's step as they went up the stairs and into his impossibly true dream.

Teddy and Mouse were so plump now, at eight months, that people said they should be on a football team — or sumo wrestlers. Beckett had put them in the double stroller, as they were due to meet Eve at Brothers' Legacy.

Today was the big day, the opening. One month after the walk-through, he checked Mouse and Teddy's little belts again and pushed the stroller up the sidewalk. It was crowded. There were dignitaries, business owners, social workers, and friends, plus the promise of cookies and lemonade after the grand tour.

Eve trotted up beside him, having come from the bank after closing on another new rental property, and placed a kiss on each of the babies before giving him one as well. After an appraising glance over the crowd, she took over the stroller, and Beckett found Blake and Cole toward the front.

The place looked great. He knew inside there were pristine bedrooms, game areas, and two kitchens. It was a great place to have a fresh start, and the list of those hoping to be admitted was already larger than the rooms they had available.

McHugh waltzed up with Kathy on his arm. "Gentlemen."

Beckett knew they'd likely never be close, but as long as they could work together, exist in the same space, he could manage. At the party Livia had hosted for the babies' homecoming a few months ago, John and Bill Langston had gotten on like gangbusters. It had soothed the rift between them a bit. John seemed to like everyone around Beckett, so Beckett held out a small hope that the man would accept him someday. Bill and Cindy were clearly still sad, but they took their job as grandparents seriously and were doing their very best to move on.

Ryan and Midian waved, her left hand sparkling with a recent diamond addition, and Ryan mouthed "cock flicker" in honor of the occasion. Beckett ignored him and nodded to Tashika as well. Recently, after Eve had disclosed her full situation and remaining eggs to the women, Tashika had volunteered to be the surrogate for a baby comprised of Eve from the past and Beckett from the future.

Though he was beyond grateful for this chance, the irony was not lost on him. The means to the eggs had been taken from Eve before she knew she wanted to kill Beckett. And now? Now they were a family with a family life like neither of them had ever dreamed would be possible. They rotated houses with his brothers on Sundays for family dinners, for God's sake.

And now, with a brother on either side, he faced the cameras to showcase their future. The Poughkeepsie Brothers' Legacy would be one of hope, one of brotherhood and sisterhood.

Cole, Blake, and Beckett wrapped their arms in a handshake and then together cut the ribbon on a whole new chapter ahead.

THE END

Sneak Peek from *Poughkeepsie Begins*,
a prequel to the Poughkeepsie Brotherhood series
by Debra Anastasia

Beckett put his head down and waited for Rick. Other kids his age would be calling girls to go on dates right now. Maybe playing a video game. Looking at colleges. Under a year left on this sentence a "caring" judge had issued for him, and in his head, he was plotting his first murder.

The fall leaves crackled under the man's approaching feet, steady. Beckett would never say out loud that he preferred the punch to the anticipation of it. He had to play by these rules, these fucked up rules, to keep the other kids inside his foster home safe. After all, Rick had a great track record with "hard" kids. And that was exactly how Beckett would be described by pretty much anyone except the two guys on either side of him.

Arm's reach. They were within arm's reach on either side of him. This Thursday dusk had cloud cover, so Blake Hartt stood tall, protected by the shade, on his right. Cole Bridge was on his left, silent and able to take obscene amounts of pain before buckling. He always went last. Cole was the closer.

But it started with Beckett. Rick's fist connected with his stomach, and then the wait was over. Sometimes, as he punched, Rick went on diatribes about kids these days, or explained how he was helping the boys to keep to the straight and narrow.

His words were instantly dismissed. His victims had lived too much life in their short years to believe his lies. Rick was a hitter. A beater. A sadist in the purest form.

The blows came as predictably as a drumbeat, and Beckett let his body be a target—never running, never even trying to. He had a deal with Rick: all beatings happened here. Never inside. Rick and his wife had ten kids in their clutches at the moment. Their motives were not obvious to those on the outside.

When Beckett was done, when he could take no more, he shifted his hand to hold his forearm instead of his other hand. And Blake, so observant, would step forward. Rick would switch targets then, taking on a new victim with vigor.

Beckett hated himself and loved Blake like a brother in those moments when he heard Rick's fist, or belt, or switch from a tree rain down on someone other than him.

And Cole never let it last long—sometimes waiting for Blake's hand to shift to his forearm, sometimes stepping forward before then. Today was one of those days. Cole's eyes flashed when Beckett glanced over at his face.

Cole stepped forward aggressively. And Beckett had to watch, because Cole would never grab his forearm to indicate he needed a break, or that something hurt particularly bad. *Just enough to catch my breath, to buck up*, then Beckett would step up again, he promised himself.

After all, before these guys, it had been only him to take the beatings.

Tonight Rick petered out before Beckett had a chance to take another turn. The man looked at the ground as he turned and staggered, probably ready to go back and screw his spineless bride. Nothing got Rick more excited than witnessing pain. *Fucker.*

They waited, motionless, until he was gone. Beckett listened to Rick's footsteps retreat until he heard them no more. Next business in order was a "first aid check," as Blake called it. He'd stashed ice packs in the hollow of one of the trees, and he now dug them out and passed them to Beckett and Cole. The nature-loving Blake somehow always had the packs cold and ready, even in the burning heat of summer. If there were any bleeds, they'd bandage them up, if they had those supplies. Finally they'd critique Rick's performance in a dark bit of humor that Beckett was pretty sure kept him sane.

Blake iced a spot on his chest while Cole put pressure on a bleeder on his bicep, his shirt pulled up.

Beckett put ice on his jaw, soothing a rare hit to the face from Rick, who knew how to hide marks like a master. "That bitch is getting sloppy," Beckett commented. "I think he's hitting menopause."

Cole rolled his eyes. "As long as menopause doesn't hit back, I'm sure he'll take another swing."

They all moaned as a laugh bubbled up.

Blake passed his ice pack to Beckett, who used it on his throbbing rib. "Got you in the money spot, huh?" Blake observed.

Beckett nodded. "Always finds my rib. Like a homing pigeon. Motherfucker."

The full dark descended, and all of them had school in the morning. Beckett tried not to be jealous of the kids who came into school in new clothes with a lunch packed by their moms. Their nights had to be as taxing as a fart. Nothing like this. Never like this.

Blake pulled out his cardboard piano, which Cole and Beckett hardly noticed anymore. This quirk was as much a part of Blake as his hair color. Cole continued to move, pacing around the clearing, restless when he usually sat still.

Beckett had seen the scars on the kid. Ol' Rick was not his first rodeo. Cole had been tortured when he was younger—so much so that the pain of hate almost felt soothing to him. The crack of a fist was likely as close as he got to a lullaby.

"What's up, brother? You got scabies or some shit like that? You're shifty like a meth head." Beckett tossed the extra ice pack to Cole.

"Nothing to worry about." Cole put the pack near his kidney.

Blake shook his head. "Not what I heard. How come Dunns told me some guys are planning to fight you after school?"

"Dunns has a big mouth." Cole shook his head slightly, closing down.

"Baby, you know I'm gonna annoy the fuck out of you until you tell me." Beckett held his hands up like it was obvious he'd get the answer he sought.

"No. No. We're not letting you go back to Boys' Village again." Cole handed Blake the ice packs. "This place is enough of a prison."

"Tell me." Beckett stepped in front of him.

"No." Cole backed away.

"Do it." Beckett tilted his head to the side.

"No!" Cole half shouted.

"You know I'll find out. And I'll start with Dunns tomorrow." Beckett folded his arms over his chest.

"I can handle it." Cole pushed past him.

Beckett and Blake watched as Cole stormed off, then abruptly turned on his heel and returned.

This was what they did. Eventually they told each other the shit they usually kept hidden inside. They were comrades, friends—in the same military unit, in their heads.

"It's the guys from over in Westlake—the fancy neighborhood. They're sure Blake's going to snap—saying he's a serial killer and stuff. After PE they want to meet him in the locker room. They say tomorrow they're hitting him until he fights back." Cole put his hands in his jeans.

"You got PE fourth period, right?" Beckett spoke to Blake but put his hand on Cole's shoulder. He wasn't sure how the hell he was going to fix it, but he would.

"I can fight my own battles." Blake look supremely embarrassed.

"Yeah, but there's ten of them. Too many. Even for you." Cole shook his head. "I won't let Blake go into the locker room."

"Can you ditch class tomorrow? I need you to not be there." Beckett looked at Blake who shook his head.

"Not alone. No way," he told Beckett. "All three of us or none." Blake looked like he might beg if he had to.

"We can't get caught," Cole reminded them. "If we do, the kids here get what we don't take for them." He motioned toward the house with his thumb.

"I got this, baby," Beckett assured him. "I think I was born for it. I already have a plan." He pounded fists with Blake and Cole.

Beckett smiled as he walked into the locker room. The Westlake kids had picked their day well: there was a substitute PE teacher, currently handling an injury to one of the smaller Westlake kids, who was pretending to have a concussion. By covering their tracks, they'd given Beckett his opportunity.

Blake entered the locker room after class, as they'd discussed. Cole showed up right behind Beckett, a bathroom pass in his hand. The attackers had followed Blake in, just a few feet behind, slapping lockers on their way. The Westlake kids were on the football team, and their testosterone was new and flooded their systems when they were in groups. Like now.

Blake walked past his locker and came to stand next to Beckett and Cole. The numbers were off, but if Beckett had money, he'd still bet it on his side of things.

"Oh, you think those two are gonna help?" one of the Westlakers taunted. "We don't want your kind here. Fucking foster kids. Parents hate you so they dump you in here, and we have to deal with you in your hand-me-down clothes."

"Shit, my parents probably pay the taxes that buy your goddamn food every night," offered another.

The insults came fast and free.

Beckett was about to start, to intimidate them, threaten them, but Cole was quicker, and he kept his courage at the end of his fist. He jumped and hit the nearest kid with a punch that nailed the top of his skull.

Beckett watched the kid's eyes roll up in his head.

"Shit." Beckett came in hard. This wasn't his first fight, and it wouldn't be his last. Blake, who the Westlake guys had wrongly assumed was an easy mark, came back swinging as well. Beckett picked off the guys closet to him, but became distracted when he saw Blake falter. As a result, two of the meatheads got him in a restraint, a third landing a punch in his fucking rib.

Meanwhile, Cole wasn't Cole anymore. There were no rules to how he fought, no line he wouldn't cross. Like a bull with a laser focus, he got to the guys by Blake and took them down. Now standing, Blake came in with Cole, stopping Beckett's assailant from getting in another shot. All the aggression, all the punches they were never allowed to return to Rick came to the surface now. This was a battlefield, and while the kids from Westlake had wanted to bully someone, Cole, Beckett and Blake knew how to fight to survive.

Together they worked, and even with the crappy odds of three against ten, they dominated.

The substitute teacher ran into the locker room, hollering, "What's going on? You shouldn't be in here. You didn't have to change out."

There were bruises and blood everywhere. No one spoke. The Westlake kids knew better. They all just waited the teacher out. Finally one of the smartasses piped up, "Didn't want our clothes getting sweaty. We'll get dressed. We're cool."

The other boys in the class peeked in the doorway. Obviously the show Mr. Fake Concussion had put on was over. When the teacher finally gave up and told them she'd meet them outside when they were changed, the Westlake kids helped each other up. The ringleader walked over to Beckett, hand extended.

"Hey, we're cool, dude. Right?"

Beckett took his hand and squeezed it tight, pulling the guy close, whispering just for him in his ear. "You want a serial killer? You fucking found one."

He maintained eye contact until the guy finally looked away, wrenching his hand free. "You're crazy. Jesus."

Cole, Blake, and Beckett let the Westlake guys leave first, staying in the locker room until it emptied out.

"You think they'll stay quiet?" Blake wondered.

Beckett nodded. "They will." He didn't tell them he was planning to visit the ringleader tonight at his home. Or that he'd found a starter pistol in Rick's basement and painted the orange tip black. Beckett had every intention of threatening the guy until he crapped his pants and made sure his football friends never pulled this shit again. On his brothers. On anyone. He looked at Cole, then Blake.

Each of them had blood streaming down their forearms. The part of their arms that signaled a need for solace in the forest now dripped with violence.

Beckett held up his arm in an arm-wrestling stance. "Grab on."

Blake complied, then looked to Cole. "You too."

The three-way handshake brought them close together. Beckett was hopped up on adrenaline, but he knew this was real. He knew it deep.

"Brothers?" he asked.

"Brothers," Blake responded, smiling.

"Forever," Cole added solemnly.

Sneak Peek from *The Revenger*, a stand-alone novel
by Debra Anastasia, coming in 2015

CRACKED

Sitting in a car had never been this tough before. God, it was hard. The man next to her had a red aura and demanded a pounding for that alone. Savvy sat on her hands and tried counting the trees that passed. It failed to calm her.

She kept taking peeks at the driver. He seemed pretty shaky too.

When he spoke, she jumped. "My name's Bugs. I handle the computers and surveillance cameras at the house."

Savvy was afraid to talk. She didn't want to lose control, and she was so very close to doing just that. As they drove, the clock ticked off twenty painful minutes on the dashboard. They were heading toward the beach; she could smell the change in the air coming through the vents. Bugs pulled out this phone and hit send, and Savvy could hear everything coming through it. Her senses were enhanced so close to his red aura.

The ringing stopped, but the person now on the other end of Bugs' cell said nothing. He filled the silence with hurried words. "Yes, I have her right here. She came peacefully. Do you want her delivered straight to your bedroom?"

Bugs' hand clenched and unclenched around the phone.

Savvy could hear the silky reply as if the man speaking were whispering in her ear. "No. Put her in the Blue Room. Bring her through the back entrance."

The phone clicked as Bugs' boss hung up.

Another ten minutes passed before Bugs pulled up in front of a gated entrance. He lowered both their windows, and a screen appeared from the ground on each side. Bugs put his hand on the closest one and a laser tasted his fingerprints. Savvy wanted to tear the screen on her side of the car from its pole and beat Bugs with it. *Steady, girl.*

"Put your hand up to the screen, please." Bugs waved in the direction of the technology.

Savvy turned her head slowly and met his eyes. "Kiss my ass. I'm not putting my hand on that thing."

Bugs looked from the clock to his phone, obviously running through his options. "Look, if you don't put your hand up soon, this car will explode with gunfire. It's programmed to kill us."

Savvy smiled at the thought of Bugs being physically removed from his evil aura.

"Okay, I get it, you don't care if I die," he said. "You don't care if you die. But my boss? If he doesn't talk to you because you're dead? He'll kill your brother anyway." Bugs pointed to the screen again.

He could very well have been lying, but the sweat on his forehead told her he was at least scared.

She shook her head. She'd already lost two battles: getting in the car and now this. She placed her hand on the square. The laser engaged, and it felt like a butterfly's wings were tickling her palm. She was marked in their system now. Who knew what they could do with her fingerprints. The gates slid open, and Bugs gunned engine. Even before opening fully, they were closing again behind them.

The driveway was insanely long, and the greenery transitioned to more and more sand as they got closer to the house. Bugs was talking again. Warning her about rules and etiquette that she guessed she should listen to, but she couldn't. The mansion in front of her called her name and demanded her righteousness.

She knew there were many, many red auras inside. So many. She looked at her knees and tried to breathe. Bugs had parked the car in a huge circular driveway with a spouting fountain in the center of it.

"We need to go in the back entrance, so you're not seen." Bugs had come around to her side of the car.

Savvy got out and walked past him. He hurried alongside, begging her to follow him, but he was too smart to put his hands on her. He'd seen the surveillance videos of her beating criminals senseless with a superhuman strength, after all.

Savvy's high heels clicked loudly on the marble staircase that led to the two-story tall front doors. When she was close enough, she kicked the doors and smiled as they easily obeyed her command, smashing wide open.

She waltzed into the foyer and looked from person to person. Almost every man had a gun drawn or was in the process of doing so. The women were stifling screams and hitting the floor.

Savvy tracked an imaginary path of destruction, wondering how many she could tear to pieces before their bullets felled her. A man jumped in front of her and blocked her body from the men defending the mansion.

"No! He wants this chick alive. Put your fucking guns away." The man's neck was Savvy's only view at the moment, and she wanted to snap it in half. His aura stopped her because it was confusing. It was definitely red, but closer to his body, it was gold.

She reached a hand out to touch it. The red outline was hot, and it fed her strength, but a little deeper, the gold felt cool. His peculiar aura was the only thing that kept him alive.

He turned to her. "I take it you're the new one? He wants you in the Blue Room. My name's Boston. I'll show you the way."

He had dark hair and deep blue eyes. When he smiled to encourage her, he revealed his dimples as well. She didn't move. The wave of red auras was taking her good sense. Her eyes were drawn to each of the men surrounding her again. Even some of the women had red.

To be loose in here for five minutes would be amazing.

Her brother's name brought Boston's face into focus again. "Tobias will only be safe if you cooperate," he said.

The gold got darker around the man. So confusing.

"Can you walk with me?" he asked.

He wasn't being polite, she knew he could tell she was paralyzed from the inside out. Savvy had to recover — she had to. Tobias's life might depend on it. She looked at the floor and nodded, keeping her gaze down, free from all the temptation around her.

But her skin knew the red was there, could still feel the pull.

One step, another step.

It took forever to get to the Blue Room, but finally, Boston opened a large door. Savvy noticed belatedly that Bugs had gone. Keeping to his namesake, he'd disappeared when the action started.

"Just go in and sit down." Boston closed the door behind her, and she heard a large bolt slide into place.

Savvy couldn't sit if she tried, so she stood in front of a conference table hedged by fancy boardroom chairs.

She waited. The room was blue, as was expected. Its only decoration was a large mural of the surf that Savvy figured was right outside the mansion, judging from the smell in the air.

She had no idea how much time passed, but she knew it was a mind game, and frankly, she sucked at those. There was so little of her rational mind left.

Finally, the mural crackled to life. Savvy stepped into her fighting stance and watched. Instead of a picture, she was now looking at a flat-screen TV — much like the ones Tobias ogled in Best Buy when he dreamed of hitting the lotto.

Soon it had a picture again, but it took a few seconds for Savvy to put the images in context. It was Tobias on the very screen he dreamed of buying. He was parking in the lot at the police station and dialing his cell phone. After what must have been an unsuccessful call, he cursed. Although there was no sound, Savvy recognized her name on her brother's lips. He spotted her car and trotted over. The video faded out as Tobias used his elbow to break her driver's side window.

The mural returned. This was happening in real time, and they weren't bluffing. Someone from this place was watching her brother. Screaming began in her head, and she fell to one knee while holding her hair.

The sound was so clear and so desperate. It was Sara's scream during the accident. Savvy hadn't heard it since that night — her brain had saved her from recalling it. Or maybe it was her soul's survival instinct that kept her protected from the sound. Until now.

Now Sara, her daughter — scared and screaming — filled Savvy to the brim.

"No," Savvy whispered. "No, no, no, no."

The screaming became a pinpoint, the center of a black hole located just behind the mural. She snapped her head up and looked closely. She could make out his outline. Sara's screams were coming from him. His aura was her exact pain.

Sagan stood in his office waiting, watching the surveillance camera Bugs was running. The girl's name was Savannah Ann Raine, according to the information derived from her license plate number. She had deliberately defied him and kicked in the front doors of his house. Sagan bit his lip as he watched her entrance again on the monitor.

Boston had worked his magic and calmed the beast that she was. Yet she stood instead of sitting in the Blue Room. Antagonizing him yet again.

God, it was refreshing.

He had watched her fidget for eighteen minutes before he had Bugs run the footage of her brother's arrival at the police station. He loved letting his new acquisition know he was everywhere and that his power was more potent than any law.

She was furious and clearly worried by the time the painting had returned to its passive seascape. He checked his hair and straightened his tie, even though both were already impeccable. He nodded at Boston as he entered the observation room and shut the door behind him. It was located just behind the mural, and the picture served the purpose of disguising the watcher from the watched.

The minute he set foot in the small, narrow room, Savannah fell to one knee in obvious pain. At first Sagan was just fascinated to see this seemingly invincible girl in such a vulnerable position. The room was well wired, so he could hear her whisper, "No, no, no, no."

He decided then to call Doc. Savannah was experiencing something that obviously required medical attention. She looked right into his eyes, and she was feral. Her hair was wild from where she'd raked her hands through it punishingly, and her face was set in determination. Sagan licked his lips in anticipation. It was like watching a hungry tiger in a zoo.

Her movements were so flawless, it was like she had choreographed them and practiced for weeks. She grabbed the back of one of the chairs and stepped up to the mural. The chair didn't make a dent on its first downward strike. But Savannah didn't stop. She kept pounding on the bulletproof screen until it started to crack. Boston stepped into Sagan's private sanctuary.

"Sir, you need to get out of here." Boston pulled out his handgun and aimed it at the girl.

Sagan waited.

Her gaze had never left his eyes, as if she could see right into his mind. The screen cracked again, a sure fissure from top to bottom. She was actually going to break through the impenetrable glass.

Finally the chair dropped from her grasp. She walked to the mural and put one hand on it. Sagan mimicked her motion despite Boston's protests. Hand to hand they stood, and he could feel her hot hatred. This close to her face, he could see into her cloudy, gray eyes. They held so much pain.

Sagan almost felt sympathy.

Her perfect lips, rose-colored from exertion, began moving. He hoped the camera was still functioning so he could replay her words again and again. Her voice was reverent, a promise wrapped in a threat.

"Know this: I will kill you. Take these words and carve them onto your horrible soul." She looked from his lips to his eyes and smiled. "I will be the one who kills you."

Savvy could only see sand and a stationary ocean, but she could feel his eyes. She knew where his lips were like they were the center of her universe. Her daughter still screamed over and over in her head as she promised to kill the man who stood inches from her. *He* had made Sara scream somehow. Instead of hugging her daughter's memory and feeling her soft hair, Savvy could only remember her agony as crisply as if it were happening again.

Whoever was behind the screen had to die. Savvy stepped away so she had enough power to punch. Feeling the glass crunch under her fists was much more pleasing than the chair attack had been. She was making headway, but then it hit her: *If he's on the other side, there's a door.* She gave away her intention as she headed for the exit to the Blue Room. She leveled kicks at the door's sweet spot, but the bolt held for a few extra seconds. Finally, with a crack, she was free. She turned toward the most likely place for a secondary room. The door stood ajar, and the narrow room was empty. Savvy closed her eyes as she heard the clatter of approaching defenders, those she'd already scared enough to have them draw their guns when she busted into their world.

Sara's screams lead the way, and Savvy ran down hallways she'd never seen before. Finally, the screams led her to a terrace, and she busted through the glass doors to stand on the balcony. The ocean crashed against the shore below her, in motion and alive. From the roof she could hear a helicopter's blades pounding the air. She tilted her face to see it rise above the house. The man who held Sara's screams sat in the passenger seat and looked right at her.

Right into her.

He was devastatingly handsome, and his green eyes showed a hint of a sparkle as he realized he was getting away. Behind her, the army of red auras leveled all types of weapons, but she paid them no mind. She was trapped in the eyes of the evil man above her. He winked at her now as the helicopter began to rise.

Savvy pointed at him from where she stood. She mouthed her next words so only he would get her message. "Run. Run far. I'll find you. I'll always find you."

She smiled then as his triumphant demeanor fell like a leaf from a tree. In a heartbeat, he was gone from her sight. Savvy turned to face the angry mob. There was so much red she couldn't even make out their faces.

Savvy gave them the finger and did a perfect backflip off the fourth-story balcony.

Watch DebraAnastasia.com and @Debra_Anastasia
for updates on *The Revenger.*

ACKNOWLEDGMENTS

To my readers. You know you are my heart, and you make my farts sing. Thank you so much for being here and letting me frolic in your imagination, even though you know you can't trust me.

Midian, for your name and spirit. JM Darhower, for Toni Lynn. Teresa Mummert, because of the veto. Helena Hunting, what's for lunch? Shalu, my gorgeous friend, for the tattoo. Kiya, I love you down under. Nina, never stop kicking ass. TK, for all the pics on my phone. Tijan, you know cocker spaniels rule. Sara C, you are our researcher. Kelly, as one of your many internet moms. LB, smile!! Jamie, I miss you! Erika, CVS. Amanda, I see you! Karen, the beach is waiting. Pam, you and me on Sunday night. Mom and Dad S, thanks for the morning FaceTime. Mom and Dad D, thanks for letting me use you again. Beverly Cindy, my amazing Mayor. The Poughkeepsie Street team!!! No one is better. Carol Oates, my Irish sister. My filets. My Omnific Sisters, I love you. What a great year! Nise, Patti, and Alicia, tats forever. Silly Jilly, you are the best.

Many thanks to: The Sub Club, The Smut Club, Maryse, Aestas, The Rock Stars of Romance, Michele, Beverly, GraceDZ, Jen M, Sarah, Noemi, Trayce, Eve and Ayeisha, Clista, Lori, Nicki, Bookish Temptations, Neda, Thessamari. Uncle T and Aunt J, you are so much fun. All the uncles, aunts, and cousins! TammyVoiced! We make great partners. Hootie and Glo, The Autumn Reviews, Nancee Cain, Chele, Slim Shaydy, Ron Pope and Blair, Catherine Millington, Andarta, Read Love Blog, Fics2Flics, Dymps, XO_BB_XO, Iza Matei, Literary Gossip, Lisa Jane LJ, Xtina, Fred, Sandy G Southern, Lisa, Feather, and to so many I'm forgetting, know that I adore you, and I'm an asshole.

To Omnific Publishing, for taking risks and putting dreams first every single time. The quiet strength of women who believe in each other can change the world, starting with Elizabeth. To CJ, who reminds me a of a certain revenger. Lisa, Traci, Kim—the beating heart of a dream. To my favorite bitch, Micha, I love the time we get to laugh together. Coreen, thanks for making words pretty too!

Jessica Royer Ocken, thank you for telling me I was overthinking things. That's the first time anyone has ever told me that. Please give Debra Jr. my love. Kimberly, I love that your eyes go over all the boys have to offer. Thank you!

About the Author

There are a lot of eyes in Debra Anastasia's house in Maryland. First, her own creepy peepers are there, staring at her computer screen. She's made two more sets of eyes with her body, and the kids they belong to are amazing. The poor husband is still looking at her after 17 years of marriage. At least he likes to laugh. Then the freaking dogs are looking at her — six eyeballs altogether, though the old dog is blind. And the cat watches her too, mostly while knocking stuff off the counter and doing that internal kitty laugh when Deb can't catch the items fast enough.

In between taking care of everything those eyes involve, Debra creates pretend people in her head and paints them on the giant, beautiful canvas of your imagination. What an amazing job that is. The stories hit her hard while driving the minivan or shaving her legs, especially when there's no paper and pen around. And in all of the lies she writes hides her heart, so thank you for letting it play in your mind.

Debra is eternally grateful to Omnific Publishing, which has now published five of her books: two in the Seraphim Series and three in the Poughkeepsie Brotherhood Series, as well as her novella, *Late Night with Andres*. That one is special because 100% of the proceeds go to breast cancer research. (So go get it right now, please!)

You can find her in the following places. But be prepared…

Amazon: amzn.com/e/B0051BO7I4
Amazon UK: amzn.to/1ycAhUT
Barnes & Noble: tinyurl.com/pvtf2rp
Goodreads: tinyurl.com/qces7w3
Website: www.DebraAnastasia.com
Facebook: tinyurl.com/ndzy6hc
Twitter: @Debra_Anastasia
Instagram: instagram.com/debra_anastasia
Pinterest: www.pinterest.com/debraanastasia/

Other books by Debra Anastasia:

Late Night with Andres:
Amazon: amzn.com/B00NO138VK
Barnes & Noble: tinyurl.com/p8seuzv
iTunes: tinyurl.com/orwr345

The Seraphim series:

Crushed Seraphim
Amazon: amzn.com/B00NO13AWM
Barnes & Noble: tinyurl.com/nadjbjr

Bittersweet Seraphim
Amazon: amzn.com/B00NO13ENC
Barnes & Noble: tinyurl.com/qx383e4

The Poughkeepsie Brotherhood series:

Poughkeepsie
Amazon: amzn.com/B00NO136IU
Amazon UK: www.amazon.co.uk/dp/B00NO0ZSUA
Barnes & Noble: tinyurl.com/ls2ec8j
iTunes: tinyurl.com/nopvezj
Audio Book *Poughkeepsie*: amzn.com/B00B1NW9AO

Return to Poughkeepsie
Amazon: amzn.com/B00NO138WO
Amazon UK: www.amazon.co.uk/dp/B00NO0ZXGE
Barnes & Noble: tinyurl.com/p257k2t
iTunes: tinyurl.com/pg5t2tg
Trailer 1: youtu.be/q-17oi_Suzc
Trailer 2: youtu.be/O7g-9pWUBmw

Poughkeepsie Enhanced Collector's Edition for iPad
iTunes: tinyurl.com/qanr871

Poughkeepsie by Debra Anastasia has been a cult hit bestseller since 2011. A homeless guy counting the smiles of a kind train commuter spiraled into a novel that was nominated by The Rockstars of Romance as one of the most romantic stories ever and won second place! It was a story that deserved getting a jumbo-sized enhancement. Extra scenes out the ying yang was, of course, a huge part of the fun. Getting to spend some of those previously undiscovered first moments with Blake and Livia or the moment he proposed was worth exploring. In Debra's wildest dreams she imagined *Poughkeepsie* with its own soundtrack, anchored by her favorite musicians. When blockbuster talent Ron Pope signed on with fourteen songs and then Rustic Overtones agreed as well, she knew things were going to get crazy cool.

After almost two full years of development, the enhanced *Poughkeepsie* is ready. Debra, and the developer, lost count of the hours poured into this. It was a beast and more amazing than she could have ever imagined. This app became the most exceptional reading experience Debra could devise for her readers.

Immerse yourself in the world of Debra Anastasia's *Poughkeepsie*.

Experience this bestselling novel for the first time…again as you break all the rules about books with Omnific Publishing and Debra Anastasia. In this enhanced version of the novel, you'll enjoy insights from the author, music by Ron Pope and other artists to set the mood, and images and video that bring the scenes to life as you read. You'll delve deeper into the world of *Poughkeepsie* through nearly 50,000 words of added scenes (more love, more drama, more romance!) and informative insights into how this marvelous story and its characters came to be.

Check out what's in store for you: youtu.be/b6kmXLP5jo4

Self-contained in this app (no wifi needed after downloading):

•complete novel *Poughkeepsie* by Debra Anastasia
•author/director's pop-up commentary
•music by Ron Pope, Rustic Overtones, Monoxide G, Violet Winter, Bo Heart, and Jeff Epstein and the City Line Singers
•more than 100 images to enhance the story
•videos of your favorite characters in action
•special animation

- sound effects
- interviews with the characters, author, and more
- interactive games
- trailers for the Poughkeepsie Brotherhood series
- how-to knitting instructions
- how-to instructions for making a paper rose
- recipe for the dinner Livia makes for Blake

Praise for *Poughkeepsie* Enhanced Collector's Edition for iPad:

"Oh. My. God. This is an interactive reading experience like nothing we've ever seen before. If you thought Debra's characters came to life on the written page, just wait until you get your hands on the app!" *~FicstoFlicks.com*

"This easy-to-navigate app/website lets you read the book, but adds photos, custom music and art, tons of background on the writing process, and little notes from Debra throughout. I think my favorite part of all is the little comments Debra leaves about certain lines in the book and how they are special or significant to her personally." *~Ana's Attic.com*

"What is this magical slice of reading heaven I have in my hands? This is my dream come true! As well as falling in love with Blake and Liv all over again, this app was bursting full of bonus material. The bonus scenes were marked in black and by click on these boxes it would take you to an extra scene or bonus content like recipes. It was easy to flip between the bonus content and the story. I loved reading about all the intimate moments and revelations I didn't get to witness in detail the first time around." *~Biblio Belles Book Blog*

"Anyone who is a fan of *Poughkeepsie* and or Debra Anastasia's work will instantly fall in love with this app—it is the best thing I've ever seen!" *~Curious Kindle Reader*

New Adult Romance

Three Daves by Nicki Elson

Streamline by Jennifer Lane

The Shades series: *Shades of Atlantis* & *Shades of Avalon* by Carol Oates

The Heart series: *Beside Your Heart, Disclosure of the Heart* & *Forever Your Heart* by Mary Whitney

Romancing the Bookworm by Kate Evangelista

Flirting with Chaos by Kenya Wright

The Vice, Virtue & Video series: *Revealed, Captured, Desired* & *Devoted* by Bianca Giovanni

Granton University series: *Loving Lies* by Linda Kage

Paranormal Romance

The Light series: *Seers of Light, Whisper of Light* & *Circle of Light* by Jennifer DeLucy

The Hanaford Park series: *Eve of Samhain* & *Pleasures Untold* by Lisa Sanchez

Immortal Awakening by KC Randall

The Seraphim series: *Crushed Seraphim* & *Bittersweet Seraphim* by Debra Anastasia

The Guardian's Wild Child by Feather Stone

Grave Refrain by Sarah M. Glover

The Divinity series: *Divinity* & *Entity* by Patricia Leever

The Blood Vine series: *Blood Vine, Blood Entangled* & *Blood Reunited* by Amber Belldene

Divine Temptation by Nicki Elson

The Dead Rapture series: *Love in the Time of the Dead* & *Love at the End of Days* by Tera Shanley

Romantic Suspense

Whirlwind by Robin DeJarnett

The CONduct series: *With Good Behavior, Bad Behavior* & *On Best Behavior* by Jennifer Lane

Indivisible by Jessica McQuinn

Between the Lies by Alison Oburia

Blind Man's Bargain by Tracy Winegar

Erotic Romance

The Keyhole series: *Becoming sage* (book 1) by Kasi Alexander

The Keyhole series: *Saving sunni* (book 2) by Kasi & Reggie Alexander

The Winemaker's Dinner: *Appetizers* & *Entrée* by Dr. Ivan Rusilko & Everly Drummond

The Winemaker's Dinner: *Dessert* by Dr. Ivan Rusilko

Client N° 5 by Joy Fulcher

Historical Romance

Cat O' Nine Tails by Patricia Leever
Burning Embers by Hannah Fielding
Seven for a Secret by Rumer Haven

Anthologies

A Valentine Anthology including short stories by
Alice Clayton ("With a Double Oven"),
Jennifer DeLucy ("Magnus of Pfelt, Conquering Viking Lord"),
Nicki Elson ("I Don't Do Valentine's Day"),
Jessica McQuinn ("Better Than One Dead Rose and a Monkey Card"),
Victoria Michaels ("Home to Jackson"), and
Alison Oburia ("The Bridge")

Taking Liberties including an introduction by Tiffany Reisz and short stories by
Mina Vaughn ("John Hancock-Blocked"),
Linda Cunningham ("A Boston Marriage"),
Joy Fulcher ("Tea for Two"),
KC Holly ("The British Are Coming!"),
Kimberly Jensen & Scott Stark ("E. Pluribus Threesome"), and
Vivian Rider ("M'Lady's Secret Service")

Sets

The Heart Series Box Set (*Beside Your Heart, Disclosure of the Heart* &
Forever Your Heart) by Mary Whitney
The CONduct Series Box Set (*With Good Behavior, Bad Behavior* &
On Best Behavior) by Jennifer Lane
The Light Series Box Set (*Seers of Light, Whisper of Light, Circle of Light* &
Glimpse of Light) by Jennifer DeLucy
The Blood Vine Series Box Set (*Blood Vine, Blood Entangled, Blood Reunited* &
Blood Eternal) by Amber Belldene

Singles, Novellas & Special Editions

It's Only Kinky the First Time (A Keyhole series single) by Kasi Alexander
Learning the Ropes (A Keyhole series single) by Kasi & Reggie Alexander
The Winemaker's Dinner: RSVP by Dr. Ivan Rusilko
The Winemaker's Dinner: No Reservations by Everly Drummond
Big Guns by Jessica McQuinn
Concessions by Robin DeJarnett
Starstruck by Lisa Sanchez
New Flame by BJ Thornton

Shackled by Debra Anastasia
Swim Recruit by Jennifer Lane
Sway by Nicki Elson
Full Speed Ahead by Susan Kaye Quinn
The Second Sunrise by Hannah Downing
The Summer Prince by Carol Oates
Whatever it Takes by Sarah M. Glover
Clarity (A *Divinity* prequel single) by Patricia Leever
A Christmas Wish (A *Cocktails & Dreams* single) by Autumn Markus
Late Night with Andres by Debra Anastasia
Poughkeepsie (enhanced iPad app collector's edition) by Debra Anastasia
Poughkeepsie (audio book edition) by Debra Anastasia
Blood Eternal (A Blood Vine series single, epilogue to series) by Amber Belldene
Carnaval de Amor (The Winemaker's Dinner, Spanish edition) by Dr. Ivan Rusilko & Everly Drummond

coming soon from
OMNIFIC PUBLISHING

The Hidden Races series: *Incandescent* (book 1) by M.V. Freeman
The Legendary Saga: *Claiming Excalibur* (book 2) by LH Nicole
The Runaway series: *The Runaway Ex* (book 2) by Shani Struthers
The Forever series: *Forever Autumn* (book 1) by Christopher Scott Wagner
Something Wicked by Carol Oates
Going the Distance by Julianna Keyes